LUCY FLOYD

YESTE

PAN BOOKS

In association with Macmillan London
First published 1991 by Macmillan London Limited
This edition published 1992 by Pan Books Ltd
Cavaye Place, London SW10 9PG

9 8 7 6 5 4 3 2

Copyright © Lucy Floyd 1991

The right of Lucy Floyd to be identified as author of
this work has been asserted by her in accordance with the
Copyright, Designs and Patents Act 1988.

ISBN 0 330 31532 3

Typeset by Pan Macmillan Production Limited
Printed and bound in Great Britain by
Cox & Wyman Ltd, Reading, Berkshire

For Mike, with love

ONE

Prague, December 1950

Viktor woke up to the sound of his mother crying.

He lay still for a moment, regretting his vanished dream, torn between pity and irritation, like a weary parent preparing to humour a sleepless child. The nightlight was struggling against the swirling draughts from the rotting window and ill-fitting door. It was very cold.

He took temporary refuge under the covers, breathing in sustaining gulps of his own warmth. Then he got out of bed, shivering, and crossed to where his mother lay, his socks snagging against the splintering wood of the bare floorboards. She was quiet again, curled up with her back to him, shuddering with silent sobs.

'Mama?' The freezing air rasped against his throat. He began coughing.

She turned to face him and wiped her eyes on the sheet. 'It's all right, Viktor,' she murmured. 'It was just a bad dream.' She pulled aside the bedclothes and tucked him into the crook of her arm. 'Go back to sleep now.'

Mama's bed felt damp, which made it hard to get warm again. But, as always, his presence seemed to soothe her. Wide awake now, Viktor lay very still so as not to disturb her. Tomorrow was a Sunday, when they both stayed in bed all day to keep warm. Sundays were boring, but at least he didn't have to go to school.

Viktor hated school. None of the other children would play with him, on account of his father being in gaol. They would dance round him in the playground, chanting 'Traitor, traitor, traitor!', and he averaged at least one hefty punch or vicious kick per day. At first he had fought back, played into their hands. But these days he pretended not to care, just to spoil their fun. The last year had taught him a lot about survival.

He didn't miss his father, although he knew he was supposed to. Already his memories of that dark, fearsome figure were fading. The sound of his key in the latch had filled Viktor with sullen dread, although luckily he was usually asleep – or pretending to be asleep – by the time his father got home. Tati had always been angry about something; Viktor had often heard him shouting at Mama in the middle of the night. He assumed that they were arguing about him, because he was such a dunce.

'You're a stupid, lazy boy!' his father would roar as he stumbled and stuttered over his reading primer, a Sunday evening ordeal which he no longer had to endure. 'You must work harder!'

Mama would always stick up for him and say things like 'Be patient' and 'Give him time', which only made his father even angrier. He still couldn't understand why they had sent him to prison, because Mama and Babička said he hadn't done anything wrong. It was one of the many things he wouldn't understand till he was older, even though, to Viktor's mind, eight was a great age.

His stomach rumbled loudly. It was difficult to sleep when you were hungry, and his evening meal of soup and bread seemed an awfully long time ago. He comforted himself with thoughts of Christmas at his grandmother's cottage in Bohemia. There would be carp and goose and a dozen different kinds of special biscuits; there would be eggs and boiled chicken and big fat dumplings, and Babička would say, 'Eat up, you two! Eat up!' He would play in the snow with the children from the village, who didn't know or care about Tati, and enjoy the dry, clean cold, knowing that the woodstove burned day and night, that he could always get warm again. Babička had asked him once if he would like to come and live with her, but he knew that Mama had to work in Prague, and that she would be lonely without him.

2

He tried again to get back behind the locked doors of his dream. He had dreamed that he was playing his grandmother's piano. He could see the polished wood reflecting the glitter of the chandelier, hear the sweet sound filling the big, bright room. Babička had shown him how to 'read' music, except that it was nothing like reading, because it made perfect sense. It was like looking at a moving picture of your own fingers on the keyboard. He only had to look at those squiggles on the stave and he could hear the notes in his head. It was the first thing that had ever been easy. When Babička had had to give up her apartment in Prague and move to her tiny cottage in the country, Viktor had inherited her piano. But when he and his mother had been turned out of their home, they had had to leave it behind. There was no space for a piano here and, in any case, it had been 'confiscated', which was what happened to all your things when your father went to prison.

'That's Communism for you,' Babička had told him grimly. 'What's mine is mine, and what's yours is also mine.' Viktor knew not to repeat the things that his grandmother said. You never repeated anything anyone said at home, in case somebody informed on you.

The vanished keyboard tinkled in the distance, like sleigh bells, luring him into a chilly sleep.

Morning came with a tap on the door. Mama grunted in her sleep and turned over. Viktor slid out of bed.

'Who is it?'

'Viktor? It's Věra. Let me in.'

Viktor liked Věra. She was the only person who still came to see them. She was always cheerful and smiling and, more importantly, she usually brought him something. He was rather less enthusiastic about her baby, Eva, who, undaunted by his indifference, gurgled at him in delighted recognition.

'What's the matter with your mama?' asked Věra. 'Is she ill again?' She lifted Eva out of her pushchair and crossed over to the bed.

'Say good morning to your Auntie Milena, Eva! Say, "Wake up, lazybones!"'

3

'Věra!' His mother sat up, and her face broke into a huge sad smile. 'Hello, Evicka darling!'

Viktor took advantage of the diversion to put his clothes on over his pyjamas, anxious to avoid the daily torment of washing in ice-cold water. He braced himself for a visit to the filthy privy in the yard, home to a thousand beetles, and decided he could put it off a bit longer.

'Come and say hello to Eva, Viktor,' called his mother. She was always urging him to play with Eva, much to Viktor's disgust. He didn't find babies remotely interesting. He had never been at all clear where this one had came from, because Věra wasn't married.

'Hello, Eva,' he muttered, offering her a reluctant finger, appraising the fat, rosy-faced infant with something like envy. It must be nice not to have a father. He wished his mother hadn't got married, that she'd managed to have him all by herself.

His mother stood the child up on the bed, with her hands under the girl's armpits, trying to encourage her to walk. Eva squealed in delight.

'I remember when Viktor was small,' she said to Věra. 'I remember thinking we must be mad to bring a baby into such a dreadful world. Every day I was terrified that Karel would get himself arrested and shot. And now . . .'

'I brought her with me to cheer you up, not to start you brooding! And I brought something else, too. Come here, Viktor.' Věra thrust her hands deep into both pockets of her coat.

'Which hand?'

'Left.'

Věra displayed an empty palm and shook her head mournfully.

'Too bad.'

'Right!'

'Too late.'

'Right! Right!'

Relenting, she withdrew a large red apple. Viktor grabbed it, almost forgetting to say thank you, and took a huge greedy bite before retreating to a prudent nibble, anxious to make this treat last as long as possible.

'How long since you two last had a decent meal?' said Věra,

4

offering his mother a cigarette. 'And why haven't you lit the stove? It's freezing in here.'

'I'm behind with the rent,' said his mother in a low voice. 'It's impossible to live on what they pay me in that place. I've been trying to find an evening job. But no one will take me on.'

'You shouldn't be working at all.'

'The doctor says there's nothing the matter with me. "Nerves, my good woman. Nerves!" Well, he's right, of course.' She let out a thin, cracked laugh. 'Aren't you beautiful?' she resumed, picking up her refrain. 'Who's a beautiful girl, then?'

'Have you heard from Karel?'

Viktor saw his mother jerk her head in his direction and put her finger to her lips. She got out of bed, ran a comb through her long fair hair, put her coat on over her nightdress and began boiling water for coffee over the Primus. Viktor wrapped up the rest of his apple in his handkerchief for later and got his own breakfast – two slices of dark rye bread spread thinly with plum jam. His mother said she wasn't hungry, and smoked another of Věra's cigarettes. Following his usual Sunday routine, he got back into bed, drawing the covers right over his head. After a while he heard Věra say quietly, 'Well, what Karel suggests makes sense. It must have been a difficult letter for him to write.'

'I suppose so. But if I do as he asks, I'll feel as if I've betrayed him. At the beginning I tried to fight it. I wrote letters to everyone I could think of, even Gottwald, telling them there must be some mistake. But now I feel so useless . . .' She raised her voice. 'Viktor?'

Viktor lay very still, playing possum. A moment later, his mother was leaning over him, pulling the sheet away from his face. He didn't stir.

'He's fast asleep,' she sighed. 'He was awake half the night, coughing. It's been one cold after another.' She tucked him up again. 'What's this?'

'Take it. Eva's father sent me some money.'

'Věra, I can't!'

'Course you can.'

'You need it for the baby.'

'There's plenty more where that came from. I've been

5

threatening to tell his wife unless he gets me a better job. If you must get involved with a married man, make sure he's a good Party member.'

'I'll pay you back.'

'No hurry. Look at the state of you. Use it to bribe the bloody doctor to give you a few weeks off work.'

'What's the point? I think the job is all that keeps me sane. I mean, I hate it, I hate every minute I spend in that place, but at least it's something to do. If it wasn't for Viktor . . .' Her voice dropped to a murmur. Viktor kept very still. 'But then, what use am I to Viktor? Half the time it's him looking after me. He wakes me up in time for work, gets my breakfast, does the shopping . . . what kind of life is that for an eight-year-old?'

'Then why don't you do as Karel asks?' said Věra in a low voice.

'Divorce him? Publicly denounce him? I couldn't.'

'What more harm can it do him now? If I were you, I'd write an open letter thanking the Party and the State for bringing yet another traitor to justice. For Viktor's sake. That way, they might give you a proper wage and a decent place to live.'

'You want him to grow up thinking his father was guilty?'

'Ssh. Keep your voice down.' Feeling two pairs of eyes on him, Viktor continued to feign a deep, deaf sleep. 'He confessed, remember,' continued Věra. 'Viktor's going to have to live with that.'

'But it wasn't true! It couldn't have been true! Karel risked his life time and again, working for the Resistance. He's a patriot! Why would he suddenly betray his country by leaking information to the West?'

'Isn't that what the Resistance did during the war? Leak information to the West?'

'But that was different!'

'Only because the West isn't our ally any longer. Not that it ever was, if you ask me. As for patriotism – that's called nationalism now, didn't you know? They say that anyone who was in the Resistance is under investigation. I can't believe he's guilty either, but that's beside the point. You have to cut your losses. There's no point in being a martyr.'

'If he'd put me and Viktor first, instead of the wretched

Party, none of this would have happened! After the war, all I wanted was a quiet life, a life without fear. Sometimes I feel so angry with him, so angry with myself. I should have left him. I should have left him years ago. If my parents had been alive . . .'

'Milena, I wish I could do more. I'd take you and Viktor home with me like a shot, but you know how nervous my mother is. She doesn't even know I come here. As for my father . . .'

'If he finds out he'll probably beat you.'

'I'm used to being beaten. When he found out I was pregnant with Eva, I thought he was going to kill me!' Věra's voice rounded out into her irrepressible laugh. 'But I'm still alive, aren't I? And so's Eva. And so are you and Viktor. And Karel, come to that. He could have been hanged.'

'I'd rather they'd sentenced him to death than to life. Can you imagine what his life must be like in that labour camp? As for Viktor – he'd be better off without me.'

'Don't be silly. If anything happened to you—'

'I know. They'd put him in one of those homes for political orphans. I've heard about those places. If it wasn't for that . . .' Her voice dropped and she began talking very fast. 'The other day, while I was waiting for the tram, I felt sort of . . . dizzy. I found myself thinking how easy it would be just to throw myself in front of it.'

'That's a wicked thing to say!'

'Wicked and cowardly and pathetic. That's me all over. Full of self-pity. But we can't all be brave and strong like you. You would have made Karel a much better wife than me. He always liked you.'

'Rubbish. He had eyes only for you. Even though all the girls in the factory were after him. I often think those days would have been quite fun if we hadn't been working for the bloody Nazis.'

'I never thought I'd have to work with my hands again.'

'Tut, tut, tut! What about the dignity of labour? Besides, it will mean Viktor can truthfully claim that his mother is a manual worker. That should get him into university, whether he can read and write or not.'

'He's so bright in other ways. I can't understand it.'

'That's the least of your worries.'

Viktor kept very still, taking it all in. The written word might evade his grasp, but he never forgot anything he heard. He wished he was old enough to earn money, so that his mother didn't have to work on that machine, so that there would be enough fuel for the stove and plenty of food on the table. When he was grown up they would leave this horrible room. He would find a nice apartment like the one they had lost and then Mama would stop crying in the night and wanting to throw herself in front of a tram.

Fear always made him angry. His fear of his father, of the bullies in the playground, of his mother dying, all dissolved into a melting pot of secret rage. Not wanting to hear any more, he poked his head out of the covers and set about finishing his apple.

Marta sat by the window, watching her grandson build a castle in the snow. He had plumped out in the Christmas holiday, lost that little-old-man expression. It was a pity he had to go home tomorrow. She would have liked to have taken him in, and his poor mother too, and support them out of her savings. But Milena wasn't strong enough to work on the land, and to be unemployed was to commit the crime of 'parasitism'. To think of an educated girl like that putting spokes in bicycle wheels!

Poor Milena. So gentle, so highly strung, so vulnerable. Marta had always known the marriage would never work. Karel had needed a tough nut, someone who would stand up to him. But in wartime people fell in love for all the wrong reasons.

Marta had sent her daughter-in-law back to Prague with enough cash to keep her solvent for a while. The gesture had involved the discreet sale of another of her rings – not a difficult transaction, even in this backwater, given the peasant mentality. The endless rumours of devaluation made gold the hardest currency available, and Marta's was not the only feather mattress with buried treasure hidden in its depths. Karel would have disapproved, of course. Her jewellery had been bought with old money by her grandparents and passed from generation to generation in the best capitalist tradition.

Karel hadn't shown a shred of sympathy when the National Committee had turned her out of her spacious apartment, her home for over thirty years, and pensioned her off to this miserable shack in the middle of nowhere.

'There's a housing shortage,' he had snapped. 'What do you want with five rooms? Two families could live in that place! If you don't like it, you can move in with us. We all have to make sacrifices.'

But she had known better than to accept the invitation. By that time she had become a liability, a sinful relic of his bourgeois past, the past that had finally been used in evidence against him. Father: a Bohemian nationalist and later a Social Democrat; First World War veteran and ardent admirer of Tomáš Masaryk, the nation's first president; linguist, historian, a professor of Charles University; frequent visitor to Paris, Berlin and Vienna, often accompanied by his wife and son; author of many learned papers on the founding of the Czechoslovak Republic; flamboyant, idealistic, dead of a heart attack at fifty-two, mercifully spared the betrayal of Munich, the Nazi occupation, the Communist takeover, and the disgrace of his son.

'Times have changed, Mother,' Karel kept saying. 'Communism is the only way for the future. The old democracy didn't work. It allowed the growth of Fascism, it couldn't defend us against Hitler. To whom do we owe the greatest debt – the Western capitalists or the Soviet Union? You're living in the past.'

His love for Milena was like his love for the Party – a triumph of passion over reason. Once Karel set his sights on something nothing would deflect him. Even now, rotting in that gaol on a trumped-up charge, he probably still believed the Party could do no wrong.

'Viktor!' She tapped on the window to summon him inside, and began ladling out soup for the midday meal while he took off his outdoor clothes. He was rather subdued today, well aware that tomorrow his mother would arrive to take him home. Milena finished work at noon on Saturdays; she would arrive pale and exhausted, wanting only to sleep, sleep, sleep. The girl had a kind of sleeping sickness: it was the nearest she could get to dying. Sometimes Marta got impatient with her,

9

but it was hard to cheer someone up without offering them some crumb of hope for the future. And there was no future. As the wife of a self-confessed imperialist agent, she was an outcast, one of the public scapegoats the regime so badly needed. There was nothing wrong with the system, despite the shortages and the queues and bureaucratic chaos. Once all the enemies of the people had been weeded out, and their wives and children reduced to penury, the new socialist paradise would be revealed in all its splendour.

'Are you looking forward to seeing your mama tomorrow?' said Marta brightly, trying to invest his departure with some positive element, doggedly hiding her own misery at the thought of the lonely months ahead.

Viktor nodded, the characteristic furrow of anxiety settling between his brows. He worried about things that should never concern a child: that without him there to wake her, his mother would oversleep and lose her job; that without him to stand in the early morning queues for food, she would not have anything to eat; and sometimes, in the night, he would wake suddenly, jolting Marta out of her slumber, having dreamed that he could hear his mother crying.

It began snowing. Marta put more wood on the stove. In the dark winter afternoons she would read aloud to him – the noble, tragic stories of King Wenceslas and Jan Hus, and Hasek's satirical tales of *The Good Soldier Švejk*, the wily underdog, the embodiment of passive resistance. After supper they would play chess. It was a pity that Karel had never found time to teach his son; it might have convinced him he was less stupid than he thought. Viktor's concentration was absolute: he had a positive gift for entrapment, displaying a cold-blooded guile that spelt death for Marta's king. But from time to time, he would let her win, subtly manipulating her every move towards undeserved victory. 'Well done, Babička!' he would crow, jumping up to kiss her, as if trying to atone for his earlier ruthlessness. If there had been money on the table, he would have cleaned her out, and then cheerfully lost the lot. And then, as the evening drew to a close, they would sing folk songs by the light of the oil lamp until it was time to snuggle up under the goose down, and try not to think of happier times.

The snow was falling very fast, in thick, fat flakes. Marta hoped that Milena would not arrive at the station to find the road blocked by snow. The countryside looked so beautiful, hiding the harsh realities of survival. Without kindly neighbours to carry wood and water for her, what would have become of her? Without a bit of money salted away, how would she have survived? Why didn't they just kill off old people and be done with it?

Viktor pressed his nose up against the window, staring at the whiteness outside, while Marta cleared the dirty dishes, delicate Dresden china with fluted edges dipped in gold. She had just begun brewing a murky mixture of ground rye and barley when there was a yelp from Viktor and a sudden rush of cold air.

'Viktor! What are you thinking of? Viktor?'

She ran to the door to see Viktor stumbling in the snow towards a figure approaching slowly on skis, dragging its feet painfully, clearly near to exhaustion. Marta peered over the top of her glasses. It wasn't Milena. It was a short, stocky girl, too well insulated to be recognisable. But as she entered the house, puffing, with Viktor at her heels, and drew her scarf back from her face, Marta smiled in welcome.

'Věra! We were expecting Milena tomorrow – I was just worrying about the weather. Have you come to collect Viktor for her?'

For once Věra wasn't smiling. 'I got here as fast as I could,' she said, looking around her, as if searching for something. The snow from her boots began melting into a dark stain on Marta's Persian rug. She seemed rooted to the spot. 'Is this the only room?' she whispered. Marta nodded, realising from the expression on her face that she wanted to talk to her in private. She would have sent Viktor outside, but it was snowing.

Viktor's eyes grew huge. 'Is Mama ill?'

Věra knelt down on the floor, pulled off her gloves, and took hold of both his hands.

'Viktor . . . your mama had an accident.'

Marta felt suddenly very cold.

'Is she hurt?' demanded Viktor. 'Who's looking after her?'

Věra bit her lip and bent her head. 'She was crossing the

road, and she got hit by a car . . .' Her voice tailed off. Marta sat down numbly. 'Viktor, darling, I'm terribly sorry.' She took a deep shuddering breath as if to dislodge the words from her throat. 'Your mama is dead.'

Marta let out an involuntary cry, and swooped on her grandson, crushing him to her bosom, staring at Věra with disbelieving, hostile eyes, condemning her as the bearer of bad news.

'I'm sorry,' said Věra again. Her plump face was blue with cold, wet with snow and tears. Viktor wrenched himself free.

'A car?' he demanded tonelessly.

'She was knocked down and banged her head very hard.'

'Did you see it?'

'No. I went to visit your mama at home last night, and a neighbour told me what had happened.' Věra turned to Marta, unable to hold Viktor's fierce, interrogative gaze. 'I went to the hospital,' she mumbled. 'She was unconscious. I sat with her till she died, early this morning. She never woke up. She didn't have any pain.'

'Are you sure it was a car?' demanded Viktor in a strange, sharp voice.

The two women exchanged glances, disturbed by the odd expression on his face, the irrelevance of the question, the anger in his voice.

'Are you sure it wasn't a tram?' he persisted, accusingly. Věra stared back at him, apparently tongue-tied.

'Viktor,' said Marta gently. 'Don't think about how it happened. A car, a tram, it makes no difference. Your mama is in heaven now, at peace. Your mama . . .'

Viktor accepted her embrace stiffly, his eyes bright with unshed tears. 'Will they send me to an orphanage now?' he asked woodenly.

'Of course not. Do you think I'd let them take you away from me? Your Babička will look after you.'

'You promise? You *promise*?'

'Of course I promise. Viki, don't look at me like that. Let me hold you. You're quite safe. You're quite safe.'

But for how long? she thought. For how long?

12

TWO

Paris, January 1968

Cassie hadn't eaten for two days. She had never thought much about food before, nor, incidentally, about money. The connection between the two commodities – or lack of them – had come as a revelation.

She lay on the lumpy bed for a moment, contemplating her new-found hunger and poverty. Thin sunlight shone patchily through the hideous curtains, informing her that she had overslept again. The faded fabric, which matched her counterpane, depicted a pink pastoral idyll, its shepherdesses simpering smugly at her tardiness. Cassie's alarm clock, which had been unable to penetrate her drug-induced slumber, confirmed to one half-open eye that she had missed her eight o'clock class for the third week running. Her neglected pupils – an unruly bunch of thirteen-year-olds – would have taken their usual uninhibited delight in advertising her absence. She would be summoned yet again to Mme le Censeur's office and upbraided in the declamatory tones of a character in a Racine play. Her empty stomach would rumble loudly throughout the interview, reducing the drama to farce.

She kicked the bedclothes on to the bare floorboards, concertinaed the single, skimpy curtain and yawned at the romantic view from the grimy window, a cold grey landscape of frosty Parisian roofs. The dingy attic room was suddenly full of reproachful, threatening morning, its privacy invaded by the cruel searchlight of another day. Today I will definitely clean up in here, thought Cassie. Today I will go to the launderette and buy myself a dustpan and brush. Then she remembered with some relief that of course she had no money.

Still groggy, she rummaged in her bag for her tranquillisers, popped one in her mouth and, finding the Evian bottle empty, swallowed it dry. Grimacing, she crossed over to the cracked washbasin and turned the solitary tap full on; it belched rusty air and grudgingly delivered a trickle of cold brown water. Cassie splashed her face and neck – no time to boil water for a proper wash – and put on the new skinny sweater which had caused her present penury. In the dimly lit boutique in Saint-Germain-des-Prés, it had passed for a bright, defiant, pillar-box red, calculated to lift her flagging spirits. But now, viewed against the harsh white light of a winter sky, it revealed itself as a dingy terracotta which did nothing for Cassie's English-rose complexion and tarnished the blondeness of her long, fine hair.

Frowning, she took it off again and settled for a trusty black Marks & Spencer jumper, a well-worn workaday garment which had acquired a sudden unexpected chic. Her fellow-teachers had hailed it enviously as *un shetland ravissant* and had commissioned her to purchase a dozen similar items during her Christmas holidays, warning her to cut off the labels to thwart malevolent customs men. The equivalent of a fifty-nine-and-eleven woollen sweater retailed for a good two hundred francs in Paris. Cassie could have allowed herself a comfortable profit margin and still delivered a bargain – but then Cassie had never thought much about money.

Black jumper, black skirt, black tights, black boots. You should always wear black, Wilfred had said. Perhaps because black made her look older, reducing the twenty-five-year gap between them. She had always been overly conscious of the difference in their ages. For her, as for him, no doubt, it had been part of the attraction. Wilfred couldn't come to terms with middle age; Cassie had never felt young.

Yes, she looked sober and soulful now, pale and ethereal. She would plead a migraine and look vague and victimised until the old bag had run out of steam. The threat of dismissal was purely a matter of form. Mme le Censeur was well aware that Cassie was of *trés bonne famille*. Her father, Dr Lawrence

14

Blakeney, moved in the best academic circles, and Cassie's appointment as English language *assistante* to the Lycée Alphonse Cluny – one of the most prestigious girls' schools in Paris – had been fortunate rather than fortuitous.

'*Merde!*' muttered Cassie, appropriately enough, finding the malodorous communal squatter clogged solid with *France-Soir*. Once she had attempted to share a fat imported roll of Andrex with her fellow-tenants, more out of self-interest than generosity, but it had duly disappeared within minutes of installation, and since then Cassie had learned to swallow her embarrassment and transport her own supply back and forth along the length of the corridor. Inevitably she would encounter a neighbour while thus encumbered, and it was mortifying to have to exchange the ritual *Bonjour* and *Ça va?* in such an obviously pre- or post-lavatorial state. Thanks to the frequent blockages, she had become a regular patron of the café across the road, where the *Toilettes–Téléphones* sign tactfully obfuscated her intentions.

Cassie's family supposed her to be living in a 'bedsitter', but the word gave quite the wrong impression. There was no English equivalent to her present accommodation, which possessed a tawdry glamour unique to Paris. The erstwhile servants' quarters of the city's apartment blocks – minuscule mansarded rooms on the seventh floor – now served as the cheapest form of rented accommodation, usually devoid of hot running water or other such sybaritic luxuries. They were inhabited by students, low-paid workers, and, occasionally, by the maids of the families who lived in comfort below; although maids were a vanishing breed, the generic name for an attic room was still a *chambre de bonne*.

Cassie ran down the seven flights of stairs, doing calculations in her head. She had half a carnet of Métro tickets and five school-meal vouchers and three francs forty, and these had to last till she was paid at the end of the month. She hadn't been particularly hungry over the weekend, having slept and read her way through most of it, but today she would clear her plate, for once, and filch some extra bread to take home.

Other people, of course, sent home for illicit funds, flouting the currency restrictions. Anxious parents sent ten-pound notes in thick brown envelopes; fellow-students returned from visits home with banknotes secreted in their shoes. Cassie had been brought up to know that such behaviour was reprehensible. Dr and Mrs Blakeney were committed supporters of the Wilson government, their lifelong socialist principles having survived the heavy burden of inherited wealth and accommodated, by immaculate reasoning, an expensive private education for all three of their thoroughbred offspring. A substantial house in Hampstead, a weekend cottage in the New Forest, and a sizeable unearned income were offset by a conspicuous social conscience. Extravagance and acquisitiveness were deemed immoral, not to say vulgar; Cassie's pocket money had never been lavish and her carefully calculated allowance had been designed to 'teach her to manage' – which she always had done, until now.

There was no excuse for her present insolvency. Eight hundred francs a month – the salary for an *assistante* – was well above the baguette-line. It was considerably more than the national minimum wage for a forty-eight-hour week. It was a handsome return indeed for twelve hours' work (if conducting English conversation lessons could reasonably be called work), a schedule designed to leave the visiting student ample time to study and read and attend mind-improving lectures at the Sorbonne. Eight hundred francs a month was more than enough to live on, even if it didn't run to designer knitwear. The red sweater was the latest in a ruinous rash of impulse buys – a shocking-pink feather boa, a big, floppy, purple hat, and a ridiculous pair of tarty silver shoes – none of which had succeeded in cheering her up. Predictably, they had had the reverse effect.

Cassie ran across the road without looking, provoking a furious hoot from a taxi. Her local café was a gloomy place with tan vinyl banquettes and ultra-surly waiters. The appetising coffee-and-croissant aroma did not descend to the subterranean gloom of the *toilettes*, where the familiar odour of unbleached U-bend made her empty stomach heave. Unable to recall putting on her deodorant, Cassie dabbed some duty-free *L'Air du Temps* under each arm; galvanised by her dishevelled reflection in the spotted mirror, she dragged a brush through her shoulder-length fair hair and peered through her long fringe to thicken up yesterday's mascara. Cassie's vanity, albeit well developed, was mercilessly self-critical and rather than develop a style of her own she had embraced an anonymous dolly-bird disguise. Her large, clear, grey eyes were lost in a pit of sooty eyeshadow, her full mouth rendered all but invisible by the palest of pale lipsticks, her long legs exposed almost beyond the bounds of decency, but the overall effect was spoiled – or possibly enhanced – by a tousled lack of conceit. Cassie knew she looked sexy, but she didn't feel it; when men whistled at her in the street, she felt a fraud.

On her way out, she caught sight of an abandoned coffee cup, with two wrapped rectangles of sugar lying neglected by the saucer. Running her hand along the edge of the table as she passed, she surreptitiously removed them, popping one into her mouth as soon as she was safely outside. The pure sugar revived her, inspiring her to walk the two Métro stops to the school rather than surrender another precious ticket. She would still be in time for her nine o'clock class, an earnest clutch of *lettres supérieures* who had read more English literature than she had – or rather, not more, but more thoroughly, able to quote Shakespeare and Dickens by the metre, regurgitating approved lit. crit. without an original thought in their heads. Original thought formed no part of the syllabus at the Lycée Alphonse Cluny. Original thought did not pass the *baccalauréat*, the savage matriculation exam that separated the winners from the losers. Success at the *bac* guaranteed automatic university entrance; failure consigned the failee to a dead-end job. The system was cold-bloodedly designed to eliminate half the candidates and hung over the senior pupils like the sword of Damocles.

Cassie underestimated the length of the walk and arrived, panting, at three minutes past nine, running straight into the majestic bulk of Mme le Censeur, the vice-principal.

'Mademoiselle Blakeney!' she hissed. 'In my office at once, if you please.'

Cassie opened her mouth to protest that her class was waiting but the excuse died in her throat, given that her eight o'clock pupils had waited, once more, in vain.

17

The words of the lecture never varied. Next time she defaulted on a class, she would be required to make her excuses to Mme la Directrice herself. Was her timetable so onerous that she could not present herself on time for the requisite number of hours per week? Was she aware that her absence had necessitated intervention by a *surveillante*, who had found her pupils laughing and chattering and unattended when they should have been engaged in earnest discourse about English culture and customs?

Cassie was a good deal taller than Mme le Censeur – a long-limbed five feet eight against a squat one metre fifty-five – and these hectorings made her feel like a giant, gawky child. The enviably long legs that had come into their own with the mini-skirt seemed suddenly coltish and ungainly again. It was humiliating to be reprimanded week after week, like a recalci-trant postulant facing an irate mother superior, but Cassie's meekness was the product of prudence, not penitence. The hier-archy of the Lycée Alphonse Cluny was rigid even by English public school standards, and a display of abject contrition, how-ever false, was *de rigueur*. While the Censeur droned on, her voice precise and cold, as if she were giving a particularly tortu-ous *dicteé*, a faint odour of boiling artichokes wafted upwards from the school kitchen. It was early to be boiling artichokes. Presumably they would be served cold with vinaigrette today, not hot with hollandaise. The smell of boiling artichokes at nine o'clock in the morning had the gradual but inexorable effect of some sinister mind-numbing gas. Not for the first time in her tall, thin, perennially anaemic life, Cassie fainted.

The games mistress was sent for to administer first aid, the two women clucking round her half sympathetically, half sus-piciously. It occurred to Cassie that perhaps they thought that she was pregnant, and if so, their suspicions were a good year out of date.

'I haven't had breakfast, that's all,' she admitted plaintively. 'I woke up too late.' The Censeur sent down to the kitchen for coffee and a roll which Cassie, normally a diffident eater, wolfed down with immoderate haste, provoking the wry ques-tion, 'And when did you last eat, mademoiselle?' A note of matronly concern crept into her voice. Pretty girls were all obsessed with dieting, and this one was prettier, and thinner than most.

'Friday,' admitted Cassie, enjoying herself now. 'I am rather short of money at the moment.'

'Then you must write home and request that your father send you more!'

'It is not permitted,' explained Cassie piously. 'We are only allowed to bring out fifty pounds sterling per year. I have already spent it.'

The Censeur raised a cynical eyebrow, well aware, no doubt, that such laws were made to be broken.

'I am not authorised to give you an advance on your salary,' she said, as if pre-empting a request. She extracted a fifty-franc note from her purse and extended it regally. 'Please treat this as a personal loan. Meanwhile, if you cannot manage on your salary, may I suggest that you give private lessons. But kindly do not solicit pupils from this school – their parents will think that you have a vested interest in neglecting your duties.'

Cassie tried to refuse this unsought handout, but the Censeur made an impatient gesture.

'Do not force me to bring this matter to the attention of the Directrice,' she said. 'She might find it necessary to write to your tutor in England. Now please proceed to what remains of your nine o'clock lesson. I suggest you visit the British Institute in the rue de la Sorbonne next time you attend a lecture at the faculty. They keep a list of persons seeking private tuition. Who knows, you may even be able to save, mademoiselle. Now that your English pound has been devalued, you are fortunate indeed to be able to earn money in francs.'

With this parting shot she opened the door wide, dismissing her.

Miserable old cow, thought Cassie, smiling sweetly. Though perhaps private lessons weren't such a bad idea, if only to fill a few of the endless hours she currently spent lolling around in her room doing nothing. The incentives to study were poor. The lectures at the Sorbonne were grossly over-subscribed, and with her tendency to lateness she invariably had to join the crowds listening to the loudspeakers outside the lecture hall, there not being enough seats to accommodate everybody. Sometimes she had to stand, and standing for long periods meant that she would faint, so that in the end she had not bothered to go any more; no attendance records were kept in any event. Yes, giving private lessons would help kill a bit of time, replace one form of boredom with another.

Boredom was Cassie's favourite vice; living alone had reinforced her naturally anti-social tendencies. The previous term she had lived in a hostel for English students in the *cité universitaire*, where she had shared a room with a fanatically tidy girl from Leeds who had objected loudly to Cassie's slovenly habits. Communal living had never suited her; years of boarding school – where she had been deemed a poor mixer, lacking in team spirit, and prone to malingering – had fostered an ability to insulate herself from the people around her which had earned her the epithets 'shy' and 'stuck-up' in roughly equal proportions. University had driven her even deeper into her shell. Cassie had failed Oxford entrance so spectacularly that no amount of string-pulling could put matters right. After consulting with their trendier academic friends, her parents had steered her towards Southwold, a new university with a radical image, where her disappointing A-level results were deemed unimportant and where her presence could be passed off as a deliberate, anti-élitist gesture.

Cassie had found the liberal atmosphere at Southwold almost as oppressive as the one in which she had grown up. The lecturers wore their hair long and were addressed by their Christian names; the students were mostly grammar school types from suburban semis, trying to pass themselves off as working class. Sex and Marxism intruded into every lecture and seminar; political and moral conformity was rife. Cassie, used to being a misfit, had kept herself to herself, a technique which had travelled well.

But after three months of living in the *maison anglaise*, hemmed in as always by fellow-students – all having a wonderful time – it had occurred to her, belatedly, that there was nothing to stop her living on her own, other than a shortage of funds. The squalor of her *chambre de bonne* was the price she had paid for her recent extravagances; it had been all she could afford. But at least when she shut her door she could please herself, a luxury which more than made up for her other deprivations.

Since moving in, after the Christmas vacation, Cassie had effectively cut herself off from the student population of Paris, both indigenous and foreign, while continuing to shun well-meaning overtures from her colleagues. The English teachers at Alphonse Cluny had been eager to involve her in extramural activities, but Mlle Blakeney had shown no inclination to accompany class outings to Olivier's film of *Hamlet*, nor to involve herself in a school production of Shaw's *St Joan*. She might do less than her twelve hours per week, but never more; her excuse was always the pressing need to study and her preoccupied, absent-minded air lent credibility to her midnight-oil image. But the real reason was an overpowering apathy, a man-made condition which had successfully drained her huge reserves of nervous energy.

The tranquillisers had first been prescribed to get Cassie through her A levels. She had never been able to sit an exam without weeks of preparatory terror, involving loss of appetite, sleepwalking and, once, hysterical amnesia. Her new, artificial calm had been a great relief to her parents, who had been assured that her medication was non-habit-forming and harmless, one of a revolutionary range of new, safe drugs that could be prescribed long-term without any ill effects. Since then, thanks to a repeat prescription from the progressive student health clinic at Southwold, sleepless nights and anxious days had become a thing of the past. Thanks to an identical repeat prescription from her tame GP at home, Cassie had quietly doubled her dose without provoking any embarrassing questions. The woolly vest she had been given to stop her shivering no longer kept her warm – so she had added a jumper and an overcoat, as any sensible person would. That winter now lasted all year round was a minor inconvenience. At least she was safe from sunburn.

The rest of the morning passed in the usual blur. Cassie never prepared her lessons; when inspiration failed, she would recite Edward Lear or Lewis Carroll with the utmost gravity and get her pupils transcribing words like 'brillig' and 'runcible',

translated as the fancy took her, into their vocabulary notebooks. When she got back to her room that afternoon, leaden
with too much lunch, her concierge handed her a letter from
Wilfred.

> ...every chance I might make it over to Paris for a
> weekend later this term. I'll let you know the dates and
> you can book us a hotel. Meanwhile, for God's sake get
> out more. I don't expect you to live like a nun...

This was Wilfred's way of telling her that some other nymph
was currently consoling him for his wife's sagging breasts and
coarsening upper lip (entranced, no doubt, by the mature
charm of his baggy eyes and dinky little bald patch).

She would have to put him off. Meeting him in London at
Christmas had been one thing – he had borrowed a friend's flat
for the purpose – but having him here, in Paris, invading her
precious isolation, was quite another. She had expected, even
hoped, that he would drop her after the abortion. Perhaps he
would have done, if she hadn't made things so damned easy
for him. She had made no embarrassing fuss, she had been a
brave girl, she hadn't told her parents or anyone else, and she
had followed his instructions to the letter. A softly spoken doctor had talked to her about her period pains and recommended
a scrape; Cassie had not compromised him by mentioning her
pregnancy: it had all been perfectly legal. After this minor
interruption they had carried on as before, with Cassie safely
on the Pill. Well, not safely perhaps. She was only to take it for
two years, initially. And by that time she'd probably be
married, the doctor told her jovially. What would happen if
she took it for longer than two years? Oh, most probably nothing but, of course, there would have to be regular checks.
Why? Was it dangerous? No, of course not, the checks were
just routine. Wilfred said that the Pill heralded a new era of
freedom for women. Cassie thought that it heralded a new era
of freedom for men.

It was Cassie, not Wilfred, who had felt bloated and nauseous, Cassie, not Wilfred, who had suffered blinding
headaches, and she had stopped taking the horrible things the
day she left for France. At Christmas she had quietly got her-

self a new cap, but fear that it would let her down again had made it even harder than usual to go through the motions of lust. Besides which, absence and abstinence had taught her that she did not need Wilfred, that she did not, in fact, need sex. It was the Blakeney in her that had needed sex, as part of a programmed quest for knowledge, and she had been glad to lose her ignorance at the hands of an experienced man, not a groping contemporary. There had been no folly, no passion, no risk of falling in love. For Cassie there had been the immeasurable relief of finding something she was apparently quite good at, even if she didn't much enjoy it – which was why she had balked at breaking things off with Wilfred.

While Wilfred was her so-called lover she could kid herself that she was normal. Her ritual moans and spasms evidently convinced him – with a little help from his ego – and that in itself was a kind of reality. It would be too daunting to risk exposure with someone else, someone who might, because he actually cared, realise she was faking, someone who might, because *she* actually cared, make her feel dishonest. Here in Paris, she needed no one, because she was no one. But when she got home, she would be, inescapably, a Blakeney again.

Viktor Brožek tossed the monogrammed pigskin wallet into the Seine. By chance it was engraved with his own initials, which had tempted him, briefly, to keep it. But discretion, or rather professionalism, had prevailed. It had until recently belonged to a Mr Virgil Bernstein, a camera-laden American tourist who had been discreetly relieved of the contents of his back pocket while he was changing his film outside Notre-Dame. It had proved a good haul, as the good Mr Bernstein had recently converted some two hundred dollars into francs. The remaining travellers' cheques, along with his Diners' Club and American Express cards, had already been fenced – less profitable than forging the signatures, but unquestionably safer. Viktor combined a natural recklessness with cultivated caution; he valued his freedom, and the way he earned his living was a celebration of it.

He had done enough business for one day. Or rather, some innate superstition told him not to push his luck. He had the

23

professional gambler's instinct for knowing when to quit, and besides, he had earned an evening off. Last night had been hard work. The blue-rinsed widow he had picked up in the bar of the Crillon had proved less gullible than most; it had taken three hours and five champagne cocktails before she finally gave in and invited him up to her room. Not that Viktor had had the slightest intention of screwing her, other than in the metaphorical sense. Her brief visit to the bathroom had given him more than enough time to relieve her of a thousand francs in petty cash and sundry items of jewellery before beating a hasty retreat. Such crimes were rarely reported to the police, who had a habit of asking embarrassing questions; Viktor had a nose for respectable women. Nevertheless, one couldn't be sure, and it gave him a good excuse to lie low tonight and desert the tourist track for a dingy bar in the back streets off the rue Monge, where he could get quietly drunk and pick himself up a tart. But first he must call in on Babička.

Viktor's grandmother, Marta, lived in a modest three-roomed apartment in the Gobelins, her home since their escape from Czechoslovakia in 1951. She had stubbornly refused to move, despite Viktor's repeated offers to set her up in more stylish accommodation. She wanted no part of his ill-gotten gains and still earned her living, doggedly, as a dressmaker, despite her advanced years and failing eyesight. She had taken no charity from anyone, asked nothing of France except liberty, and it pained her that young Viktor had never done an honest day's work in his life (even though he was a good boy at heart).

She growled a greeting at him, dished him out a bowl of stew, and sawed half a dozen chunks of bread, watching him as he ate. His thick, dark, glossy hair flopped forward over his forehead as he bent over his plate. He attacked his meal like a man in overalls, even though he wore a Cardin shirt, a silk cravat, and an expensive hand-made suit. Such a good-looking boy, so like Karel had been at that age.

'I had a letter from your father today,' she said. 'He's off work with his bronchitis again.' As always, Viktor displayed no interest. 'He asks after you.' She put on her reading glasses. 'Would you like me to read it to you?'

'Not particularly.'

'He thanks you for the twenty dollars.'

He threw her a mocking look and helped himself to another piece of bread. 'You could have sent him a hundred, you old skinflint.'

'And where would I tell him it came from?'

'Tell him the truth. Tell him I share his touching devotion to Communist doctrine. How does it go? "What's mine is mine and what's yours is also mine."'

'Things are changing at home. There's a bit here about this new man, Dubček. Your father says—'

'This is terrific Roquefort. Have a piece. You're all skin and bone.'

He squashed a lump of it on to a piece of bread and handed it to her, as if to shut her up. Marta waved it away, sighing, and watched him wash it down with another glass of wine. Viktor treated any news from home with the same cynical indifference. Even his father's release from gaol, following the 1957 amnesty, had provoked little more than a shrug. His rejection of his origins would have been easier to bear if he had adopted his new country wholeheartedly. But he affected contempt for it – an understandable syndrome in older exiles, racked by guilt and nostalgia, but unusual in the younger generation.

'This country has been good to you,' she would rebuke him, during his routine diatribes. But Viktor would repeat that France was corrupt, class-ridden, complacent. He took a pride, he said, in feeding off its fat. He had never quite forgiven Marta for taking out French citizenship, automatically conferring this dubious privilege on to him and thus condemning him to two interminable years of *service militaire*, prison by any other name. He had been busy making up for lost time ever since.

'Make sure you're in tomorrow morning,' said Viktor casually, wiping his fingers on his napkin.

'What's happening tomorrow morning?'

'It's your birthday. We had an agreement, remember?'

Marta sighed, half annoyed, half touched. Viktor's attempts to refurbish her flat from top to bottom, to kit her out with every conceivable luxury and to replace the assets she had lost twenty years before had been obstinately thwarted by Marta's unshakeable principles. But on special occasions she relented and allowed him to spoil her. She had been unable to resist a fur coat at Christmas ('A present from my grandson. He's doing so well at his job, you know'), and her jewellery box bore witness to other festive moments of weakness. Marta was every bit as vain at seventy-six as she had been at seventeen, and Viktor knew it.

'My birthday? I'd forgotten. You stop counting the years at my age.'

Viktor grinned, got up and began removing the pile of records from inside the old-fashioned radiogram, which had recently given up the ghost.

'Viktor, you haven't!'

'It's the latest model. Stereo. For God's sake don't touch it till I get here and show you how it works.'

'How much did it cost you?'

'Not half as much as I spent on mine.'

'Really Viktor! Just an ordinary machine would have done. You know how I hate you spending money on me. Not that I'd mind if you came by it honestly . . .'

She set her jaw in the fierce, disapproving line Viktor knew so well. In the old days it had heralded a thrashing with a man's leather belt bought specially for the purpose. It had never hurt much – Marta had the physique of a sparrow – but Viktor had pretended that it did, as a mark of respect. If she had been a man he would have borne the beatings with Spartan indifference, plotted revenge, hit back. But her very weakness was her greatest strength.

Little by little, he would wear her down. He had always envisaged setting her up in a nice place once she got too old to argue. Somewhere with a maid to cook and clean for her, and a nurse to look after her when she was sick. Somewhere with a bit of luxury to make up for all the years of making do.

'Don't be such an old misery. It's your birthday! If you dare send the van away I'll tear up those concert tickets for tomorrow night. And that's a promise.'

'Concert tickets?'

'Stern playing Dvořák's Violin in A Minor. The best seats of course. But only if you behave yourself.'

Marta got out her handkerchief.

'Oh, Babička, don't start snivelling, please. Twice a year I get to give you a lousy present. Don't spoil it.'

'I've told you before, Viktor. I won't visit you in gaol.'

'You won't have to. Only fools end up in gaol.'

The significance of this barbed remark was not lost on Marta but she chose to ignore it for once, overcome with furious affection for him. Viktor bent to kiss her, evidently anxious to get away. He hated tears.

'Poor Babička. What a trial I am to you. I'd better leave you in peace.'

She creaked to her feet and saw him to the door, watching him as he sauntered across the street. To annoy her, he whistled at a girl in a very short skirt. Viktor's taste in women was appalling. Marta's hopes of his settling down with a nice girl seemed unlikely ever to be realised. Sometimes she wondered if she had done the right thing in bringing him to the West; at home he would have been forced to work, at least. What high hopes she had had for him! Hopes that had driven her to risk her life and his.

They had been luckier than many escapees, many of whom had fallen foul of Operation Kamen, a false escape network set up by the state security forces to ensnare the unwary. But her relief at finding safe harbour, after weeks of waiting in a West German refugee camp, had not been shared by young Viktor. She had remembered Paris with pleasure, recalling the year she had spent there with her husband and son in 1932; it still held happy memories for her. But to Viktor it had seemed a strange, hostile place, whose language he could not understand. At home he had been a pariah, yes, but here he was a foreigner, which was worse.

After years of persistent truanting, pilfering, and vandalism, Viktor had been hauled before the juvenile court and sent to a reform school. He had come home unreformed but a great deal wilier, and ever since he had been careful not to let the law outwit him again. Yet throughout his delinquent youth, throughout repeated beatings and lectures from Marta, he had remained an affectionate grandson, as co-operative within the home as he was rebellious outside it, inspiring in her a dogged loyalty, an unshakeable belief in his intrinsic worth. With hindsight, his love for her, and hers for him, had somehow fuelled his hatred for the rest of the world. After she was dead there would be no one for him to love, leaving only the hate . . .

Viktor walked back to his apartment, hands thrust deep into the pockets of his fur-lined camel coat. He had been planning to stay longer, but news of the letter from Prague had made him keen to get away. Any word from his father would start Marta off on the same old singsong. At this very moment she was probably hunched over her kitchen table, writing one of her embarrassing letters full of absurd lies.

'Don't you think your poor father's suffered enough?' she would challenge him, her stubborn excuse for an elaborate fiction involving Viktor's industry at school, his success at the *bac*, and his responsible, well-paid job. Even her friends and neighbours had been conned into believing that he had made good and qualified as an accountant; periodically they would solicit his advice about their income tax. Luckily, this was a subject on which Viktor was reasonably well informed. He filed an immaculate return each year, and paid his dues like any honest citizen, having secured himself a bogus job as a waiter at the Chez Clément, a favoured watering hole whose proprietor had been glad to vouch for him for a suitable consideration. Viktor liked to be one jump ahead of the bureaucrats; to be 'self-employed' was to invite investigation.

Camouflage was all-important, hence the immaculate cut of his working clothes, a uniform which proclaimed him to be bourgeois, respectable and law-abiding. Once he had stolen a woman's purse in a crowd outside the Louvre, and bungled it. He had not been quite light-fingered enough, choosing the wrong angle of approach, and she had realised her loss almost immediately. He had found his escape route blocked by a throng of bodies and had been obliged to stand frozen to the spot while she shrieked hysterically, attracting a nearby gendarme who had duly rushed to the scene and collared some innocent, long-haired youth. It had been an object lesson in the value of disguise, and Viktor had thought of himself ever since as a saboteur, a resistance worker, an undercover agent, thwarting an oppressive regime, duping its flunkeys, depriving its collaborators of their spoils. It had been tempting, after that, to take unnecessary risks in order to increase the thrill, but that one salutary taste of incarceration had taught him the better part of valour.

Still, there had to be some element of danger or the whole exercise became pointless, and adrenalin was addictive. He loved to stroll into the foyer of the Georges V or the Ritz, make himself comfortable with a newspaper, and watch the movements of the porters before choosing his moment and helping himself to a small item of baggage. He would walk out with it at a leisurely pace, sometimes stopping to make an enquiry of the desk clerk or admire the trinkets in the hotel shop or consult the restaurant menu. Once he had tipped the doorman to hail him a taxi and, shaking with suppressed laughter, had watched him load the misappropriated item into the boot. Often he didn't net anything worth having, but that hardly mattered. Picking pockets was too easy to provide job satisfaction in itself. By the same token it appealed to his sense of humour when he fooled some withered bitch into thinking herself desirable and then made off with the baubles her fat cat of a husband had bought her. Nevertheless, his operation was strictly small-time. Once you got greedy, you got caught. And once you got caught, you lost your nerve.

He smiled lazily at Mme Bloc, his concierge, an ill-tempered crone who simpered at the sight of him, and not just because he tipped her heavily. A concierge in one's pocket was a watchdog, informant and bodyguard all rolled into one, a valuable bulwark against possible uninvited guests. Viktor had lived in the same block for the last five years, a veteran amongst ever-shifting tenants; although he could well have afforded to move to a better flat in a more fashionable area, he felt comfortable here. The only concession he had made to his increased affluence was to transfer to a larger apartment, formerly occupied by a prosperous prostitute who had married one of her clients and gone to live in suburbia. This had given him room to install a bigger piano, a Pleyel baby grand, and the latest in elaborate hi-fi equipment. Viktor possessed thousands of records and stack upon stack of sheet music, although mostly he played by ear.

Apart from the piano and the hi-fi, the apartment displayed a Spartan lack of interest in home comforts. The furniture was minimal, except for an outsized wardrobe which housed Viktor's collection of impeccable working clothes. His taste for the good life took him outside his own territory to fancy bars and restaurants and nightclubs and gambling joints where he lost with a good grace. There was always more where that came from and holding on to the stuff tied you down, as did a flashy apartment. The street was his natural habitat; it was there that he felt most at home. The city was his hunting ground, and people were his prey. He would have denied that he loved Paris but Paris was in his blood. He knew all its smells and sounds and secrets. It was like a woman whose body he plundered nightly: his attachment was carnal, not spiritual; instinctive, not intellectual. Paris was like a heaving mass of flesh that helped keep out the cold.

Mentally muttering resolutions, Cassie marched into the British Institute, keeping her head down to avoid being accosted by anyone she knew. She found the notice board, which was festooned with cards advertising rooms for rent, cultural outings, clubs, lectures, entertainments and tuition. There were plenty of people offering to give lessons; none, unfortunately, seeking them. She would add her name to the board and hope for no response. She fumbled in her bag for a pen, succumbing inexorably to the familiar, creeping inertia. She couldn't be bothered. She just couldn't be bothered ... She forced herself to write a short, unappealing message.

Assistante offers private English tuition at competitive rates. Apply Blakeney, c/o Lycée Alphonse Cluny.

The lower reaches of the board were already covered and Cassie had to stretch to find a spare corner. She had just pinned up her advertisement when a voice behind her said, in French, 'Can you help me, please?' The voice was female, and addressed her as *tu* in the manner of a fellow-student. She turned to look at its owner, a diminutive, cat-like creature, sleek and self-contained, with fluid, feline movements and a bright green stare. She half smiled at Cassie in a silent miaou and handed her a piece of squared exercise paper and a drawing pin.

'I can't reach,' she said. 'Would you put it up for me? Read it first, you might be interested.' The message was written in red ink, and the writing was graceful and idiosyncratic, unlike the usual standardised French script.

'English lessons required for six hours a week for a very unintelligent lady,' read Cassie. 'Twenty-five francs per hour, with good reason. Rue du Ranelagh. Apply Madame Lemercier . . .' And a phone number. Twenty-five francs an hour seemed over generous. Cassie wondered what the catch was.

'My stepmother,' explained the girl, with a toss of her long chestnut hair. 'My father's taking her on a business trip to America and she needs to be fluent in essential phrases like "I would like a mild shampoo followed by a curled chignon," and "I shall require a three-sided mirror in my room." You look the calm, patient type,' she added, critically. 'If you like, you can have an exclusive. At least you won't have to worry about her failing her *bac*. Well?'

Automatically, Cassie went into the bewildered, stricken, can't-explain mode she used to excuse herself from importunate requests. Automatically, because there was no reason why she shouldn't at least find out more and steal a march on the competition. But her withdrawal was involuntary, not rational, almost as if this girl were a man looking for an excuse to pick her up.

'Armelle Lemercier,' she continued, shaking Cassie's hand, clearly amused at her diffidence. 'And you?'

'Cassandra Blakeney. Cassie for short. Er . . . thanks. I shall definitely telephone.'

'Good. It will get the old cow off my back.' She pointed to her notice. 'You'd better take that down again, or someone else might beat you to it.'

Cassie did so. Armelle Lemercier had an insidious air of authority about her, as if she was used to getting her own way. And yet her manner was casual enough, imbued with the ubiquitous French shrug.

'Let me buy you a drink,' she said, with another arch, mocking smile. 'To seal our bargain.' She led the way briskly into a

31

nearby café and selected a small table by the window.

'Cigarette?' She smoked untipped Gitanes, the cause, perhaps, of that husky, purring voice. Cassie accepted one and asked for a small black coffee. Armelle ordered a *diabolo menthe*, a bright-green peppermint fizz. Green was definitely Armelle Lemercier's colour, thought Cassie, just as black was her own. Black was full of denial, black was retreat and privacy and fear. Green was lush and greedy, full of growth and envy. There was something bright and threatening about Armelle Lemercier.

'Are you at the faculty?' demanded Armelle, arching her neck and blowing smoke at the ceiling.

'Officially, yes. I'm supposed to attend six lectures a week. But I never go. And you?'

'Second year sociology. At Nanterre.' She pulled a face.

Cassie nodded sympathetically. The overflow campus, in the north-west suburbs, was a utilitarian, modern complex set in the midst of the *bidonville*, the insalubrious shanty town of tar-paper huts inhabited by immigrant workers. Cut off from the diversions of the Latin Quarter, beset by petty restrictions and governed by bureaucrats, Nanterre students were known for their militancy and had recently staged a major boycott of lectures.

'Still, it's a good excuse not to live at home,' continued Armelle. 'Since my father remarried, I've felt *de trop*. Odile, your new pupil, used to be his secretary. God knows how – she's illiterate. Men adore inferiority in women, don't they? Especially intelligent men. Do you pretend to be inferior, with men?'

Rather floored by this unexpected question, Cassie's first reaction was to say no, in that she had always sought Wilfred's good opinion. But the easiest way to secure that good opinion was to defer to him. Wilfred was clever, well informed, mature and articulate, which was why Cassie slept with him, there being no physical incentive to do so. It was as if, by virtue of sleeping with him, she had abdicated dissent, accepted him as her intellectual overlord.

'Yes, I suppose I do,' she said, seduced into agreeing, unconsciously mimicking Armelle's offhand manner and worldly wise smile.

'A man has to think himself superior,' continued her mentor, 'otherwise ... pfft.' She made a noise like a balloon deflating. 'Don't you find? Alain!'

She jumped up, and ran to embrace a thin-faced, sallow young man who had just entered the café. He nodded stiffly at Cassie as Armelle introduced him, evidently rather ill at ease. The proffered hand was rough and calloused; the uncertain smile revealed crooked teeth and creased his dark eyes into a fan of crow's feet. His nose had a pronounced bump, as if he had once broken it, and his hair was very short and slicked down with grease. His ill-matched ensemble of dark-blue donkey jacket, brown home-knitted jumper and narrow grey trousers which had lost their crease suggested a lack of vanity, or taste, or money, or possibly all three. But despite his unprepossessing appearance he projected a tangible, if understated charisma; there was a brooding intensity about his eyes that lit up an otherwise unremarkable face.

His arrival produced an instant metamorphosis in Armelle. Still inescapably feline, she changed from imperious Siamese to fluffy kitten, linking her arm with Alain's and scratching her little snub nose against his stubbly cheek.

'*Tu veux boire?*' she enquired, geisha-like. She lifted her drink, inserted one of the two straws in his mouth, and they sucked in unison, evacuating the green glass with all the intensity of a couple engaged in *soixante-neuf*. Cassie began making her excuses.

'Don't run away,' said Armelle.

'I have that phone call to make,' said Cassie.

'Cassie's going to give English lessons to Odile,' said Armelle.

Alain smiled thinly. 'You're a student?'

'Yes. And you?'

'Alain works in my father's factory, at Boulogne-Billancourt,' interjected Armelle. 'Twelve hundred people working for a pittance, making automobile parts. Hundreds of wives and children dependent on my papa for their daily bread.'

Alain lit a cigarette.

'We are trying to radicalise them,' continued Armelle

eagerly. 'Make them see that it's not enough to be bought off with petty rises and a works canteen. Make them realise that power is theirs for the taking. Make them—'

'That's enough, Armelle,' said Alain. His expression was hard, perceptive, wary, telling Cassie politely that he did not want her to know his business, that he did not trust her. Presumably he was a union militant of some kind. Cassie had never met a union militant before – the Blakeneys viewed the proletariat and its spokesmen from a safe, respectful distance – but she felt instantly humbled in the presence of anyone who participated in the world of Real Work: work that people did from necessity, not choice; work that no one would do from choice.

Armelle accepted the reprimand with a *moue* of disgruntlement. Alain ruffled her hair.

'I hear there was trouble at Nanterre yesterday,' he prompted, as if to steer her on to safer ground. Armelle's tight little mouth spread into a thin, wide grin.

'A little. Forty of us decided we'd had enough of the plain-clothes *flics* spying on us. So we gathered in the main hall and marched up and down for a bit with a few banners, just to test them out. That brought the real vermin out of their holes. Uniforms everywhere. Talk about a police state. Well, they started the usual provocation, but we'd already put the word about. Before they knew what had hit them there were a thousand or more of us, so they took fright and buggered off. It was beautiful. There will always be more of us than them. Always. And this is only the beginning.'

She was like a naughty schoolgirl recounting an escapade; her glee was ingenuous.

'A thousand students don't make a revolution,' said Alain.

'Maybe not. But there are half a million of us in France alone. And it's happening everywhere. Rome, Madrid, Berlin . . . '

'Students don't make a revolution,' repeated Alain, rather irritably. 'Workers make a revolution.'

'Except that the unions will make sure they never do. What do you think, Cassie?' she asked, flooding her with the favour of her smile.

Cassie searched her brain for some tenet of Blakeney socialism which would adapt itself to the discussion. She came up with a feeble, 'Well, if the unions do their job properly, there shouldn't be any *need* for a revolution, should there?' only to meet with a stony silence. '*If* they do their job properly,' she repeated hastily. 'Are you in the union?' she asked Alain anxious to take the heat off herself.

'In it, but not of it,' he said dryly. 'Unions are just another power structure. The worker gets squeezed between the union and the employer, they both exploit him. And in the end they always sign the equivalent of some Nazi–Soviet pact.'

Realising that she was getting well out of her depth, Cassie mumbled that she really must be going and this time Armelle, as if responding to some silent cue from Alain, did not try to detain her. 'You will phone Odile, won't you?' she reminded her, almost skittishly, as she stood up to shake Cassie's hand. 'I hope I haven't put you off.'

'Not at all. I need the money.'

'Look upon it as a conspiracy,' continued Armelle. 'A way of bleeding the rich, of diverting capital. And be hard. An hour is an hour. If she spends ten minutes on the telephone during a lesson, or she's late starting, that's too bad. Demand overtime. And remember,' – her face plumped out into a malicious grin – 'whatever you teach her to say she'll repeat without question. She's too stupid to learn any other way. Think of the power that gives you.'

'Power?'

'Power,' repeated Armelle solemnly. It was like a mission, a sacred trust. It almost sounded like fun.

Viktor hung up his suit carefully and changed into mufti – blue jeans, a white cable-knit sweater and a black leather jacket. He stuffed some notes into his pocket and left the rest of his petty cash in the piano stool. Living it up was all very well, but it required a conscious effort, and tonight he felt like a bit of relaxation.

The Chez Clément was a five-minute stagger away, discreetly tucked into a dark alleyway. A workers' café with no pretensions to chic, it was a raucous, smoke-choked, evil den of a place; its *raison d'être* was serious drinking and gambling. The *patron* hawked pornographic magazines from under the counter, paid the local *flics* to stay away, and welcomed the lowest class of *pute* and punter. Viktor had just made his turning off the rue Mouffetard when he was accosted by a tall, bearded, red-haired youth seeking directions. A haversack was slung across his back and a guitar over his shoulder; he looked stoned.

'I'm looking for a hotel in the rue Émile,' he said, beaming vaguely at Viktor through a pair of granny specs. 'Is it near here?'

'There's no hotel in the rue Émile,' said Viktor curtly.

The hippie fished a piece of paper out of his pocket. 'I asked a waiter for the name of a cheap place to stay. He said that the Chez Clément had rooms to let.'

Clearly a waiter with a sense of humour, thought Viktor. Clément let out the upstairs rooms by the hour rather than the day, and tourists formed no part of his clientèle.

'In that case, follow me,' he said, amused. 'But I shouldn't ask for a room, if I were you, till you're sure you want to stay. It's a bit of a dive.'

The man grinned through a mass of freckles. 'That's okay. I can't afford to be fussy.'

Viktor led the way, allowing the stranger's long stride to overtake him while he took an automatic inventory of his assets. There was a visible bulge in the back pocket of his jeans, advertising the whereabouts of his wallet, but he didn't give the impression of being particularly well off; Viktor never knowingly robbed anyone who couldn't afford it.

'This is it,' he said indicating the insalubrious frontage of the café, all chocolate-brown paint and dirty windows. The man peered through the steamed-up glass and towards the smoke-fogged bar.

'Thanks a lot,' he said, evidently undaunted. 'Can I buy you a drink?'

Viktor shrugged assent and preceded him inside, where an impromptu cabaret was in progress. Clément, the proprietor, was haranguing a hapless-looking Algerian, shaking him by the shoulders and emitting a stream of obscenities. Viktor recognised his victim, Hafaïd, a regular customer and dedicated patron of the pinball machine. He was slightly backward, not that his lack of grey matter cut any ice with the burly Clément, who was gesturing wildly at the 'no credit' sign and baring a set of bad teeth. Poor Hafaïd was cowering in terror while others looked on and laughed.

Viktor murmured something in Clément's ear. The landlord snarlingly accepted what he was owed, while Hafaïd grinned in imbecilic gratitude. Viktor shoved a few francs into his pocket and made his way towards a vacant table. His protégé had the grace to look slightly uneasy. A perfectly civil exchange was taking place between a group of card players near by, but to an untutored ear it no doubt sounded as if bloodshed was imminent.

The bearded man unslung his guitar, got his wallet out of his back pocket and extracted a twenty-franc note, revealing a thick wad of money to whoever happened to be within eyeshot. Viktor began to have second thoughts about his scruples: if he didn't do the job himself, someone else undoubtedly would.

'*Vous voulez boire?*' he asked Viktor. The wine at Clément's was thirty centimes a glass; twenty francs would see them both under the table.

'*Rouge,*' affirmed Viktor and called the order out, not bothering to ask him what he wanted. It arrived in a litre bottle, drawn straight from the barrel. The stranger filled both glasses, raised his in salutation, and knocked back the wine in one swallow, like beer. Then he began rolling a cigarette but appeared to think better of lighting it in public. He excused himself and headed off towards the *toilettes*, returning ten minutes later full of serendipitous bonhomie. 'I'm Rob, by the way,' he said affably, extending a hand. 'And you?'

'Viktor. You're American, aren't you?'

'That's right.'

'You're avoiding the draft?' queried Viktor, one jump ahead of him.

'Resisting it,' Rob corrected him. 'I was told France, Sweden and Switzerland were most likely to grant long-term permits. So I chose France, because I knew the language.'

To Viktor's mind, draft dodgers were just cowards with a

moral overcoat, but Viktor approved of cowards. Cowards were survivors.

'You speak very good French.'

'I learned it as a child. My mother's from Quebec.'

'Wouldn't Canada have been easier?'

'Yes. Too easy.'

'You want it to be difficult?'

'If I wanted it to be difficult I'd have gone to England. No chance of a work permit there. I'm hoping to find a job, till the summer anyway. Then I want to hit the road. What do you do?'

Viktor smiled, anticipating his reaction. Despite the beard, the long hair, and the marijuana, the American had an air of respectability that seeped through the disguise.

'I'm a thief.'

Rob registered no surprise, reluctant, perhaps, to appear uncool.

'So what do you steal?' he asked, conversationally.

'I pick pockets. Tourists, mostly.' He pointed at the guitar. 'How about a song?'

Rob looked a bit sheepish. 'To tell you the truth, I only bought this thing just before I left home. I've been learning from a book. Can't actually play anything much.'

'Can I try?' said Viktor, reaching for the instrument. Rob moved round the table and demonstrated some basic chords, which Viktor reproduced correctly, first time. Before long, he was brushing the instructions aside, fascinated by his new toy. Rob left him to it, returning to his wine, retreating into some private, peaceful place of his own, untroubled by the lack of conversation. Viktor didn't notice him make yet another trip to the WC, nor did he register his return. He was still bent over the guitar, brow furrowed, trying to master the scale, when a voice said, 'Very funny. Now give it back.'

Viktor looked up. 'Give what back?'

'My wallet. My money.' His voice was calm, reasonable, but his face was like thunder.

Viktor stood up and held his hands above his head.

'Search me,' he said. 'Go on, frisk me. I haven't got your lousy money.'

'You mean you've already passed it to someone else?' He

was calling Viktor *vous*, the polite mode of address according ill with the accusation. Viktor was assailed by a sense of the ridiculous. That would teach him to admit to his trade in future.

'Of course I haven't,' he said, with helpless sincerity, struggling in vain to keep his face straight. Rob's murderous expression struck him as hilarious. This would be a good test of his claimed pacifism.

Unamused, Rob seized hold of his jacket. 'Don't laugh at me,' he snarled, losing his cool abruptly. 'I'm warning you. I said, *stop laughing*!'

Viktor shook his head and tried to explain, tried to find the words to share the joke, but the words came out as more laughter, laughter that persisted even when Rob sent him reeling backwards with a blow to the jaw.

No one intervened. Fights were part of the free floor show *chez* Clément. Clément made a tidy profit on breakages and never risked getting caught in the crossfire. Viktor staggered to his feet. Rob was swaying slightly with the effects of booze and pot, shaking his head as if to clear his vision. Then, with incongruous care, he took off his spectacles and put them down on the table, blinking owlishly. Viktor got down on his knees, cowering with mock terror.

'*Je ne suis qu'un pauvre Vietnamien,*' he bleated, pulling back the corner of both eyes with his thumbs. '*Ayez pitié de moi, Monsieur Soldat-Américain. Ayez pitié de moi!*'

A bellow went up from the spectators, who echoed the plea in a raucous singsong. Rob hauled Viktor to his feet and hit him very hard on the nose. Viktor collapsed on to the floor, snorting blood.

'Fight, damn you!' bellowed Rob, in English, dragging him upright. 'Whassa matter with you, man? You want a war, you fucking well *fight* one!'

Too late, Viktor decided that he had better defend himself. Too late. He saw the big man totter to the floor like a felled tree, revealing a grinning Hafaïd, perched atop a chair, still wielding the jagged stump of a once-full bottle of *rouge*. There was a moment's perfect silence while the blood from Rob's head trickled warmly into the pool of wine.

'Go home, Hafaïd,' said Viktor, taking the remains of the

bottle from him. 'Go home quickly now.' Clément endorsed this advice by seizing the culprit by the scruff of the neck and ejecting him on to the pavement. Viktor rolled Rob on to his back. The expression on his face was beatific. Meanwhile Clément was yelling at Viktor to get out and take the thrice-cursed body with him.

Viktor slapped Rob's face and poured a carafe of water over him, eliciting no response. It took ten minutes for one of Clément's emissaries to lure a taxi into the alleyway, two people to lift the dead weight into the back seat, and ten francs to persuade the driver to help Viktor carry it up to his apartment.

'I won't be home till late,' Alain told his mother, dipping a piece of bread into a bowl of sweet, milky coffee. 'I'll be going into town straight after work.'

He had swopped shifts again, to give himself a free afternoon; his father and two younger sisters were still asleep. His mother always rose at dawn, even though her job at the laundry didn't start till eight thirty. Neither her husband nor her son had ever been allowed to get his own breakfast.

'You're meeting that student girl again?'

Alain nodded.

'Why don't you ever bring her home to meet us?'

'It's not serious, Maman. You know what girls are like. If I brought her home she might think I want to marry her. Perish the thought.'

'All these books you read,' sighed his mother, resuming her familiar refrain. 'You could go to night classes, get a better job. Then you could afford to get married and live in a nice place. If only you'd worked harder at school . . .'

'I don't want to work in an office, I don't want to join the bosses. I don't even want to be a foreman. It's against my principles.'

'You want to end up like your father? Thirty years of slaving away, day after day, with nothing to show for it but this?' She swept an arm around the room.

The Moreau family lived in a soulless municipal block in the south-western suburbs, one of the modern, monolithic structures which had shot up to meet the post-war population boom. Nevertheless, it was an improvement on the slum Alain had grown up in, and he was disinclined to move out; finding his own accommodation would have deprived both himself and his family of income. There were only two small bedrooms, however. Alain slept on a divan in the cramped, fussy living room, next to a wall lined with shelves of second-hand books. Being entirely self-educated he was an insatiable reader, devouring thick tomes on political thought and philosophy and psychology as if they were thrillers. This should have given him something in common with Armelle, but paradoxically the reverse had proved true. He avoided and curtailed intellectual discussions, ever fearful of exposing his ignorance – especially in front of a woman.

Introducing Armelle to his family had always been, and remained, out of the question. No need to tell them who she was: they would see for themselves what she was. Alain's father, a union diehard and a lifelong member of the *Parti Communiste Français*, would have dismissed her as a posturing bourgeois brat. His mother, in contrast, would have been pathetically hospitable, subservient even, anxious to impress such a well-bred young lady, terrified of letting her adored son down. His two younger sisters would have giggled. It would have been intolerable.

'My family are ordinary working people,' he had told Armelle curtly. 'You would have nothing in common with them.' It irritated him that she was so keen to meet them, like a child clamouring to be taken to the zoo. She thought that he was taken in by her studied submissiveness but Alain knew that her dove's feathers clothed a bird of prey.

No, he would never bring her home. Their present arrangement suited him very well. Two or three times a week they would meet up in a café in the Latin Quarter – which remained the spiritual home of those students exiled to Nanterre – and proceed to an apartment belonging to one of Armelle's friends. Her father had refused point blank to set her up in an apartment, paying her residential fees at Nanterre direct, and keeping her short of ready cash while allowing her a monthly credit account at various approved stores. It was his way of protecting her morals and ensuring that none of his hard-earned money found its way into revolutionary coffers. Armelle's lack of her own accommodation spared Alain the necessity of finding an excuse not to move in with her. As it was, he never stayed overnight, however much she tried to tempt him. Armelle was inexhaustible and indifferent to the charms of sleep; she didn't have to get up early or put in a hard day's work.

He had met her during an anti-Vietnam war rally the previous autumn, when they had both managed to get themselves arrested and had spent an hour cooped up in the back of a police van. Two years' national service had served to harden Alain's anti-militarism. His uncle had been killed at the battle of Dien Bien Phu, the massacre which had heralded France's withdrawal from Indo-China, and a neighbour's son had been posted to Algeria, returning home blinded in one eye. Alain identified strongly with the blacks and working classes of America who couldn't avoid conscription and it frustrated him that they were not the ones burning their draft cards or demonstrating outside the Pentagon. No, that was the province of the college kids, suddenly afraid that their turn might come now that students' deferment had been curtailed. Meanwhile the blacks and workers went off to do their duty, duped into obedience.

Armelle didn't care, of course, how many Americans got killed. The more the better, in her view. They had had an argument about it, but Armelle and her brainy friends had been too busy ranting on about Chairman Mao and Ho Chi Minh to take his point. Alain was the only worker in the van; the demonstrators had been predominantly students – students having more leisure for such pursuits – and Alain had lost his temper with them, frustrated at their superior articulateness. He had called Armelle a spoilt rich bitch, an insult which had unexpectedly produced a humble apology. She had asked him meekly what he did, and where he worked; when he told her, she had gone very quiet, and it was not until several weeks later that she confessed herself to be his employer's daughter. Meanwhile, she had suggested that they meet again, and it had been impossible to refuse. He had assumed that she just wanted sex, not realising that she wanted much, much more than that until it was too late.

He still felt sore and weary from their last meeting. Armelle always made love as if it was her last day on earth. She was as irresistible and as indigestible as an over-rich meal, leaving him bilious and bloated. Yet it was she who fed off him: she grew fat and indolent on him while he sickened and starved. The whole relationship was illusion; that it could have no future was, for her, the essence of its charm. Armelle craved only the impossible, Alain hated to fail. The problem was nothing as simple as the class barrier between them; it was more fundamental than that. For Alain the struggle was real, for Armelle it was a game. And yet she made him feel like a dilettante, if only because she cared more, in her game-world, than he did in his real one. She was like a film, or a play, or a book, that made fiction more vivid than life.

Only about half the workers at the MerTech factory belonged to the union, which was affiliated to the Communist-dominated *Confédération Générale des Travailleurs*, or CGT. Female and immigrant workers were notoriously apathetic when it came to fighting for their rights. Alain had started off as a union activist bent on increasing membership, but his disaffection had grown as he studied the writings of Marx and Engels, and increased even more after Armelle had given him books by the gurus of the New Left, Herbert Marcuse and Régis Debray. For months now he had been working towards the revolution, spreading the seeds of dissent, antagonising both bosses and union, eager to provoke the kind of spontaneous action that would topple the power structures once and for all. Armelle's father was rarely seen at the works, relying on cringing minions to crack the whip while he concentrated on winning export orders and improving profitability, but industrial relations were infuriatingly good: Lemercier timed and measured every concession with Machiavellian skill.

Consequently, Alain had fallen foul of both management and shop stewards but had generated enough popular support to make them think twice about conspiring towards his dismissal. If there was only one like himself, just one, in every workplace, there would soon be hundreds, thousands, and then they wouldn't need unions or bosses. They could change the world.

Books. They were like a lens that let you see the world in

43

focus – and he'd chosen to stay blind for most of his life; he'd never read a book till he left school. School was enough to put you off books for good. It was a clever system, that.

'Does she love you, this girl?' resumed Alain's mother, replenishing his coffee bowl.

'She pretends to. She's a romantic.'

'And you?'

'No. It's just a sexual thing.'

'Don't get her into trouble, will you?'

'Have I ever got a girl into trouble? Look, I'm late.'

Jeanne watched from the window as her son mounted his *vélo* and joined the crowds converging on the works. Ever since he met this girl he had been secretive, evasive. To her mind, Alain was definitely in love. She hoped so. It might serve to explain why he had become so moody lately, why he kept falling foul of his father and his foreman. Albert thought that his son was getting above himself. Albert objected to Alain heckling at union meetings and encouraging his workmates to do likewise. Attendance at meetings had shot up dramatically; they were becoming unmanageable. In no time at all there would be a splinter group of would-be anarchists, led by his own son, undermining everything the union stood for.

'He's young,' she had soothed her husband. 'The young like to rebel. He'll grow out of it.'

'He'll get himself expelled from the union,' her husband had predicted. 'He'll get himself sacked. Sometimes I think that's what he wants.'

Sighing, she finished Alain's abandoned coffee. Fathers were so hard on their sons. Alain was a good boy. He had never been out of work, never been in trouble with the police. He handed over half his wages every week without a murmur, he was patient with his two little sisters, and, as he had said himself, he had never got a girl into trouble. While other young men were out getting drunk or gambling, he would sit quietly reading, reading, oblivious to the din of the *télé* or his sisters' chatter. Albert would drive him out if he kept picking on him like this, and once a son left home he was lost for ever.

She would have liked to meet this girl of his, if only to re-assure herself that she wasn't good enough for him.

THREE

Hearing his stepdaughter's footsteps on the stone stairwell, Karel hid the rum bottle under the bedclothes and took one final drag on his cigarette, drowning the stub hastily in a cup of cold tea. He held his breath for a moment, letting the acrid smoke caress his phlegm-choked lungs, before exhaling it under the covers.

Eva lingered on the landing for a moment while a neighbour quizzed her about the provenance of some oranges in her string bag; she had inherited her mother's knack for procuring the unobtainable. Věra's lingering death had left Eva older and wiser than her eighteen years, even though she looked young for her age, having retained her cheerful baby-faced features. She let herself in, weighed down with cabbage and potatoes, and treated Karel to a look of baleful indulgence. He lay back expectantly in cosy anticipation of a lecture.

'You'll set fire to yourself one day,' she said, removing her woolly hat and gloves. She bent to kiss him, her nose wrinkling as she caught the dark, sweet scent on his breath. But she denied him the dubious satisfaction of a second reprimand. 'I should open the windows and let you catch pneumonia.'

'Go ahead. You'd be doing me a favour.' He added a plaintive cough, which turned into a real one, as if to serve him right. Karel's winter bronchitis kept him off work for several weeks every winter. Eight years in prison had taken their toll of his health but his complaint was largely self-inflicted, the result of unrepentant chain smoking and a strong psychological incentive to be ill. He had come to look forward to this seasonal respite from the grinding monotony of his job.

Eva hung up her coat and got busy in the kitchen, a cupboard-sized area between the front door and the rest of the apartment, which comprised a single, large, draughty, high-ceilinged room with two curtained-off sleeping areas. The salon still sported its chandelier, now invariably obscured by a washing line steaming with damp laundry. The juxtaposition was appropriate; the gracious *belle époque* apartment building, pleasantly situated between the Botanical Gardens and the River Vltava and still redolent of Austro-Hungarian opulence, now masked a dilapidated and overcrowded interior. Věra, Karel's second wife, had been rehoused here with her parents in 1948, following the Communist takeover; they had thought themselves fortunate to be allocated one room in the abandoned home of a bourgeois family. Since then the original spacious apartment had been crudely partitioned into three; others, in more select locations, had been left respectfully intact to house the new élite.

'Jan asked me out this evening,' called out Eva from the kitchen, as she stirred.

'Which Jan is that?'

'Don't you remember? He sent those beautiful lilies when Mama died. He's a sub-editor at the paper.'

'Hmm. Another one who'd better start looking for another job.'

The newspaper where Eva worked was one of the many official organs which lived in expectation of mass dismissals and reappointments. Alexander Dubček, a little-known Slovak, had recently displaced the long-established Antonin Novotny as first secretary of the Communist Party; the former leader's protégés knew that their days were numbered.

Eva shrugged non-committally. 'There's been no sign of a shake-up yet. Dubček seems to be biding his time.'

'Then he won't last five minutes. He needs to get rid of all the Novotnyites, or they'll get rid of him. You mark my words.'

'Well, Jan isn't important enough to get the sack. Let alone poor little me. More's the pity. It's so boring there.' She made a face.

'You don't know when you're well off, young woman. There are worse places to work, I can tell you.'

Věra had got her daughter the job, having worked at the paper herself for fifteen years, as the result of some string-pulling by a former lover, Eva's unknown father, a respectable Party official with a bad conscience and a jealous wife. Thanks to her mother's shrewdness, Eva was luckier than most: lucky to work near her home rather than in some industrial suburb, for a newspaper rather than a factory, typing words rather than columns of figures. But she was still bored. Perhaps boredom was inevitable. There was little incentive to do more than the bare minimum. Pay differentials were small and the path to promotion was through Party membership, rather than ability. Party membership was not freely given; it required evidence of political commitment, long hours of attendance at dull meetings and functions, a stringent vetting procedure, and, above all, the ability to dissemble. Nobody seriously believed the dogma any more, as they had done in the old days, but those who wanted to get on had to pretend they did.

'Aren't you having any supper?' said Karel, as she set a tray in front of him.

'I said I'd eat with Jan. He had to work late. We'll just grab a quick bite and then we'll probably go dancing or something.'

'Dancing? You call that wriggling about dancing?'

'If you disapprove, I won't go. I'll tell him my wicked stepfather won't allow it.'

She gave him that bright, all-knowing, stubborn smile, the smile that kept him sane. Her mother had kept smiling to the bitter end, even while she was dying, humouring him, tolerating his vile moods, indulging his monstrous selfishness. He had come out of prison to find that all his former friends had disowned him; only Věra had stayed loyal, loyal enough to invite him into her home as a lodger, then as a lover, then as a husband. He had taken her for granted, given her nothing in return. And now he was doing the same to Eva.

'You should go out more,' he muttered. 'You should find yourself a sensible young man and marry him. I'll move out, find myself lodgings somewhere, you don't have to worry about me being in the way.'

'Don't be ridiculous. I've no intention of getting married yet. And anyway, you'd be helpless on your own, you poor old thing.'

'There's nothing the matter with me. And less of the "old". I'm not fifty yet and I'll probably live to be a hundred. If you're so keen to be a nurse, you should find yourself a job in a hospital. You're a fool, Eva, like your mother.'

Eva stopped smiling. It had been a cruel remark to make, albeit unintended, the product of one of those spurts of helpless anger that Věra had deserted him. Four long months after her death he was still taking it out on her daughter. Karel opened his mouth to apologise, to put it down to the morbid side effects of the rum, and then shut it again, knowing she would forgive him, not wanting her to. But her truly formidable glare was too much for him. If her mother had known how to glare as well as smile he might have treated her better.

'I'm sorry,' he growled. 'And don't say it's all right. Because it isn't.' Two large maudlin teardrops began rolling down his cheeks. Eva wiped them briskly away with a tea-towel and made great play of sniffing it.

'Why don't we recycle this stuff and save some money? Alternatively, you could always pee straight back into the bottle. Your soup's getting cold.'

Chastened, he picked up his spoon while she set to work rolling dumplings. Her hands were covered in flour when the doorbell rang.

'Stay where you are,' she said, as if addressing a restless canine. 'I'll get it.'

She opened and shut the door quickly, as the visitor entered on a blast of cold air.

'Come in, Miloš,' she said cheerfully. 'Have some soup, it will warm you up.'

Miloš, a gregarious old bachelor, invariably contrived to arrive at mealtimes. Eva always made him welcome as one of Karel's few friends. They had met in the notorious Vojna labour camp, where thousands of political prisoners had mined uranium ore in conditions of unspeakable hardship. Miloš, a local politician in his native Bratislava, had been one of the earliest victims of the Stalinist purge. Having fought with a

Slovakian partisan unit during the war, derailed trains, blown up bridges, lost all his family in Nazi reprisals, and been a life-long Communist, he had been quickly identified as a man of strong principles and a potential troublemaker. Like Karel, he had been arrested, tortured, and forced to confess to a shopping list of anti-state activities; unlike Karel, he had survived the ordeal with his self-esteem intact.

After Khrushchev's dramatic denouncement of Stalin in 1956, the two men had been released the following year under the first of two general amnesties which did little to clear the victims' names. There had been no public exoneration, which might have implicated powerful officials who had assisted in the convictions. Former prisoners had been pardoned, but not absolved. In consequence, Miloš, a qualified doctor, had been assigned to a lowly job as a clerk, while Karel, formerly a government economist, now assembled cardboard boxes in a packing shed.

'Still malingering, I see,' boomed Miloš, rubbing his hands together. He winked, looked to see if Eva was watching, and slyly tapped the pocket of his overcoat.

'He's already had enough for one day,' said Eva, who had eyes in the back of her head.

'Have a heart,' wheedled Miloš. 'It's only beer.'

Sighing, she produced two glasses and went back to rattling her pans. Miloš extracted two bottles.

'I came to tell you that the first meeting's been fixed for tomorrow night,' he hissed in a conspiratorial undertone.

'I'm not well enough to go to any meetings,' growled Karel. 'You can tell me what happens. I enjoy fairy stories.'

'I can tell you what's going to happen,' continued Miloš, undeterred by this sour response. 'We're going to draft a full schedule of demands. We won't settle for anything less than full rehabilitation and compensation. We're going to demand the kind of publicity they gave the show trials back in the fifties. It's not enough for them to say, sorry, it was all a mistake, here's a few crowns and a lousy job. And the time is right. If we all stick together . . . '

' . . . we can have a cosy reunion back in gaol.'

'What's the matter with you? Isn't this the chance we've

been waiting for? Now Novotny's gone we have a chance to expose him and all the other people he's been shielding. Don't forget our national motto. Truth will prevail!'

Karel gave a harsh bark of laughter, which collapsed into a cough.

'The truth? Can liars demand the truth? I confessed to half a dozen crimes I hadn't committed, I implicated other innocent people I'd never even met. And so did you. Innocence doesn't protect you against guilt and the truth is a two-edged sword. I've learned to live without it.'

'Then it's high time you learned to live with it!'

'All this talk of rehabilitation and free speech and abolition of censorship – I'll believe it when I see it. This new man will never pull it off. And even if he does, I give it six months at the outside before Moscow puts the boot in.'

'No time to waste then, is there? I calculate that our potential membership could be in excess of forty thousand.'

'Plus how many informers?'

'Oh, for pity's sake . . . '

'What are you two whispering about?' demanded Eva, dispensing bacon and *knedlíky*.

'Miloš is telling dirty jokes again,' said Karel. 'I would laugh myself silly, only I've heard them all before.'

He began chopping and mashing his food into a shapeless pulp; he had lost all his teeth in prison and his ill-fitting dentures made chewing a chore.

'Thank you, Eva,' said Miloš, accepting a steaming plate. 'You cook like an angel. Will you marry me, let me take you away from all this?'

Eva smiled patiently. It would be nice if someone *could* take her away from all this: from Karel and his moods, from the drudgery of keeping house, from the humdrum job. Some hope.

'Excuse me,' she said. 'I must go and change.'

She disappeared into her cubicle, glad that Karel would have company while she was out. Miloš was always in a good humour, especially once fed, and seldom came empty-handed. He had various contacts on the black market and would often produce treasures from the depths of his capacious overcoat – a lump of fine Prague ham destined for export, or some South

American coffee or Swiss chocolate which had lost their way *en route* to the state-run Tuzex shops, where they could only be bought for hard currency. Fiddling was not dishonest, as far as Eva could see. Anything that undermined the system had to be a good thing.

She couldn't be bothered to change. It was only Jan, after all. Eva squinted in the mirror, re-drawing the thick black line on her upper eyelid. She added a couple of inches to her height by way of vigorous backcombing – she was, to her frustration, short and plump, like her mother – and put on a thick head-band to keep her ears warm without crushing her hair. By the time she emerged Miloš and Karel were engrossed in one of their interminable chess games. Her departure raised barely a grunt.

Going out in the evening was still something of a novelty. Eva's mother's long illness had severely curtailed her social life and she had never had a steady boyfriend. It was a pity that Jan wasn't good-looking, because he was educated, intelligent and polite. But, of course, if he'd been good-looking as well, some educated, intelligent girl would have snapped him up by now. He was also painfully shy, the result, no doubt, of an unfortunate stutter which had gone straight to Eva's heart.

Jan had joined the paper the previous summer, straight from Charles University. While the other girls at work had teased him mercilessly, Eva had gone out of her way to be nice to him. Jan had sent flowers when her mother died; they had become friends. Now, inevitably, he wanted to be more than friends, which would probably ruin everything. But she was hardly besieged by admirers, and it was better than staying at home.

She caught a tram to Wenceslas Square, where Jan was waiting for her outside the Koruna Automat as arranged. They queued for *klobasy* sausage and sauerkraut and ate it standing up at the counter. Eva knew that Jan was hard up. He had to pay rent for a room in someone else's apartment – his family lived in a remote village in Moravia – and was obliged to eat out all the time. If it hadn't been for Karel she would have invited him home and cooked him a decent meal.

'What would you like to do?' he asked.

'Whatever you like.'

51

'Would you like to listen to some j-jazz? I know a good jazz club.'

'That would be nice.'

'Shall we w-walk? It's not far.'

It was a dark, low-ceilinged basement in the Old Town, a favoured haunt of students. Jan was immediately hailed by some old college acquaintances, who made room for them at their table. A trio of piano, drums and clarinet had just finished playing to loud applause, succeeded by a clink of glasses and a buzz of animated conversation.

Eva wasn't a jazz fan – she much preferred pop – and she found Jan's friends rather overpowering. There were three men and two girls, all of them vociferous and well informed. They argued endlessly about what was going to happen under Dubček. Eva kept quiet so that she wouldn't show herself up by saying something ignorant.

'Did you read Smrkovsky's piece in *Prace*?' Jan was saying eagerly.

The others had; Eva was forced to admit that she hadn't. She knew little of the flamboyant liberal spokesman – to her mind all politicians were alike – nor had she ever read *Prace*, the trade union weekly, which she had assumed was every bit as dull as any other newspaper, including the one she worked for. But as she listened to the lively discussion of the article – a sensational call for democratisation, free speech, economic reform and national rebirth – she noticed that Jan's stutter had miraculously improved.

After another musical interlude the conversation moved on to the question of summer holidays. Exit permits, once heavily restricted, were going to be easier to get, so they said; everyone seemed to be planning a visit to the West.

This was a subject nearer to Eva's heart. Visiting Karel's mother in Paris had been one of her when-I-grow-up fantasies for as long as she could remember. And now she was grown up. She had pushed the idea to the back of her mind during her mother's illness, but now there was really nothing to stop her bringing the subject up. Karel, as an ex-political prisoner, was debarred from travelling abroad; Marta, as an illegal emigrant, had been repeatedly refused a visa to revisit her homeland. It seemed logical to Eva that she should bridge the gap, bringing

Marta a breath of Prague, and taking back with her, willy-nilly, news of Karel's long lost son.

Eva had mixed feelings about Viktor. It irritated her how Marta sang his praises in every letter and how Karel lapped it all up, even though Viktor never bothered to write, never deigned to acknowledge his father's existence except with dollar bills. Given that these fetched several times their official worth on the illegal currency market and gave access to luxury goods in the Tuzex shops, they were not to be sneezed at, but Eva considered conscience money a poor substitute for family feeling. Karel, for all his faults, was the only father she had ever known, and it galled her that Viktor, who clearly didn't give a damn about him, still was, and would always be, the favourite.

'An accountant,' Karel would mutter, with that peculiar, grudging pride of his. 'He must have inherited my head for figures.'

'Let's hope that's all he's inherited from you,' Eva would respond crisply.

But the photographs of him showed a striking physical resemblance, when you made allowances for Karel's grey hair and sunken cheeks. Eva couldn't remember Viktor, who was some eight years her senior. There were several pictures in the family album, showing him as a bonny baby, as a gap-toothed toddler, as a sullen little boy. The latest one – which Karel kept by his bedside, like an icon – showed a smartly dressed, rather arrogant young man-about-town, with his father's long, straight nose, deep-set dark eyes, and slightly sinister smile.

The annoying thing was that whenever she allowed her mind to fall into the furrow of its most familiar reverie, Viktor was always part of it. There was an air of mystery about him that was the very stuff of fantasy. He gave shape and substance to the most ridiculous of her secret daydreams – that in Paris, city of glamour and romance, she would fall madly in love, get married, acquire a French passport, and thereafter never return to Prague except as an affluent tourist dressed in fashionable clothes, with a handbag full of hard currency and a return ticket back to her new home in the West . . .

'What are you thinking about?' said Jan, in her ear.

'The ironing. The shopping. What to make for tomorrow

night's supper. What else would I be thinking about?' She could hear the note of self-pity creeping into her voice, and despised herself for it. But she spent so much of her time trying to keep Karel cheerful that it was a relief to sound petulant and discontent.

'If you're bored, we can go somewhere else.'

'I'm not bored. I'm just a bit depressed today, that's all.'

'You must miss your mother.'

'Yes. But Karel misses her even more than I do. And now I'm all he has left. It gets me down sometimes. The responsibility of it. Knowing that he couldn't manage without me.'

'Doesn't he have any friends?'

'Not really. He's not very sociable.'

'Does he mind you going out?'

'Probably. But he would never admit it.'

'So he won't object if I s-see you again on Saturday?'

'I shouldn't think so.'

He took this negative as giving assent and caught hold of her hand, which he caressed and squeezed throughout the next bout of music. Eva shut her eyes. His hand was dry and warm, and she would have liked to feel it elsewhere on her body – not as part of him, but as a disembodied instrument of pleasure, the physical extension of the thoughts that intruded on her sleep. Then she opened her eyes and saw Jan, with his high, bulbous forehead, protruding ears and thin, wispy, prematurely receding hair.

'It's getting late. Time I went home.'

'I'll take you.'

'No need. It's right out of your way. Just see me to the tram.'

He walked to the stop with her and, as the tram approached, kissed her goodnight. Eva made short work of it, keeping her lips firmly closed, feeling mean. She didn't have to see him again on Saturday, of course, but she didn't have anything better to do and if she said she wanted to be 'just friends' he would be bound to take it as a rejection.

She hauled herself aboard, punched her ticket, and smiled at him through the window, wishing she'd been nicer to him. Jan stood waving as the tram rattled on its way. Eva shut her eyes and began composing a letter to Marta.

* * *

Rob woke up piecemeal. First his aching head, then his desiccated throat, then his bursting bladder, and then, reluctantly, his brain. He was lying on top of a double bed, fully dressed except for his desert boots, and covered with a patchwork quilt. Thin rays of sunlight leaked through the curtain, revealing a blurred, bare, white-walled room. A large old-fashioned wardrobe loomed at the foot of the bed like an upright coffin. He had no idea where he was.

He hauled himself to his feet, head spinning, and padded barefoot into a small, square hallway with several doors leading off it. One of them was open, identifying the bathroom, where he relieved himself endlessly and held his head under the cold tap, wincing as he loosened the clump of hair matted with dried blood. He could hear someone picking out a tune on a guitar. His guitar, he hoped. He followed his ears to the sound.

His host was sitting cross-legged on the floor with the instrument across his knees, his brow furrowed in concentration. The room was dwarfed by a baby grand, its open jaws full of long white gleaming teeth, laughing at him. The events of the previous evening all came back in a rush. He rubbed his eyes and groaned.

'So,' said Viktor, without looking up, 'you're alive.'

'Just about. Sorry about last night.'

'I'll bet you are. Pity about your money. No point in going to the police. They'll laugh when you tell them where you lost it.' He grinned unsympathetically. His nose was red and swollen, causing Rob's knuckles to come out in sympathy.

'I'd better go,' he muttered.

'Where to, without money? You can stay here, if you like, till you get some more.'

'Well . . . thanks. Did I . . . hurt you?'

'It was worth it. Call me *tu*, for God's sake.'

'Right. Er . . . have you seen my glasses?'

'On the piano, over there. You were lucky they didn't get smashed. Was it cash you lost, or travellers' cheques?'

Rob put on his spectacles and blinked for a moment, as if waiting for his brain to focus.

'Cash. I'd just hocked in my return air ticket.'

'I take it you're not insured?'

Rob shook his head. 'I was on a tight budget. Not as tight as the one I'm on now.' He rummaged in his pockets, producing some ten francs in loose change.

'What will you do? Cable home for some more?'

'Can't do that. My folks aren't well off. Their business is in trouble. And besides, they don't approve of me being here.'

'They'd rather you went to Vietnam?'

'No. My brother was killed there, in sixty-five.'

Viktor raised an inquisitive eyebrow, but Rob didn't elaborate.

'I've got an address to write to, here in Paris,' he continued. 'Some student set-up that helps draft resisters. Perhaps they can give me a loan, get me a work permit. I'll make out. I can always sell the guitar.'

Viktor got up, opened the lid of the piano stool, and thrust a wad of notes into his hand. Rob looked at him stupidly for a moment.

'For your guitar,' said Viktor patiently.

'This much would buy an orchestra. I can't take it.'

'Why not? I did. Besides, I don't need it.'

'Then ... why do you steal?'

'Why? For fun, I suppose. But I didn't steal from you, evidently.'

'Why not?'

'Oh ... because it was my night off. Put it away, for God's sake. It's only money.'

'Well ... thanks.' The word sounded wrong – stiff and formal. Viktor wasn't the kind of person you thanked. Rob shoved the notes into his back pocket, making a mental resolution to pay every cent of it back. 'Got any coffee around the place?'

'Café' and '*café*' were synonymous for Viktor. He never ate or drank at home. He led the way down the stairs and across the street into a *bar-tabac* still reeking of last night's wine and cigarettes. The coffee arrived in wide, shallow cups topped with inch-thick froth. They drank it sitting at the counter while the barman dried glasses with the dexterity of a juggler. Rob

56

couldn't face the thought of food, averting his eyes as Viktor dipped his brioche into the steaming brew and caught it, dripping, between his teeth at the point of disintegration. Viktor ignored him, evidently more interested in his breakfast than his new house guest. He seemed perfectly relaxed and yet alert as well, as if he was tuned in to some invisible wavelength, like a dog basking in the sun, ears imperceptibly cocked. His brand of cool was inborn, instinctive; it owed nothing to grass – it was real.

'I'll tell the concierge to let you back in,' said Viktor, sliding off his stool. 'Stay as long as you like, till you find a place to rent.'

'Thanks,' and then, weakening again, 'It's very kind of you.'

Viktor's lip curled. 'Rubbish,' he said, 'I'm not kind,' as if it were an insult.

Rob ordered another cup of coffee, black this time, asked for notepaper, envelope and stamp, and retreated to a table where he wrote a brief note to the contact he had been given on the National Vietnam Committee at Nanterre, explaining that he needed a *carte de séjour* and a *permis de travail*. The sooner he became legit. the better. He had been lucky not to lose his passport; if it hadn't been for Viktor he would probably have ended up spending last night in the cells and woken up destitute to find himself on the verge of deportation.

'I am of no fixed abode,' he wrote, hoping that this would produce an urgent response, 'and am currently living on borrowed money.' And then, aware that this made him sound like a bum, 'I dropped out of college two months ago and worked to finance my trip to Europe, only to have all my money stolen on my first night in Paris. I haven't been to the American consul, for obvious reasons. I will be at this café each day between ten and eleven and hope to hear from you soon.

'Thanking you in advance for your help,

'Robert F. Jerome.'

He took off the granny specs and polished them. Like the beard and the guitar, they were recent acquisitions. His discarded hornrims had belonged to a clean-cut, short-haired chemistry major, a serious young man almost engaged to a charming girl, a creditable substitute for the brilliant elder brother who might still be around today if he hadn't volunteered. Did anyone volunteer any more? To volunteer was to label yourself as some kind of Fascist, but in those days it hadn't seemed that way. Mike had been given a hero's sendoff; Rob had been envious of him, not because he wanted to fight but because he knew he would never be allowed to. What would Mike think of him now?

He'd thought a lot about his brother in the last few months. Like a lot of other clean-cut, short-haired, serious students at Berkeley, Rob had ritually burned his draft card and joined the protest march on the army induction centre in Oakland, braving squads of police and tear gas. He'd done that for Mike and all the others who'd died needlessly, not for himself. The selfish bit had been in leaving home, unnecessarily, before the army medical deprived him of his excuse to run out on Ginny and his family, to cut loose from the shackles of his old identity, to stop trying to be Mike and be himself, to sleep with as many girls as he liked, to get stoned, to forget, to be free.

'Papa!' cooed Armelle, kissing her father on each cheek. 'I'm sorry I'm late. How are you?'

The waiter pulled out a chair and enquired if mademoiselle would like an aperitif. Armelle ordered a sweet vermouth and clucked disapprovingly at her father's large Scotch and soda. 'You shouldn't drink spirits before lunch, Papa. It's bad for the liver.'

She was dressed demurely in a navy-blue suit and a pink cashmere polo neck with her hair tied back in a velvet bow; a papa's-little-girl outfit that could mean only one thing.

'It's money, I suppose?' said Bertrand Lemercier, keeping his voice stern. She was looking so beautiful today, the image of her mother, damn her.

'I wanted to see you in private. I can't talk to you with Odile there. She makes me nervous. Why is she so jealous of me? I try so hard to be civil. I put up her advertisement in the British Institute, like you asked. I went there specially. Did anyone apply?'

'Get to the point, Armelle.'

He sat back in his chair and reminded himself that he was a

wealthy, successful, powerful man. A man who had started with nothing, no money, no education, no influence, and beaten the bourgeois at their own game by being tough, determined, ruthless. A man who had homes in Paris and Provence, a bulging portfolio of legitimate investments, and millions of untaxed francs in a Swiss bank account. He reminded himself of all this because Armelle made a weakling of him, reminding him of the one failure of his life.

'Partly it's money, yes.' She made a face, as if he had been indelicate in bringing the subject up.

'Only partly?'

'Is that the tie I gave you for Christmas?' She leaned across the table and felt the silk between her fingers.

'How should I know? I have so many ties.'

'It suits you. I knew it would. I'm starving! What shall we have? Will you order for me, Papa? I'll have the same as you. Just an entrée, though.'

Bertrand barked an order for *médaillons de veau*. Armelle found it difficult to gauge his mood. His face, as always, gave nothing away. Wine tended not to mellow him; rather the reverse. She decided to press ahead.

'I'm so depressed,' she began. 'It's impossible, trying to study at Nanterre. It's so crowded and noisy. I'd be better off if I had a place of my own and travelled out each day. Somewhere I can study quietly, with plenty of room for my books. Somewhere—'

'Somewhere you can hold court to your little *groupuscule* and accommodate your latest boyfriend at my expense. The subject is already closed, Armelle. If you dislike living at Nanterre so much, you can always move back home.'

'I'd move back home tomorrow, if it wasn't for that bitch. You know that.'

As always, he failed to take the bait. He did little to discourage the antipathy between the two women, almost as if he took pleasure in their rivalry.

'And whoever the man is', he continued, 'who has put this idea in your head, tell him I cannot prevent you living with him, provided he pays the rent.'

'What man?'

'How should I know, what man? That's your affair.'

'Papa—'

'Listen to me, Armelle. It's not just the money, it's a question of principle. I have tolerated your absurd political rantings, your involvement with all these pressure groups and undesirable companions, because you are young and the young must rebel. I have allowed you to abuse me and call me a Fascist, even though your hand is always open for its share of my ill-gotten gains. I allow you to insult Odile because she is not as beautiful as your mother or as intelligent as you. But I will not allow you to take me for a fool. You think I am deceived when you simper at me? I prefer you when you are honest.'

'I don't simper. I only said that your tie suited you . . . '

Armelle's mouth began to wobble.

'It is hard for me to deny you anything, Armelle, if only because I grew up having nothing. But enough is enough. Your monthly outgoings are already double what I pay the average worker—'

'Then perhaps you should pay your workers more!'

'—and I do you a disservice in indulging you.'

'I don't want to be indulged! You can cancel all the charge accounts tomorrow, if you'll only give me a proper allowance to spend as I like. It would cost you less in the end! As it is, I buy things just to spite you!'

'As it is, you lack for nothing. You have everything you need, and more. You are beginning to annoy me, Armelle.'

His eyes flashed warningly and Armelle felt the familiar tingle of anticipation. Bertrand Lemercier's anger was rigidly controlled, packed down like high explosive. All her life Armelle had been trying to find his flashpoint, only to find hers first. Any confrontation would end with Armelle screaming and sobbing while Bertrand looked on, impassive, rigid, as if to prove his superior strength. For a small man he had enormous physical presence; the brutal line of his jaw, the heavy, crossed eyebrows, the broad, square shoulders and massive hands all suggested an unused capacity for violence.

Armelle took a deep breath. 'Please, Papa. I've found the perfect place, in the 5ème. It's only four hundred a month. What difference can four hundred francs make to you?'

60

'Peace of mind.'

'Because the dormitories at Nanterre are segregated? It's hardly as if I'm a virgin—'

Bertrand cut her short with an icy look. 'Sex is one thing, money is another. Like it or not, you are an heiress.'

'Like my mother, you mean?'

'I didn't marry for money, Armelle. I married money, which is different. Your mother inherited a small business. I made it into a big one. She gained on the transaction, believe me.'

'Why must you always judge all other men by yourself? Alain despises money. He believes in the reallocation of wealth.'

'Then I must assume he would stand to profit by it.'

'Oh, what's the point in trying to explain? You hate all my boyfriends.'

'So do you, eventually.'

'Can I help it if all men are shits? This one's different.'

In a moment she would start titillating him, feeding his morbid, masochistic curiosity with crumbs of detail, filling him with primitive jealousy. She was so like her mother. She needed a strong man. But she remained susceptible to poseurs, to dilettantes, to effete political playboys. There would be a brief first marriage to some left-wing fortune hunter, a child, and a divorce; then, belatedly, she would grow up, marry some solid youth of good family, become a pillar of society. Both eventualities depressed him; he would have liked her to meet the kind of man he had once been. But these days young men were content to attack the system instead of making it work to their advantage. She needed someone older, wiser . . .

Bertrand tasted the Burgundy he had ordered and rejected it as being too cold. A clipped exchange followed, the sommelier torn between deference and contempt. The most expensive tailor in Paris couldn't hide Bertrand's origins: it was like putting varnish on unsanded wood. A different bottle was duly fetched which the waiter assured him had been brought up from the cellar that morning. Armelle drummed her fingers on the table top. Wine bored her. She always diluted it with water, however rare the vintage.

'He reminds me of you,' she said at length. 'He doesn't compromise. He doesn't care what other people think of him.

He's self-sufficient. Independent. And he doesn't love me. Men like that can't love.'

'And this appeals to you?'

'It's not a question of choice. I can't control him. I don't want to control him.'

As usual, she neglected to mention the slightest detail of the man's appearance. For Bertrand, sexual attraction was a tactile, visual affair, but his daughter seemed to pick men with her eyes shut, caring only for their philosophies, their personalities, their politics.

'He's a student, I suppose?'

Bertrand despised students. He had wanted his daughter to have the best possible education and he was proud of her academic ability, but that was because she was his daughter.

'No. A worker.'

'What kind of work does he do?'

'Boring, dull repetitive work on a production line. Like you used to do, remember? Like you'd still be doing, if you hadn't married my mother.'

'He works . . . with his hands? In a factory?'

'That's right. I knew you'd approve.'

Bertrand tore off a piece of bread and chewed it slowly, letting the bland flavour fill his mouth, concentrating on it.

'What new game is this, Armelle?' he said eventually.

'A game? Oh, you mean history repeating itself.'

Bertrand pushed his plate to one side. 'Very well. Don't expect me to play the ogre and forbid you to see this man. You will never settle down until you have at least one disastrous relationship behind you. Go ahead and make your mistakes. Live with him, have his baby, marry him if you must. As long as you do so at his expense, not mine.'

'I'll ask Maman for money.'

'You can ask. But remember she has another child to think about now. Not to mention her layabout of a husband.'

'Giovanni's not a layabout! He works for a living, which is more than you can say for Odile!'

Bertrand signalled for the bill, leaving his meal untouched. 'I have work to do. Order coffee and dessert if you wish.'

'Papa!'

Armelle stretched out her hand and gripped his.

'Why are you always so cold towards me? After Maman left, we looked after each other, didn't we? We were so close. And now . . .'

She turned away and fumbled for her handkerchief. The tears were always a last resort, but none the less real for that.

Bertrand got out his wallet. 'Here's fifty,' he said curtly.

'I don't want it!' She flung the note back at him.

'Then redistribute it to the poor.' He scribbled his signature across the bill. 'I have a meeting. Excuse me.'

He bent to kiss her. Armelle did not return his embrace and waited till he had gone before putting the discarded money in her handbag, defiantly adding a silver knife and fork, right under the eye of the waiter.

'Would mademoiselle like dessert?' he enquired stiffly, noticing that she had left the spoon.

'Put a dozen profiteroles in a box. I'll take them with me. And hurry.'

She marched out of the restaurant, swinging the box of pastries to and fro. Money. Everything in life depended on money. Every war was fought to gain or retain it, every social ill was caused by an excess or a dearth of it. People lied and cheated and killed for it. And you could understand why. Money was like blood: a lack of it left you listless and anaemic and feeble; too much of it made your heart beat faster; losing it left you dizzy and light-headed.

Alain was waiting for her at their usual table, engrossed, as always, in a book.

'Why are you all dressed up?' he said, thinking how inaccessible she looked. If she'd been dressed like that the first time they'd met he wouldn't have dared to speak to her.

'I've been having lunch with my father.' She began undoing the string on the box. 'I told him all about you.'

'What?'

'Not that you worked for him. But I told him what you did.'

'Why?'

'Why not? Have a profiterole.' She had swung the box so violently they had congealed into a soggy mess. She offered him a finger laden with *crème pâtissière*.

'Are you trying to get me the sack?'

'Isn't that what you want? It would be unfair dismissal. It would give you just the excuse you need for a walk-out.'

'Don't interfere in my affairs, Armelle. You don't understand how things are on a shop floor. You and I are something separate.'

'Why is it you won't discuss things with me? Why is it you won't let me get close to you? Don't you trust me?'

She sweetened her words with another dollop of cream-soaked pastry and then closed her mouth round his and shared it with him, flicking the fragments to and fro with her tongue.

'Let's go,' said Alain, swallowing. Armelle would quite happily have made love in public and sometimes she came pretty near it.

'Nowhere to go to.'

'What about your friend's place?'

'She has visitors,' said Armelle mournfully. 'And I can't take you back to Nanterre – the warden stands guard like a watchdog. If only we had somewhere of our own . . .'

'That's not possible,' said Alain stiffly, well inured to this familiar refrain.

'Never mind,' said Armelle coyly, running her finger along the inside of his thigh. 'We can stay here, and just talk.' Her hand travelled to his flies and began kneading relentlessly.

'Armelle. Not in here.'

'The orientals can achieve orgasm without even touching or speaking. Did you know that?'

She withdrew her hand, closed her eyes and feigned a trance. Alain caught a look from the waiter behind the bar who stood watching them with prurient cynicism.

'Let's get out of here.'

'It's so cold outside.' She began rocking to and fro and humming to herself, her brow furrowed.

'Armelle . . .'

'Ssh. You're spoiling my concentration.' Her breath started to come faster and she began squirming in her seat as if impaled. Alain looked away, embarrassed. It was impossible to watch her without remembering the real thing – Armelle purring and licking, Armelle with her back arched and her eyes like green slits, Armelle soft and savage, all sleek fur and sharp claws.

'Armelle!'

She was bouncing up and down in her chair now, swivelling her hips, panting and moaning, her hands high above her head, her fists clenched, as if clinging to some invisible bedstead. People turned, stared, clucked, muttered.

'Armelle, stop it!' He grabbed one of the upstretched arms and tried to pull her to her feet.

'No, don't stop. Don't stop, Alain. Don't stop!' She began grinding her teeth and working up towards her final frenzy. Two men sharing a bottle were riveted to the free peep show, too engrossed even to snigger. Grunting, she threw her head from side to side, releasing her long hair from its pins, lips parted, teeth bared. Alain slapped her face, twice, in quick succession, which only seemed to increase her fervour. Desperate now, he stood up, lifted her bodily off her chair and carried her out of the café, while she clung to him and sank her teeth into his shoulder, before finally jerking all her limbs and going completely limp, doubling her weight and making him stagger.

'Bitch,' he hissed. 'What was that supposed to prove?'

'You'll see in a minute,' she murmured. 'My father gave me some money. Let's go to a hotel.'

Mme Lemercier's telephone voice was high-pitched, staccato and precise, like a speaking clock, an impression which was reinforced when she granted Cassie an interview for a quarter past sixteen next day.

The rue du Ranelagh was a high-class residential street in the 16ème, a stroll away from the leafy expanses of the Bois-de-Boulogne. Unusually for Paris, it featured houses as well as apartments. The Lemercier residence proved to be a substantial three-storey villa, the ultimate status symbol in Haussmann's seven-tiered city. It was surrounded by high wrought-iron railings, threaded with barbed wire, and a heavy iron gate which clicked open, after a short delay, when Cassie pressed the buzzer.

The front door was opened by a strapping, rosy-faced young woman in a starched apron.

'Madame has not returned from the *coiffeur*,' she said in a thick Spanish accent. 'Would mademoiselle like to wait? I will bring some tea.'

The salon gleamed in the pale sunshine which highlighted every spotless surface, searching in vain for dust. It was a wintry sort of room. Armelle's stepmother favoured cold colours – greys and ice blues – and hard, shiny finishes. The upholstery and curtains were of a pale, satiny fabric which reflected the light as though polished. The furniture was all bandy-legged, cloven-hoofed antique; genuine, but so carefully matched for period and style that it might almost have been repro. The whole place reeked of *nouveau riche*, a class Cassie had been brought up to despise.

'It's a beautiful house, isn't it?' said the maid, returning with a pot of very weak Lipton's which she dispensed reverently into a paper-thin shallow cup.

'It's lovely,' said Cassie.

'Are you Armelle's English friend? She told me about you.'

'Er . . . yes. That is, I only met her once, at the British Institute. She told me about Madame Lemercier wanting English lessons.'

'I am Pilar,' said the girl, shaking Cassie's hand gravely. 'Armelle is my very good friend. She visits me sometimes, when Madame is out. *Elle est très gentille, n'est-ce pas?*'

'*Très gentille,*' agreed Cassie. 'Where are you from, Pilar?'

'Cantabria. The wages here are much better than in Spain. Do you live at Nanterre also?'

'No. I have a *chambre de bonne* in the 7ème.'

'I have a very nice room, upstairs. Would you like to see?'

Bemused, Cassie followed her up two flights of stairs to a very small, very clean room of which Pilar was pathetically houseproud. She had painted it herself, in lilac emulsion, made her own floral curtains and lampshade, and put down a cheap patterned carpet. The furniture, in sharp contrast to the stuff downstairs, was tacky bargain-basement, but it had been lovingly polished to mirror brightness and was festooned with knick-knacks.

Cassie, still wallowing in bare floorboards and naked light bulb, felt duly humbled. She still hadn't got round to cleaning her room – like her mother, she was totally undomesticated.

The house in Hampstead was never really clean; Mrs Blakeney was ever wary of upsetting her surly, fag-puffing char for fear she might have to do the job herself. Mme Lemercier clearly had no such inhibitions, though doubtless Pilar didn't need telling twice.

'This is my little sister María,' she began, itemising the numerous framed photographs adorning every surface. 'That is my mother and father with my uncle León.. that is my other sister, Inéz . . . ' Cassie tried to picture her parents and brothers and Wilfred, and found they had all merged into one big forgettable smudge. 'And this,' concluded Pilar proudly, pointing to a Billy Fury lookalike, 'is my boyfriend, Jean-Claude. *Il est beau, n'est-ce pas?*'

Cassie was spared the need to endorse this view by the sound of the gate squeaking open and shut. They hurried back downstairs, Cassie taking refuge in the salon while Pilar went to open the front door. Mme Lemercier issued an immediate volley of querulous instructions which was followed by the ping of the telephone receiver being lifted and ten minutes of social squawks. Cassie popped an extra pill, a talisman against any ordeal.

'Forgive me for keeping you waiting, mademoiselle,' trilled Madame at last, drifting in on a cloud of hair lacquer. 'My hands, alas, are always full.'

The hands in question were exquisitely manicured and quite empty. Cassie had been expecting someone middle-aged, but she couldn't have been much more than thirty, even though her *grande dame* manner made her seem older, as did the hideous, though no doubt expensive, fur-trimmed pink suit, liberally adorned with heavy gold jewellery which looked cheap and showy enough to be the real thing. She had the stiff, erect posture of a dummy in a shop window, and the painted perfection of a china doll; her hair was bleached almost white and mounted in an ornate chignon, set off by thick, matt make-up and a fixed, frigid smile which didn't quite reach her false eyelashes.

She drew up a chair and, after a cursory interrogation as to Cassie's academic credentials, launched straight into a detailed résumé of her requirements, as if reading out an order to a tradesman.

'I shall be accompanying my husband on a business trip to the United States,' she informed Cassie briskly. 'It is most important that I make a good impression and be able to converse with the wives of his associates. I wish to learn correct, cultivated English, as spoken by the Queen. To save time, I have prepared a list of all the phrases I shall require.'

She extracted some headed notepaper from a bureau and handed Cassie an ill-written list of essential conversation topics, which might well have been headed 'In the beauty parlour', 'At the hairdresser's', 'My home', 'My husband' and so on. It didn't appear to concern her whether she understood other people or not; such a skill would presumably be superfluous to her needs. She attributed her limited grasp of English to many months' missed schooling; she had suffered from delicate health as a girl. Whether this was true or not, Odile Lemercier was, as Armelle had warned her, not very bright. It would be a bit like teaching a budgie to speak. Cassie felt a wave of overpowering inertia.

'Many applicants have telephoned, you understand,' continued Mme Lemercier, exposing herself as a liar, 'but as you teach at Alphonse Cluny I am willing to give you the benefit of the doubt. Six lessons per week, ninety francs. *Entendu?*'

Arithmetic had never been Cassie's strong point. She puzzled a long moment before saying, 'A hundred and fifty, surely?'

'Six times fifteen makes ninety,' said Madame, proud of her superior numeracy.

'But the advertisement said twenty-five francs an hour.' Cassie scrabbled in her bag to find it. Twenty-five might be excessive but fifteen was well below the going rate.

'Mademoiselle, I wrote it out myself. My husband gave it to my stepdaughter to display at the faculty.'

Cassie blinked at the bold, literate handwriting, re-read the reference to a 'very unintelligent lady' and remembered Armelle's mocking smile.

'I must have made a mistake,' she muttered, feeling a fool. Madame's smile grew brighter, falser. Her smile was like a shield, thought Cassie, investing the most dastardly of intentions with spurious goodwill. 'If I'd known it was only fifteen,' she added, rallying, 'I wouldn't have wasted your time.'

She stood up to go, glad to have an excuse to forget the whole thing. The woman was obviously a bitch. And yet . . .

'Eighteen,' said Madame, in the poker voice of one who was used to haggling.

What was it Armelle had said? 'She'll repeat everything you say. Think of the power that gives you.' Cassie wavered, tempted by the challenge of moulding such a willing pupil, of interspersing her pretty-Polly drivel with innocent little swear words, of teaching her a lesson in more ways than one.

'Howdy there,' she would greet her American hostess, smiling. 'What a perfectly shitty dress you're wearing . . . '

'Twenty,' said Cassie languidly.

Madame sighed wearily, signifying assent, and rang for more tea. Cassie showed her appreciation by giving her a free mini-lesson and soon had her chirruping 'a nice cup of char'.

'Toodle-oo,' she said, as she took her leave, indicating that Madame should repeat.

'Toodle-oo, mademoiselle,' said Madame, smiling.

This strenuous encounter left Cassie exhausted, so much so that she flopped down on the bed as soon as she got home and dropped off for a couple of hours. But that still only took her up to half past seven. Hell was to stare at the hands of a clock for ever, waiting for them to move.

She ought to get out of here, spend some of Mme le Censeur's money. She ought to go to the theatre, or the cinema, or drag herself along to the Restaur-U for a subsidised student meal and engage in stimulating conversation with the natives. Failing that, she ought at least to read something edifying and boring like Proust, or write a letter home, or tidy the room. She ought to do something. But she was assailed by the old familiar feeling of being stranded in a fog, knowing that if she moved she would collide with some invisible obstacle, clinging to the safety of immobility, and yet dreading the dispersal of that comforting mist that hid so many dark and threatening shapes.

Sleep. Sleep was the best medicine. She reached for the medicine marked sleep.

She woke again in the small hours to the familiar sounds of neighbouring copulation. The Moroccan waiter next door had recently installed a full-time mistress, a pasty girl who worked

69

behind the lingerie counter at Prisunic. Cassie had never seen her smile. She had a permanently sullen expression, a bruised look around the eyes and the vacant, passive air of a long-abused wife. Once or twice Cassie had wondered whether he beat her – not just because of the hangdog air, but because of the screaming. She would scream obscenities at the top of her voice in time to the rhythmic collisions against the partition wall. The proceedings would culminate in a blood-curdling 'aargh' suggesting a severed jugular, and then all would be silent again, till the next encounter. Perfectly silent. She never heard them quarrel, never even heard them speak, never saw them go out or come in together. It was as if they lived hermetically sealed existences, emerging only to fornicate, albeit frequently, as strangers. Perhaps they didn't much like each other. Or perhaps it was easier to enjoy sex when it was totally impersonal. Perhaps if she didn't have to talk to Wilfred, listen to Wilfred, try to please Wilfred, perhaps if she didn't respect Wilfred's superior brain, perhaps if she didn't treat each encounter with Wilfred as a sex seminar, she might achieve some insight into what ordinary, fairly stupid people got out of it. She tried to imagine herself yelling that kind of abuse of Wilfred; it would be impossible to do, of course, but it was quite easy to imagine the kind of relief she might find in screaming and screaming and screaming . . .

Yawning, she got out of bed, put on the light, and tried to put her thoughts down on paper.

> I heard a woman screaming to the rooftops,
> Heard her guttural celebration of disgust,
> Heard the sound of squelching life and croaking death
> Music and lyrics written in hell
> For voices driven by ecstasy and woe
> Towards the screeching orgasm of rage . . .

Poetry was a product of the night. It seemed to flourish in the dark, unlike prose, which tended to curl in upon itself like a plant deprived of sunlight, thwarting Cassie's nocturnal attempts to astound her family with a Brilliant First Novel. Cassie would have died rather than let anyone read her outpourings; in the morning, she would discard them like dreams,

70

but like dreams they helped the brain's sorting process, bypassed rational analysis, cleared her mind of debris. Certainly it was less painful to write a so-called poem about the lovers next door than to speculate on her own lack of libido.

Fearful of oversleeping again, she didn't go back to bed, and arrived untypically early for her eight o'clock class, finishing lessons at noon. Her first session with Mme Lemercier wasn't till four; she decided to kill time by relinquishing her last school-meal voucher and treating herself to a decent cup of coffee.

The senior English mistress, spotting her in the staff dining room, descended upon her table and started banging on about *St Joan* again; Cassie explained soulfully that since taking on private pupils her schedule was even more hectic than before. A one-sided discussion ensued about the progress of her *troisièmes* – Cassie could never remember any of their names – delaying her planned getaway to the local café. It turned out to be thronged with junior teachers and senior pupils who had massed for their weekly meeting of the *Comité d'Action Lycéen*, another group activity which Cassie had taken pains to avoid. Thwarted, she turned to go.

'*Non, non, tu peux entrer,*' called a fellow-teacher in welcome, one of the young radicals who had joined the lightning strike last term. Not wishing to cross their picket line, Cassie had stayed in bed for three days and been seen as sympathetic to the cause. The group had been born out of the anti-Vietnam war campaign and concerned itself with educational and political reform; it held all the tenets of the bourgeois establishment in contempt and was viewed with unmitigated disapproval by the Directrice and the Censeur.

'There's plenty of room,' hissed her colleague, squeezing along the banquette to make room for her. Cornered, Cassie sat down. A burst of applause went up to greet a visiting delegation from a pressure group committed to the furtherance of the Vietnamese revolution and the victory of the National Liberation Front. The speaker – a Latin-looking type flanked by two groupies taking notes – spoke of the need to create 'Vietnam base committees' which should be 'militarised' as necessary. Cassie stifled a yawn. There were some dissenters from the floor who favoured the official peace-at-all-costs Communist Party line, but they were out of joint with the mood of the meeting, and were shouted down. An announcement was made about a rally of all the CALs in Paris with a view to mobilising joint resources; leaflets were circulated giving full details. By this time it was nearly two thirty and Cassie, who was bored stiff, was just preparing to sneak off when a familiar voice murmured, 'Cassie! *Ça va?'*

It was Armelle, who was making her way from table to table distributing literature. 'I was hoping I'd see you here,' she added, *sotto voce*. 'Wait for me after the meeting, okay?'

She sat down near the door, effectively blocking Cassie's intended exit. Armelle would now assume that she had come to the meeting from choice and expect her to be horribly enthusiastic. So she ought to be, given her upbringing. The *Comité d'Action* was precisely the sort of thing a Blakeney ought to get involved in; that was what put her off. A childhood spent mournfully tagging along on Aldermaston marches, distributing Labour election propaganda and listening to her parents' fellow-intellectuals pontificating over the Royal Worcester had been more than enough to put her off politics for life. She had withdrawn, rather than rebelled. If she'd wanted to rebel she could have done something really shocking, like joining the Young Conservatives. But there had been no point. It would simply have been seen as an adult variant on bad behaviour. Bad behaviour was never censured, never punished, it was merely ignored, which took all the point, and the fun, out of it.

As the meeting dispersed, Armelle conferred briefly with her comrades before making her way over to Cassie's table, mercifully alone.

'How did it go with Odile?'

'You set us both up nicely. But I won, I think. I managed to push her up to twenty an hour.'

Armelle grinned. 'Good for you. When do you start?'

'Today. Four to six p.m. three times a week. If I can stick it.'

'She's vile, isn't she?'

'Well . . . yes.'

'I knew you would loathe her,' said Armelle smugly, as one

arbiter of good taste to another. 'Sometimes I despair of Pilar. Odile treats her like dirt and she doesn't seem to notice. I've said to her a million times, why don't you pee in the soup to show your contempt? But she can't see the necessity. Do you live near here?'

'About ten minutes' walk.'

'You owe me a coffee. Why don't we have one at your place? I'd like to see it.'

'There's nothing much to see, except a bit of a mess,' began Cassie. But Armelle was already on her feet.

'You're so lucky, having somewhere of your own. How much do you pay?'

'Two hundred and fifty a month.'

'That's cheap. But it's still more than I can afford. My father shells out more than that for me to live in that stinking room at Nanterre. But he can't bear the thought of me having any independence. What about yours?'

'Oh, he's quite generous. But he can't send me any money while I'm here because of exchange control.'

'What does he do?'

'He's a writer.'

'Is he famous?'

'He's sort of renowned, I suppose. He writes highbrow stuff. Biographies, literary criticism, that kind of thing.'

'And your mother?'

'She helps my father with his research, and does a bit of book reviewing on the side.'

'Any brothers or sisters?'

'Two older brothers. They're both journalists.'

'How horribly bourgeois,' sighed Armelle, commiserating.

'I wouldn't call them that,' said Cassie, rather defensively. 'They're all very left wing.'

'Communists?'

'Heavens no. Labour.'

'You mean they vote for Harold Wilson?' Armelle seemed unimpressed. 'He's just an American puppet.'

'The alternative, in England, is voting Tory.'

'Exactly. What's the point in voting at all if both parties are as bad as each other? Look what's happened in Germany.

Right and Left in bed together, so there's no difference any more. Everywhere it's the same story. Coalition. Compromise. Consensus. And here in France there's no opposition worthy of the name. The old Left is finished, *foutu*. Elections, parties, leaders, they all stink. So-called democracy stinks. You should come to some of our meetings at Nanterre. We have some very good speakers . . .'

She continued in this vein passionately until they reached Cassie's block, where the stairs put paid to her proselytising. Gazelle-like, Cassie ran ahead. It was too late now to regret not cleaning up. But Armelle didn't seem to notice. She sat down on the bed and looked round enviously while Cassie rinsed out two dirty cups under the cold tap.

'It must be great, being able to invite whoever you like,' she said. 'We're not allowed to have men in our rooms. And we can only visit the men's block if we have a letter of permission from a parent or guardian. Which needless to say my father won't give me. It's like a prison.'

'Well, at least you have hot water and baths and so on.'

'I wouldn't care where I lived as long as I could come and go as I pleased. Alain and I are like nomads. We have to make love where we can. My father won't even let me have a car. Just because I had a silly little prang in Odile's. What times did you say you were teaching her?'

'Tuesdays, Wednesdays and Fridays,' repeated Cassie, unsuspectingly. 'Four till six.'

Armelle thought for a minute.

'Alain works shifts, you know. When he's on earlies he gets up to town at about half past three.' Cassie poured boiling water into the mugs and reached for the powdered milk. 'Would you mind if I brought him here tomorrow, while you're out?'

'Pardon?'

'We wouldn't use the sheets. You wouldn't even know we'd been.'

'Well . . .'

'Just till I find a place of my own. I'm looking for a flat-share, but I can't find one for less than two hundred a month.'

Cassie hesitated. If she refused she would look impossibly

74

wet. And hypocritical. Her illicit affair with Wilfred had been conducted exclusively in hired and borrowed beds.

'All right then.'

'I knew as soon as I saw you that we were going to hit if off!' Armelle jumped up and embraced her. 'There's a place in the rue de Sèvres that does copy keys. I could nip down there now, if you like, it won't take a minute.'

For a moment Cassie felt warm and fluttery inside, revived by the feeling that Armelle might actually *like* her. Then she popped another pill and found she didn't much care either way.

'Well, my old friend? What did you think of the meeting?'

Karel was trembling all over with excitement, a state which he had passed off, rather unconvincingly, as the product of a chilly night and a weak chest. Miloš shepherded him into the *hospada* and ordered two tots of rum.

'Talk about a mutual admiration society,' grunted Karel. 'Anyone would think we had something to be proud of. There was a man there I recognised from state security back in forty-nine. One of the interrogators who helped convict me. And a year later, he gets arrested himself! Serve the bastard right.'

'Be fair. Can you honestly blame him for believing you were guilty, at the time? Remember how it was in those days. We all trusted the Party implicitly. We all thought that Western spies were everywhere, that another world war was about to start. When the arrests started, did it ever occur to *you* to think that the evidence might be manufactured? This isn't about revenge, Karel. It's about justice.'

'Justice, eh? That speech you made tonight was rousing stuff, you were always a good speaker. And you can bet your life that every word of it has been taken down.'

'So much the better!'

Karel drained his glass in one swallow. 'Even if they agree to mount an investigation, how far do you think it will be allowed to go? Too many top officials are implicated. If the truth came out, they would stand to lose everything – their jobs, their reputations, their privileges. So they'll close ranks. They'll do everything in their power to get rid of Dubček and all the other liberals. We're playing right into their hands.'

'They're outnumbered.'

'They have powerful friends. Before you know it, there will be a big clampdown and people who opened their big mouths will find themselves under arrest. You talked so loud tonight they must have heard you in Moscow. I have Eva to think of, remember.'

'Exactly. You have Eva to think of. If her mother was alive, she'd give you a good kick up the arse. God, you were lucky. I wish I'd had someone like Věra waiting for me. Don't you owe it to her to try and clear your name? Don't you owe it to your son?'

'My son?' snapped Karel, caught on a raw nerve. 'What difference would it make to him?'

'Well, wouldn't he like to see you vindicated?'

'Don't be such a sentimental old fool. The boy can hardly remember me. Just as well,' he added darkly.

'I'm going to nominate you for the committee,' went on Miloš relentlessly. 'We could do with an economist. To project the figures for compensation levels, and so on.'

'You can nominate me till you're blue in the face. I won't stand.'

'You're shaking. You need another drink.'

'No. I'm off home.'

'You should talk to Eva. She'd be right behind you, you know.'

'Eva? It's all ancient history to her. She's only a child. Nothing in her head except dancing and boyfriends.'

'You underestimate that girl. She's got her head screwed on.'

'If you've got any plans to nobble her behind my back, you can just forget them.'

He stood up to go.

'I might drop in for a game of chess over the weekend,' said Miloš casually.

'Still a politician at heart, aren't you?'

'And you're still a bureaucrat at heart. Always worrying about pettifogging details. But I was a doctor too, remember. And for you I prescribe a strong laxative.'

'The factory quack has other ideas,' grunted Karel. 'I got a letter this morning. I've been condemned to spend my summer leave at some godforsaken spa in the Tatras.'

Miloš roared with laughter. 'All that clean air! It'll probably kill you. They'll frisk you for fags and booze twice a day. That'll teach you to take so much time off sick.'

'Can you imagine it? A bunch of obscene old men coughing and spluttering all over each other.'

'Think about what I said,' repeated Miloš. 'Who knows, it might improve your health. Goodnight, old friend.'

Karel emerged from the comforting fug of the tavern into the cold night air. The meeting had been held under the auspices of a philately society which met regularly in a private room attached to a beer cellar near Old Town Square. The precaution had been thought wise at this early stage, even though it was probably gratuitous. Indiscretion had been in the air like vaporised neat spirits, going straight to everybody's head.

Hope was infectious, dangerously so. But apart from the odd public statement by leading liberals, there was little proof that any long-term changes were afoot. Miloš was always claiming to have 'inside information' about this and that, and for the past five years he had been confidently predicting that the old regime was on the verge of collapse. But every step forward had been dogged by retrograde measures. Writers and film-makers had made brave stands against the censor, winning success and prestige abroad, only to find their work subsequently banned at home. Economic reforms had been invalidated by rigid wage control and continuing political appointments to key managerial posts. Progressive trends in the universities had culminated in student demonstrators being beaten up by police. Novotny had been ousted as first secretary, but he was still president, and was survived by a rump of hardliners in the Central Committee. And Karel knew only too well from his colleagues at the packing shed that the workers mistrusted liberal intellectuals. Everyone was well ensconced in the system; doing as little work as possible, fiddling right and left, viewing any change as a threat.

He walked home, lost in thought, no longer cold now but hot all over, almost feverish with the old burning feelings of anger and savaged pride. He stopped for a moment by the embankment, leaning heavily against the cast-iron railings, gazing into the glassy waters of the Vltava. Across the river lay the Smichov district, where he and his first wife, Milena, had spent the final year of their marriage in a well-appointed Ministry apartment. While other families slept three and four to a room and had to queue for the most basic commodities, they had been among the privileged few, living in pre-war comfort and buying scarce goods at special shops reserved for Party officials. He had stubbornly shut his eyes to the anomalies of their new classless society, although Marta had never missed an opportunity to point them out. She and Milena had been as thick as thieves. He had been glad to see the back of his meddlesome mother with her reactionary views, her endless harping on about the good old days, her indomitable disrespect for all the things he held sacred. It annoyed him to this day that she thought she had been proved right, because, despite everything, he still believed in socialism. The ideal had been distorted by Cold War paranoia, by power-hungry despots, by cynical opportunists, but its principles were still valid, lying like sunken treasure in the depths of that cold, dark water, the water that might have claimed him years ago if Věra hadn't taken him in. Miloš was right: if she were here she would want him to clear his name.

He had no idea how long he had stood there, staring into his past, until he arrived home, dazed by too much introspection, to find Eva waiting up for him in her dressing gown, flushed and furious.

'Where have you been?' she flew at him. 'I've been worried sick. It's after midnight. You've been on one of your benders again! You stink of booze!'

'No. No, I only had one drink. I went for a walk and forgot the time. Look.'

He walked a straight line with his eyes shut to prove his good faith. Eva was unimpressed. 'A walk? In the freezing cold? Are you trying to kill yourself?'

Karel laughed.

'What's so funny?' demanded Eva, hauling off his coat and scarf.

'It's a bit late in the day for killing myself, that's all. I'm sorry I kept you up. Go to bed.'

'I wanted to talk to you.'

'Tomorrow. I'm tired.'

'You think I'm not tired? I was up first thing to do the shopping, I've been at work all day, and I spent the whole evening doing the bloody washing. I'm tired too!'

'Eva! What's the matter?'

'You might bother to tell me when you're going to be out. Or at least leave me a note. You take me completely for granted.'

'I know. I'm sorry. Miloš invited me. I didn't mean to go, but I changed my mind at the last minute. Do I have to ask your permission now before I go out? Do you ask mine?'

She glared and shoved a piece of paper in front of his nose. 'No, I don't. Not any more. I'm letting you read this as a courtesy, that's all.'

It was a letter to his mother. He sat down and read for a few moments.

'Have you applied for a permit?' he enquired gruffly.

'Not yet. But there's no reason why I shouldn't get one if Marta sends me a written invitation. Will you be able to manage without me for a couple of weeks?'

'Of course I can manage. I'm not an infant.'

'You behave like one most of the time.' And then, anxiously, 'It's difficult, inviting yourself. I wasn't sure how to put it. Do you think she'll have me?'

Karel gave her one of his suspicious looks. 'For a couple of weeks? Or permanently?'

'What do you mean?'

'You know perfectly well what I mean. What future is there for you here? It would be different if your mother was still alive. But now . . .'

Unaccountably, Eva stamped her foot, turned her back on him and burst into tears.

'What did I say?'

'You don't have a very high opinion of me, do you?'

'I'm being practical, that's all. It's not unknown for people to go on holiday to the West and not come back. I'm sure Viktor can introduce you to some nice young men.'

'How dare you suggest such a thing! You think I'd get

married just to get papers? What do you take me for? Anyone would think you wanted to get rid of me!'

'Perhaps I do. For your sake, not mine. Eva . . . don't cry. I didn't mean any harm.'

She wiped her eyes angrily and stared straight ahead of her, shoulders shaking, squeaking angrily into her handkerchief. Eva rarely cried; the very first time he had seen her she had been grinning from ear to ear, a podgy eight-year-old with rosy cheeks who laughed at the slightest thing. Karel put a tentative arm round her, helpless at the sight of her distress.

'Do you think I don't know you're unhappy?' he muttered. 'Do you think I'm that selfish and insensitive? I feel like a millstone around your neck. I didn't mean to offend you. I expressed myself badly, that's all.'

'I just want to get away for a bit, don't you see? I've never had a holiday apart from those lousy youth camps. I've saved a bit of money. Everyone else is going.'

'Everyone?'

'Jan's friends. Students. You should have heard them talking. Vienna, Rome, London, America even. Well, I want to go to Paris, that's all. And straight away you accuse me of planning to defect!'

'Eva . . . please look at me.' She turned to face him, red-eyed and sullen. 'Whatever you want to do is all right by me. I'll write a letter myself, to go with yours. And on Monday you must put in for your annual leave and lodge your application for a permit. And don't worry about money. I've been salting away those dollars Viktor sends. For your bottom drawer.'

For no good reason that Karel could see, this remark produced another storm of weeping, but she wouldn't say what was wrong. He sat her down on the sofa and put his arm around her, afraid to speak in case he put his foot in it again. She clung to him like a child, still whimpering, and he stroked her hair and wiped her face with his handkerchief, hampered by his inability to show emotion. He had always mistrusted his feelings, seeing them as a sign of weakness, not a source of strength.

'Go to bed now,' he said gently. 'I'll stay up and write my letter.'

She got up, shuddering in the aftermath of a sob, and squeezed his hand. 'I'm sorry I made a fuss. I got worked up worrying about you being so late. I care about you, you horrible old man!'

'I can't imagine why.'

'Neither can I, sometimes,' she said, almost angrily. 'But I do.'

Viktor had had a good day; a fruitful afternoon trawling the cafés in the Champs-Élysées and a profitable evening at the Lido. He had taken several calculated risks, just to keep himself on his toes. Now, as usual, he felt flat, empty with a sense of anticlimax.

He got home to find Rob patiently strumming his guitar to 'Blowin' in the Wind' and making his usual fist of it. Viktor couldn't understand why it took him so long to master the basic chords, which to his mind were common sense.

He sat down at the piano and drowned him out with an impromptu variation on 'Mr Tambourine Man', splashing around happily in the melody like a child in a bathtub. Rob put his instrument to one side.

'What did you do today?' asked Viktor.

'Hung around the café for an hour. Went to the Musée Rodin. Bought myself a sketch pad.'

He sounded fed up.

'What's the matter?'

'Nothing really. I'm just feeling kind of foreign, I suppose. I'll be okay once I get myself a job and a place to live.'

'Don't count on it. I still feel foreign. And I've been here for seventeen years. At least you're here by choice.'

Rob shrugged. 'The guys I admire are the ones who stayed home and went to gaol. That takes real guts.'

Viktor gave a derisory snort. 'The guts to do what? To endure solitary confinement, torture, brainwashing, and hard labour? To be publicly denounced as an enemy of the people? To forfeit all your property?'

'What do you mean?'

'Your President Johnson is no Stalin, whatever his critics say. I wouldn't shed too many tears for your brave buddies in gaol.'

'Hey. You're not pro-war, are you?'

'I oppose the spread of Communism. But I'm not the one who's being asked to fight.'

'That's not the point! The point is—'

'Never mind. My opinion isn't worth having in any case. Do you feel like a woman? There's a place near here that can fix us both up.'

'You mean a brothel?'

'Why do you sound surprised? If you wanted a baguette, you'd go to the baker's, wouldn't you?'

'But . . . why do you pay for it?'

'Women always make you pay, one way or another. This way you know exactly how much you're in for. Well, are you coming?'

'No thanks. It's late. I think I'll get some sleep.'

But he didn't sleep. It was true, he did feel like a woman. He cast his mind back to Ginny, who had ceded her virginity to him during his first week at college and clung to him like glue ever since. She was a nice girl, the kind that didn't sleep around, that made you feel responsible, obligated, trapped, old before your time . . . guilty. And now he found himself missing the convenience of having a girl on tap. But not enough to contemplate some cold-blooded fuck with a whore. Of course, Viktor was the cold-blooded type, except when he played the piano. When he played the piano, you could almost hear his dreams.

Viktor stayed out most of the night and slept late next morning, so Rob went to the café for breakfast without him. There had been a light fall of snow during the night; it lay sparse and frozen on the ground like a sprinkling of coarse sugar, and the sky was grey with the promise of more to come. The barman greeted him with a surly nod and produced a large black coffee and two butterless rolls garnished with a dollop of apricot jam. Rob had just ordered a second cup when a girl walked in, looked briefly round the room, came up to his table and said, 'I'm Armelle Lemercier.' She pulled off her gloves and held out her hand. 'National Vietnam Committee.'

Rob had been expecting a man. The girl was small, neat, and very feminine, with a soft, throaty voice and long, silky, chestnut hair; she wore jeans tucked into scuffed white boots, a navy-blue fisherman's sweater and a very grubby sheepskin jacket, an outfit which she wore like a fashion model, making it look mysteriously chic.

'Thank you for coming,' said Rob, and then, 'How did you recognise me?'

She laughed, revealing tiny, very even teeth. 'By looking at you. I hope we can help you. And that you can help us, in return.'

She caught the waiter's eye without difficulty and ordered herself a hot chocolate.

'You wish to settle permanently in France?'

'I don't know about permanently. Until the summer, anyway. I've got a tourist visa, but it's only valid for a month. I'm living on borrowed money, as I told you. And camping out on a friend's couch.'

'Can you stay where you are till we sort out your papers? We'll help you make the necessary applications and put you in touch with a free lawyer if there are any difficulties.' Her manner was efficient, bureaucratic almost. 'We have helped several people in your position. We also provide safe houses for GIs who have deserted from Germany. Perhaps you'd like to come to our next meeting.'

She delved into her bag and produced a leaflet. Rob read through it while she ate the froth on her chocolate with a teaspoon. It was all very heavy stuff.

'This bit here . . .' He ran a finger along a line of smudged purple print. 'You say that we should help the workers and peasants in Vietnam "continue the revolutionary struggle towards a people's victory". But what about peace? Surely we should be pressing the US to reach a peace settlement, not encouraging the Vietnamese to prolong the war?'

Armelle offered him a cigarette and proffered her own for a light.

'First of all, oppression is not peace. There can be no peace, no freedom, without the revolution. Your government knows that, and ours too. They fear that students and workers may follow the example set by the people of Vietnam. As we shall.'

'You're talking about a revolution here in France?'

'Not just in France. All over Europe the movement is preparing itself towards the overthrow of capitalism and the creation
of a classless society . . . '

She had all the implacable zeal of a missionary faced with
the sinful innocence of a heathen. Not wishing to argue with
such a pretty, serious little thing, Rob nodded politely, anxious
to keep her talking, fascinated by the movements of her mouth,
looking, not listening. After several minutes of fluent evange-
lism, she sighed and said, 'You're not taking me seriously, are
you?' Her tone was weary, resigned. 'Revolution's unfeminine,
I know. The same words would sound quite different coming
from a man. They'd sound wonderful coming from a big
strong man like you.'

Caught out, Rob made a placatory gesture. 'Listen, I'm not
all that political. I'm into non-violence, I believe in peace. It's
nothing to do with you being a woman . . . '

'Yes it is. But it's not your fault. It's mine. I have too much
sex appeal.' It was a statement of fact, devoid of conceit. 'For a
man to respect you politically you have to be sexless, preferably ugly as well.' There was a sudden, woebegone self-mock-
ery about her. 'Sometimes I think to myself, I'll stop shaving
my legs and washing my hair and wearing make-up. But I'm
too vain. Even when I look a mess, it's *soigné*. I've inherited my
mother's looks, unfortunately.' Her mother had given her
clear, unblemished skin, ears like little shells, almond-shaped
green eyes and a dainty mobile mouth that gave tantalising
flashes of a tiny restless tongue. 'Men are so lucky, not to have
to worry about such things.' She looked at him saucily, as if she
could read his thoughts. 'Would you like to meet some French
girls? You'd meet plenty of girls at our meetings . . . '

'*Salut*.'

Rob turned to see Viktor, a cup in one hand, a plate in the
other, and a cigarette in his mouth. He bowed at Armelle with
ironic chivalry, deposited his breakfast and shook her hand
while Rob did the introductions.

'I talked to the concierge,' said Viktor, taking a big bite
of croissant. 'There's an apartment to let in the rue Ortolan,
just a few blocks away. Three hundred and seventy-five a
month.'

'I can't afford that much.'

'You won't get a place with a shower for less,' shrugged Viktor. 'But there are two rooms, apparently. You could always sublet one of them.'

'Perhaps I could help you find a tenant,' said Armelle. 'In fact, as it happens, I'm looking for a place myself. That is, most of the time I live on campus. But it's vile. I need a bolthole. I can't afford much, but if I paid, say, a hundred for the smaller room, and I was hardly ever there . . . '

'You haven't seen it yet,' said Viktor, before Rob could respond. 'I doubt if it's the kind of place you're used to.'

Viktor could sniff out people's income bracket like some kind of social bloodhound; it was his job. This girl oozed money. Her handbag alone had cost a good two hundred francs and long hair didn't hang that way unless it was expensively trimmed.

'You should see the hostel I live in at Nanterre,' she snapped. 'It's disgusting.'

'Ah,' said Viktor, feigning enlightenment. 'So you're a *student*.' The word was heavy with scorn.

'Armelle's on the National Vietnam Committee. She reckons I won't have too much trouble extending my visa.'

'How uplifting. France, home of the persecuted and oppressed, haven of the refugee.'

'Well, it's about the only good thing you can say for this lousy government,' said Armelle. 'At least it opposes American imperialism in Vietnam.'

'Only because France was totally humiliated in Indo-China and can't bear the thought of America showing her up.'

'Rubbish.'

'Oh, I'm sorry. Not being French myself, I keep forgetting how touchy the natives are.'

Armelle's eyes narrowed.

'He's Czech,' muttered Rob, apologetically.

'Which hardly counts as a nationality,' continued Viktor. 'After all, the country only existed for twenty years before France sold it down the river.'

'France?' echoed Armelle. 'It was Britain who did that, not France.'

'It was France we had a so-called treaty with.'

Armelle opened her mouth and shut it again, sensing, perhaps, that she was being set up.

'Don't expect me to wave a flag for France,' she said. 'But if you hate it so much here, why don't you go somewhere else?'

'Hate it? Wherever did you get that idea? I adore its food, its wine, its women.' He moved his chair closer to Armelle's. 'I'm sorry. I didn't mean for you to take it personally.' He picked up the pamphlet lying on the table. 'Can you explain all this to me?' he continued, humble now. 'Believe me, I find this war an abomination. My country, after all, is a victim of Soviet imperialism. I identify strongly with the Vietnamese freedom fighters. But I'm not an educated man. I come from peasant stock, you understand.'

She didn't respond straight away, still mistrustful, but he held her gaze with a display of genuine contrition. After a moment's hesitation, she launched uncertainly into her little spiel again, gathering steam as Viktor listened attentively.

'You believe in the redistribution of wealth?' he prompted. 'You believe in the principle of collective ownership?'

Rob didn't hear her answer. Everything about her was coiled and compact as if it had all been folded into a very small space, like a rosebud. Her hands moved a lot as she talked, little white hands disfigured by nails bitten down to the quick. Rob found her nails absurdly touching.

Viktor was nodding now and being serious, asking questions which she seemed eager to answer. Rob assumed that he was just trying to pick her up, and felt automatically protective, not to say proprietorial. They had moved on to the Algerian war, a topic Rob knew nothing about. Momentarily they might have been speaking in an unknown language. He found himself interpreting the conversation through their gestures and facial expressions, as if watching a silent movie. But for that, he would surely not have noticed what happened next, because it was done with a sleight of hand bordering on the magical.

Armelle had left her bag lying beside her chair, to Viktor's left. It was now on his right; he must have guided it there with his foot, under the table. His eyes never leaving Armelle's, he leaned sideways and made great play of scratching his right leg as he undid the catch on the bag and thrust his hand inside it briefly, so briefly that a mistimed blink prevented Rob from spotting what he had taken. The hand was busy in his pocket now, delving for his lighter, and seconds later the bag had been skilfully dribbled back to where it had come from. Armelle, who had been talking earnestly throughout this manoeuvre, didn't notice a thing.

Rob tried to catch Viktor's eye but his attention was still fixed on Armelle. To accuse him in public was unthinkable but to let him get away with it would make him an accomplice. He looked on, quietly fuming, hoping that Armelle would visit the *toilettes* so that he could tackle Viktor in her absence and make him return whatever it was he had stolen.

'So when capital is redistributed,' Viktor was saying, 'when the proletariat come to power, you won't mind the loss of privilege? You won't mind giving up your money and possessions as the price of equality?'

'Money, possessions and privilege are the carrots of capitalist society,' said Armelle patiently. 'Those who have them flaunt them in order to trick those who *don't* have them into thinking that if they go along with the system they can have them too. It's a giant state-controlled conspiracy to hoodwink and exploit the workers in the name of so-called democracy.'

Viktor sighed in a show of scepticism. 'If you were a worker, you'd have credibility. But you're not. You're a student, a future member of the élite. And you're not poor, that's obvious.'

'I'm not rich either. My father's rich, but I'm not. That's not my fault. He made the money, not me.'

'So what do you do with the money he gives you? If I said to you, you're much better off than me, will you pay for my breakfast, what would you do?'

She thought for a moment before saying sweetly, 'How do I know that I'm better off than you?'

'You conduct a means test, naturally, in the hope that I'll have to pay for yours instead.'

'Your thinking isn't rigorous, you know. You're just playing with words.'

'That's because I haven't been taught to think, like you. I'm an ignorant, uneducated man. An immigrant. I lack your admirable French logic. But I have my pride. I would never ask for charity.'

He picked up the three separate chits off the table and put his hand into his left-hand pocket for some money.

'I'll pay,' said Armelle, relenting, reaching for her bag.

'Well ... if you insist.' Without waiting for her to discover her loss, Viktor pulled a leather notecase out of his other pocket and admired it briefly before extracting a ten-franc note which he gave to Armelle with a smile of smug munificence. Stony-faced, Armelle held out her hand for her wallet.

'What do you want?'

'My money, of course.'

'*Your* money? What about collective ownership?'

'Give it back to her, Viktor,' said Rob.

'What if I don't? Do you think she'll call the police?' He grinned satanically at Armelle. 'What would it take to make you call the police?'

Her expression dissolved from controlled irritation to desolate disappointment.

'I don't mind you stealing from me,' she said bleakly. 'What I mind is you pretending to listen to me. What I mind is you treating me like a fool. Keep the money.'

She got up to go and Rob saw that her lovely little mouth was quivering with humiliation. He resisted an urge to lay Viktor out there and then.

'Wait a minute,' said Rob, catching hold of her arm. 'You wanted to look at that room with me, remember?'

'No point now. I can't afford it. That was all the money I had.'

'I'll give you a loan,' offered Viktor, ever magnanimous.

'You're a shit, Viktor,' hissed Rob, standing up and putting a protective arm round her. 'Ignore him,' he said. 'He's a kleptomaniac.' He turned to Viktor and demanded belligerently, 'What was the address?'

Viktor gave him a mocking stare.

'Perhaps I'd better come with you,' he said.

The apartment in the rue Ortolan comprised one decent-sized room, fitted with an electric hotplate and a small sink, a cubicle housing a shower and WC, and an adjoining window-less boxroom which had two doors, one leading into the main living area, and the other directly on to the landing. This made it technically self-contained, albeit unlettable on its own. Armelle said it was just what she was looking for.

'I couldn't charge you anything,' began Rob, unhappily. Much as he welcomed the notion of having this terrific-looking girl as his flatmate, the so-called room had no furniture in it and was evidently intended just for storage.

'Don't be a fool,' said Viktor curtly, counting out a hundred francs of Armelle's money and handing them to her.

'Will this be enough?' she said, offering the notes to Rob. 'You'd be doing me a favour. I've been looking for somewhere for weeks, but there's nowhere I can afford. I promise I'll be no trouble to you, you won't even know I'm there.'

It had to be a come-on. She'd only known him five minutes and no one in their right mind would want to rent a room like that. It seemed too good to be true.

'Be my guest,' said Rob. 'Or rather Viktor's. He's lending me the rent.'

She beamed in delight, reached up on tiptoe and kissed Rob on both cheeks, leaving him giddy with her perfume.

'Will you arrange it with the concierge?' she said sweetly. 'I'll wait here. She might object to us sharing.'

Rob flung Viktor a hands-off look and left the room.

Armelle turned to Viktor. 'If you had stolen a million francs from me,' she began earnestly, 'if you took everything I had, I would never, ever go to the police. I want you to know that. The police are scum, the lackeys of the state.'

Viktor yawned.

'That wasn't the first time you've done something like that,' she continued respectfully. 'You were so quick, so skilful. Are you a professional?'

Viktor stared at her balefully, irritated. 'It's what I do for a living, if that's what you mean.'

'Have you ever been caught?'

'Only cretins get caught.'

'Tell me . . . why do you do it? Not just for the money. I can tell you don't do it just for the money.'

More flattery. Viktor sighed. 'Because it's the only thing I can do. And because I enjoy it. But mostly for the money.'

It was a luxury to confront a victim after the crime, to show his contempt openly. He disliked her intense, sincere expression, the way she was trying to adapt her strategy, to manipulate him the way she had manipulated Rob. Like most expert practitioners of the art, Viktor was critical of others' technique.

She sat down on the bed, crossed her legs oriental-style as if preparing to meditate, and held on to her feet, rocking backwards and forwards, as she said, 'Would you like the chance to steal a lot of money, without getting caught? I could help you.'

She had been to see *Bonnie and Clyde*, thought Viktor, dismissively. 'Thank you but I work alone. I don't need any help.'

Armelle reached into her bag and produced a large bunch of keys. She put the ring round her index finger and swung them round and round for a moment before saying, 'My father has a house in the 16*ème*. The week after next he and my stepmother will be in Chamonix, skiing. The maid will be visiting her family in Spain.' She threw the keys at him, forcing him to catch them. 'The place will be empty.'

Viktor looked at her coldly. 'What's that to me?'

'He keeps a lot of cash in the safe. For bribing people into giving him contracts and so on. It's money the tax people know nothing about. And then there's my stepmother's jewellery. Bought for cash, uninsured. He can't report any of it missing. That's the beauty of it, don't you see?'

'So why don't you steal it yourself?'

'I would if I knew how. I've tried every combination I could think of. Birthdays, anniversaries, that kind of thing. But nothing worked. It needs a professional touch, like yours. You do know how to open a safe, don't you?'

'That's not the point. It's too risky. He'll guess you had something to do with it.'

'Oh, I shall have the perfect alibi. I'll go skiing with them. Papa and I will do all the black pistes together. It'll ruin her holiday.' She made a swishing noise and a swooping gesture with her hands. 'And all the while, I shall be thinking, if only he knew . . .'

Her eyes were bright, pleading. They left him unmoved.

'I'm not interested.'

'Why not? Are you afraid?'

Viktor didn't answer. She took the keys from him and itemised each one. 'This one's for the front gate. That's the latchkey and there are two deadlocks – this one for the bottom lock and that one for the top. There's no burglar alarm. He's more afraid of the police than he is of burglars.'

'And how much is your cut?'

'Say, ten thousand francs? I could ask for more, but I want to keep my motives pure.'

'And what are these pure motives?'

'I just hate the power his money gives him over me, that's all. I hate the power it gives him over others.'

Viktor threw the keys up and down, tormenting her.

'It's not a trick,' she went on. 'Like I said, I'd never go to the police, and in any case I couldn't without implicating myself.'

Viktor put the keys in his pocket. 'I'll think about it.'

'You won't regret it. You should make at least fifty thousand francs, probably more, plus whatever you can get for the jewellery.'

'I didn't say I'd do it,' repeated Viktor. 'I said I'd think about it. Why do you hate your father so much?'

'Because he's a filthy capitalist. Because he exploits his workers, because he betrayed his class, because he . . . he . . . '

'Because he married this Odile woman?'

'That's got nothing to do with it. This is a political act, not a personal one.'

'Political? You delude yourself.'

'Look, it's just one tiny gesture, that's all, against the system. As a thief, you should understand. A thief is a natural subversive, the most primitive kind of revolutionary. You're only an outlaw because society sanctifies property and criminalises any threat to ownership—'

'Spare me the lecture,' said Viktor, weary of this polysyllabic harangue. 'I couldn't care less about your politics. If I do as you ask, it won't be to please you. It will be to please myself. If I do it, it won't mean you have acquired a tame criminal to service your revolutionary plans. And if I don't do it, it will be because I don't need or want that kind of money, because having too much would make me lose my edge.' To demonstrate, he took a hundred-franc note out of his wallet, flipped his lighter, and set fire to it, enjoying the involuntary look of horror on her face. 'Spoilt bitches like you make me sick.'

'I'm not your enemy,' she said, exasperated now. 'We're on the same side.'

'On the contrary. I'm a parasite on the beast you want to kill. If you succeed its blood congeals and I die, while you gorge yourself on the carcase. We can never be on the same side.'

The door opened.

'I've fixed it all up,' said Rob. 'We can move in today.'

'That's wonderful,' oozed Armelle. 'I'll get working on your case right away and I'll be in touch about the room as soon as I get back from Chamonix. I must go now. See you soon.'

She embraced him and left the room, flinging one final plaintive, provocative look at Viktor. He stared back inscrutably, not even deigning to register his scorn, fingering the keys in his pocket, tempted.

FOUR

February 1968

'Ay wood laik a cut an' blow job wiz plenty of 'air licker,'
parroted Odile, tracing the words Cassie had written with her
finger. 'An' pleeze 'urry. Ay 'ave already been wanking for ten
minutes.'

'Very good. You are a natural linguist, madame.'

'Pardon?' Madame's eyes opened wide in non-comprehen-
sion. Cassie repeated herself in French, eliciting a modest shrug.
Normally she enjoyed these exercises in semantic sabotage, but
today she wasn't in the mood. Her stomach was churning
around like a washing machine, a condition which she had at
first put down to Wilfred's impending visit, timed to coincide
with Cassie's half-term. But her malaise had proved resistant to
tranquillisers, suggesting a more banal diagnosis.

'Would you mind very much if we cut the lesson short
today?' ventured Cassie. 'I'm afraid I don't feel very well.
Perhaps I could make up the time next week, when you come
back from Chamonix.'

'That would not be convenient,' said Odile, producing her
all-purpose smile. 'I prefer to continue.' Despite her lack of grey
matter, she was proving to be an obsessively diligent pupil, if
only because she was determined to get her money's-worth.
She moved on to the next page of her exercise book. Cassie sat
very still, confirming her suspicion that the room had started to
move. She must have eaten something. If it was food poisoning,
she would have to phone Wilfred and put him off. Perhaps it
was that pâté she had bought the day before yesterday. Pâté

was always dodgy, she should have known better . . . The pungent memory of it was suddenly too much for her.

'I'm sorry, madame,' she gulped, making a dash for the nearest of the three gold-plated bathrooms. Succumbing to the luxury of a clean loo with a seat, she didn't emerge for a good twenty minutes, by which time Odile had ceded to *force majeure* and given the lesson up as a bad job.

'Madame had to go out,' explained Pilar. 'She said as she only had half an hour today . . . ' Apologetically, she handed over ten francs in very small change. 'Would you like something to drink? You're very pale.'

'I feel awful. As if I've swallowed a live rat.'

Pilar felt her forehead, declared her feverish and went into her motherly mode. She was forever luring Cassie into the kitchen and feeding her; it worried her that she was so thin. She offered to boil her some plain rice to settle her stomach, a well-meaning suggestion that sent Cassie rushing back into the bathroom.

Fearful of disgracing herself on the Métro, she blew her day's earnings on a taxi home. By the time she had climbed, or rather crawled, up the stairs to her room, the sweat was standing out in great cold beads on her forehead. She collapsed on top of the bed, fully clothed, and fell instantly into a thick, swirling semi-sleep which was cruelly, and repeatedly, interrupted. An hour and half a dozen sorties later she staggered out of the noxious cubicle at the end of the corridor to find Pilar standing outside her door.

'I was worried about you,' she said. 'So far from home, with no one to look after you.'

'You shouldn't have bothered,' began Cassie, torn between a childish need for sympathy and a paranoid sense of privacy. Never much of a good Samaritan herself, she was embarrassed by Pilar's robust, no-nonsense kindness.

'Sorry about the mess,' she muttered, opening the door to a scene of well-entrenched squalor. A bulging plastic bag full of rubbish had toppled over, spilling yoghurt pots and orange peel on to the floor. Every surface was littered with used cups, ends of bread, fossilised apple cores and discarded underwear. Books bobbed like flotsam on an ocean of crumpled clothes.

Pilar, well used to other people's dirt, didn't bat an eyelid. She remade the bed, tucked Cassie up and moved round the tiny room like a whirlwind, restoring it to some semblance of order. She squinted at the empty packet of Entero-Vioform, on which Cassie had overdosed to no avail.

'English medicine?'

Cassie nodded weakly. Pilar disappeared down the stairs and returned a few minutes later bearing a carton from the *pharmacie*. She handed Cassie a huge torpedo-shaped tablet and stopped her from swallowing it just in time.

'Thank you, Pilar,' croaked Cassie. 'It was very kind of you to come.'

'I'll come again tomorrow,' said Pilar, 'but on the day after that I'm going home for a week, while Monsieur and Madame are in Chamonix. Do you have any friends who can look after you?'

'Friends?' Cassie shuddered at the thought of any of her colleagues or long-shunned compatriots seeing her in this disgusting state. 'No, I haven't got any friends. That is, I don't need anyone to look after me. I'll be fine.'

'My room is much, much better than this one,' observed Pilar with great satisfaction. 'I would not like to live in a place like this.' She set about gathering up dirty clothes. 'I might as well wash and iron these things. I have other laundry to do.'

Cassie went through the motions of protesting but Pilar waved these courtesies aside and began admiring Cassie's scattered wardrobe, particularly the much-despised terracotta sweater, still unworn.

'You can have it if you like,' said Cassie. 'I don't like the colour.'

Without more ado Pilar whipped off her blouse and squeezed herself into it.

'You don't think it's too tight?' she queried, inspecting her voluptuous profile.

'No,' lied Cassie. 'It looks very nice. How much do I owe you for the chemist?'

Pilar shook her head, still preening herself.

'I shall wear it when I go home. My sisters will be so jealous!'

'Oh, take anything else you fancy,' said Cassie, anxious to repay her debt. 'I've got far too many clothes.'

Pilar took her literally, exclaiming at the Mary Quant and Biba and Bus Stop labels, undaunted by the necessity of holding her breath to avoid splitting their seams.

'Such a pity you're not well,' she said, stuffing her spoils into a carrier bag, 'or you could come to Spain with me. And then I could come and stay with you, in England.'

'Er . . . yes,' mumbled Cassie.

'When I get back, we should go out together, have some fun. Jean-Claude has lots of friends. Tell me, what do you do with your spare time?'

'Nothing much. I read, sleep. I like being alone.'

'You're not homesick? You don't miss your family?'

'No. We're not close. We all lead separate lives.'

'I miss my mother. But I prefer France to Spain. There's more freedom. I shall marry a Frenchman and stay here. Would you like to marry a Frenchman?'

'I can't imagine marrying anyone.'

'You don't have a boyfriend?' persisted Pilar.

'Yes. But I hate him.' The words just popped out, bypassing the thought process, taking her by surprise.

'Why do you hate him?'

Cassie shook her head, regretting this ill-considered admission. She never confided in anyone: she must be delirious.

'Did he deceive you with another woman?' urged Pilar, who was evidently used to detailed girl-talk.

'No.'

'Then what happened?'

Cassie made a face.

'I got pregnant,' she said, acknowledging the fact as if for the first time.

'He refused to marry you?'

'He's already got a wife. That wasn't the problem. I didn't want the baby in any case. At least, I don't think I did. I didn't think, at the time, I couldn't think. But . . . he just assumed that I would get rid of it. He just assumed it. There was no discussion, he just decided it for me, and I went along with it, because I thought that must be what I wanted. But . . . but . . .'

'Ssh,' murmured Pilar, sitting on the bed and smoothing Cassie's lank, damp hair.

'I'm sorry,' gulped Cassie, appalled at herself. 'I'm being stupid.'

'You did the right thing,' said Pilar. 'A baby without a husband . . . What would your parents have said?'

'My parents? Oh, they'd have taken it in their stride. If I'd gone ahead and had the baby they'd have stood by me. And if I'd told them I wanted an abortion, that would have been all right too. They're very broad-minded.'

Pilar put an arm round her and made clucking noises. Cassie tried to imagine her mother doing the same and couldn't. Mummy had always analysed rather than understood.

'Don't cry,' said Pilar. 'You'll fall in love with a good man and have lots of lovely children. And then you can forget all about this horrible *connard* and what he did to you.'

Cassie shook her head. 'I'll never fall in love,' she said. 'It's not in my nature. I'm too . . . too cold.'

'On the contrary, you have a temperature. Don't kick off the bedclothes like that, it's good to sweat, it gets rid of the poison.'

She tucked the covers under the mattress, immobilising her. 'I'll come back tomorrow and bring you some of Monsieur Lemercier's Cognac, to settle your stomach. Do you need anything from the shops before they close?'

Cassie thought for a minute.

'Will you send a telegram for me, tomorrow morning?'

Pilar fetched some paper. Cassie took a deep breath and wrote out Wilfred's name and address in block capitals. His home address, not the college.

HAVE CAUGHT THE CLAP, she wrote neatly. DIRTY WEEKEND CANCELLED. CASSIE.

'There's a letter from Prague,' said Marta grimly, handing it to Viktor.

'You read it to me.'

'You can read if you put your mind to it!'

That was hitting below the belt, a sure sign that she was spoiling for a fight. It was true, he could read if he put his mind to it, a slow, laborious and frustrating process which still made him feel like the one outsider in some gigantic conspiracy.

There were two letters in the envelope, one from his father and one from Eva. Handwriting was infinitely more difficult than print; Czech more confusing now than French. After a few moments Marta lost patience.

'Eva wants me to invite her,' she said. 'So she can get an exit permit and a visa. I might have known this would happen sooner or later. Listen to what your father has to say.' She took one of the letters back and put on her glasses.

'"Eva has been very depressed since her mother died,"' she read. '"Keeping house for an old man is no fun for a girl of eighteen. She needs to stretch her wings. I know Viktor must be very busy, but I hope he'll find time to show her round Paris and introduce her to a few young people. She's a sweet-natured, cheerful girl and I'm sure you'll enjoy her company."'

'So?' said Viktor, picking up his knife and fork again. 'What's the problem?'

'You know perfectly well what the problem is. Why do you suppose I've never invited her before?'

'I can't imagine,' goaded Viktor.

'I want you to welcome Eva, treat her as your sister. With courtesy and generosity and respect. I don't want you to let me down.'

'You don't want me to expose your pathetic lies, you mean. Just as well for you I can't write. If I could write I'd have sent my father a long letter by now and told him exactly what I do.'

'When Eva comes, you'll behave yourself. You won't give her any reason to suspect the truth!'

For reply, Viktor glared at her with the intractable stubbornness that so reminded her of his father. A mixture of arrogance and passion and sheer bloody-mindedness, an inability to move one millimetre from his chosen course, an infinite capacity for self-delusion . . .

'Please, Viktor. For me. She doesn't speak any French, remember. And you know I can't get out and about with this bad leg of mine. Think how much she must be looking forward to it! I want her to have a nice time.'

'For God's sake. What a lot of fuss about nothing. Have I ever embarrassed you in front of people?'

He was irritated with himself for being so put out. Acting out a charade for Eva's benefit was no different, in essence, from conning the punters, or the bureaucrats, or the police. His whole life was one big act, after all, and he had always pandered to Marta's sensibilities as far as her friends and neighbours were concerned.

It was the request itself that annoyed him, not the execution of it. Obligations were intolerable unless they were voluntary. At times like this he wished that Marta had carried out her oft-repeated threat and disowned him, leaving him free to misbehave with a clear conscience. And yet, he needed her disapproval; he expected and respected it. The system worked fine as long as there were only the two of them, a unit welded by love and loyalty in a world full of strangers. The invisible intruder, as always, was his father.

He would have liked to shock him, to prove that he didn't give a shit for his good opinion, to force him into a final, explicit, horrified rejection. But to do so would defeat the object of the exercise. It would show that he actually cared.

'We've invited you here as a comrade, Alain,' said Georges Leroux, folding his florid, fleshy features into a big-brother smile. As chairman of the union executive committee, Georges was used to dealing with tricky situations. He had wrung numerous concessions out of hard-nosed management by dint of persistence and guile; he knew how to negotiate a good trade-off. The rhetoric he delivered at meetings was pure theatre; he was a profoundly pragmatic man, who mistrusted his members, most of whom were too ignorant to know what was good for them – unlike Alain Moreau, who was too clever to know what was good for him.

Alain appeared unmoved by this fraternal overture. Albert Moreau, reluctantly called to the meetings as Alain's shop steward, looked fidgety and uncomfortable. Anyone observing the trio would have assumed that he was the one being hauled over the coals, and not his son.

'I hope that we can work together for the common good,' continued Georges expansively. 'The union badly needs young men of your intelligence and passion. But as you must be aware, there are those who claim that you are trying to set up a Trotskyist splinter group.'

'There's no group as such,' said Alain wearily, 'and even if there was, it wouldn't have a label.'

'You deny that you have been urging wildcat action, holding unauthorised meetings, and liaising with anti-union factions outside your place of work?'

'Why should I deny it? The workers are fed up with being fobbed off by party hacks like you. You're used to chairing meetings where fifty diehards turn up and vote for everything the executive suggests. You don't want the rank and file putting its oar in. The very people you're supposed to represent are the last ones you want to listen to. And if they dare to try to make themselves heard, you start a witch-hunt for so-called Trotskyists. But I quite understand your position, Georges. I know the kind of pressure you're under, from above.' He gazed heavenward in asinine adoration.

Georges, a wily old campaigner, didn't rise to the bait. Albert, a good Party paranoid, did.

'And who do *you* take your orders from, these days? Bertrand Lemercier? He must look upon you as his biggest ally. Someone who focuses discontent on the union, instead of the employer. If you weren't my son I'd think they were putting you up to it!'

'Can you both forget whose son I am for a moment? I intend to keep coming to meetings and saying my piece. If other workers want to come and listen to me and join in, they're surely free to do so. If we choose to extend our discussions to our free time and talk to like-minded comrades from other factories, that is our right as individuals. I repeat, there's no group and I'm not a leader. It's time we got away from groups and leaders.'

Georges put on a pair of wire spectacles and shuffled some papers.

'I have here some of the remarks you made about the recent overtime proposals,' he began. 'You are on record as saying...'

Alain gave a bark of laughter. 'So I'm being minuted, am I? My words are actually being written down?'

'You referred to the proposed agreement as a sell-out. You claimed that union and management were hand in glove to reduce manpower over the next five years, and that the men were being duped into voting themselves out of their jobs. As a result of your campaign the deal was voted down, and months of careful negotiations were laid waste.'

'You mean months of double-dealing were exposed, don't you?'

'Incidents like this destroy the union's credibility,' continued Georges, thumping the table with his fist. 'It leads management to think that we are weak and divided. For a union to be strong it has to have the full weight of the workforce behind it.'

'Then it should listen to the workforce and not treat it like a bunch of children. You are the servant of the workforce, not its master.'

'You dare to use feudal analogies to me?'

'The feudal system suits you perfectly. True collective ownership and workers' control would take away all your power.'

'If you feel this way, why don't you resign your membership?'

'Because I still believe in the principles you have betrayed.'

Georges exchanged glances with Albert, and decided it was high time they got to the point. He fixed Alain with a man-to-man stare. 'How do you feel about standing as shop steward? There's a vacancy coming up.'

Alain's initial stare of disbelief was quickly superseded by a cynical smile.

'You could serve your comrades better if you had official status,' continued Georges. 'At the moment you're just seen as a trouble-maker. We want to protect you, Alain. Management would like an excuse to get rid of you.'

'A moment ago you said they enjoyed seeing me stir up trouble. Make up your mind.'

'They need that overtime deal settled. Several export orders depend on our ability to meet heavier demand. It's better to see our members paid overtime, in this instance, than to bring in more workers. We've stood firmly against that option all along.'

'That's a very short-sighted view.'

'On the contrary, it avoids lay-offs when orders recede.'

'Rubbish. They've worked out that this way's cheaper, that's all. If they want the deal they have to pay what it's worth.'

'Well, then. Wouldn't you like to have a place in the negotiating process? Wouldn't you like an official mandate to make your comrades' views known?'

'I intend to stand down,' mumbled Albert, refusing to meet Alain's eye.

'Don't do it on my account, Papa. I'd refuse to accept the nomination. I know what you're playing at, Georges. You think that once you give me official blessing you'll be able to control me. I don't give a sou for status, or recognition, or any kind of so-called mandate. I'd rather everyone came along to meetings and spoke for themselves.'

'Anarchy has a poor track record, Alain. As an ideal, it sounds pure, seductive. But in practice it simply doesn't work. You have energy, commitment, courage. Don't waste them.'

'I don't intend to,' Alain assured him. 'Can I go now?'

'Alain!' snapped Albert. 'At least listen!'

'I have no quarrel with you, Papa. I'm sorry if I'm putting you in a difficult position. But it can't be helped.'

He kept his voice level, courteous, deceptively quiet. For a rabble-rouser, thought Georges, he was an extraordinarily mild-mannered young man, which made him infinitely more dangerous than any ranting demagogue. People trusted him.

'He's got a point about the overtime deal,' muttered Albert, as Alain closed the door behind him.

'Of course he has. But it's not worth a strike. Alain is looking for a cause to die for. A union cannot afford such luxuries. It must think of survival, not self-sacrifice.'

'I think I'll resign anyway. I'm losing heart for it, Georges. I'm getting old.'

'Older and wiser than your son. As the older generation, we have a responsibility to guide and protect the young against their own folly. Not just the responsibility, the right. A right we earned in the thirties and forties, when we had to struggle for what they hold cheap.'

'All that seems a long time ago,' said Albert.

'We've come a long way since then.'

'Too far, Alain would say.'

Preoccupied, Albert made his way to the bicycle sheds. The shift having finished half an hour ago, they were deserted apart from Chantal Durand, a pretty young machinist, and Alain, who was bent over her wheel, busy mending a puncture.

She looked up and smiled at Albert in recognition.

'I rode over a nail on my way to work,' she said. 'Lucky I had a repair kit with me.'

'I won't be long,' said Alain, addressing his father. 'If you wait a moment, I'll ride home with you.'

Albert could tell from the look on Chantal's face that she was keen to extend the encounter as long as possible, although Alain seemed unaware of her bright eyes and flushed cheeks. Which was a pity. He would have given much to see Alain settle down with a nice, sensible lass of his own class. This student girl had clearly been a bad influence. Albert mistrusted the kind of woman who read books.

'No,' he said, mounting his *mobylette*. 'You stay and make a decent job of that. I'm off home.'

The engine spluttered into life and Chantal waved to him as he rode away. She looked down at Alain, who was already pumping up her tyre. For weeks now she had been trying to get him to notice her – turning up to every union meeting, smiling at him in the canteen, making sure their paths crossed at every opportunity. But so far nothing had worked. He was always in a group, always deep in discussion about something, always in a hurry, like now.

'There you are,' he said. 'The air seems to be holding.'

'It was very nice of you.' She gave him a reproachful look. 'At least you know who I am now. Usually you look straight through me.'

'I'm sorry. Of course I know who you are.'

'I agreed with what you said at the last union meeting,' she continued, determined to delay his departure as long as possible. Her only interest in union meetings was in seeing Alain, and hearing him speak. She had understood little of what he said, but had gleaned enough to know that the way to his heart was through his politics.

'But did you notice how few women turned up?' she continued doggedly. 'Why do they always hold the meetings after work? Most women have to get home to their chores. There should be special meetings for women during meal breaks.'

She faltered, afraid that he would dismiss this suggestion as trivial. But he was looking at her properly for once, giving her the full benefit of those dark, intense, potent eyes.

'There ought to be a female representative,' she went on. She had been rehearsing this little speech for days, waiting for an opportunity to deliver it. 'Not necessarily to do with the union. Just to speak on behalf of the women.'

'Are you volunteering?'

'Me?' She affected surprise. 'Oh, I wouldn't know what to do. That is . . . I'd need some advice first. Perhaps we can talk about it some time, when you're not so busy.'

Alain thought for a moment. Armelle's sudden decision to go skiing had left his week unexpectedly free.

'How about tomorrow night?'

Chantal made a show of consulting a mental diary, hiding her delight that her little strategy had worked. 'Tomorrow? Yes, I think I'm free.'

'Okay. Let's meet at the Grand Cygne at eight thirty. You're right, the women don't get much of a say.'

Pleased with herself, Chantal mounted her bicycle, making sure that she showed a great deal of thigh and stocking-top, and gave Alain a coyly explicit look. '*À demain*. And thank you again.'

Alain watched her ride away and smiled in sudden enlightenment. He must be getting old if he couldn't spot a girl giving him the come-on. A year ago he would have been several jumps ahead of her. There had been so many Chantals, before Armelle. But Armelle had made a eunuch of him as far as other women were concerned. Despite the convoluted fantasies she was so fond of, which always put her in the submissive, helpless role, she remained paradoxically the male partner, the one with the larger appetite, the greater stamina, the predilection towards violence. And he was carried along with it, reluctantly, willingly, bewitched.

He had forgotten what normal, thoughtless sex was like.

With Armelle there was always a twist to it. She liked to pretend that she was a little girl and that he was a paedophile, a fixation that had led her to shave off her pubic hair. She liked any variation on the rape theme, she loved to fight him off and be overpowered. But throughout it all, despite his superior size and strength she was always the dominant partner. She would praise his performance excessively, shower him with obscene compliments, and still make him feel he had failed.

Chantal was indistinguishable from scores of other pretty young girls. But the look she had given him had been unequivocal. She seemed cheerful, wholesome, unneurotic. It might be refreshing to do it in the ordinary way with an ordinary girl. It might just break the spell.

Cassie extended a big toe, curled it lovingly round the gold-plated dolphin, and ran in more hot water. Then she sank back luxuriously into the pink tub, fragrant with Odile Lemercier's bath oil. She still felt weak and giddy and ill, but it was bliss to feel weak and giddy and ill and clean.

'They'll never know,' Pilar had insisted. 'Make sure you leave very early or very late, so no one sees you. I'll call round at your place when I get back from Spain to collect the keys.'

Cassie had been too weak to resist. The nadir of her misery had occurred when she had passed out in the loathsome squatter and literally fallen into the hole; no amount of scrubbing her contaminated parts with a Dettol-soaked flannel could make her feel clean again. Pilar, who had called in on her way to the Gare d'Austerlitz, had found her in the throes of these makeshift ablutions and, on hearing of her mishap, had packed an overnight case and bundled her straight into a taxi. She had left Cassie contemplating the splendour of the Lemercier guest room, complete with spotless en suite bathroom gleaming with Italian tiles and polished marble. Just looking at it had made her feel better.

Cassie cast her eye around the bathroom. Ostentatious luxury had always offended her inbred social conscience, but there was something brazenly honest about decadence. The Blakeney policy of never buying anything new and being mean about the heating and deliberately neglecting both their listed houses had nothing to do with a shortage of money and everything to do with an excess of it. What was the point of being rich if you didn't enjoy it? And she *was* enjoying it, albeit illicitly, enjoying it a lot more than staying in yet another dingy hotel with Wilfred.

Wilfred. He would have got her telegram by now. With luck his wife would have opened it first. She imagined Wilfred talking his way out of it, striking a brilliant balance between contrition and reproach. After all, if a husband strayed, it was always the wife's fault. She should have felt guilty about Wilfred's faded, fortyish wife, should have had a conscience about hurting her, but like everyone else at home, Wilfred's wife seemed unreal. It was hard to believe she existed.

It wasn't so bad, being alone. It was better than sleeping with a man you didn't even like, let alone love, better than being tempted, inadmissibly, to have a child you couldn't possibly want. High as a kite on the pre-med, just before they had wheeled her off, she had had one fleeting vision of cuddly companionship, of warm, tactile togetherness . . .

Her reverie was rudely interrupted by the shrill, accusatory summons of the telephone. Startled, Cassie reached for her watch. One a.m. Why would anyone ring at this time of night? Momentarily convinced that the caller could see her and was phoning to ask what the hell she thought she was doing, she slid beneath the water, submerging everything except her head, and lay motionless till the ringing stopped. By then the water had cooled and, like the steam, the vapour of reckless well-being had condensed into chilly droplets of anxiety. Cassie dragged her waterlogged limbs out of the bath and sat giddily for a moment, hugging a pink towel, lacking the energy to dry herself. Her throat was dry, though, and her heart was racing, thumping away like a double bass, setting the rhythm for the rest of her body.

It was proof that she was getting better. For the last few days she hadn't taken any pills, too groggy and light-headed to feel the lack of them. There was nothing like food poisoning for taking your mind off your mind. Now, suddenly, her brain was back in business, screaming like a fractious infant, demanding the empty solace of its dummy.

The adjoining bedroom struck chill after the bathroom. Cassie pulled her nightdress over her head, shivering, and slid under the covers, fighting the familiar churning rot at the pit of her stomach, visualising her cool, calm, tranquillised self, trying to make it real. Except that it had never been real. She had spent the last three years of her life in a fog of false serenity, eschewing both pain and pleasure, punctuated by desperate, futile attempts to break out of her gilded cage.

'I'm addicted,' she had pleaded, more than once. But the doctors had dismissed this amateur diagnosis and advised her briskly to carry on taking the tablets. Her so-called withdrawal symptoms were nothing of the sort: they were simply a re-emergence of her original anxiety state. Which, if it was true, meant that she was getting worse, not better, that slowly and surely and invisibly she was going round the twist.

That horrible hissing, shuddering feeling was back. She felt like a pan of milk about to boil over. Trembling, she rummaged in her bag for her sleepers and routinely exceeded the stated dose. Another few hours of her life down the sluice, neatly aborted like that troublesome foetus, a loss disguised as freedom. She felt nauseous again, her empty stomach griping under the onslaught of its chemical snack, querulously demanding a soothing potion of hot, sweet tea. She dragged herself out of bed, still wobbly and uncoordinated, and padded downstairs to the kitchen in the dark, reluctant to illuminate the house at this late hour.

She got as far as the first landing before realising to her horror that she was not alone. The door of the master bedroom was open and a bouncing torchbeam was darting around inside like a giant illuminated moth. Burglars!

Cassie tried to move, but her legs seemed beyond the reach of her brain. She ought to run down into the hall, use the telephone, call the police . . . except that she herself was a trespasser. She would end up getting arrested and Pilar would get the sack.

Heart hammering, she turned and began creeping back up the stairs, with some vague notion of hiding under the bed, only to miss her footing in the dark and land in an undignified heap back where she had started, overturning a jardinière full

107

of potted ferns and letting out an involuntary squeal of shock.

It was a dream. It must be a dream. This wasn't happening . . .

'Are you all right?'

She scrambled to her feet, blinking into the blinding light of the torch.

'Please leave,' she demanded, trying to sound formidable. 'Please leave immediately before I call the police.' Another wave of dizziness robbed her of her balance and, fearing that she was about to faint, she sat down absurdly on the floor at the intruder's feet.

'Don't be afraid. I won't hurt you.' His voice was calm, reassuring, polite. 'Armelle told me no one would be here. I'm sorry if I scared you.' He extinguished his torch and switched on the landing light, revealing a smartly dressed figure in a dark suit and camel coat.

'Armelle?'

'She gave me her keys.' He held them up, as if to prove his good faith.

Cassie stared at him in horror, wishing belatedly that he *was* a burglar, that he was the intruder and not she.

'Forgive me for waking you up,' continued Viktor, trying not to stare. Her long blonde hair was in glorious disarray and her short nightdress exposed slim white legs which were splayed either side of her, knees tightly clenched, while she sat back dizzily, leaning on her hands. 'Clearly Armelle didn't realise that her parents had invited guests,' he resumed blandly, extending a hand to help her up. But she scrambled to her feet unaided, as if afraid to touch him. 'My apologies, mademoiselle.'

Cassie's brain struggled to break free of its bonds, unable to grasp the finer details, wanting only to protect Pilar.

'Please . . . please don't say anything to anyone. Armelle's parents don't know I'm here. Nobody knows I'm here.'

He looked puzzled, and then amused, and then suspicious.

'What are you then? A squatter?'

He seemed dauntingly stern and respectable standing there in his immaculate clothes. Cassie was horribly aware of her bare feet and grubby nightdress.

'I'm a friend of the maid's,' she gabbled, unable to dream up anything less damning than the truth. 'I've been ill, you see, and I don't have a bathroom where I live. She was trying to be kind, I don't want her to get into trouble.'

'I see.' His lips twitched. 'Well, I suggest we make a deal. I didn't see you, and you didn't see me. Agreed?'

'What?'

'If you'll just give me a moment, I'll put things to rights in there.'

He went back into the main bedroom, switching the light on and leaving the door open. Cassie stood watching him, more bewildered than ever. A carriage clock, a silver cigarette box, and various pieces of Odile's jewellery were neatly arranged inside an open attaché case. The stranger removed them with leather-gloved hands and put them carefully back where they belonged.

'No harm done,' said Viktor chattily, enjoying her confusion. How could anyone so prim be so provocative? His own horror at being discovered had been quickly supplanted by a mischievous desire to shock, to watch those huge grey eyes dilate in disbelief. 'Good job you came down before I left,' he added, shaking his head. 'Otherwise you might have got the blame.'

It was definitely a dream. Cassie leaned heavily on the door jamb, wishing for once that she could wake up.

'Forgive me,' he continued smoothly. 'You must be wondering what's going on. Yes, I am a burglar, but Armelle really did give me her keys. It's what you might call an inside job. So there's not much point in going to the police, now is there? It would just get us all into trouble. You, me, Armelle, and your friend the maid.'

'I don't believe you,' said Cassie, in a small, tight voice, taking one step backwards. 'You stole the keys from Armelle. You—'

'Armelle's in Chamonix, remember? With her father and Odile. And the maid is in Spain for the rest of the week. Do you believe me now?'

He carried on with what he was doing as he spoke, shutting drawers and cupboards, restoring the room to perfect order, looking up at her now and again, half expecting her to disappear, like a ghost. 'I'm very sorry if I gave you a fright. I did telephone first, but nobody answered.'

'Well, I couldn't have answered, could I? I told you, I shouldn't even be here.' The sentence came out all wrong, collapsing into a linguistic shambles.

'You're not French,' observed Viktor, much to Cassie's annoyance.

'I'm English,' she acknowledged sullenly.

'How do you do?' he said, in that language. 'I am very pleased to meet you.'

'I'm fine, and I understand French perfectly, thank you. And now will you please go?' She regretted the request as soon as she had uttered it. His departure wouldn't end the nightmare: quite the reverse. If anyone noticed him leaving, they might ring the police. In no time the house would be surrounded by armed gendarmes. She would be discovered and taken off for questioning. Armelle would deny all knowledge of this man, articles would be found to be missing, and she, Cassie, would be arrested and tried and convicted and deported in disgrace.

She ran upstairs and started flinging on clothes on top of her nightdress, stuffing her belongings back into her overnight bag in a clumsy frenzy of activity, like a motorised rag doll. She had meant to change the bed and leave the place tidy, but there was no time to waste. She would have to leave that to Pilar. She had to get out of here, and quickly, before it was too late.

'Where are you going?' demanded the burglar, accosting her in the hallway.

'Home,' said Cassie stiffly.

'Please don't leave on my account. I promise I won't come back, if that's what's worrying you. I'll leave the keys behind, if you like.'

'They're your responsibility, not mine. Excuse me.'

She swept past him, only to find that she couldn't bring herself to open the front door. The thought of stepping out into the dark was suddenly more terrifying than staying put.

'Then at least allow me to escort you,' he said. 'You can't possibly wander the streets on your own at this hour.'

'I'll get a taxi.'

'Assuming you can find one. After you.'

He held the door open for her, relocking it carefully with Armelle's keys, looking perfectly legitimate and unconcerned.

Then he did the same with the gate. Don't run, Cassie told herself, walking quickly away, you'll attract attention. If he was going to hurt you he'd have done it by now.

'I'll carry that for you,' he said, catching her up and taking her bag from her. 'I'm Viktor, by the way.' He offered her a hand.

'Cassie.' She returned his grip very briefly, as if fearing contamination.

'Cassée?' he echoed, mispronouncing it. 'What an unusual name.'

Cassée, past participle used as adjective, meaning broken, cracked, shattered, worn out ...

'So, what are you doing so far from home, Cassée?' His manner was urbane, avuncular, patronising. No one would have taken him for a criminal. What was Armelle playing at? Was it some kind of practical joke?

'Cassie,' she corrected him. 'I'm here for a year, teaching English in a lycée.'

'And are you enjoying it?'

'Not really.'

'What do you enjoy?'

'Nothing much.'

'What – nothing? Not food, wine, love, music?'

His voice seemed disembodied, as did hers; it was like listening in on a crossed line.

'Not food,' said Cassie, shuddering. 'I've been sick as a dog for five days.' Another wave of light-headedness made her stop and catch her breath. He put a hand under her elbow.

'Is it just that you're not well? Or is there something else?'

'Something else?' Momentarily, her mind went blank. She couldn't remember what she'd just said to him, or what he had said to her, couldn't be sure that she hadn't made some crass, self-revealing remark. But she was spared the need to reply by the appearance of a cab at the junction of the rue du Ranelagh and the Avenue Mozart. Viktor promptly flagged it down and got into it with her.

'You don't mind sharing a taxi, do you? They're so difficult to get at this time of night. Where do you live?'

Cornered, she mumbled her address and sat looking fixedly

out of the window to deter further conversation, fighting the giddy feeling of unreality and yet embracing it as well, in the vain hope that she was still cocooned in those vulgar satin sheets, inviolate and alone.

The taxi took off at what seemed like breakneck speed. Before long, Cassie had completely lost her bearings. She had no sense of direction at the best of times and invariably travelled by Métro. The streets looked alien, threatening, filling her with a sudden fear that she was being abducted. No, not fear. She felt oddly resigned to her fate and was almost disappointed when the cab drew up, rather sooner than she had expected, outside her block, bringing her abruptly back to earth.

'Will you be all right now?' queried Viktor. She nodded vaguely without replying and scrambled out of the cab, all arms and legs, without offering the customary valedictory handshake. If she hadn't been English she would have seemed rude. Viktor shouted *au revoir* after her but she didn't return it, disappearing into the tradesmen's entrance without a backward glance. He ordered the cab to take him on to his apartment, amused by the way things had turned out.

He had been in two minds about his visit *chez* Lemercier. In the end he had only gone to prove to himself that he had the nerve, knowing that safe-cracking was right out of his league but intending to help himself to any cash or valuables that happened to be lying about. He had proceeded very cautiously, telephoning the house first, and working by torchlight, heart in mouth. God, that girl had given him a shock . . .

Poor kid. She was like a frightened foal, angular and awkward, but graceful as well. And so thin! She was all wrists and ankles and cheekbones. It was the first time he could ever remember feeling curious about a woman. She was like a little unsolved mystery. Now he knew where she lived, it would be an easy matter to bump into her again.

She wasn't his type, of course. He liked coarse, cheerful, well-covered women for sex. This girl was too fragile, too ethereal, to think of in carnal terms. She was remote, untouchable, unhappy. She was irresistible.

112

FIVE

March 1968

Rob put down his sketch pad and stretched his arms towards the sky in a gesture of well-being. A fresh, clean wind fanned his face, and the Seine smelt of spring. The *bateaux-mouches* were filling up with tourists again, tourists he could afford to look down on now that he wasn't one of them. His permit was valid for a year and he was legally employed, not as a dishwasher or streetsweeper, as he had expected, but as a part-time lab assistant at the science faculty – a post fixed up for him by a left-wing lecturer sympathetic to the anti-war cause. The pay wasn't much, but it was just about enough to live on and left him plenty of free time to show his appreciation by 'joining in the struggle, here in Europe' as an honorary *apparatchik* for the National Vietnam Committee, distributing leaflets outside schools, factories, and faculty buildings, banner-waving at demos, and volunteering for anything that gave him an excuse to spend time with Armelle.

He was beginning to feel accepted now, even though his appearance marked him out as an oddity. Ironically, he would have fitted in better in his old persona. French radicals wore their hair short and dressed like bank clerks; nobody turned on. There were no Jerry Rubins or Abbie Hoffmans in Paris; if there had been, no one would have taken them seriously. Drugs were solemnly denounced as mind-clouding and strength-sapping, the palliatives of a diseased, effete society. Sex was a serious business, too. As Armelle had promised, he had met lots of girls. But politically active women, he had discovered, fell into two distinct categories: the good-looking ones, who were all attached – and the dogs. As for Armelle . . . Armelle was another story.

'It's so sordid, borrowing other people's beds or going to grotty hotels,' she had said. 'Privacy's so important, isn't it?'

Rob had got the message loud and clear. Alain's arrival was his cue to clear off and leave them to fornicate in peace; if he arrived home to signs of occupation, he would go out again and kill time till they had gone.

'What an innocent you are,' Viktor had said. 'Any fool could have told you what she wanted the room for. Why don't you kick her out? She hasn't paid you a sou for this month's rent – she's just using you.'

But she still looked at him in a way that made him hope. And at meetings, they were almost like a couple. Not wishing to associate herself with the 'spare' women, Armelle would make a point of sitting next to him, endorsing his suggestions and generally playing the supporting female role.

'It's so good to be friends with a man,' she would purr, tactfully warning him off. But it was better to be her friend than blow the whole thing by jumping on her. Twice, recently, Alain had stood her up; with any luck she'd soon be on the rebound.

In the meantime, he made love to her in her absence, made her sigh and whimper and cry out, felt her soft slipperiness surrounding him, swallowing him, filled her full of limitless energy, practised for the real thing. It was more satisfying than some soulless one-night stand with a pick-up; less risky than getting embroiled with another Ginny. Ginny had written to him twice, promising to wait for him, making him feel like a prize shit; he hadn't replied. His mother wrote every week – bright letters filled with trivia and underlaid with despair. The store was continuing to lose money as the new out-of-town shopping mall took more and more customers; they were looking for a buyer, but so far there had been no takers.

That, together with Mike's death, seemed to make their whole lives pointless. They had worked hard for twenty-five years, sunk most of their savings into helping their sons through college, and now they would end up living in a trailer park and doing any crummy job rather than go on welfare. They had never had any fun, and now they never would. They had hocked the best years of their lives to finance the future, and now they had lost the ticket. Well, that wouldn't happen to him. To hell with the future. All that mattered was the here and now.

It began to rain. The wind blew the fine spring drizzle into thin sheets, combing the surface of the river into ripples, propelling strolling couples towards shelter. Rob folded his sketch pad and turned his long stride homewards, watching the cobbles wink and gleam. Armelle had warned him that she was expecting Alain tonight, so he had arranged to go out drinking with Viktor, always an enjoyable prospect, even though they disagreed about practically everything – particularly Armelle. Rob couldn't understand why Viktor disliked her so much, unless it was because he had the hots for her. This suspicion had cost him several anxious moments, until Viktor had got stuck on this weird English girl. Weird because she had so far proved impervious to the practised Brožek charm. It had taken a great deal of rough wine to loosen Viktor's tongue on the subject, and even then he had told him next to nothing. When it came to things he cared about, Viktor was as tight as a clam. Which gave the impression he didn't care about anything, until you got to know him.

He exchanged the necessary pleasantries with Mme Bloc, whose *tricoteuse*-like demeanour gave him the creeps, and took the stairs two at a time. He could hear the piano hammering out 'All you need is love' in the style of the *Warsaw Concerto*. Viktor loved to take the piss out of the music he played, as if denying its power over him. He could make the most soulful melody sound pompous, or satirical or, occasionally, unbearably sad . . . when he thought no one was listening.

'You're early,' said Viktor, inhospitably.

'I was sketching down by Notre-Dame, but it started to rain. How was she today?'

'I didn't see her today.'

'Still playing hard to get, is she?'

'Pretending to.'

'And I thought I was the patient one.'

115

'I'm not patient.'

'Obsessed, then.'

'Look who's talking. The original lapdog.'

'You've got Armelle all wrong, you know.'

'I assure you I haven't. The boyfriend is giving her the runaround. She's on the lookout for a new victim.'

'You think I don't know that? Why do you think I've hung around her this long?'

'What makes you think you're her first choice of substitute player?'

'I'll take my chance on that.'

'You know how I could do us both a favour? By beating you to it.'

Rob grinned good-naturedly, determined to take this as a joke. 'You've got no chance. She thinks you're a Fascist. At first she respected you for striking a blow against ownership. But now she's disillusioned.'

'Just because I refused to help her spite Papa? Or because I know a little whore when I see one?'

'Take that back.'

'I don't want to see you get hurt,' snapped Viktor. 'God, you're so naïve sometimes. What do I have to do to convince you?'

'I'm warning you, Viktor. If you try anything on with Armelle . . .'

'Take my advice. Find yourself another room and get her out of your life.'

'Mind your own fucking business. Just because you won't admit that you want her too.'

Viktor opened his mouth to say something, and then appeared to think better of it.

'I happen to care about her,' continued Rob, menacingly. 'And if I catch you laying a finger on her I'll kill you.'

Viktor raised an eloquent eyebrow, as if to say, What about anti-violence? What about peace and love? Already those Californian concepts seemed six thousand miles out of place. Besides, they needed grass, and plenty of it, to sound convincing.

'I don't feel like going out tonight,' said Viktor, abruptly

116

changing tack. 'There's an ice-hockey game on the box. Let's get in a few bottles.' It was meant as an apology.

'Only if you let me pay this time. I've had enough of your big Robin Hood act.'

'All right. Make it Scotch, then. Johnnie Walker Black Label.'

Rob shrugged off this latest bout of ill humour; the exchange of insults had become a ritual. But he meant it about warning Viktor off Armelle. Alain had never struck him as a serious rival: their brief meetings had reinforced his impression of a very ordinary, rather greasy-looking guy who couldn't believe his luck. Viktor was another matter altogether. Viktor was charming, confident and ruthless. Worse, Viktor was his *friend*.

He delved in his pockets for some money and made for the nearest *alimentation*, intending to pick up a couple of litres of cheap wine. He had five francs on him, which was more than enough, but it seemed like a good excuse to go back to the apartment to fetch some more. There was always the chance that Alain had let her down again, and the thought of her languishing up there, chewing her non-existent nails, was tantalising. Last time he hadn't known about it till next day, and then only on account of her red-rimmed eyes. 'Don't tell anyone,' she had pleaded. 'I feel such a fool.' And he hadn't told anyone. So how did Viktor know?

The question was headed off by the sudden appearance of his rival, heading towards him and away from the apartment, and clearly in a hurry. Too much of a hurry to give the usual cursory greeting, racing past him without a second glance, apparently unaware that his face was bleeding. Red blobs stood out like bright beads along the line of a deep scratch from the corner of his eye to his chin.

Rob ran the rest of the way, took the stairs three at a time and let himself in, stepping over the pile of broken plates which had evidently been hurled against the door, and entering the main room to find chairs and table overturned.

'Armelle?' He tapped on the door of her room. The response was a growling, squeaking noise somewhere between anger and anguish. 'Are you all right?'

There was a scratching sound, like an animal in a burrow. 'Come in,' she mewed.

She was face down on the mattress on the floor, both arms stretched out above her head, bitten-down nails dragging at the floorboards. She lifted a hand in blind salutation. Rob knelt down beside her.

'What happened?' He put a comforting arm around her shoulders. 'Was there a fight?'

She twisted her head towards him, her face streaked with mascara. 'I'd like to kill him,' she hissed, sitting up abruptly and winding her arms around herself. Rob felt a surge of primitive triumph.

'Want to talk about it?' he said. 'Come next door, it's more comfortable.'

She sniffed assent, and rose to her feet slowly, as if in pain.

'Did he hit you?'

'I hit him first.'

'Where did he hit you?'

'He slapped me across the face. He said I was hysterical. Whenever a woman gets angry, she's hysterical.'

'Are you hurt?'

She indicated her shoulder. 'I wrenched it a bit. If I'd had a knife on me he'd be dead. If I were a man, he'd be dead. If only I was big and strong, like you!'

It was like an invitation. It was as if she'd said, 'Kill Claudio!'

'Do you want me to do anything?'

'No need. He's gone. He's gone for good.'

She followed him limply into his room. Rob righted the chairs but she had already flopped down on his bed.

'So what happened?'

She shrugged, her mouth still working in distress. 'You can see for yourself. Sorry about the plates, I'll buy some more. I knew it would happen, sooner or later. He's afraid of me. Men always end up afraid of me. Tell me, what is it about me that's so frightening?'

Rob thought for a moment, choosing his words carefully. 'Well . . . you're beautiful. That can make a man feel insecure. And intelligent. That makes him even more insecure.'

She shook her head. 'No, it's more than that. He said I asked too much of him. That's a joke. I never asked anything of him. All I ever did was give, give, give. We only met when it was convenient for him, I missed meetings and cut lectures, I found places for us to make love. But he wouldn't do anything for me. He never let me meet his family, he didn't want to know any of my friends, or introduce me to any of his. And I went along with all that. I let him have his own way in everything!'

'Then he didn't deserve you. You're better off without him.'

'What does it take to satisfy a man? You do everything he could possibly want of you – *everything* – and it's never, ever enough. It was the same with Étienne. And Marcel, the bastard. I'm not promiscuous, you know. There have only been four men in my life, just four, and every single one of them has betrayed me. Do I look like the sort of girl who gets dumped? Why does it keep happening to me? You're a man, you tell me!'

'Because you were too good for them. Because you made them feel inadequate.'

It seemed, momentarily, to be the right answer, but after holding his gaze intently for a moment, she shook her head. 'No,' she said. 'Not in Alain's case. I was so careful not to damage his precious ego. I played the idiot female to the hilt. It's just that men are greedy, that's all. I bet he's found himself some little tart of his own class, someone *genuinely* stupid enough to make him feel superior. My father was unfaithful to my mother all their married life, with ugly bitches like Odile. And my mother's really beautiful. Look.'

She opened the locket around her neck and displayed two photographs: one of an older version of herself, the other of an unsmiling, coarse-looking man with the squashed, belligerent features of a boxer.

'Yes,' agreed Rob. 'Yes, she looks just like you.'

'My father's not at all handsome, is he? But women find him attractive. Because he treats them like dirt, I suppose. We're supposed to love that, aren't we? Well, my mother didn't. She got her own back. That's all you can do, in the end. Get your own back.'

'Forget this guy,' said Rob, sitting on the bed beside her. 'He isn't worth it.' He took her hand, reminding himself that it was too soon to take advantage of the situation. He felt guilty, seeing the pain in her eyes, at his ill-concealed delight. This was too good to be true ...

119

'I know what you're thinking,' she said, jolting him out of his complacency. 'That this is your big chance. You want me, don't you? I've known that right from the start. Well? Do you deny it?'

Her voice was still full of venom. Right now, he was just another man, one of the enemy.

'Of course I don't deny it. I never tried to hide it. I won't pretend I'm sorry to see the back of Alain. But that doesn't mean I'm glad to see you miserable.'

She turned away from him. 'I bet you'd treat me well,' she said in a tight, twisted voice. 'I bet you'd be kind and gentle and loyal. I like you, you know. I've always *liked* you.' She made it sound like a problem, and perhaps it was. 'I never liked Alain,' she added. 'And now I hate him. God, how I hate him.'

She put her arms around his neck and began weeping piteously. Rob held her close, rocking her to and fro till the tears subsided, wishing that she liked him less, envying Alain the passion of her hatred. He would have given anything to make her cry like that.

Eva was so engrossed in her newspaper she nearly missed her tram stop. These days she read it from cover to cover, not just to keep her end up with Jan and his clever-clever friends – although that was how it had started – but because, for the first time, it was actually full of news. A year ago, when she had started work, it had been just another organ of Party propaganda, stiff with predictable dogma. But in the last month long-frustrated journalists had found themselves suddenly free to investigate and report the truth, while the censors, now unofficially redundant, filled their time with card games and crossword puzzles.

Every day, it seemed, brought news of some new scandal. There were sensational tales of corruption in high places, involving blackmail, sexual orgies, embezzlement of public funds and theft of government property. Novotny's own son was implicated in the unfolding drama of the *dolce vita* excesses of the old regime. Plans for a military coup to unseat Dubček were exposed and universally censured. The Novotnyite faction of anti-reformers was in disarray. At long last the new administration had shown its teeth: dismissals and resignations were now a daily occurrence as those who had risen under Novotny fell like ninepins. The old man still clung to the office of president, but already there had been mass demonstrations demanding that he stand down. Every morning Eva woke up thinking, What will happen today? And other people must have felt the same, because every newspaper in Prague was sold out by six a.m.

She arrived home to find Karel already tuned in to the radio for the seven o'clock news. No longer a party political broadcast, it now carried its audience from one cliffhanger to the next.

'You're late again,' he said.

'I know. There's so much extra work at the moment. I couldn't leave till I'd finished.'

'Still bored, are you?'

Eva punched him playfully. 'There's a rally in Old Town Square tonight. Why don't you come with us?' She put her hands on his shoulders. 'Repeat after me: Novotny out! Novotny out!'

'There's no need for all that. He's finished and he knows it.'

Eva lit the gas under a pan of potatoes and began chopping cabbage. 'We've got to keep the pressure up. Besides . . . it's fun. I typed a draft survey this morning for the senior editors. We're sending it out to forty thousand people. You wouldn't believe some of the questions! Let's try some of them on you. Do you support the establishment of free opposition parties?'

Karel grunted.

'Go on,' pressed Eva, tipping the cabbage into hot fat. 'You might even be one of the people we canvass. We want a cross-section, including ordinary, unimportant people like you.'

'Free opposition parties? Well . . . in principle, yes. Because the Communist Party ought to be strong enough to withstand dissent. But I'd be dead against any return to capitalism. What do you think?'

Eva burst out laughing. 'What do *I* think? What's got into you?'

Karel had the grace to look sheepish. 'If my opinion matters suddenly, then so does yours, presumably.'

'I think . . . that everybody should have a say in what

121

happens. That's what socialism means, isn't it? Everyone being equally important. Everyone working together. You wouldn't believe the atmosphere at work. People giving up their lunch-breaks, getting in early, staying late, because they want to!'

'Try spending a day making cardboard boxes. You wouldn't feel like staying late then.'

'I might if I had a say in how the factory was run. I might if there was some point, some pride in doing a good job.'

'What it is to be young and naïve.'

'You were young once. And a lot more naïve than me. How could intelligent people be so . . . so brainwashed?'

'We had faith,' Karel corrected her crossly. 'We had to have faith in something, after the war. We wanted to rebuild a new, strong society . . .'

'Well? Now's your chance!'

'You think I don't know that? But we have to move forward by degrees, slowly, with moderation. We're going too far, too fast.'

Eva shook her head and smiled her 'poor old man' smile. The speed was part of the fun. It was as if a whole nation of cripples were taking up their beds and running, too impatient to walk. There was a new spring in her step, a new quickness and dexterity about her movements, as if she were in a hurry. You couldn't blame the young for being impatient. He had been impatient himself, once, before the baggage of the past had slowed him down. But, as Miloš kept reminding him, plenty of people had suffered even more than he had.

'There's a big inaugural meeting of this new club at the end of the month,' he informed Eva gruffly, not looking at her. 'Anyone imprisoned under the old Law 231 is eligible to join. We've got some very good speakers lined up. We're hoping for a big crowd.'

'We?'

Karel shrugged. 'Well, I might as well be involved as not. Can't leave these things to old fools like Miloš. I think some-thing happened to his brain in gaol.'

Eva hugged him delightedly. 'You old hypocrite. All those evenings playing chess. I knew you were up to something.'

'Don't ask me too much about it. If things go wrong . . .'

'There you go again. Eat your supper.' She sat down and joined him, with one eye on her watch, while they listened intently to the news. Only when she had cleared the table, put on her coat, and was halfway out of the door, did she turn round and say casually, as if it were a matter of no importance, 'I almost forgot to tell you. My visa came through today.' And then, more urgently, 'Are you sure you won't come to this rally?'

'Have you been waiting long?' asked Viktor, just to annoy her. There was never any prior arrangement to meet.

Cassie had been sitting in her local café since lunchtime, killing time till her four o'clock lesson with Odile. She was always half expecting him, but never sure when and where he would turn up. He would neglect her for days at a time, and then tail her for a whole afternoon like some seedy private detective. Either way, he had a knack of materialising suddenly, out of nowhere, like a will-o'-the-wisp.

She looked up from her book and feigned her usual surprise and indifference. She felt unnaturally wide awake today, despite two consecutive nights without a wink of sleep. The sun had seemed so bright that she had had to put on sunglasses; the noise of the waiter rinsing glasses behind the bar sounded like a bath running with both taps full on. Viktor ordered her another *express*, and a *demi* for himself.

'Why are you wearing shades? To escape your fans?' He reached across the table and took them off her face. Cassie snatched them back.

'My eyes are sore.'

'You don't look well.'

'I'm fine.'

'For a skeleton. How about a slap-up dinner at Maxim's tonight? That'll put some meat on your bones.' He delved in his pockets and produced two bulging wallets which he tossed on to the table. 'Both Germans, I'm glad to say. Not bad for a morning's work.'

Cassie caught the waiter looking at them. 'For God's sake, Viktor. Put them away.'

'Nag, nag, nag. If you disapprove of me so much, why don't

123

you get up and walk out? Or would you like me to leave? I'll leave if you ask me nicely.'

'I don't disapprove of you. What you do is none of my business. Stop trying to shock me.'

'You enjoy being shocked. It turns you on. Or it would do, if you let it.'

He reached for her handbag, put the swag inside it, fished out her pills and held them up to the light.

'A brand new bottle,' he observed.

'I found a very nice doctor in the rue du Bac. He gave me another prescription. So what?'

'Did you tell him how many you take?'

'Do you tell someone you're about to pick their pocket? Leave me alone.'

'Did you like the flowers I sent you yesterday?'

'You mean the wreath? I thought it was in very poor taste.'

'So is ending up splat in the middle of the road. Don't you ever look where you're going? I saw you come out of the school the other day and walk straight in front of a bus. It missed you by this much.' He held up his finger and thumb.

'I wish you'd stop spying on me.'

'Sorry I didn't come yesterday, by the way. I thought I would play it cool for a change. Pathetic, really. Well, you should know. Poor Cassie. Did you miss me?'

'*Fous-moi la paix,*' snapped Cassie. She would never have dreamt of telling someone to fuck off in English, though perhaps she would if the someone had been Viktor. She was always rude to him, but for once it wasn't just for show. Today she was in an untypically filthy temper.

She resumed ferocious interest in her book. The minute French print was even harder to read than usual, but then everything was slightly blurred today and no amount of blinking would clear her vision. It had been forty-eight excruciating hours since she had last popped a pill, since she had last seen Viktor. It was like seeing him for the first time against a dazzling light. He looked evil, threatening, ruthless, dangerous . . .

'I don't know why I waste my time on you,' he sighed. 'It must be the attraction of opposites I suppose. Me so polite and well bred. You with your uncouth ways and bad language.' He leaned across the table, looked this way and that, and hissed out of the corner of his mouth, 'Come off it, Cassie. I know you're crazy about me. Why don't we go back to my place?'

As always, he made it sound like a joke, knowing she would reject him.

'No thanks,' said Cassie, attempting to hide her face in a minuscule coffee cup.

'What exactly are you afraid of?'

'I'm not afraid.'

'I could understand if you were a virgin. But a woman of the world like you . . . ' He clucked disapprovingly.

Cassie scowled. She had only mentioned Wilfred to shut him up, to make herself seem normal. But being unused to talking about herself, she had found it difficult to control the flow of words. He had made her talk and talk and tell and tell. Afterwards she had had that familiar, unnerving feeling of not being able to remember exactly what she had said.

'I may be a thief, but at least I'm honest,' he had said, paradoxically. But honesty had nothing to do with it. He had been testing her, that was all. 'If what I do bothers you, just tell me to get lost. I'll understand.' It had been like a dare, a threat, an insult. And his so-called honesty had another purpose too – it had provoked the competitive need to make some equally startling revelation, fostered the kind of reckless intimacy that can only exist between strangers.

It was all foreplay, of course. He had obviously marked her out as an easy lay. English girls had that reputation, thanks to popular notions of *le swinging London*, resulting in the Anglophobic nickname *poubelles*, literally translated as dustbins. Cassie had expected him to lose interest rapidly once he realised there was nothing doing, but he seemed to take a perverse pleasure in being given the brush-off, or rather inviting it. It was all part of the game . . .

In a moment, he would get up and go, with his usual curt goodbye, leaving her compromised by the stolen property in her handbag. She would wrap the wallets in a stout manila envelope and post them to the police. Twice he had offloaded items of jewellery – a string of pearls and a solid-gold bracelet – which she had similarly dispatched, but not before she had tried them on in front of a mirror, cherishing them briefly, like love tokens.

Viktor sat drinking his beer, watching her, still trying to work out what it was about her that made him want to be kind to her, cruel to her; what it was that made him care. He liked robust, earthy, uncomplicated women. But this one was like a wraith: formless, elusive, inaccessible, full of buried glitter and hidden pain. Her hold on life seemed tenuous; she had the air of someone who was doomed to waste her life, or die young. But today she seemed twitchy, restless, almost reachable.

'Are you absolutely sure you don't want to come back to my place?' he repeated, keeping his voice dead-pan. 'This could be your last chance.'

She shook her head, her attention still riveted on her book. Her habitual fascination with her book would have annoyed him rather a lot if he had thought for one minute that she was reading it.

'What a lot she carries around with her,' he muttered, as if to himself, inspecting the contents of her handbag. 'Passport, *carte de séjour, permis de travail,* money, cheque book, Métro tickets . . . and her pills, of course. What a panic she'd get into if somebody pinched her bag. And how convenient she doesn't know where I live.'

In the split second it took for the penny to drop, he had gone, taking her handbag with him.

'Viktor!' Cassie sprang to her feet and ran after him. 'You swine! Give it back! I'm late for a lesson with Madame! Give it back!'

He stopped, turned round, danced on the spot, clapped a hand to his mouth in mock terror, and hid the bag behind his back. Cassie made a lunge for it but he sidestepped her neatly, forcing her to run circles round him like a dog chasing its tail.

'Careful of the traffic,' he chided, seizing her hand and dragging her across the road, nimbly dodging her continued attempts to snatch back her property. He let go of her in front of the entrance to the Métro and leapt several feet backwards in one balletic bound.

'*Au voleur!*' he yelled, holding the bag high above his head.

126

'Catch me if you can!' He tossed her carnet of tickets at her and disappeared down the stairs.

Cassie scrabbled to pick it up and ran after him, wrenching her sunglasses off in the gloom and jostling her way on to the platform just before the automatic gates shut, in time to see Viktor waving smugly from the doorway of a first-class compartment. Flushed and fuming, she leapt aboard the nearest carriage and jumped off and on again at every station until she saw him alight at Cardinal Lemoine, where she gave chase again, fighting through a crush of bodies, losing sight of him until she reached street level, only to hear a loud whistle summoning her in the right direction.

They seemed to run for miles. He kept turning round, waving her handbag aloft, and urging her on like an athletics coach. 'Come on, Cassie! You can do it! Faster now!' And then he would duck into a side road, leading her she knew not where, round and round, back and forth, until she collided breathlessly with a barrowload of oranges and fell over in an exhausted heap.

The brightly coloured globes rolled all around her like waxen effigies of sunshine, glowing on the grey, gritty pavement, smiling inanely at her. Cassie reached out for a squashed fruit and inhaled its scent, succumbing to a delicious wave of euphoria, indifferent to the stallholder's angry abuse. She was barely aware of Viktor shoving some money at him. She had lost interest in retrieving her handbag, she would have been happy to sit among the oranges all day . . .

'Cassie?'

She looked up to see two narrow green eyes staring down at her.

'Hello, Armelle,' she said, too dazed to register any surprise. 'What are you doing here?'

'My room is just round the corner. The place I told you about, remember? Are you all right?'

'Of course she's all right,' said Viktor, approaching and hauling her to her feet.

'I didn't know you two had met,' said Armelle.

Cassie blushed scarlet. She had never mentioned that awful night, not so much to protect Pilar as to protect herself from ridicule. Viktor had been similarly discreet, unwilling to admit to the first failure of his professional life. He had returned Armelle's keys – which was more than Armelle had done with Cassie's – on the grounds that if she wanted ten thousand francs she would have to steal them for herself.

'I'm late,' muttered Cassie, stupidly, looking at her watch. 'What for?'

'A lesson with Odile.'

'Let the evil bitch rot for once,' said Armelle. 'Come and have a drink. You look as if you could do with one.'

'You dropped this,' said Viktor, handing her bag, looking at the two spots of colour on her cheeks and the sheen of sweat gluing her eye-length fringe to her forehead. It had been wonderful watching her run, seeing those long white legs of hers flex and stretch. It had been like Coppelia coming to life.

Bad luck they had to bump into Armelle. They had been within a stone's throw of his apartment, and that wasn't the kind of stunt you could pull off twice. He wondered if the chase across Paris had had the same effect on her as it had on him. But if so, she gave no sign of it. Armelle had a sisterly arm around her now, whispering in her ear.

'I'm with Rob now,' murmured Armelle, indicating a tall, red-headed man talking to Viktor. 'So whatever you do, don't mention Alain. It all turned to shit. But I haven't finished with that bastard yet, believe me. Rob,' she said, raising her voice, 'let me introduce you to my friend Cassie, from London. Rob's from California. He's resisting the draft.'

'Pleased to meet you, Cassie,' he said, in English, looking at her curiously. 'Viktor's told me a lot about you.'

'You never told me Cassie knew Viktor,' challenged Armelle. 'I didn't know you knew Cassie,' shrugged Rob.

'So how did you two meet?' repeated Armelle. Cassie exchanged looks with Viktor, who gave her no help at all. She felt as if she had been dragged on stage in the middle of a play without knowing any lines.

'Through a mutual friend,' she said, almost truthfully.

'Nice friends you keep,' said Armelle, relinquishing Cassie's arm in favour of Viktor's. 'Does this poor girl know all about you?' she whispered maliciously in his ear.

'Of course. Ask her yourself.'

But Cassie and Rob had fallen behind, talking together in their own language.

'What on earth does she see in you?' continued Armelle archly. 'Does she like a bit of rough?'

'Don't judge others by yourself.'

'You're too late,' she hissed, vindictively. 'I'm with Rob now.'

Viktor stared at her with unconcealed dislike. He found her eternal flirting tiresome. As for her visit to his apartment last week – if it hadn't been for Cassie he would have happily screwed the shit out of the sex-mad little bitch, just to keep her away from Rob, even if it meant losing his friendship for good.

'*You're* too late,' he said coldly. 'Don't look to me to help you hurt him.' He withdrew his arm.

'. . . I've got a job in a lab,' Rob was saying. 'The pay's not much, though. These private lessons sound like a good racket. Do you suppose anyone wants to learn American?'

'Madame Lemercier does. I've been doing my best. She can say "I 'ave to take a leak," and "Sank you for a god-awful meal."'

There was a splutter of mutual mirth. Viktor looked round, wondering what Rob had said to amuse her, irritated that he had managed to make her laugh after less than two minutes' acquaintance.

'Stop speaking English, you two,' commanded Armelle, leading the way into the café. 'Mine is nearly as bad as Odile's.'

Cassie sat down between Rob and Armelle, facing Viktor, and asked for a *citron pressé*. Armelle had her usual *diabolo menthe* while the men drank beer.

'How are things at Alphonse Cluny?' asked Armelle, passing round Gitanes.

'Same as usual.'

'That has to be the most reactionary dump in Paris. Still going to the *Comité d'Action* meetings?'

Armelle's attempts to radicalise Cassie had mercifully been limited to brief harangues in the Lemercier kitchen, where Pilar served the movement by doing all Armelle's washing and ironing, feeding her, and filling her in on the latest matrimonial squabbles.

'Now and then,' lied Cassie. 'But they're usually after lunch, and I only teach in the mornings.'

'No excuse. Rob, have you got one of those leaflets on you? There's a big anti-war demo tomorrow. Why don't you join us?'

Rob fished around in his pockets and unfolded a dog-eared sheet of paper.

'It should be good for a few laughs,' he said. 'Specially if the Maoists show up. They're into heavy stuff, like Molotov cocktails.'

Armelle shook her head in exasperation. 'Rob is incapable of taking anything seriously.'

'Come off it, Armelle,' said Rob, ruffling her hair. She arched her neck, like an angry cat. 'It's always the same old clique that turns up.'

'Say you'll come,' went on Armelle. 'We need some new blood.'

'Specially if you're willing to spill some,' put in Viktor.

'All right,' said Cassie, just to needle him. 'Why not?'

'Great! Meet us here and we'll take you with us. Can you get here by two?'

'I suppose so. I finish school at twelve on Saturdays.'

'Try to bring some of your pupils with you. We're hoping for a big crowd.'

Soon Armelle was spurring her hobby-horse to a gallop. Her voice sounded loud but unintelligible, like a radio blaring in another room. Cassie didn't look at Viktor, but she could feel him looking at her. It made her feel hot and breathless and damp again, as if she were still running. She fought to concentrate, to ignore the swelling tide of panic, the multiplicity of aches and pains all over her body, the fluttering feeling in her chest, the tranquillisers in her bag, and Viktor.

'Are you okay?' he said, reaching for her hand across the table.

'What's the matter?' asked Armelle, who had not noticed anything wrong.

'I'm all right,' said Cassie, standing up. 'I must just . . . go to the loo.'

She ran downstairs into the basement, desperate to evade

their collective scrutiny, and locked herself in a cubicle, trying to gather her wits. There was a tight band of pain around her eyes and both her feet had gone to sleep, they felt soft and spiky, like pincushions. It was much worse than yesterday. Yesterday she had felt so bad that she had actually telephoned home, on impulse, succumbing to a childlike need for comfort, teetering on the edge of tears. But by the time she had waited her turn in the post office and been summoned to a booth she couldn't think of anything to say.

As usual, her mother had filled the breach by putting words into her mouth. How romantic to be living in a garret, what fun to be studying at the Sorbonne, and if Cassie wanted to spend the Easter holidays with her chums in Paris, she and Daddy would quite understand. There had followed a glowing account of how both Cassie's elder brothers had been to the anti-war demonstration in Grosvenor Square. They had duly sat down, got themselves carted off to the police station, met some terribly interesting people in the cells, and been fined £3 each next morning . . . Follow that one, thought Cassie despondently. It had almost been a relief when the pips had gone and cut the conversation short.

Everyone else managed to rebel. The sudden warm breeze of comradeship from Armelle had been sensual, seductive; she had the come-into-my-parlour charm of a moral carnivore. It was always tempting to join a club, to suspend one's critical faculties as the price of acceptance. But if she did, it would be very much like going to bed with Wilfred. In politics, as in sex, she would have to fake orgasm.

No, there was only one way to hit back at the system, to reject apathy, compromise and oppression, to spit in the face of authority. And this time she would see it through to the end. She would do it. She would prove them all wrong. *She would stop taking the pills . . .*

She emerged from her hiding place, splashed cold water on her cheeks and dried them with her handkerchief. Then she mounted the stairs very slowly, one numb, prickly step at a time, and rejoined the others.

'I'm taking Cassie home,' said Viktor, standing up. 'She's not well.'

'It's just a migraine, that's all,' said Cassie.

'Why don't you come back to our place and lie down for a bit?' said Armelle, concerned.

'No. Thanks anyway. I'd better go.'

'Don't forget about tomorrow, will you.'

'Tomorrow?'

'The demo.'

Her mind had gone a complete blank, but she nodded anyway. Viktor took her arm, and led her out into the street like a blind person.

'I'm sorry I made you run,' he said. 'Are you ill?'

'It wasn't the running.' The running had made her feel better, if only briefly. 'It was afterwards.'

'Well, listening to that silly bitch rant on about the revolution is enough to make anyone sick. My place is just across the road. I swear to God I won't touch you. Come on.'

She followed him into a dark courtyard which gave access to an unprepossessing four-storey apartment block.

'Can you manage two flights of stairs? There's no lift. Perhaps I should have got Rob to carry you. He's much stronger than me.'

'I told you, I'm all right,' growled Cassie. 'Stop fussing.'

She had expected his place to be vulgar, a bit like him. Viktor's line in sharp suits verged on the spivvy, as did his appalling taste in jewelled cufflinks, loud ties, and overpowering male cologne. Even when he was in civvies – cords and a black leather jacket – he did cringe-making things like paying for two coffees with a hundred-franc note and leaving exorbitant tips. But the room he showed her into was tidy and understated, with white walls, polished floorboards, and very little furniture, apart from a settee, a Bang and Olufsen hi-fi, a small television, and a large piano. She hadn't been expecting a piano. There was a built-in shelf unit covering an entire wall, housing rows of long-playing records and stacks of sheet music, but not a single book.

'Would you like a drink? There's only Cognac. I never thought you'd come, you see.'

'Neither did I.' She sat down dizzily.

'Hadn't you better have one of your thingumajigs? I'm sorry

I teased you about them. I suppose the bloody doctors must know what the hell they're doing.' He went into the kitchen and returned with a glass of water.

Cassie shook her head. 'No. I don't want one. I've stopped taking them. I haven't taken any for two days.'

He sat down beside her. 'What exactly happens when you don't take them?'

'In practice? Or in theory? In theory, I go back to the way I was before. I can't remember that far back. But before I was in control. Putting it on, more or less. To get attention, I suppose. Sometimes I think all I wanted was for my parents to stop being patient and sympathetic and tell me to stop being such a bloody pain in the neck.'

'Stop being such a bloody pain in the neck,' said Viktor. 'You've been driving me crazy, do you know that? I'd just about given up on you. I wanted to put a bomb under you, to shake you till your teeth rattled, to scare you half to death. Anything to wake you up. But I was scared of making you cry.'

'I never cry.' Cassie got her pills out of her bag and handed them to him. 'I've got loads more at home. Plus the sleepers. They're the same stuff, more or less, only stronger. If I give you the lot, will you keep them for me?'

'Why don't you just throw them away?'

'Because I'll end up asking that nice doctor in the rue du Bac for more. And he'll give them to me. This way, I can ask you instead. And you can say no.'

'Cassie—'

'I've tried before, you know. I hate feeling like a bloody zombie. But I couldn't stick it, it was awful. It *is* awful. It's like going mad. And everything hurts. My hands, my feet, my eyes . . . my skin feels as if there are things crawling over it. And my hands shake.' She held them out and watched them in disgust.

Viktor felt a thrill of triumphant fear. This way, he would have a hold over her. And he wanted that power, of course he did, but not the responsibility that went with it. 'I'm not happy about this. You should be talking to a doctor.'

'Haven't you been listening? The doctors keep telling me the pills can't hurt me. They say it must be *me*.'

133

'Don't start crying on me. I'm warning you. Don't cry.'

She didn't cry. She stared at him through her fringe, grey eyes glistening with unshed tears. He wanted to put his arms around her and say, 'Don't worry. I'm here. I'll look after you. It'll be all right.' But he knew that wasn't what she needed. And in any case, looking after someone didn't make them strong. Quite the reverse. He had learned that at an early age. Worse, looking after someone left you vulnerable to resentment, failure, and above all, guilt.

'Okay. But one condition. If you ask me for them, I'm going to say yes, not no.'

'Then I won't ask for them.'

'Yes you will.'

'No I won't, damn you!'

'Look at my hands,' he said. He held them out, rock steady, and grasped hers, as if linking a fragile shrub to a wooden stake. 'That's what it feels like when you don't care. And not caring is how you survive.'

Her hands were very cold. She twisted her fingers through his as if testing their strength. 'You do care,' she said. 'Just a little bit. I can feel it.'

'Just a little bit's okay. As long as it doesn't show.'

He wanted to keep her here and watch over her, protect her, use her fear and need to enslave her, and perhaps himself as well. Instead he said, 'I'm going to take you home now. If you want to give me the rest of those pills, it's up to you. I'll see you sometime tomorrow, or the next day, I'm not sure when. I expect you'll be climbing the walls by then. Come on.'

Cassie gritted her teeth and followed him out, perplexed that he had not pressed her to stay. He didn't want to be involved, not really. She had embarrassed both herself and him. It was the first risk she had taken in years . . .

Sooner or later they would put the stuff in the water supply, inoculate everyone against protest. Would Armelle's revolution come in time? It was a relief, at last, to share in the struggle, to cast off real shackles, to confront the endless terror of the rest of her life. But all that was secondary, nebulous, abstract. Viktor thought she couldn't do it. And she would prove him wrong.

* * *

'What's the matter with you, Alain?' demanded Mme Moreau, clearing away his untouched plate. The question had become routine, expecting the answer 'nothing'. Alain had been pre-occupied for weeks now, but there was no hope of any explanation, not that one was needed. That student girl had obviously broken the poor boy's heart; his mother's sympathy was tinged with relief. Young Chantal Durand seemed a nice lass; it must have been difficult for her to share him with another woman. But she had put up with it meekly, cleverly, and now her patience was beginning to pay off.

'Washing up, you two,' she said, dispatching her daughters into the kitchen. Albert got up and fetched his pipe. Jeanne began folding the tablecloth.

'Wait a moment,' said Alain quietly. 'I've got something to tell you.' Albert exchanged glances with his wife, sharing a simultaneous split second of premonition. 'I'm getting married.'

His mother's face broke into an uncertain smile. 'Married? To ... to ...'

'Chantal,' said Alain woodenly. Albert sighed noisily and returned his attention to his pipe. 'She's pregnant,' he added superfluously.

'Well ... you could have done a lot worse,' said Mme Moreau stolidly, taking the news in her stride. It was too commonplace a situation to rate as a drama.

'Yes. So, now you know.'

'After all I said to you ... ' muttered Albert.

'Albert! The boy has to get married sometime. Do her parents know?'

'She's telling them tonight. They won't be surprised. It runs in her family. The same thing happened to her sister.'

Albert got to his feet and poured a hefty slug of *marc* into Alain's empty wine glass. 'Women are all the same,' he grunted. 'They'll do anything to trap themselves a husband.'

'Albert!'

'It was my fault,' said Alain. 'I was careless.'

'It's for the best,' soothed his mother. 'Chantal's a nice, sensible girl. I'm sure she'll make you a good wife. We must go and see her parents, Albert. Discuss the guests and so on. There won't be much time to arrange everything, in the circumstances.'

'There's nothing to arrange,' put in Alain sharply. 'Just the civil ceremony. I'm not going through any religious rigmarole afterwards.'

'Alain, please. Your sisters will want to be bridesmaids. They'll have to give up their room for you, remember. There won't be any space for you with her family.'

'No. As good Catholics they have bred like rabbits. One good reason not to carry on the tradition. I'm not having any child of mine brought up to believe all that claptrap.'

'Show some respect!' thundered his father. 'You bring disgrace on this girl, and on us, and now—'

'Don't be a hypocrite, Papa. You haven't been inside a church since Françoise was christened.'

'Poor Chantal,' clucked Alain's mother, unperturbed. They would talk him round soon enough. 'A wedding day is the happiest day of a woman's life. To deprive her of a proper ceremony . . . '

'What do you want of me? I'm acknowledging the child, aren't I? I'm prepared to sign away the rest of my life as the price of one stupid mistake . . . '

'You've been seeing a lot of the girl,' his mother reminded him. 'You must have liked her at the beginning. Enough to start two-timing the other one. Just be thankful it wasn't *her* you made pregnant.'

'For God's sake. You make me sound like Casanova.'

'Stop acting hard done by,' put in Albert. 'Take it like a man. Responsibility is what you need. It's time you grew up.'

'Ah, I see. You think I'm going to start toeing the line now. A man with a wife and child can't afford to risk his job. He keeps on the right side of the boss and trusts the union to take care of him. His ambition is to become a foreman so that he can earn a few francs more than his fellow workers. And he'll jump at any chance of overtime, no matter how lousy the deal is, because the kids need new shoes and the wife is nagging and—'

'That's the real world, Alain. Men supporting their families. It's time you learned to live in it. It's hard enough to raise a family when you're in work, let alone when you're on strike or unemployed. Once the child is born, you'll need a place of your own, you'll have to find money for rent, for furniture, for—'

'We'll buy you a bed, son. We'll buy you a bed, as a wedding present, won't we, Albert?'

'What do we need a bed for? She managed to get herself pregnant without one.'

'Don't be crude in front of your mother!'

'I'm going out. I need some air.'

Alain flung down his napkin and left the flat. There was the usual din from his sisters' bedroom, the Rolling Stones emanating at full blast from their record player. The paper-thin walls were festooned with pictures of pop stars, the tiny room was a shrine to ebullient youth. Now they would be banished from their lawful territory so that he and his new wife could enjoy an illusion of privacy.

How could he have been so bloody stupid? But it had been such bliss to be with a girl who expected so little of him. Or appeared to expect so little of him. Warm, compliant, undemanding, Chantal had humbly accepted his right to carry on seeing Armelle. Because it had proved quite impossible to stop seeing Armelle. And equally impossible to stop seeing Chantal. Chantal was like a digestif after a rich meal, like a Sunday after a hard week's work, like a warm towel after a swim. But without Armelle, she was redundant, meaningless.

It was his own fault. He had reverted to class, inexorably; mated with one of his own species, followed the most hackneyed tradition in the book. He would 'do the right thing by her'. She had got her man. It was the kind of craven compromise that made the world go round. Armelle would have despised him for it. He had not been able to bring himself to tell her the truth. On the contrary, he had been deliberately cruel to her, excessively so, left her feeling that she was the one at fault. He had enjoyed making her suffer, relished the sense of power and release it gave him. He might have lost his freedom but he still had his pride.

Armelle was high on adrenalin. Saturday's *manifestation* had borne rich fruit. Superficially, it had seemed a tame-enough affair, culminating in the demolition of the glass frontage of the American Express office, but the consequences had proved dramatic.

There was a hum of excitement and chatter throughout the student assembly at Nanterre as speaker followed speaker on to the platform. For six people to be arrested *after* the demonstration, at their places of residence, was seen as proof positive that the Dean maintained a blacklist of activists. The thought that her own name almost certainly appeared on it filled Armelle with pride and frustration. If only she had been one of the six! Now, as always, she suspected that her background accorded her unwanted immunity. If she were foreign, or Jewish, or an orphan, or working class, they might see her as more of a threat.

'If this motion is carried,' continued the speaker, 'we must proceed with caution.' There were a few catcalls. 'There are at least a couple of hundred police on campus, some in plain clothes, and people have already been hurt.' Armelle linked arms with the people either side of her as a gesture of solidarity. 'If we occupy the admin building, let's concentrate on the ground floor. There aren't enough of us to hold the whole block. Better to stick to a small area and refuse to budge.'

'No!' yelled a man from the floor. Armelle craned her neck and saw that it was Étienne, her former lover. 'That's a futile gesture. We need to take over the Dean's office and get hold of the blacklists. We need to go to the top, literally!'

There was a roar of support. Armelle could barely keep still from excitement. The Dean's office was right at the top of a concrete ivory tower. Its lofty position seemed to symbolise hierarchy, élitism, inaccessibility, everything that was wrong with the system. She had a sudden vertiginous vision of throwing the Dean out of the window, on to the concrete forecourt. She felt a trickle of excitement between her legs. Never had she wanted Alain more.

Rob had made it worse, not better. Rob with his good nature and gentleness, Rob who saw it as his mission to repair the damage other men had done her, to be loyal and kind and generous to her, even though she didn't deserve it.

'The motion is carried!' The words were drowned in the

noise of the exodus as people advanced, shoulder to shoulder, towards the admin block, some chanting slogans, some singing the 'Internationale', some just laughing, like Armelle, in an overflow of joyful rage.

The police held back, watching sullenly, as the small student army advanced towards the ugly modern block and mounted, unmolested, to the top floor. The Dean had already gone home for the weekend, as had most of his minions. His office was soon crammed with bodies as drawers and cabinets were rifled for the blacklists. Armelle dipped her finger in a bottle of ink and began writing slogans on the walls.

'Armelle,' said a voice in her ear, mocking her. It was Étienne, the ex-boyfriend who had dumped her the previous year.

'Étienne,' she acknowledged, without turning round.

'I hear it's all over with what's-his-name.'

Armelle put an inky finger in her mouth, savouring the metallic, blood-like taste.

'Yes,' and then, too quickly, 'I'm with Rob now.'

'The American?'

'That's right.'

'That's a pity. When I heard, I thought perhaps you needed a shoulder to cry on.'

'Hardly. I was the one who broke it off,' said Armelle, hating him. Just the sight of him filled her with white-hot memories of jealousy and humiliation. It was his promiscuity that had attracted her, of course. His final rejection of her had been a self-fulfilling prophecy, an obsessive re-enactment of her deepest insecurities. Even now, she was tempted. There was no point in wanting things unless they were off limits.

'The trouble with Alain', she began tartly, intending to deliver some scathing if-the-cap-fits remark, 'was that he—'

But Étienne turned away from her in mid-sentence to respond to a query from one of his fellow-activists, and was soon in the middle of another discussion, leaving her mouthing soundlessly like a goldfish. Pink with fury, Armelle released her frustration by yanking a picture off the wall, throwing it on the floor and jumping up and down on the glass.

'I sympathise,' murmured a girl standing near her. 'Étienne has that effect on me too.'

Armelle's blush deepened as she recognised the speaker as Étienne's former girlfriend, the one she herself had displaced.

'Claudine Bonnard. A fellow-victim,' she reminded her dryly.

'I know who you are.'

She was a dark-complexioned girl of *pied-noir* origin, swarthily attractive in an earthy, unfashionable way. Étienne had kept Armelle on her toes by telling her how good Claudine had been in bed. Every time Armelle looked at her, she found herself trying to imagine her naked.

'All Étienne's exes ought to stick together,' continued Claudine. 'There must be enough of us to start a revolution. Imagine, all the women of the world in revolt against male imperialism! It would make Vietnam seem insignificant.'

Armelle looked at her curiously. There was a mole at the corner of her mouth and a fine, dark fur on her upper lip. Her large, loose breasts were unharnessed, bulging haphazardly but explicitly under the thin blue pullover.

'Male imperialism?'

'Every time the men start talking about the revolution, just replace the word "worker" with "woman". You'll soon see what I mean.'

The two girls sat down on the floor side by side as the meeting was called to order. A move to wreck the office was rejected, much to Armelle's chagrin, and after several hours' debate it was decided to hold an 'anti-imperialist day' the following Friday, with the object of splitting into groups and occupying as many classrooms as possible. This agreed, the discussion went on all night; every group had to have its chance to speak and no one who wanted to make a point was denied the floor. Armelle eventually fell asleep, waking up just as people began to disperse. Claudine helped her to her feet.

'What happened?' Armelle yawned and stretched and realised that she was hungry.

'We've formed a new organisation, to act as an umbrella for all the different groups. Communists, anarchists, Trotskyists, Maoists ... from now on we're *le Mouvement du vingt-deux mars*. After you fell asleep we drafted a manifesto setting out our aims.'

'You mean we finally managed to agree on everything?'

'On the contrary. We disagreed on everything. So much so that no one felt able to sign the document on behalf of his group. Hence the new name. It represents everyone and no one. No leaders, no dogma, no official policy. We're working towards continuous revolution. Do you feel like some breakfast?'

Armelle hesitated on the brink of an excuse.

'It would annoy Étienne to think that we were friends,' said Claudine, putting an arm round Armelle's shoulders just as he passed by. Sure enough, he turned and looked.

'All right.'

Claudine took her back to her room and served her instant coffee, *biscottes* and greengage jam.

'He seems nice, your Rob,' she observed, sprinkling powdered milk into Armelle's mug. 'Rather quiet. You'd never notice him, if he wasn't so tall. Is that what attracts you to him?'

'His size? Or his quietness?'

'You tell me.'

'Both. He's very dependable. I never knew where I was with Alain.'

'Neither did anyone else. Talk about the invisible man. I began to wonder if you'd invented him.'

'I didn't know you took an interest in my affairs.'

'I can't help hearing gossip. And you did talk about him rather a lot. I suppose it's difficult, having a man you can't show off to the others.'

'Alain doesn't have much time for students. He says we don't understand the real struggle.'

'I dare say he's right. I mean to say, we have too much fun. Even in this dump. It can't be much fun being a worker. So . . . is that why you broke up with him?'

'Not exactly. It was the same problem as always. I was afraid to express any ideas or opinions of my own. When I was with Étienne, I was in the *Jeunesse Communiste Révolutionnaire*. Before that, I was supposed to be a Trotskyist, because I was with Marcel. For the last six months I've been calling myself an anarchist, because of Alain. And then I realised how ridiculous it all was. Do you ever see a man changing his politics to match his girlfriend's?'

'What about Rob?'

'Rob has nothing to learn from me,' said Armelle sweepingly. 'He sacrificed everything for his principles before we even met.'

'Do you imagine I would think less of him if I thought you had influenced him?'

'You might not. But other men would. And other women too.'

'You're right. It isn't just men who oppress us, it's other women. So many of us collaborate, without even realising. I did it myself, for years, just like you. Sex, politics, the same attitudes prevail. Women are there to be used, to service the men. Everyone knows it's true, but no one does anything about it.'

'Then do something. Why don't you interrupt the next meeting and suggest . . . suggest that the men type the leaflets and make the coffee and listen to the women for a change?'

Claudine looked at her intensely for a moment, as if gauging the seriousness of the question.

'I did once, in so many words. I prepared my speech in advance, saying much the same things I've just said to you, went along to a student union meeting, and spoke from the floor.'

'And what happened?'

'I was shouted down. Jeered at. Accused of being a lesbian. That was the hardest part.'

'What a cheap insult. You were very brave.'

'Not brave enough to admit in public that the cheap insult might be true.'

'What?' Armelle's mouth fell open.

'Not brave enough not to be ashamed. There. That'll give you something to gossip about. Don't look so stricken. I didn't bring you here to seduce you.'

'I'm sorry,' said Armelle. 'When I said it was a cheap insult, I didn't mean—'

'Of course you did.'

'No I didn't! And if you thought I did, why did you tell me?'

'Because I hoped you might be different from all the other

groupies out there. Because I thought you had an independent mind. Because I'm fed up colluding with the system. I used to think I couldn't exist without a man. That's why I let that bastard Étienne fuck me half to death, and he wasn't the first. And the more I did it, the more I despised myself. And then I got to thinking about how things were in Algeria, how people like my parents despised the people they oppressed, how imperialism thrives on fear and paranoia ... and I realised that I was oppressing myself. That I wasn't free. Are you? More importantly, do you really want to be?'

Armelle stared into her cooling coffee for a moment. She wanted to fight, certainly, but was that the same thing? Every war needed a pretext. Perhaps the struggle was an end in itself. She wanted enemies more than she needed friends. One way or other she always ended up alone ...

'Yes,' she admitted finally, wishing it wasn't true. 'I want to be free.'

SIX

Viktor had left Cassie sleeping, and the memory of it still haunted him, ruining his concentration. He had planned a profitable evening at the Lido, a regular hunting ground, where he would find himself a likely prospect, get her tiddly, whisk her round the floor a few times, and make off with her purse. But at the last minute he had thought better of it. It was fatal to work if you weren't in the mood. Or perhaps that was just an excuse to go back and see how Cassie was doing.

He had been particularly cruel to her today. After ten days of abstinence her suffering was almost more than he could bear to watch, and yet he deliberately made it worse, knowing that it helped her to have something tangible to focus her anger on. Cassie was a minefield of unexploded anger. That afternoon he had counted out her entire stockpile in front of her – one hundred and twenty-three yellow tranquillisers and fifty-eight white sleepers – arranging them in two tantalising heaps and murmuring, 'They can't hurt you, Cassie. They'll make you feel better. You know they'll make you feel better. They're nice pills, kind pills, clever pills. Go on. Stop being silly. Be a good girl and take your medicine . . . '

She had stared at them for a long time, stirring them around with a finger, and for a moment he had thought that she was about to weaken. But then she had painstakingly rearranged the tablets into the shape of a swastika and given him a look so full of accusation that she had made him feel ashamed.

Her head had begun to nod soon afterwards and he had

taken her back to her room where she had flopped on to the bed fully clothed and fallen asleep with startling suddenness. He should have been glad for her after ten days of raging insomnia, and yet he had begrudged her the sensual embrace that robbed him of her company.

He could have stayed, lain down beside her, seized the moment, but there would have been no satisfaction in it, not while she was still in such a vulnerable state. Or perhaps that was yet another excuse. The closer he got to her, the more untouchable she became. Her mind was like a deep moat, protecting the fortress of her body, sucking him down into its dark, muddy depths, forcing him to swim round and round in a travesty of forward motion.

He paid off the cab and raised his eyes roofward, contemplating the seven flights of stairs. He had found her a decent apartment, offered to pay the difference in rent, and got nothing but a sullen scowl for his pains. He pressed the buzzer, releasing the catch on the door, and switched on the *minuterie* which flooded the back staircase with dim yellow light. It annoyed him that she chose to live in this crummy place. If she'd been forced into a slum like the one he had shared with his mother, she might have learned more respect for comfort. Voluntary hardship was an affectation reserved for the overprivileged. Infuriatingly, she had admitted as much.

He paused outside her room to get his breath back. She was awake. He could hear the hum of a hairdryer from inside her room, could see in his mind's eye that long hair hanging in damp disorder around her bare white shoulders... He knocked extra loudly, so that she would hear above the noise of the motor. She switched it off.

'Pilar?'

'It's me.'

There was a suspicious, hostile silence. 'What do you want?'

'Just to see how you are.'

'I'm fine. You can't come in.'

'Why not?'

'I'm not decent.'

'So much the better.' She switched on the hairdryer again. 'Cassie? Put some clothes on and stop acting up.'

145

'It's not that. Go *away*.'

'Is something wrong? What are you so angry about?'

'Nothing. I don't want to see you. Leave alone.'

A man emerged from the next room, a barrel-chested Moroccan in a string vest.

'What's the matter with you?' persisted Viktor. 'Are you sulking again?'

'Go away!' yelled Cassie above the noise of the dryer. 'Don't you understand French? Piss off!'

'Why don't you do what the lady says?' suggested Cassie's neighbour mildly, scratching at the holes in his vest.

'Mind your own business,' snapped Viktor.

'You heard what she said. We all heard what she said. Now beat it.'

'Are you going to make me?'

'Are you looking for a fight?'

'Did you hear that, Cassie?' bellowed Viktor. 'I'm about to have a fight with the bloke next door. Do you want to watch?'

The door opened a fraction. 'Bastard,' she hissed. 'I have to live here, remember.'

Viktor snarled a smile at the Moroccan and went in. 'You don't have to live here at all. What's that smell?'

Cassie was wearing a dressing gown and appeared to be in the throes of changing the bed. A pile of sheets and blankets lay on the floor and a hairdryer lay on the bare, stained, lumpy mattress. The room reeked of ammonia.

'The window won't open,' said Cassie, as if in explanation, and then, hopelessly, 'Oh, what's the use. I wet the bed.' Her face twisted with the humiliation of it. 'Trust you to turn up at a time like this. Do you suppose that's progress? To sleep so deeply that you wet yourself? That'll teach me to let you buy me three *citrons pressés*. That's the other thing. I can't face the thought of eating anything but I'm thirsty all the time. Even though it hurts to swallow. I'm beginning to hate my body almost as much as I hate my mind.'

There was a wavering, vicious edge to her voice that alarmed him.

'You can't sleep here tonight. Leave the bed to dry out and come back to my place. I'll sleep on the settee.'

'What, and pee in your bed too?' She switched the hairdryer back on and aimed it savagely at the damp patch in the middle of the mattress. Viktor took it from her and switched it off.

'Listen to me. I know I said I'd go along with this, but it's gone far enough. I can't stand to see you like this.'

'You wouldn't have seen me like this if you hadn't barged in uninvited. I wasn't expecting you. I don't want you coming here again, do you understand? This is my space. This is private.'

'Look.' He wheeled her round to face the mirror above the washbasin. There were huge circles under her eyes and her mouth was cracked and swollen. 'Can't you see what you're doing to yourself? What are you trying to prove? That you're not ill? Well, you *are* ill. You've got to accept that.'

'If you tell me once more, just *once* more that I ought to go to the doctor . . . That's like *me* telling *you* to give yourself up to the police!'

'It's not the same thing at all. I feel responsible. If I hadn't called you a junkie—'

'Don't try to take all the credit. Or the blame. This is nothing to do with you. I'd have done it anyway. I don't need your help, I should never have asked for it. I might have known you'd run a mile.'

'I'm not running anywhere. I—'

'*You're* the one who needs help,' she continued, eyes flashing. 'Because you're every bit as hooked as me. You steal things the way I pop pills. Because it's the only way you can live with yourself. Because there's nothing else. Because you're empty.'

'That's enough.'

'It's your way of opting out, isn't it? Of convincing yourself that you're not really a failure, of getting your own back on all the people you think are to blame. You're a coward, that's all. It takes one to know one.'

'Don't ever tell me why I do what I do,' hissed Viktor, rattled now. 'Don't ever presume to understand me or explain me.'

'But it's so obvious! If you were an exam question you'd be so easy!'

'An exam question? You rich, educated bitches are all alike. You think you're so damned clever, don't you? What do you know about me? Only what I've chosen to tell you. Nothing!'

'Why's that? Because you're afraid to look inside yourself? Or because there's nothing there?'

There was a loud knock on the door. 'Are you all right in there, mademoiselle?'

'Bugger off!' yelled Viktor.

'Mademoiselle?' Another knock.

Cassie clenched her teeth and threw open the door. 'Will you please leave us alone?' she yelled at the public-spirited Moroccan. 'Your girlfriend screams her head off half the night and I don't complain, do I? Well, now it's my turn! I'll make as much noise as I like, do you hear me?'

Viktor hid his head in his hands. Cassie slammed the door.

'Calm down, for God's sake.'

'Calm down? You used to go on at me for being a zombie. Make up your mind.' He put his arms around her and squeezed, immobilising her. 'No, don't. Don't . . . ' The second 'don't' was barely audible, like a silent imprecation to herself.

'It's okay,' he said, meaning, 'Don't worry, I'm not going to try to get you into bed,' because he knew that was what she must be thinking. She would never believe that he was doing this for any other reason; she already felt as if she owed it to him. And that wasn't good enough, for him, or more importantly, for her. Meanwhile, the only erogenous zone that mattered was buried somewhere deep inside her head.

He had asked for this. He had gone into it knowing that he wanted more than sex. For weeks now he had circled and backed off and advanced, gone so far and no further, as ruthless as a predator, as circumspect as prey. He had lured her into indiscretions, used his own false frankness as a lever to open her up, delighted in each new discovery, each new proof of a life as hollow and artificial and barren as his own. He had wrung every detail out of her, hungrily, pitilessly, while revealing nothing that mattered about himself, knowing that she would open up to a stranger more readily than to a friend. He had never pretended to be a friend. He hadn't been sympathetic: quite the reverse. Sympathy would have been a sop. He had offered himself as a scratching post, a counter-irritant, not a balm.

148

It had pleased him to know that she was unhappy. He had enjoyed milking her complexes about her parents, her siblings, her ex-lover, her aborted child, painstakingly picking the lock of her mind, greedy with anticipation. She was the loneliest person he had ever met, lonelier even than himself. Her isolation was the most attractive thing about her. It meant that he didn't have to share her with anyone, not even her family, who didn't appreciate or need or deserve her. She was like a beautiful piece of jewellery, impaled on the bosom of a rich, fat, ugly woman, crying out to be stolen.

She broke away from him and sat down on the floor, arms folded, with her back against the bed and her long legs stretched out provocatively in front of her. 'There's no need for you to put up with all this, you know,' she said sullenly. 'God knows I've got no excuse for being such a bloody mess, I've had every unfair advantage you can think of.'

'So you keep telling me.'

'It takes all the point out of everything, don't you see? Even if I flunk my finals, it won't matter. My father knows all the right people, he'll fix things so that I can have any job I want. And even if he didn't, it wouldn't matter. When I'm twenty-one, I come into my money, I won't *have* to do anything at all.'

'Poor Cassie. Life's been really cruel to you, hasn't it? What a pathetic, self-pitying baby you are.'

It was the kind of remark that made her feel better. She flung him a grateful glare and resumed her attack on the mattress.

'Why don't we do a deal?' she said. 'See who can hold out longer?'

'What do you mean?'

'You could try not stealing for a week. See how twitchy you get. It would give me an incentive, if you were going cold turkey too.'

'Very funny.'

'It's not a bit funny,' she said quietly. 'Try it and you'll find out.'

As fixes went, she would have done instead, but to tell her that would have sounded like blackmail. He sat watching her for a moment, inhaling the hot, acrid air, knowing that he ought to get out of this elaborate trap he had set for himself, before she infected him with a need for self-knowledge, before she deluded him with hope. She was much too proud to run after him. And she probably would manage on her own. Seeing her so raggedly determined made him feel redundant, useless . . .

'Don't try to change me, Cassie.'

'I can't change you. Only you can do that.'

'I'm happy as I am.'

'If you say so.'

'Do you want to sleep at my place or not?'

'No thanks. Please go now. I'm okay.'

'I'll see you tomorrow.'

'Or the next day. I know.'

He bent to kiss the top of her head, breathing in the lemony smell of her hair, but she was locked inside herself again, a million miles beyond his reach. Already he needed her more than she needed him. And the little bitch probably knew it.

Jan was waiting outside the cinema, engrossed in the evening paper. There not being any public meetings fixed for that evening, they had arranged to see Elizabeth Taylorova in *Cleopatra*.

'Have you had anything to eat?' Eva greeted him.

He looked up and smiled. 'I had a couple of sausages, off a stall.'

'You'll end up with scurvy. Look . . . Karel's gone out for the evening. Do you want to come home and have something to eat? There's plenty left over.'

'We'll be late for the film.'

'We don't have to go to the film.'

'Are you sure?'

'I'm sure about making you dinner, yes. That's all.'

'I didn't mean . . .'

'Of course you did. Come on.'

'Won't your stepfather mind?'

'He thinks you're as harmless as you look. I noticed how careful you were the other night to agree with everything he said.'

'Was it that obvious?'

150

'Well, it worked, didn't it? You got your invitation to the meeting. If he knew you were "one of those young hotheads" he'd have kept you well away.'

'A hothead? Me?'

'By his standards, yes.'

Jan shrugged. 'You can't blame his generation for treading carefully. Most young people don't know about the things that happened under Stalin. That's why *Spring Tide* is so important.'

The proposed new magazine was Jan's pet project. It would be independent, unofficial, answerable to no one, and aimed specifically at young workers and students. Nothing and no one would be immune from censure, least of all Dubček himself. He had talked about nothing else all week.

'How are you going to raise enough money to print it?' asked Eva, practical as ever.

'I know where I can get hold of some surplus paper.'

'Where you can pinch it, you mean.'

'And we've got access to a duplicator at the university. And we'll all be working for free, of course. We'll give it away at first, to establish a readership, and then we can charge a nominal price, just to cover our costs. You could help, you know.'

'By typing the copy? That would make a nice change.'

'Come on, Eva. I didn't mean it like that. You're much too bright to be stuck behind that machine all day. You know, when you're with me you talk nineteen to the dozen, you're full of opinions and ideas. But whenever any of the others are there, you never say a word.'

'That's because I'm listening. And stop trying to butter me up, because dinner is all you're getting.'

It was a mild evening and they walked the long way home, via the embankment. The grey water of the Vltava was jewelled with setting sunbeams and the ochre stucco glowed with reflected gold. Spring was in the air. Soon there would be blossom on the trees. The seeds that lay dormant in the ground would be lured out of cold storage by warmth and light, reaching skyward like the city's innumerable spires. It must hurt, thought Eva, for a shoot to fight its way out of the hard earth. A bursting bud surely felt pain . . .

Every so often Jan stopped and kissed her. She enjoyed kissing Jan, in a detached kind of way, but as always something was missing, which frustrated her because she badly wanted to fall in love with him. Now that he stuttered less, smiled more and walked that bit taller – which she liked to think was partly down to her – his unfortunate looks didn't seem to matter. Eva wished that she liked him less, or more. In between was so difficult.

'What I'm really after,' continued Jan, 'is some personal interviews with ex-political prisoners, so I can compile a few case histories.'

'If you're thinking of Karel, you can forget it. That's why he's getting involved in the official side of things. So that he can depersonalise it. He's never talked about those years, not even with my mother.'

'The ones who don't want to talk are the ones with the most to tell. I see this as a long-term project, not a one-off feature. I want to follow things through from the campaign stage onwards. There are an awful lot of skeletons rattling in cupboards. I should think we're in for another spate of scandals. Think of all the judges and state security people who were involved. They can't *all* claim they didn't know what was going on.'

'I'll bet *she* did,' muttered Eva, smiling sweetly at the *domovnice* as they walked past her cubby-hole. She was an old sourpuss, one of the brigade of official watchdogs installed twenty years before to report everything she saw and heard back to the authorities. No wonder she was looking so fed up these days. She flung Eva a baleful look, as if to say, 'I know what you two are up to.' Eva responded by giving Jan a smacking kiss which dissolved into a giggle.

'What's the joke?'

'Did you see her face? Every time I look at her I want to do something outrageous.'

She let him in and lit the gas under the saucepan of stew and *knedlíky* she had prepared that morning.

'That smells good.'

'Oh, I'm a wonderful little housewife. Please don't remind me of it.'

'Okay, I'll shovel it in without a word.'

'I'm used to that.'

'Karel will miss not having you to look after him. It's not long now, is it?'

'Two months.'

'I bet you can't wait.'

'On the contrary. It's nice to have something to look forward to. It'll probably be the best part.'

'I envy you. If I wasn't so hard up, I'd tag along.'

She sat down next to him, thinking how well he fitted into this shabby room, how comfortable he looked in that old arm-chair. He had 'husband' written all over him. She returned his embrace rather stiffly, remembering the number of times she had led him on and let him down.

'I'm really fond of you, Jan,' she said, awkwardly. 'I know I'm not always very good at showing it.'

'I respect that. I don't expect you to do anything you don't want to do.'

Sometimes she wished he did expect it. Sometimes she wished he would push his luck, be strong and decisive and selfish. Which was silly of course, because if he was like that he wouldn't be Jan: he'd just be another domineering male with a one-track mind. She knew exactly how it would be tonight. He would go just so far and no further, respecting her nice-girl protests, and she would be relieved and disappointed. Afterwards, lying on her own in her single bed, she would relive the encounter and find her hands straying and wish that she had gone through with it. Then, next morning, she would tell herself that she ought to break it off with him, because he was really stuck on her and, if she didn't feel the same way, he would end up getting hurt. But she didn't want to lose him, because somehow Jan was all bound up with the changes in herself, and in other people; he was part and parcel of what was happening all around her. She remembered their first evening together in that jazz club, and how fed up she had been, and how she couldn't follow the conversation. Now, with his help, she was finding that there was more to life than empty daydreams, that reality was worth something after all. He was wise and kind and amusing and clever. Not for the first time, she wondered what on earth he saw in *her*.

'What are you thinking?'

'How hungry you look,' said Eva, smiling, and went to fetch his supper.

'Are you coming back here tonight?' asked Rob, reaching for his glasses and polishing them with the sheet. It worried Armelle that she had begun to notice his little habits and find them endearing.

'I don't know.' She had meant to say probably not, or just plain no. She got out of bed and put on her dressing gown quickly, afraid that he would want her again.

'Something on your mind?'

'Just all the things that are happening today. The occupation and so on.'

'You sure you don't want me there? I finish work at midday.'

'You can do more good distributing leaflets in the Latin Quarter. We want as many students coming out to Nanterre as possible.'

'You're saying you don't want to see me today, right?'

'I didn't say that. I said—'

'I know what you said. It's okay.'

Armelle shut herself in the shower cubicle and turned the spray full on. Last night was supposed to have been her last night with Rob, but she had been too much of a coward to end it. After all she had said to Claudine about wanting to be free! She had wanted to quit while she was winning; as it was she was merely running away.

He made her feel like a child again. Safe and loved and innocent. And that in itself was a threat, because she knew it couldn't last. The innocent child had become a bad girl, and bad girls didn't deserve to be loved. Especially by a good man, a man she couldn't bring herself to hate . . .

She dried herself and rubbed away the condensation on the mirror, admiring the accidental beauty of her face and figure. That was what Rob loved about her; what else did she have to offer? It was her hold on him, her disguise, the thing she most valued and most despised about herself. Without it, she was

154

nothing. Carefully, she applied her make-up, improving on nature, taking no chances. Her looks might last another twenty years, if she took care of them. After that . . . It was like contemplating death.

She found Rob making coffee. He handed her a mug but she waved it aside, anxious to get away.

'Rob . . . try to understand.' Her voice sounded false, even to her. 'This is a bad time for me. So soon after Alain and so on. I should have given myself a bit of breathing space before getting involved with someone else. I never meant things to get serious. I don't want to hurt you.'

'I know. You want *me* to hurt *you* instead. Like Alain and all the others. Why? Why are you so scared of being happy?'

'Stop trying to psychoanalyse me! I'm going.'

'I'm not stopping you,' he said mildly. 'And I'm not going to beg you to come back.'

Weakening, she put her arms round him and offered her lips for a kiss, telling herself again that it would be the last time, and then, again, because it would be the last time, wanting to make it last as long as possible, wanting more, for the last time . . .

'No.' It was his voice, not hers. All the times she had shrieked 'No!' to excite herself, and now he was turning her weapon on herself. 'No,' he repeated. 'I'm late for work. But I can probably fit you in tonight.'

'I told you, I won't be back tonight.'

'Tomorrow then. Whenever. Or never.'

She looked at him mutinously for a moment, wrong-footed, and then left the room quickly. Rob stood at the window, waiting to see if she would look up, and sure enough, she did. It was like a promise, contradicting her words. Words were for lying with.

There were two Armelles – the insatiable wet-dream temptress and the shrinking virgin – both roles played out simultaneously in some weird masturbatory fantasy that reduced him to a stooge. If you went along with it, she blew your head off; if you didn't, there was nothing doing. But last night he had finally managed to crawl under the hoops, catch her unawares . . . that was why she was so jumpy. She couldn't work without a script.

In any case, sex was just a preliminary to the real lovemaking, when she would curl up in his arms, defenceless, trusting, if only because she thought that the danger was over. Make love not war. For Armelle they were the same thing; she wouldn't recognise peace if she saw it. But he wasn't about to give up on her. If he didn't have faith in her, how could she have any in herself? This was what he had been waiting for. This was the real thing . . .

He washed and dressed, picked up the latest bundle of posters and leaflets and set off for the science faculty, where he spent the morning setting up equipment for experiments and clearing up the detritus of the day before. In between lectures he pinned up notices and canvassed passing students in the corridor but, as he had expected, interest in the 'anti-imperialist day' was minimal. Nanterre seemed a remote outpost to the city-based students, who felt little kinship with their less fortunate brethren; with the Easter break coming up, people had their minds on the vacation and cramming for the summer exams.

At midday he positioned himself in the central courtyard of the Sorbonne, hoping for a better response, and spent the next couple of hours doggedly spreading the word, without much success.

'Join the struggle against capitalism!' he urged a worried-looking youth, who shook his head at him irritably and hurried on his way, a pile of books under each arm. Rob quite saw his point of view. If someone had shoved that leaflet at him a year ago, he wouldn't have bothered to read it. And then it occurred to him that he hadn't actually bothered to read it this time either.

'Show solidarity with – Hi there.'

Cassie blinked at him, as if unable to place him.

'Hello. Er . . . thank you.' She looked at the leaflet blankly. 'I'm sorry I didn't make it to the demo last week,' she said, all in a rush, as if trying to pre-empt an accusation. She seemed different when she talked English. It showed up details like a magnifying glass.

'It's okay. Viktor said you weren't well.'

'I'm better now,' she said, adding quickly, 'but I don't think I can make it out to Nanterre today. I've got lectures all after-noon.'

'Cut them.'

'I can't. I've missed every lecture this term.'

'Then why not today?'

'I was bored. I felt like doing something.'

'Then *do* something!'

'Are you going?'

'Well . . . no. Someone has to drum up business. But Armelle will be there.'

She took a leaflet and read it. 'Sounds almost as boring as existentialism,' she commented. 'Not to mention the nine-teenth-century novel. Who writes this stuff?'

'They do it collectively. It takes half the night to draft one of those things. They debate every sentence.'

'You don't take it seriously do you?'

'Not really.'

'Well, in that case . . . do you want any help?' She stuck out a hand, almost belligerently, tossing back her hair to expose a stubborn, square jaw which belied the fragile quality of her curtained-off, oval face. The revelation was as startling as an unexpected striptease.

'Well . . . sure, if you like.' He handed her a bundle of leaflets. 'Do you want me to put your files in my haversack?'

She gave him two ring binders, both neatly labelled on the spine, one as 'Sodding Sartre' and the other as 'Bloody Balzac'.

'Are you sure you're up to it?'

'What do you mean, up to it?'

'Nothing. It's just that . . . Nothing.' She looked pale and exhausted, as if she had been up all night.

'I'm okay,' she muttered irritably. 'Don't you start. I get enough of that from *him*. What is it I have to yell at people?'

'Whatever you like,' said Rob, bemused, wondering what had come over her.

'How about *À bas les aristos*?' she suggested. 'Will that do? No, *À bas la bourgeoisie* is better, isn't it?'

She began hawking her wares with sullen gusto, chanting her chosen refrain, evidently untroubled by the odd looks she was getting. It was almost as if she was taking the piss out of herself, and him. But she had barely got into her stride when the courtyard emptied abruptly as everyone crowded into the ampitheatres for the two o'clock lectures.

'We might as well knock off till three,' said Rob. 'Let's go and get some coffee. Unless you want to try to catch your class.'

'No. There won't be any seats left now.' She seemed glad of an excuse to skive off. She followed him out into the rue de la Sorbonne, rather slowly now, like a clockwork motor that had run down.

'You seemed to enjoy that.'

'I felt like shouting, that's all.' She thrust out an arm at a group of stragglers. 'Join the struggle at Nanterre, comrades! Speak out against the capitalist conspiracy!'

'Why don't you clear off back to Germany?' demanded one of the youths, tearing up the leaflet. His companion varied the message by screwing his up into a ball and throwing it in Cassie's face.

'Germany?'

'Cassie . . . ' Rob tugged at her sleeve. Four against one and a half was no contest. 'Let's get out of here.'

'And take your boyfriend with you,' put in one of the others, shaking a fist in Rob's face. 'Go on, bugger off back to Nanterre. We don't want any of you dirty reds round here.'

'Move,' hissed Rob in Cassie's ear. 'They're *Occident*.'

'They're what?'

'Right-wingers. Fascists. Come *on*.'

'American!' hooted one of the gang, hearing them talk English. 'An American hippie and a whore.'

Rob pulled Cassie away, but the men followed closely, whistling and jeering.

'Stay cool,' murmured Rob. 'They're just trying to wind us up.'

'Whore!' they chanted in unison, one of them reinforcing his words by putting his hand up Cassie's skirt. Ignoring Rob's advice, she wheeled round and clouted the culprit in the face with her bag, provoking a triumphant collective war cry. Rob tightened his grip on her hand.

'Run!' he said.

She ran, but not quite fast enough. One of the youths kicked her hard on the rump and sent her flying headlong, banging her head against the cobbles. A couple of passers-by crossed pointedly to the other side of the road. Rob knelt down beside her, alarmed.

'Cassie? Are you okay? Cass—'

Four pairs of hands dragged him to his feet. Rob struck out automatically, knowing it was useless. A vicious punch to the jaw, a knee in the balls and a volley of blows to his chest felled him to the ground, only to be pulled upright again. While one of the men pinioned him in a vicious arm lock, the other three worked him over like a punchball, sending his spectacles flying.

Suddenly the street was deserted. No one came to his aid, apart from Cassie. Through a blur, he saw her stagger to her feet and tried to shout at her to get away, but couldn't collect enough breath between blows. He wasn't sure what happened next. He heard a scream behind him, felt his arms fall free, and struck out, only to find there was nothing there.

'Quick!' shouted Cassie, seizing his hand. One of the men was lying on the ground, squealing like a stuck pig; the other three were bending over him. 'Before they come after us!'

They didn't pause to look round, running hell for leather, not pausing to speak until they were out of breath and safely in the crowded thoroughfare of the Boulevard Saint-Michel.

'I think we've lost them,' panted Cassie. She put her arm out for a cab. 'Are you all right?'

'I've lost my glasses.' Blood was gushing from his nose and he could barely see. 'What about you?'

She displayed a pair of grazed knees.

'Sorry I was so slow on the uptake. I banged my head quite hard. I thought they were going to kill you.'

'What did you do to him?'

'Stabbed him in the back with my nail scissors. I don't suppose they went very deep,' she added ruefully.

'Christ almighty. I mean . . . thanks.' He rubbed his eyes, still dazed. 'I have to go back, see if I can find my glasses. And my haversack. Your files are in it . . . '

'Don't be silly. They might have another go at you.'

'But—'

Bossy now, she pushed him into the cab and gave the driver directions.

'Your face is a mess.' She fished a handkerchief out of her bag and offered it to him. 'Armelle will throw a fit when she sees you.' She seemed suddenly very brisk and doughty and in her element, the kind of Englishwoman who helped win wars. Overruled, Rob sat back, while the anaesthetic effects of adrenalin wore off and every part of his body started protesting at once.

'Perhaps you ought to go to hospital,' she said, seeing his face contort in pain.

'No. We might run into the guy you stabbed.'

'I can hardly remember doing it. I've never even hit anyone before. It makes you think, doesn't it? If I'd had a gun on me I'd have shot him, I was so *furious* . . . My God. Suppose a policeman had come along? I'd probably have been arrested.'

Rob had a sudden hilarious vision of Viktor visiting Cassie in gaol, but it hurt too much to laugh. Moments later, the cab deposited them outside his apartment. She insisted on paying the fare.

'I can't leave you like this,' she said. 'Let me help clean you up and then I'll go and see if Viktor's in.'

Rob crawled upstairs and lay down thankfully on the bed. His head ached viciously, he felt sick from swallowing blood, and it hurt to breathe. Cassie fetched a bowl of hot water and a towel and began mopping up the worst of the damage.

'Who exactly are *Occident*, then?'

'Nationalist types. That's why they picked on us. Because we're foreigners.'

'It was my fault. I'm sorry.'

'You weren't to know.'

'What happens when they see you again? They'll want to get their own back.'

'Don't worry. I'll see them first.' Except that he wouldn't, not without his glasses. 'Can you do me a favour?' Painfully, he eased himself into a sitting position, pulled his teeshirt out of his jeans, and unstrapped the money belt round his chest.

'Viktor gave it to me,' he explained, self-consciously. 'I was robbed the first night I was here.' He closed one half of his

160

mouth round an imaginary Gitane, mimicking the gravelly smoke-charred voice and clipped enunciation. 'Paris is full of thieves, my friend.'

'Well, he ought to know,' she said sitting down on the bed.

'He told you?'

'Told me what?'

'What he does for a living,' said Rob carefully.

'Of course,' she said, adding scathingly, 'He's proud of it.'

'Better than being ashamed of it.'

'I suppose so. What's this?'

'It's my prescription,' he said, handing it to her with a bundle of notes. 'Can you find an optician and get it made up for me?'

'What about the frames?'

'Oh, whatever's cheapest. You choose. Can you ask if they can have them ready as soon as possible? It's kind of urgent.'

'You mean you can't see without them?'

'Sure I can. But I need them for work.'

'Okay. Anything else?'

'Just something for a headache.'

He lay back again, letting out an involuntary cry as his ribs protested.

'Perhaps you ought to have an X-ray.'

'I'm okay. We don't want the bureaucrats asking any questions. Not with your nail scissors sticking in this guy's back. I'm only here on sufferance remember. They'd jump at any excuse to deport me.'

'You ought to shave that beard off and cut your hair. Then those thugs might not recognise you.'

'I'll think about it.'

She left him, returning half an hour later with a bunch of daffodils, a bottle of Cognac, and half a chemist's shop.

'Viktor was out. I left a message with the concierge. And your glasses will be ready tomorrow.'

'Tomorrow? How did you manage that?'

'They took one look at your prescription and asked me if you had a spare pair, and when I said you hadn't . . . Your eyes are pretty bad, aren't they?'

'I get by. Don't . . . don't say anything to Arm – I mean anybody, okay?'

161

He couldn't focus sufficiently to read her expression.

'Of course I won't,' she said.

'You're a lucky man, Alain,' said Jeanne. 'To have found a girl who's such a good cook.'

Chantal beamed prettily and began gathering up the plates. Jeanne laid a motherly hand on her arm, restraining her.

'You've done enough, *chérie*. You mustn't get overtired. You should take better care of her, Alain.' Alain grunted non-committally. He was getting more like his father every day. 'It's not good for her to be on her feet all day,' continued Jeanne, turning to her husband. 'Albert, the union ought to get her a sitting-down job. Can't you have a word with someone?'

'Nothing to do with me,' mumbled Albert. Alain looked up sharply. 'I'm resigning as shop steward. It's time for a younger man to take over. Jacques Rivière is keen to stand. No reason why he shouldn't be elected.'

'Rivière?' echoed Alain, appalled. 'Whose bright idea was that?'

'Come and sit down, Chantal, and leave the men to their politics,' put in Jeanne. 'The girls will wash up.'

'This concerns Chantal too,' said Alain. 'She's still a worker, isn't she?'

'I wish you would stand for election,' ventured Chantal shyly. Her interest in politics, as always, was minimal, except insofar as they affected her husband. 'You're so popular and ...' She caught the warning look in his eye and faltered. Jeanne bore her off to the settee and switched on the television. Alain's sisters began clattering at the sink.

'Rivière will be a disaster,' continued Alain.

'He's a good union man,' shrugged Albert.

'He's an imbecile.'

'He doesn't read books, granted. But then neither do I. Perhaps I too am an imbecile?'

Alain sighed. 'It's nothing to do with education. It's to do with integrity. You always did what you thought was right. Rivière is just a yes-man. His first duty is to the union, not to the workers.'

'There's a difference?'

'You know perfectly well there's a difference!'

'Then stand against him.'

'Is that the idea? It's a trick, isn't it?'

'Why should you care who's elected? It will be someone else for you to attack, to win cheap points against. A rebel is always a popular chap. But any immature kid can be a rebel. It takes a real man to build rather than destroy.'

'You can't build until you've destroyed. You can't build on rotten foundations!'

Jeanne leaned forward and turned up the sound on the television. Chantal was placidly knitting bootees, affecting not to listen.

'Let's go out for a drink,' muttered Albert. 'All this noise is driving me mad.' He hustled his son into the hallway. A gang of children were playing on the stone stairwell, shrieking and yelling at each other. Seeing the two grim-faced men, they parted to let them pass.

'The foundations may not be as rotten as they seem,' said Albert gruffly. 'I married your mother for the very same reason you're marrying Chantal, as you must have worked out long ago. I felt trapped, just like you. I felt I'd lost my youth, my freedom. But when I look back, I think to myself, what if I'd married for love? It wouldn't have lasted. As it is, I have a family and a comfortable bed to come home to. Compromise has its compensations.'

'Why are you dragging Chantal into this? We're discussing work, not women.'

'Your ideals are like a love affair, Alain. Flirt with them all you like, but for God's sake don't marry them. They won't last you into middle age.'

'You're telling me to embrace the political equivalent of a Chantal?'

'It's better than the political equivalent of a broken heart. You're not still seeing that other girl, are you?'

'No. But I still think about her. It's not a question of choice.'

'You're going to hurt that poor little wife of yours. She's devoted to you.'

163

'I won't hurt her. What little she wants from me, I can give her. That's the trouble, Papa. That's the whole problem. She doesn't want *enough*.'

'Have you heard the news? Johnson's not standing for re-election!' Armelle dumped a pile of shopping on the table and flung her arms around Rob, making him wince in pain.

'No kidding?'

'He's put out an order to limit the bombing and called for peace talks.'

'That's terrific!'

'It's pathetic, you mean. He must take the Vietnamese people for fools.'

'How the hell do you make that out?'

'Isn't it obvious? It's a bribe, that's all. Once the Americans realise that the National Liberation Front isn't for sale, they'll drop twice as many bombs, you'll see.'

'You sound as if you hope they will.'

'What's the point of peace on American terms?'

'You mean, what's the point of peace, don't you?'

War was sexy, of course, the blueprint for all lesser fantasies; his injuries had proved that. But for those friendly *Occident* thugs she might have moved on by now. As it was, she had proved the most diligent of nurses, like a gentle little squaw ministering to her wounded brave before sending him back to battle. A Chinese student had concocted an ointment for her, a malodorous concoction of herbs, which she applied religiously at three-hourly intervals with more sensuality than skill. She had filled the room with hothouse freesias and gardenia to mask the smell. Viktor had likened it to a funeral parlour. 'She's embalming you like a corpse for burial,' he had remarked, holding a handkerchief to his nose. 'Be warned.'

The apartment was now decked out with additional drapes, cushions and knick-knacks; Armelle's erstwhile bedroom was crammed with unopened boxes of china, linen and glass. 'I've nowhere else to put them,' she had told him plaintively. 'Odile told me to get all my things out of the house. You know how jealous she is of me. It's the stuff my mother gave me when she left. I can't bear to part with it. And my room at Nanterre is like a nun's cell, no room to swing a cat.'

These storage arrangements were her way of telling him that she had come to stay. He knew her better than to make her spell it out and frighten her into a denial.

'I adore it when you're grumpy,' she continued as she unpacked her shopping.

'I thought you liked me because I was kind and gentle?'

'I do. But I'm sure there's a brute inside there somewhere, fighting to get out.'

'And if there isn't you'll create one?' She had come pretty near it. He wanted to squeeze all the actressy pretence out of her, frighten her into being herself. She had an unfailing instinct for bringing out the worst in him, in everybody. She was like a sculptor fired by some grotesque vision, patiently chipping away with her chisel, knowing the hardest material would yield to subtle, skilled persuasion. 'Why can't you just act natural?'

'What a bad-tempered patient you've become. It must be a good sign.'

'For God's sake, Armelle,' said Rob, as she advanced purposefully with her jar of pungent balm, 'not again. I've just had a shower.'

'Don't you like me touching you?'

'Not when you plaster me with that stuff.' He took the jar out of her hand. 'Besides, I don't need it any more. I'm feeling a lot better. Well enough to go to Nanterre with you today.'

'No. We're expecting a lot of trouble. You've got to get properly fit again before you can fight.'

The anti-imperialist day had provoked a huge police presence and the summary closure of the lecture halls and library. Today's demonstration was a response to that, the last big assembly before the Easter break.

Armelle sat down on the bed beside him. 'I like your spare glasses,' she cooed, taking the dark frames off his face and kissing his swollen nose. 'Much better than those Sergeant Pepper things. They help disguise your face. Cassie's right, you know. You ought to shave off the beard and cut your hair. Those vermin will be looking out for you.'

She fetched a pair of scissors, a Delilah-like gleam in her eye.

'No,' said Rob.

'Don't be so vain. Besides, I don't like you looking like a hippie.' She swivelled his head and he felt the steel cold against his neck.

'Are you trying to make me angry?'

'Of course not. I won't do it if you don't want me to. But I care about you. I don't want you to get hurt again. You're so conspicuous with that red hair of yours. Perhaps we could dye it black.'

'I'll dye mine when Dany Cohn-Bendit dyes his,' said Rob, referring to the flamboyant student leader, popularly nicknamed Dany le Rouge. 'Not before.'

'Can I have just a snip of it? For a keepsake?' He heard the blades click, pre-empting his consent.

'That's enough. If I want it cut I'll go to a barber.'

'I can't imagine what your face is like under that beard. Perhaps shaving it off will make you less attractive.'

It sounded like a warning, or possibly a plea. She retreated, put the scissors away, and snapped the lock of hair into her locket, pausing briefly to look at the two photographs inside it. Rob should have been flattered, but again he felt a stirring of unease, as if he had just been laid to rest in a mausoleum of lost love.

'My mother gave me this,' she murmured wistfully, extracting a paperweight from the big box of unsorted items on the floor. She handed it to him reverently. A blue and gold butterfly was trapped for ever in the glass, its wings locked in eternal flight.

'She loves beautiful things,' continued Armelle. 'Giovanni – that's her second husband – is a painter. They live in Rome. He's done some fantastic studies of her.' She unwound the layers of sheet protecting one of the pictures she had stacked against the wall, and held it up in front of her, displaying a wistful nude. 'We're very alike, aren't we? I might go and stay with them this summer. Perhaps I'll ask Giovanni to paint me. It would be nice if he did one of us together.'

This was his cue to leap at her and tear her clothes off, against her will, of course. Rob looked away.

'It must be wonderful to have talent,' she resumed. 'You should be less shy about your sketching. I could pose for you, if you like.' She picked up his guitar, which Viktor had returned, and strummed it tunelessly. 'I wish I had a gift. Will you teach me how to play? I used to learn the piano, but my hands were too small. I couldn't span the octave.'

She spread out her fingers, short and slender with bitten-down nails. He felt a wave of hopeless, angry tenderness.

'Come here.'

'Come and get me.' She took one step backwards.

'Stop playing games. Stop trying to turn me into some kind of rapist. Is that the only way you can enjoy it? When somebody forces you?'

'Why are you so inhibited?'

'You're the one who's inhibited, not me.'

'I told you, I'll do whatever you ask. Which is more than can be said for you.'

She turned away sulkily. Rob got up and put his hands on her shoulders. 'Anything I ask?'

'Of course. I don't understand all your hang-ups. It's only sex.'

'I'm not interested in only sex. Not from you.'

She let out a short, exasperated sigh, her face hardening into that child-whore look he hated. 'And I'm not interested in what you call love.'

'Why not?'

'Because the word is meaningless.'

'You know what it can mean, if you let it happen. Why won't you? What was it that screwed you up so bad? Perhaps if you told me about it . . .'

She shook her head and pressed her face against his chest, as if to muffle the tiny squeak of distress, to drive the genie back inside the bottle. Rob put his arms around her and began doing things his way, provoking a reluctant response. It was temptation she was really afraid of.

'I don't want to,' she murmured, as if to convince herself.

'Then you don't have to.'

He shucked off his bathrobe, leaving her fully dressed. His pale, freckled skin was piebald with bruises; she couldn't resist feeling them, kissing them. Her fingers, clean of the oriental unguent, were cool and tentative, her lips were soft and innocent. More than ever, he wished that he had been the first.

'I will if you want me to,' she conceded humbly.

'No hurry.'

'But you're ready.' She clasped her hand around his erection, as if to take charge of it.

'I've been ready ever since I woke up this morning. You made sure of that. I can wait a bit longer.'

'You make me sound like a tease.' She began giving him a textbook hand-job. 'I don't care about myself. Only about you.'

'I can do that for myself. That's not what it's about.' He unclasped her fingers. 'Forget it.'

'Now *you're* teasing.'

'Am I? Prove it.' He walked away from her, lay flat on his back on the bed, put his hands behind his head and shut his eyes. After what seemed like a long time he heard a sharp intake of breath, the sound of shoes being kicked off and the rasp of a zip.

'Bastard,' she hissed.

'Go away. I don't feel like it any more.'

'Liar. I could finish that thing off in two minutes flat. Less.'

'Why would you want to do that? Because it scares you?'

She knelt astride him.

'Look at me.' She wore her nakedness the way she wore everything else, like a model haughtily flaunting her wares on a catwalk. Rob kept his hands under his head. 'I'm beautiful, aren't I? Look at my breasts.' She squeezed her nipples between finger and thumb. 'Don't you want to touch them?' She stood up on her knees and advanced towards his head till her shaven crotch was level with his mouth. 'Why don't you kiss me?'

He'd been caught that way before. She would start screaming and squirming as if his tongue were red hot, consumed with aphrodisiac disgust.

'Because you don't really like it. Sometimes I wonder if you like any of it.'

She sat back on his chest. 'What is it you want of me?'

'I want you to stop pretending. I want us to do it for real.'

168

She plucked at the hairs on his chest for a moment, biting her lip, evidently embarrassed, as if he had just suggested some gross perversion. Then, almost tentatively, she manoeuvred herself on to him. She felt tight and dry.

'Relax,' said Rob, bracing himself for another elaborate game of cat and mouse. 'Take it slow.' She sat still for a moment with her eyes tight shut, as always, contracting and releasing her muscles like a musician flexing her fingers before playing.

'Open your eyes,' said Rob. 'Don't shut me out.'

Reluctantly, she obeyed, blinking like a mole emerging from its burrow. Then, quite unexpectedly, she began to cry, profusely but almost silently, sending delicious tremors through him. Rob took hold of her hands and held them while she sobbed, welcoming her tears as a token of trust, happy for her to stop right there. But then she began to move. Usually she moved like a demented fish trapped in a net, jerking and writhing in a dumbshow of defiant death. But this time she moved with slow, uncertain precision, like someone afraid of falling, keeping her eyes fixed on his, as if trying to retain her balance. Curbing his impatience, he matched his rhythm to hers, gratified that she wasn't rushing it, for once. Gradually, she loosened up, forced a shy smile. He could feel her desire trickling out of her now, could hear the soft liquid sound of it as she swayed. He wanted this to go on for ever . . .

'Christ, Armelle, I'm sorry.'

She bowed her head in something like relief. 'It's all right.'

'It's not all right.'

She slid off him and lay down beside him. 'It doesn't matter. Truly, it doesn't matter.' She picked up his hand and put it away. 'There's no need for that. I feel fine.'

'But—'

'Don't say anything. Just let's be quiet for a moment.'

She sounded languid, genuine. Rob stroked her hair, furious with himself. The first time that had counted for anything, and he had loused it up. 'Don't go to your demo. Stay home today. We'll—'

'No. I'm not in the mood. I only did it to please you.'

There was just a hint of malice in her voice, sweetened with sadness. There was no point in forcing a retraction out of her; it would only make things harder next time. She got up and dressed.

'I'll be back late. Don't forget to eat.' She itemised the collection of paper tubs from the *charcuterie* – grated carrot, cold ratatouille, potato salad, mushrooms à la grecque, *tête de veau*. There was fruit, a wedge of Brie, a bottle of wine, a baguette. If he was still hungry she would cook him an omelette on her return. You Tarzan, me Jane, thought Rob.

'Wish us luck,' she continued briskly. 'We're hoping for the TV cameras. And if I don't come back tonight, don't worry. It will just mean I've been arrested.'

'Don't get yourself hurt,' said Rob roughly. 'Don't go looking for trouble.'

'If I'm hurt, you can nurse me. And I'll be just as ungrateful and ill-tempered as you.' Her lips brushed his cheek. 'It's all right,' she murmured again, rubbing it in. 'It doesn't matter.' She blew a kiss at him from the doorway and left the room, leaving him burdened with longing for her return.

He went into the bathroom and looked at his still-swollen face. He had two black eyes, a split lip and his nose was agony to touch, possibly even broken. If it hadn't been four against one, he would have given as good as he got. It was easy to say you wouldn't fight until someone actually attacked you, and then you realised there was nothing to it, it was the most natural thing in the world. In primitive societies they felt good about killing, they thought they inherited the dead enemy's strength, they roasted and ate his flesh. Even a harmless little thing like Cassie was capable of murder. Perhaps this anti-war thing was all shit. It was different once you were in the thick of it. He could just imagine the poor saps out in Vietnam, scratching notches on their guns, eager to avenge their buddies, to underwrite their own mortality with as many dead gooks as possible, hating the peace brigade back home that sanctified the enemy . . .

There was a knock on the door. Rob pulled on his jeans and went to answer it.

'I thought her ladyship might have dragged you off to Nanterre,' remarked Viktor, walking in.

'How are you feeling?' asked Cassie.

'Bored,' said Rob, reaching for his shirt. 'Would you two like something to eat? Armelle went out for a couple of croissants and brought back all this stuff.'

Viktor tore a piece of bread off the loaf and tossed it at Cassie.

'Eat something,' he said tersely. 'Here, have one of these nice china plates.' He picked one up from the tissue-wrapped stack on the table and threw it into the air like a frisbee; Cassie dropped her bread and jumped to field it, with the sudden, fluttering movement of a bird. She missed, and it shattered on the floor.

'Oh God,' she wailed, bending down to pick up the pieces. 'I can never catch things. Was it one of a set?'

'It's only property,' jeered Viktor, inspecting a matching cup. It was fine Limoges porcelain, delicately patterned. It irritated him to see Armelle's belongings strewn all over Rob's apartment. She was as invasive as lice, colonising everything she touched. 'You've just struck a blow against ownership.'

'It's some stuff her mother gave her,' said Rob, wearily taking his point. 'She'll be upset.'

'You're a bastard, Viktor,' said Cassie crossly. 'I'll take one away with me and get it matched,' she added, turning to Rob. 'Tell Armelle I'm really sorry, won't you?' She unwrapped another plate and helped herself to some mushrooms. Viktor added some *tête de veau*.

'I hate offal,' she protested, squirming at the pallid lumps of meat.

'It thickens the blood,' said Viktor, spearing a morsel on a fork. He prised her mouth open and force-fed her without ceremony. 'I bet you were a faddy child.'

'Only till I went away to school,' she said, screwing up her face as she chewed experimentally and swallowed with evident distaste. 'At home I was allowed to serve myself at table and not take things I didn't like. But if I left anything on the plate, my mother would dock my pocket money and give it to famine relief. So I never took any chances.'

'No wonder you're so thin,' said Rob.

'I . . . ' She groped for the word she wanted and slipped lazily into English. 'I metabolise quickly. I can eat any amount of chocolate and not put on any weight.'

171

'Milk or plain?' asked Rob.

'Oh, milk. The sicklier the better.'

'Hard or soft centres?'

'Soft. Specially Turkish delight. I don't like the nutty ones.'

'What are you two talking about?' demanded Viktor.

'Wouldn't you like to know?' said Cassie. She turned to Rob. 'Keep talking English,' she said. 'Just to annoy him.' Rob caught the paranoid glint in Viktor's eye and grinned.

'Since you're such a demon with the scissors,' – she collapsed into theatrical giggles – 'will you cut my hair for me?'

She looked startled. 'Me? Oh, I don't think I'd better. I haven't got a very steady hand. Why don't you ask Armelle?'

'I'd rather surprise her.'

'Well . . . at your own risk, mind.'

He fetched the scissors and sat down in an upright chair by the window. Cassie began snipping. She carried on chattering, aimlessly, just to exclude Viktor.

'What was the row about?' murmured Rob, fishing.

'What row?'

'Come off it.'

'Oh, he's just in one of his funny moods, that's all. Just ignore him. He hates that.'

She flung Viktor a goading look, to let him know she was discussing him. Viktor responded with an unconvincing sod-you smirk.

'Why is he in a funny mood?'

'Because I've been getting on his nerves, as usual. I was going to leave him to it, but he dragged me round here instead. I hope you don't mind.'

'Any time.'

'Last night . . . last night he dragged me along to this crummy disco in Montparnasse, even though he knows I can't dance. That is, I can, but I've always hated it.'

'Why?'

'Same reason I hated PT at school,' she said, leaving him none the wiser.

'So why did you agree to go?'

'I didn't agree. We were supposed to be going to see *Un Homme et Une Femme*.'

'That's a great movie. At least, I enjoyed it. Armelle reckoned it was corny.'

'I like corny films. Anyhow, he's always doing things like that. The minute he found out I was scared of heights, he suggested an innocent little walk in the Champ-de-Mars and dragged me up to the top of the Eiffel Tower.'

'Sounds like you enjoyed it.'

'I pretended to, just to spite him.'

'Good thinking. He's just a bully.'

'Rob says you're a bully,' she translated, eliciting a modest shrug. 'Is that short enough at the back?' she resumed in French, signifying an end to hostilities. 'I'm not much of a *coiffeuse*, I'm afraid.'

'Here, let me,' said Viktor, taking over. 'Let's make him really beautiful for Armelle.'

'He'll scalp you,' remonstrated Cassie. 'Do be careful, Viktor.'

'I might as well have a shave, when you've finished,' said Rob, affecting indifference to Viktor's twitching blades. 'Get it all over with at once.'

'You should wait for the swelling to go down,' said Viktor. 'You'll bleed like a pig. But then, blood excites her, doesn't it? Sorry if I don't have Cassie's light touch,' he added, slicing away brutally with the scissors.

Cassie smiled, and something fleeting passed between her and Viktor, hanging in the air like a plume of smoke, making Rob feel like a voyeur, filling him with envy. He wanted to knock their heads together, to tell them to go home and make love and stop wasting time. But he didn't, and they stayed for the rest of the day.

SEVEN

April 1968

'On 10 January 1950,' wrote Karel, 'at five a.m. precisely, the doorbell rang.'

That was the worst part. The first sentence. Just looking at the words was like prodding a tumour. The cheap lined paper and leaking ballpoint seemed appropriate enough as surgical instruments. He would operate without skill, without method, without anaesthetic. It would be a real kitchen-table job, brutal, clumsy and slow. But this was kill or cure.

> I had been asleep barely three hours. The deepening financial crisis put enormous pressure on my department in the Ministry of Economic Affairs, and it was my habit to work late and to bring papers home. I woke with a start, as did my wife Milena, who was very frightened. A knock on the door at that time of morning could mean only one thing.
>
> Three men were waiting for me on the doorstep. They said that my presence was required immediately in order to assist in an official inquiry. I tried to reassure my wife that this was purely a routine matter. She clung to me and began weeping. I felt a strong need to see my son before I left but, not wishing to alarm her, I did not do so. I was never to see my family again.
>
> I was taken by car to a building on the outskirts of Prague, where four men were waiting to question me. They explained that both my post and my department

were currently under scrutiny. I was asked to write an account of my life, both before and after joining the Party. Having nothing to hide, I replied that I would be pleased to do so. A brief summary of my statement is set out below: unwittingly I damned myself with every word I wrote.

I was born in Prague, in 1919, the only child of Jaroslav and Marta Brožek. My father was a distinguished historian and the author of several learned academic works. I was educated at a private academy run by Jesuits. In 1932–3 I spent a year with my parents in Paris, where my father was a visiting professor at the Sorbonne. Two years later my father died of a heart attack. In 1937 I began reading for a degree in mathematics at Charles University.

My studies were curtailed by the Nazi occupation and the subsequent closure of the faculty; I was sent to work as forced labour in a tramcar factory in the suburbs which had been requisitioned for the manufacture of military vehicles, and where I was to remain until 1945. Naturally I was bitterly envious of those of my compatriots who had managed to leave the country and enlist with the Allied forces, and I soon became active in the Resistance. During this period I met and fell in love with the woman who was later to become my wife; our son was born in 1942. At the time I was unable to marry her or acknowledge my child, for fear that they would be victimised if I was ever arrested.

As the war progressed, I began to question the bourgeois values on which the old Republic had been built. I became disillusioned with the reactionary attitudes within the Resistance movement, and in particular its refusal to co-operate with the Communists in the fight against Fascism. In 1944 I became a Party member.

I took part in the uprising, sustaining a flesh wound to my leg. The day after Soviet tanks liberated the city, I married the mother of my child. I was anxious to contribute such skills as I possessed to the rebuilding of our society, and applied for a junior post in the Ministry of Economic Affairs, where I was fortunate enough to receive rapid promotion. My present post involved analysis of sensitive and classified information.

Having completed this statement, I was told that I could not return home until the investigation was complete. I was refused permission to telephone my wife, and remained unaware that my apartment had already been searched and a large quantity of official and personal documents taken away for examination.'

Karel paused. He had quite lost the habit of writing; his hand was no longer supple, the letters were badly formed and uneven. Poor Milena. Time and again she had begged him to resign, weeping and pleading far into the night. On several occasions it had been a relief when the telephone extension in the bedroom had interrupted her rantings to summon him to an emergency late-night meeting. He hadn't listened to her, of course. But *they* had listened, both to her heresies and to his replies, which were later quoted back at him, out of context, and made to sound like treason. The black ministry telephone sitting sentinel by their bed had picked up every word.

Late that night I was taken by car to another building near the airfield at Ruzyne, where two plain-clothes security men formally arrested me and charged me with offences against Law 231 for the Defence of the Republic. I protested that I had never committed any crime against the State and asked for specific details of the charges. I was told that they already had proof of my association with Western agents; my only hope for clemency was to make a full confession and reveal the names of all my accomplices.

I was stripped naked, made to put on filthy, ragged garments stained with blood and urine, and told to rewrite my statement, this time incorporating details of my activities as a spy, the names of my fellow-conspirators, and responses to various specific questions arising from my original statement.

I could not deny that my late father had been a social democrat and a supporter of Tomaš Masaryk. But I refuted the suggestion that he had ever been in contact with Western agents, or that he introduced them to me during our stay in Paris, or that I had kept in contact with these non-existent agents thereafter.

I confirmed that I had once taken part in a student debate, during which I had attacked the principles of Marxism–Leninism, but pointed out that I had on another occasion been equally critical of capitalism. At that age I had prided myself on my objectivity, but this was before the betrayal at Munich and the experience of the war years had radicalised my thinking.

I conceded that many intellectuals had been sent to German concentration camps, where many of them had perished, and agreed that I had indeed been fortunate in escaping a similar fate, but strenuously denied that I had collaborated with the Nazis in order to buy my own life, or that I had infiltrated the Resistance as an *agent provocateur*.

I further refuted the allegation that my recommendations to the Ministry were calculated to damage the national economy in line with instructions received from Western saboteurs.

Having read my second statement, my interlocutors concluded that I was being stubborn in my refusal to cooperate. It therefore became necessary to question me more thoroughly.

This questioning continued for the next three months and lasted for eighteen hours each day. I was required to remain standing throughout the interrogation, and within a couple of weeks my feet became blistered and swollen, causing me constant pain. During the six hours' sleep allowed me I was woken every few minutes and required to stand to attention before lying down again. On some days I got nothing to eat at all; such food as I was given was merely pig-swill.

Day and night, I could hear the cries of other prisoners being tortured. But still I refused to confess, knowing that if I were condemned as a traitor, my family would become social outcasts. Then one day my interrogators informed me that my wife had instigated divorce proceedings against me. I later discovered that this was a lie, but at the time I believed it. My first reaction was shock, my second a kind of bitter relief. I told myself that she was doing the sensible thing, to protect herself and our child, whether or not she truly believed I was guilty. Nevertheless, I felt bereft, betrayed. I began to lose my will, and my incentive, to resist.

I had been told repeatedly that my accomplices had already given written evidence against me; my earlier hopes of convincing a court of my innocence seemed naïve. Worse, I could no longer convince *myself* of my innocence. The Party had demonstrated its god-like omnipotence; I was like a sinner condemned to hell and consumed by a vision of forgiveness. To 'repent' seemed the only way to salvation.

Twelve weeks after my arrest I wrote out a full 'confession' and named various innocent colleagues as fellow-counter-revolutionaries. This done, I was allowed to sit, given books to read, and fed proper food. Freed from hunger and physical pain, my strength returned and my brain cleared; a few days later I formally retracted my confession, only to be told that the evidence against me was sufficient in itself to guarantee my execution. I resolved to die with dignity, protesting my innocence to the end.

At the time I had no way of knowing that I was one of the victims of a wholesale purge, masterminded by Stalin and carried out with ruthless efficiency through his henchman Beria and hand-picked members of the secret police. We 'traitors' were to be scapegoats for the failures of the post-war regime: the terrible shortages, the worthlessness of our currency, and the unrelenting hardships suffered by the vast majority of the population, who were led to believe that all these things were the fault of Western agents, of black marketeers, of bourgeois sympathisers. To maintain credibility, however, everything had to be done with the strictest legality, and no one could be permitted to shed doubt on his conviction by denying his guilt. Being ignorant of this conspiracy, I had no inkling that what happened next was merely a charade, calculated to break my spirit.

Every night thereafter I was woken, blindfolded, and led into a room where a gallows had been set up, there to await a telephone call authorising them to hang me. At first I was not afraid, because by that time I wanted to die. But as night followed night and the phone call did not come, I began to understand the true meaning of despair. To deprive a man of sleep and food is aimed at his mind, not his body; to deprive him of death, when that is all he craves, is aimed at his very soul.

It was during this period that I finally lost all sense of my own identity. The person masquerading as myself finally broke down and made a fresh confession, more detailed and damning than the last, convinced that in some way this would be for the good of the Party, and of the State.

My trial was a mere formality. None of the many accused who were to follow me, in the big show trials of 1952, said one single word in their own defence; only those of us who lived through the experience can begin to understand why. I was sentenced to life imprisonment and joined 1,500 other political and common criminals in a labour camp in southern Bohemia.

In 1957 Comrade Khrushchev ordered the first of two general amnesties, and the first contingent of condemned men was released. No public explanations were given; we were 'free' and at the time that seemed enough. But many of us are still not free of the self-disgust, the bitterness, the guilt and anger. Memories do not fade with the passing years; as we age, the past seems ever nearer.

But I must relinquish all thoughts of revenge. It would give me little comfort to seek out and persecute all those who colluded and condoned, because I too colluded and condoned, however unwittingly. And until I can forgive myself, I will always be living in the past.

He was a small fish, a man no one had ever heard of, too ordinary, too insignificant, for his story to matter to anyone but himself. That was what made it worth writing. It was to be the first true confession of his life.

'That's beautiful,' said Cassie dreamily, as Viktor launched into the reprise of a haunting, unfamiliar melody. The piano acted as a kind of buffer between them; while he was playing, there was no need to talk, let alone argue.

Viktor looked over his shoulder as she lay back sleepily on the settee. The most inappropriate tunes were effective lullabies, soothing her into voluntary torpor. Once she had dozed off to the endless, repetitive coda of 'Hey Jude!', and hadn't woken up till morning.

'It's the Czech national anthem.'

He began singing along, as if to shut her out.

'What do the words mean?'

' "Where is my country, where is my home ... " The usual sentimental bilge.'

'Haven't you ever felt like going back, for a visit?'

'Oh, Marta's been trying to set up a pilgrimage for years. Luckily they wouldn't give her a visa.'

'But now they would, surely? Did you read that newspaper cutting I gave you?'

'For God's sake. You're getting as bad as my grandmother. There's nothing there for me now. I'd just be another bloody tourist.'

He switched abruptly to a boogie-woogie version of the 'Marseillaise'.

'Why are you so touchy today?' said Cassie.

'That's terrific, coming from a fishwife like you.'

Cassie swallowed the automatic denial. Since coming off the pills, her temper had shortened alarmingly; the harder she strove to control it in public, the more she let rip with Viktor, picking gratuitous quarrels just to let off steam. For someone

180

so volatile he had displayed remarkable forbearance, although Cassie was not deceived. To retaliate there and then would have been to admit that some of her more vicious remarks had struck home. He preferred to bide his time and get his own back later, when she least expected it.

'Touchée,' she muttered, chastened. And then, on one of her sudden ungovernable impulses, 'Thank you for putting up with all the crap I dish out. I couldn't manage without you . . .'

'What a terrible fate. Not to be able to manage without a . . . what was it? . . . a small-time crook with a chip on his shoulder. An overgrown juvenile delinquent. A psychopath. An unscrupulous exploiter of innocent women. I'm vulgar, promiscuous, arrogant, immature . . .'

'Oh, shut up.'

'Why should I? You never do.'

'If you want me to go, just say so.' He carried on playing, ignoring her. 'Viktor? Will you please look at me when I'm speaking?'

'Why? I know what you look like. A bag of bones with greasy hair and a dress that looks as though you've slept in it for a week. Can't think what that dirty old man of a boyfriend saw in you.'

'You can be incredibly cruel sometimes,' said Cassie coldly, cursing herself for the tremor in her voice.

He swivelled round on the piano stool to see the effects of his cruelty. Cruelty was the easiest, quickest way to bring that angry flush to her cheeks, to draw all her inner poisons to the surface. It enchanted him that he had the power to play on her like his keyboard, to produce sweetness or discord at will. No, not quite at will, because in certain circumstances she was unpredictable, she would display surprising self-restraint, accepting abuse as fair comment, rejecting reassurance as a sop. The one thing that always worked was indifference: indifference wound her up as tight as a spring.

He turned his back on her and began playing again. Rising to the bait, Cassie banged down repeatedly on the treble keys until Viktor seized both her hands and pinioned them against the keyboard.

'Let me go.' But the words were hollow; she made no

attempt to free herself. He released one wrist and kept hold of the other one, dragged her roughly on to the settee and pushed her on to her back, suddenly aware of why he was so angry with her. He had never, ever in his life had any problems with sex, never experienced this paralysing fear of failure, until he ran into this ball-breaking little bitch. Just looking at her made him sweat with wanting her, and she knew it. She had been expecting something to happen right from the start; she was expecting it at this very moment. Every opportunity he let slip by increased his sense of impotence.

Cassie didn't react at all, other than to go very limp. He knew she wouldn't refuse him, which only made things worse, because not refusing him wasn't the same as wanting him; it was precisely the kind of passive response he couldn't bear to contemplate. He would have liked her to resist, to kick and scream and plead, so that he could deliver the final insult of letting her go, watch her fear collapse into tell-tale disappointment. But she just stared at him meekly, calling his bluff, mocking him. Annoyed, he got up and lit a cigarette.

'It's all right,' she said, showing that she had understood, and misunderstood. 'I honestly don't mind. In fact I wish to God you'd get it over with.'

Viktor swore under his breath. He had envisaged it flowering out of one of those rare, exquisite moments of perfect harmony when he felt he held all her well-being in the palm of his hand. But such moments were so threatening, so disarming, that he had wantonly destroyed their melody with deliberate discord, confusing both her and himself. Sometimes, when she lapsed into one of her exhausted daytime dozes, he had a curious sensation that she was watching him through her closed lids, observing her power, the power that had spoiled him for the honest pleasures of the flesh. It wasn't her flesh he wanted, it was the strange, tormented soul that lay within it, the key to the understanding of himself.

She held her arms in silent invitation, rendering him helpless, hostile. He had always regarded a woman's body as the human equivalent of a money-stuffed pocket: he would select the angle of entry, choose the most propitious moment of insertion, delight in varying and perfecting his technique, seeing it as a cold-blooded exercise in self-gratification. There had never been any question of being preyed upon in return.

But then he saw in her wide, appeasing eyes that she wanted nothing back, that this was a simple gift, a penance even, that she had never enjoyed it and did not expect to enjoy it, but wanted to make things up to him, show goodwill, settle her debts, win approval.

'I'm sorry,' he said. 'I didn't mean to take advantage of you.' The phrase sounded ridiculously old-fashioned. 'That's not the reason I spend time with you. Not the only reason, I mean. And anyway, you're not well.'

'I'm much better now,' she protested, swallowing the hard knot of panic in her throat, fearful that he would realise just how bad things really were and give up on her. She buried her face against his chest, and felt his hand run through her hair, and thought, now. Before the moment passed again, now.

She wound her arms round him and tilted back her head, suddenly blessing Wilfred, because whatever Viktor wanted, she would know how to provide it; ignorance was the one problem she didn't have. She covered his mouth with hers, first a tentative kiss, then a brazen one, seized with a reckless sense of the inevitable, afraid that if she didn't do this now she would lose him for ever. His lack of reciprocation didn't worry her at first; Wilfred had liked her to do all the work, if only because he needed all the help he could get. Wilfred believed in women taking the initiative and continually bemoaned his wife's inhibitions. Wilfred was a lazy slob.

'Stop it.' He pulled her hand away from his flies, as if it were some revolting parasite, and threw it back at her. 'Don't you understand anything at all? I don't want any favours or charity. I don't want to be *paid*. Anything I want, I take it. I help myself. If I feel like a fuck, I'll go out and find myself one without all this bloody drama. You're neurotic enough as it is.'

Cassie flushed a deep, blotchy red, leapt to her feet, and stormed into the hallway. Viktor followed angrily and grabbed hold of her arm.

'And don't ever try to manipulate me again. I don't ever do anything I don't want to do. Not for you, not for anybody.'

'Hypocrite. You wanted to all right. You've wanted to right

183

from the start. Why else would you bother with me? I'm quite good at it, you know. You missed a freebie. I was taught by an expert, I know how to raise the dead. Perhaps I missed my vocation. If I charged you a hundred francs would you reconsider?'

'Shut up!'

'You don't believe me, do you? You want to think of me as innocent and shy and trusting. Well, you're wrong. There's nothing I won't do in return for a bit of attention, and I don't expect anything for nothing, specially not love. Is that what you're afraid I'm after? *Love*?' Her voice sank into a sneer. 'You must think I'm an idiot. No one else has ever loved me, why the hell should you?'

The words poured out of her like lava, showering him with spittle. Viktor seized her by the shoulders and tried to shake her into silence, but she was unstoppable, ablaze with her own articulateness.

'Armelle was right about you!' she yelled. 'She said you were afraid of women. She said you were a repressed homosexual!'

Viktor let go of her abruptly and walked back into the living room, knowing that she would follow him and apologise. She wouldn't have the nerve to walk out on him now, not after a remark like that. He sat down and waited, and after a moment's silence she appeared at the doorway, right on cue.

'I wish you were,' she said sheepishly, by way of retraction. 'Then I would know where I stood.' Her voice wavered perilously on the brink of tears.

'Don't start blubbering on me, for God's sake.'

'Have you ever seen me cry?'

He hadn't. In a rare moment of weakness he had told her about his mother weeping in the night, disguising his phobia as a warning. She had respected it rigorously ever since, despite endless provocation. A huge wave of remorse knocked him flat.

'I'm sorry, Cassie.'

'So am I. Can we be friends again?'

She sat down beside him, head tilted forward so that she could hide behind her hair.

'Listen to me,' he said carefully. 'I spend time with you because I want to. No other reason. I never do anything unless I want to, remember?'

He put his arm round her, and she turned towards him and mumbled something into his shoulder.

'What was that?' He pulled back the curtain of hair so that he could see her face.

'I meant what I said just now. About not being able to manage on my own. I'm scared. Sometimes I feel I can't bear it any more. That I'm going mad.'

Viktor thought of her pills, safely stowed away in his sock drawer, and wondered yet again whether he was wrong to think that between them they knew better than the entire medical profession. He was probably the only person in the world who would endorse her private revolt as being worthwhile, important – no, *essential*. Revolution was the price of freedom and lasting peace, if you believed the gospel according to Armelle. The doctrine was sound, for all its false disciples. Freedom and lasting peace. They were surely worth a bit of pain.

'I'm so glad you could make it,' gushed Armelle. She strolled over to the cocktail cabinet and poured *pastis* and water into a tall glass, which she handed to Alain with the graciousness of a born hostess. 'I would have contacted you sooner, but there's been so much going on at Nanterre. Second year sociology are boycotting the exams. We're hoping other departments will follow suit—'

'You didn't ask me to your father's house to tell me about Nanterre.'

'Why not? I thought it might give you some ideas. We occupied the large lecture theatre the other day. Some German activists came to give a talk. We've got lots of ideas for next term. Have you ever thought of occupying the factory until my father meets all your demands?'

'Get to the point, Armelle. If you ever write to me at my parents' place again . . . How did you get my address?'

'From your personnel record, of course. The same old trout's been running the department ever since I was knee high. I told

185

her I was doing a project for my sociology course and she gave me the run of her files.'

Alain shifted uncomfortably in his chair. He had convinced himself that the only reason he had come was to prevent her turning up, unannounced, at his home and causing an embarrassing scene. But that wasn't the reason at all. Just the sight of her was a reminder that his motives were much simpler and baser than that.

'How's your new girlfriend?' asked Armelle sweetly.

'What new girlfriend?'

'Come now. You surely don't expect me to believe you've been doing without it all this time?'

Now was the moment to tell her about Chantal. But the admission stuck in his throat. Her fury he could bear, but not her scorn.

'What's this in aid of, Armelle? Is your father going to walk in any minute? Is that what all this is about?'

'I told you, Papa is away on business. And Odile has taken herself to the house in Provence for Easter. That's why I couldn't meet you at Cassie's place – she's not giving lessons this week. And I can hardly take you to the apartment. Rob wouldn't like it. He's been so good to me. I think I love him.'

'I'm glad to hear it.'

'Rob understands me. He respects me as a person, as a woman. But then he's an American, of course. He's used to American women. No American woman would put up with the kind of treatment we take for granted in Europe. My friend Claudine says that—'

'I don't care what your friend Claudine says. What is it you want from me, Armelle? We're wasting time.'

'What's she like in bed, this girl of yours?'

'My sex life is no concern of yours.'

'I hope she's on the Pill. Or is she a Catholic?' She crossed herself and assumed an expression of idiotic piety. And then, with the smug rictus of some satanic madonna, 'Did you honestly think I wouldn't find out?'

Alain didn't answer, loathing her, wanting to wipe that taunting look off her face.

'I assume she's pregnant?' continued Armelle sweetly. 'I

can't believe there's any other reason. You may be stupid, but not *that* stupid.'

'I would have broken it off with you anyway. I gave you my reasons. It's finished.'

'Liar. Do you remember the last time we made love?' How could he forget? It had stuck in his mind like a piece of gristle caught between two teeth. 'Does she let you do things like that?'

'Shut up.'

'I understood you right from the first. All your life people have walked all over you. You're trapped, and you know you're trapped. The only thing that can save you is the revolution, but until that happens you need someone else to take it out on. Someone who makes you feel . . . powerful.'

'If-you're thinking of blackmailing me, you can forget it. Chantal isn't a hysterical bourgeois bitch like you. She'll stand by me whatever happens.'

'She hasn't got much choice, has she, poor swollen sow. I expect she lost the sight of one eye the day you married her.'

'That's enough.' His palms began itching. 'You've had the last laugh, as you think. Now go to hell.'

Alain marched into the hall and tried to open the front door, without success.

'It's locked,' purred a goading voice behind him.

He pulled uselessly at the handle.

'Where's the key?' he hissed, furious now. He had walked straight into a trap, but of course he had known that; that was why he had come . . . 'Give it to me, or I'll beat the shit out of you until you do.'

Armelle smirked.

'Why do you suppose I went for a pee as soon as we arrived? The key is in a very safe place. But you're welcome to look for it.'

Slowly, she unzipped her skirt and let it fall to the floor, revealing her lack of slip or panties. She stood with her legs apart and stuck an exploratory finger into her vagina.

'It's still there,' she confirmed sweetly. 'Help yourself.'

'Give me the key,' repeated Alain, eyes flashing. Armelle bared her teeth in anticipation. She had never made him genuinely angry before. Before it had all been for show. But now she had nothing to lose. With one swift movement, she pulled open the front of her blouse, tearing off all the buttons, took it off, and ripped it in two. Then she crossed her arms over her bare breasts and shouted feebly, 'Rape! Rape!' And then louder now, '*Au secours! Au sec—*'

Her voice rose to full-blooded shriek. Alain clapped one hand over her mouth, swivelled her round and held her immobile while he tried to force his hand between her legs, but she squeezed her thighs together, barring his entry, and flailed wildly with her elbows. How often had they played this game before? How often had he had to 'overpower' her? He thought of Chantal with her placid compliance, as cosy and wholesome as new-baked bread. Chantal, who thought that his sudden loss of libido was out of respect for her pregnancy, who had thanked him for being 'considerate'. Thinking of Chantal was his undoing . . .

'Armelle,' he began, hopelessly, but then she began sobbing, and kissing him frantically, sinking to her knees and dragging him on to the floor. And then she was crawling all over him, her mouth and hands were everywhere at once, like a swarm of locusts gorging on his flesh. Only when she was sure of him did she fall away from him, like a corpse, and lie there, waiting for him to impose his wicked will on her.

The key slid out of her, warm and wet, on a torrent of desire, unlocking her. For once she forgot her ritual moan of virginal pain, unable to keep up the pretence of violation. Brutally, savagely, he unleashed all his misery and frustration, frightening her, disgusting himself. It had been intended as a punishment, but she took it as a reward. It had been meant as revenge, but he knew it was capitulation. Before it had always been an act, but this time it was genuine. She had got what she wanted at last.

Prague, 10 April 1968

Dear Babička,

Thank you for suggesting that I call you that. And for your very kind letter. As you say, this way we can get to know each other a little before I arrive. As for your warning to be 'discreet', you really don't need to worry any more. Your letter arrived untouched and this one will reach you the same way.

I have now had clearance from my supervisor on my holiday dates. I will be leaving on the Saturday morning train and arriving at the Gare de L'Est on Sunday, 19 May, at four minutes past seven, a.m. Sorry to be so horribly early! Naturally I'm very excited about my visit, but I'm sure the next few weeks will pass in a flash. There is so much going on at the moment that the time just flies. The other day Jan, my boyfriend, and I went to a youth rally at the Exhibition Hall, and so many people turned up that they had to use the adjoining buildings for the overflow – there were over 20,000 of us in the main hall alone. The politicians sat on the platform and answered questions from students and young workers for eight solid hours. We gave them quite a grilling, I can tell you, as we weren't prepared to be fobbed off with empty promises. The discussion got quite heated at times, specially as we knew there were loads of police outside, but they were obviously under orders to keep a low profile and didn't give us any trouble. To think that only six months ago students got beaten up and sent to prison just for taking part in a peaceful demonstration! This gives you some idea of how much, and how fast, things have changed.

I don't expect people in the West take much interest in what goes on here – as Karel says, they never did in the past! – so I thought you'd be interested in hearing the news first hand from your own personal foreign correspondent. Besides, it's good practice for me. Jan has said I ought to try writing a feature on my visit to Paris for his new youth magazine. It's called *Spring Tide* and we are hoping to get the first issue out by the end of this month. I say 'we' because I am typing the stencils, although I do change the odd word here and there, on the quiet!

Karel's bronchitis is much better. I hardly see him at the moment, as he's been elected to the committee of the local branch of Club 231 and is out nearly every evening.

The inaugural meeting was a huge success, and incredible numbers of people are applying to join all over the country. I don't think anyone realised just how many political prisoners there were. It will be wonderful if Karel can clear his name at last. They're pressing for full personal, social and political rehabilitation plus financial compensation, of course, to include loss of earnings, value of confiscated property and damage to health. It's good to see him taking an interest in life again, even though he's as much of an old pessimist as ever – or pretends to be.

Anyway, a lot of people are obviously terrified that their sins will finally find them out. Every day this month some bigwig or other has committed suicide – mainly members of the secret police who were in office during the fifties. The papers here are full of it. Naturally the old guard are closing ranks and accusing the progressives of encouraging a witch-hunt and trying to win cheap popularity. But now that it's all coming out about what went on under Stalin and Gottwald – not to mention Novotny – they've lost all credibility. At public meetings there are usually a few diehards who try to barrack the speakers, but on the whole people don't bother to shout them down, because after all, free speech means free speech, and they are entitled to have their say along with everyone else.

Don't tell Karel I told you, but he has started writing his memoirs. He didn't want me to know, but he couldn't very well hide what he was doing, scribbling away far into the night. I am honour bound not to sneak a look until he has finished, but I have offered to type his manuscript for him. The way things are going, he might even manage to get it published!

It's very nice of Viktor to offer to take time off to show me round Paris. But I really don't want him to go to any trouble on my account. I'm sure he can find better things to do than entertain a poor relation, and—

Eva shook her head and crossed out the last two sentences. It sounded as if she were being sarcastic, and so she was. But

Marta was the founder member of the Viktor Brožek fan club, and she would have to pretend to like him, for her sake.

Please tell him how much I appreciate the offer. I suppose he still remembers me as a snotty little brat. I sincerely hope he won't recognise me!

Not that she had changed that much. She was still as round-faced and plump as ever. In any case, she didn't care what Viktor thought of her. Jan never stopped telling her she was beautiful. Which only went to show that love was blind.

Perhaps she ought to sleep with him before she went to Paris. Then she would feel properly grown up, more confident, less nervous. It sounded feeble to admit she was nervous, but she was. Just as she was beginning to find her feet, to think of herself as an adult, to take an active part in what was going on, to consider her own opinion worth expressing, she faced the daunting prospect of going back to being a child again. In Paris she would feel, and seem, ignorant, unsophisticated, and boring. It seemed ridiculous to say that in some ways she would rather have stayed at home when this trip had been all she had dreamed of for years. Everyone kept saying things like 'When are you off?' And 'Lucky you' and 'Not long now', and superficially she found it easy to be enthusiastic, to tell herself what a wonderful time she would have. But then she thought of all the things that would be happening while she was gone and cursed herself for her bad timing. Only a few months ago she had flirted shamefully with the notion of never coming back. Now the idea seemed as ludicrous and outdated as her childhood ambition to be a ballerina. She even found herself worrying that the new, self-assured Jan might find himself another girlfriend in her absence, one who could give him what he wanted.

She looked up and saw the framed photograph of Viktor looking down at her from the wall with that supercilious smile of his. Its position was such that she could feel his eyes upon her every time she and Jan had a snogging session on the settee. Sometimes she could almost hear him laughing at their clumsy, juvenile gropings, filling her with a reckless desire to shock. And yet she still held back, mistrusting her own motives . . .

Viktor. How idiotic it was to be so hung up about someone she couldn't even remember. She hoped that he would turn out to be as conceited and snobbish as she imagined him. And once she had arrived she would find plenty to do without having to rely on him to entertain her. Various elderly Czech ladies were apparently looking forward to meeting her. That sounded like loads of fun . . .

Counting the days till 19 May,
All my love,
Eva.

'I feel so confused,' wept Armelle. 'I don't know what to do.'

'Sounds to me like you just can't function without a man in tow,' said Claudine sceptically. 'Or preferably two men in tow.'

Armelle wiped her eyes. 'When I got back, Rob was waiting up for me. He asked me where I'd been, so I lied, of course. And then almost immediately I began to feel guilty. I thought that this way I wouldn't be dependent on either of them, but it's only made things worse.'

'Why don't you tell him the truth?'

'He'd never agree to share me. He'd throw me out.'

'Rob? I doubt it. He looks the type to put up with almost anything.'

'You don't know him like I do. When I first met him I thought he was just another American hippie, you know, one of those drop-outs who thinks you can change the world with drugs and rock music. But that's just a front. He's very demanding, you know. Very passionate and possessive.'

'Then stop seeing Alain.'

'I can't.'

'Then break it off with Rob.'

'I can't do that either.' Alain might be the cake she wanted to eat, but Rob was the one she had to have. And adultery had a sweetness all its own.

'Then you'll have to carry on as you are, and swallow your guilt,' shrugged Claudine. 'Do you have somewhere to take him?'

'I've still got Cassie's key.'

'Can you trust her?'

'Not really. She might tell Viktor. He'd jump at any excuse to get Rob away from me. But I know when she teaches Odile, so if we time it right she needn't find out.'

The risk of discovery appalled and excited her, adding a new and devilish twist of danger. Last night, after Alain, Rob had asked, quite casually, where she had been and she had found herself blushing, and caught the penetrating look in his eye and felt deliciously afraid. He looked so different without the beard. She had hoped that the vanished hair would reveal some hidden weakness, but the line of his naked jaw was hard, uncompromising; the Christ-like benevolence had fled. The beard had softened his face, not strengthened it; it had been a mask, not plumage.

'Is it really worth it? Or do you enjoy feeling guilty?'

'Perhaps. It wouldn't be surprising.'

'Meaning?'

'Nothing.'

'You can tell me. I'm not a rival, remember.'

That much was true. Perhaps that was why she felt so comfortable with Claudine. Armelle had a poor track record with female friends. Some man always seemed to get in the way. And men friends, of course, were a contradiction in terms. Even Rob. Especially Rob . . .

'I can't tell you. I've never told anybody.'

'I told you my secret, didn't I? So if I split on you, you can do the same to me.'

Armelle began crying again. Claudine took it in her stride, handing her a clean hanky and waiting patiently for her to collect herself.

'Promise you won't be shocked.'

'Not possible. We've both slept with Étienne, remember. If he did the things to you he did to me, you wouldn't need to ask me that.'

'Did he . . . ?' Armelle whispered the rest of the question. Claudine nodded and whispered something back. They both collapsed into giggles.

'Now tell me. Or don't. It's up to you.'

Armelle hovered on the brink of confession, testing the icy waters of her shame.

'Oh . . . it's nothing original. I was raped, that's all. Except that I didn't report it, I didn't even resist. So I suppose it wasn't really rape at all.'

'How old were you?'

'Fourteen. It wasn't his fault. I led him on.'

'You're making excuses for him. You were only a child!'

'I carried on letting it happen, for nearly two years. So I suppose I must have liked it. Even though I hated doing it. Does that make sense? And then he finally dumped me for another woman. I should have been relieved, but I was hurt, and angry. There was a row. He called me a little slut. That's what I am. That's what I'll always be. A slut.'

Claudine put an arm round her. 'That word was invented by a man. Don't let me hear you use it ever again. Why didn't you tell your parents?'

'It was soon after Maman left home. I was pretty screwed up at the time.'

'What about your father?'

Armelle didn't answer.

'Armelle?'

'Don't make me say it, okay? Isn't it bad enough without th-that? Besides, it was my fault!'

'Oh God. My poor baby.'

'I wanted to tell Rob. But I couldn't do it. He's a man. He'd despise me.'

'Yes,' agreed Claudine bitterly. 'Yes. He probably would.'

Hearing the unmistakable rap on the door, Marta hurried to let Viktor in, her jaw falling open as she saw that he had a girl with him.

'This is my friend Cassie,' he said, in the most offhand way possible. 'Cassie, meet my old tyrant of a grandmother.'

Cassie presented her with a huge, rather ragged bunch of spring flowers – daffodils, red tulips and narcissus. Marta hid her surprise behind a flurry of thanks and hospitality. Not just surprise that Viktor had, at long last, brought a girl home to meet her, but surprise at the girl herself. She was pretty enough, in a pale, haunted kind of way, despite the fashionable fringe obscuring half her face, the two sooty holes for eyes and the blotted-out lips. But she was much too tall for a woman, and terribly skinny – hardly the buxom, blowsy type she would have expected Viktor to go for, not that that was any bad thing. And it was charming of her to bring flowers. She must have chosen and paid for them herself, because Viktor always brought big, extravagant hothouse blooms wrapped in cellophane.

'I'm very pleased to meet you,' said Marta, extending a bony hand. 'Will you stay for lunch? I don't have anything special ready, but ...'

'Viktor keeps telling me what a good cook you are,' said Cassie. Despite her limp appearance she had firm grip and a nice, shy smile. 'I hope you don't mind me coming without an invitation.'

'Not at all. I love company. Any friend of Viktor's is always welcome.'

She fetched a vase, and began arranging the flowers with evident pleasure.

'By the way,' said Viktor, 'Cassie knows what I do. I told her you'd taught me everything I know, so there's no point in pretending to be respectable.'

Marta's smile metamorphosed into a ferocious glare. Cassie tried too late to disguise a strangled giggle as a cough.

'It's no laughing matter,' Marta rebuked her sharply, waving a daffodil at her guest. 'I advise you to have nothing to do with him. No decent girl should give him the time of day.' And then, belying her words, 'Sit down, sit down.'

Cassie deposited herself in a squashy armchair which groaned under her weight and completely swallowed her up.

'So what do you do, mademoiselle?' Useless to expect Viktor to tell her anything afterwards. She would have to pump the girl herself.

'Oh, please call me Cassie. I'm a student.'

Marta nodded approvingly. A nice, educated girl. What on earth was she doing with a boy like Viktor?

'And your family – do they live here in Paris?'

'No. I'm from London. I'm only here until July.'

'Really? I would never have guessed. You speak very good French.'

'Rubbish,' snorted Viktor. 'It's just that you speak it even worse than she does.'

Marta flung him a behave-yourself look. But at least the girl didn't seem to take offence.

'London is somewhere I've always wanted to see,' she continued, anxious to make the poor child feel welcome. She must have come expecting some kind of thieves' kitchen. 'My husband and I were due to visit Oxford in 1935. He was a distinguished scholar, you know, of very good family. We haven't always lived like this.' She cast an apologetic arm around the room. 'But he died, quite suddenly, a few weeks before we were due to travel. His heart just gave out, without any warning. And he was only fifty-two.' She gave the vase pride of place on top of the television set. 'I often wonder how things would have turned out if I'd taken Viktor to England, instead of France. When my husband was alive, we spent such a pleasant year in Paris. It was quite a different city in the thirties, much more refined and civilised. Of course, those days will never come again, here or anywhere else. I put it all down to the war.'

'Here we go,' said Viktor. 'The life story.' He gave Cassie a sly, cruel look. 'That'll teach you not to gatecrash in future.'

Cassie didn't deign to acknowledge this remark, except by an involuntary flush. For the first time ever she had been bold enough to call round at Viktor's apartment on the off-chance, several hours ahead of their agreed rendezvous, only to encounter him on the staircase, already on his way out. But after a second's indecision, he had said, quite casually, that she might as well come with him, without telling her where they were going until the last minute. By then it was too late to back out and now, inevitably, she felt in the way, as he must have known she would. It was yet another variant on the Eiffel Tower, or the disco in Montparnasse, or any of the other ordeals he had devised for her.

'I just heard from Eva,' said Marta, turning to her grandson. 'She's arriving in the middle of next month. I'll read you her letter later. She thanks you very nicely for offering to show her round.'

'I didn't offer,' muttered Viktor. 'You press-ganged me into it.'

'My son's stepdaughter,' explained Marta. 'She was only a baby when we left Prague. This is her first visit to the West.'

'Where the streets are paved with gold,' put in Viktor, 'and fried chickens sing in every treetop.'

'He doesn't know when he's well off,' said Marta. 'When I think of the life he would have had, if we'd stayed –'

'If we'd stayed, they'd have taught me the dignity of honest socialist toil,' agreed Viktor. 'I'd be slaving away all month for less than I make in an afternoon. But thanks to your foresight, Babička, I'm my own boss. Long live private enterprise.'

'Just wait till you have children of your own. You'll learn what it is to worry. Do you have any brothers and sisters, Cassie?'

'Two brothers. Both older than me.'

'That's nice. Only children are always spoilt.' Viktor raised his eyes to heaven and helped himself to an apple. 'I hoped to have a big family, but it wasn't to be. We only had the one. Though perhaps it was just as well. I knew women who lost all their children in the war.' She shook her head. 'Those were terrible years. My apartment was a weapons store you know, in readiness for the uprising. Guns under the floorboards, ammunition sewn into the mattress. The factory where my son worked even had a secret underground vault. People think we Czechs just sat the war out, but ordinary people were risking their lives every day. The Resistance transmitted thousands of messages to the Allies, not that they got thanks for it.'

'For God's sake, Babička. She doesn't want to hear all that stuff. Can't you see she's bored stiff?'

'No, I'm not,' said Cassie with spirit, greedy for any pointers to Viktor's past.

'I'll tell you all about it, my dear, one day when Viktor isn't here to interrupt. Of course, those years were as nothing compared to what followed. After what happened to Viktor's father, we had no choice but to flee the country. But I still dream of my beautiful Prague.'

Viktor began playing a mock violin with a smile of seraphic cynicism.

'When are we going to eat?' he demanded. 'That's the only reason we came here, after all.' Marta sighed and creaked to her feet. Noticing the bandage on her leg under the thick lisle stocking, Cassie jumped up.

'Can I help?' she asked, hoping that her minimal domestic skills would not be put to the test.

'Thank you, dear. I always have food ready. It won't take us a minute. Viktor, go out and buy some wine.'

Viktor looked at her suspiciously, shrugged, and sauntered off. Marta opened a cupboard and extracted a saucepan, revealing an unopened bottle of Bordeaux.

'I feel dreadful putting you to all this trouble,' said Cassie.

'I like going to trouble. I like to see Viktor enjoy his food. Don't you ever eat? You're so thin!' She looked Cassie up and down. Her tight ribbed jumper emphasised her lack of curves, as did the minuscule apology for a skirt wound round a non-existent bottom.

'I burn it up quickly,' said Cassie, steeling herself to clear her plate. She badly wanted this old lady to approve of her. She imagined them discussing her next time Viktor came here, alone: 'That's a strange girl you brought the other day, Viktor. What do you see in her?' 'Nothing, Babička, she's just a little bit crazy, that's all.' 'Crazy? What's the matter with her?' 'Well, for a start . . .'

Perhaps he told his grandmother everything. Perhaps he had already passed on all her secrets, betrayed her trust. Did telling the person closest to you count as a breach of trust? 'I won't tell a soul,' people said, meaning, 'I won't tell a soul apart from my husband/mother/sister/best friend', or whoever else had a greater claim to loyalty. Which meant the only people you could count on were the ones who had no one at all . . .

'It's nothing special, I'm afraid. If I'd known you were coming . . .' She tossed two thick chops into a pan of hot butter.

'Aren't you having any?' asked Cassie.

'Oh, at my age I only eat one meal a day. Have you known Viktor long?'

'A couple of months.'

'He's never invited anyone home before. Not once. It must be serious.'

'Oh, he didn't invite me, exactly. I just turned up at his place and he said I might as well tag along. I don't usually see him in the mornings. But today . . .'

Today I woke up at three a.m. in a blind panic. I had to get out of bed, I couldn't lie still. And then I thought, I'm not the only person awake, so I walked to Les Halles, in the dark. Awake wasn't the word for it. So much noise and colour, everybody shouting and jostling, and somehow I was part of it, inside it. It was exactly the opposite of the way I've been feeling lately, like I'm the only person in the universe, whizzing round all on my own in space. And before that, for years, I just felt sort of indifferent to everything, like it had nothing to do with me. But suddenly . . . it reminded me of how it used to be ages ago, when I went to the funfair as a kid, or read a good book or saw something terrific at the theatre. I'd forgotten how it felt, it was like the wires connecting up again, it was like black and white turning to colour. And then I had a huge plate of onion soup, just for fun, even though I don't much like onions, and went home and slept right through till eleven o'clock. And when I woke up I was so pleased with myself, that I had to rush off and tell Viktor about it. And then on the way, this flower seller smiled at me, and I realised that she was smiling back – so I bought a huge bunch of flowers . . .

' . . . But today I just happened to be passing, so I thought I'd see if Viktor was in. He would never have brought me otherwise.'

Marta looked unconvinced. Probably she thought they'd spent the night together and he hadn't been able to shake her off.

'Viktor never does anything he doesn't want to do,' said Marta, with feeling. 'You look like a nice, quiet sort of girl. You could be a good influence on him.' The inference was clear. The most hopeless case could be redeemed by the love of a good woman.

'I doubt it. He doesn't listen to anything I say.'

'You have to stand up to him. Don't be afraid of that sarcastic tongue of his. He's much too used to getting his own way. My fault, I suppose. But he's all I have left. Did he tell you what happened to his parents?'

'Just that his mother died when he was a child,' said Cassie. 'He never talks about his father, though. And he doesn't like me asking questions.'

'Karel was a difficult man. Very wrapped up in his work. For the first three years of Viktor's life he barely knew him. I think it was difficult for him to adjust to being a father. And of course, he had no experience of children, no younger brothers or sisters. He was far too strict with Viktor, and his mother spoiled him to make up for it. Or perhaps it was the other way round. You mustn't judge him too harshly. But you mustn't make too many allowances for him either.'

She transferred the chops to the oven and threw some sliced cooked potatoes into their juices. The pan hissed loudly.

'I'd like to see Viktor settled before I die,' she continued, turning down the heat. 'Do you . . . care for him at all?'

Cassie didn't answer.

'I'm sorry. I'm embarrassing you.'

'I'm not embarrassed. Viktor's the one who'd be embarrassed. Yes, I do care for him. But I can hardly tell him that, can I? Please don't say anything to him. He'd run a mile.'

Marta sighed. 'There's a lot of good in him.'

'I know.'

'But of course your family wouldn't approve of him.' It was a weary acknowledgment of fact, devoid of rancour.

'He wouldn't approve of my family. He—'

The front door slammed, indicating Viktor's return. Marta sent Cassie to join him.

'What's she been saying about me?' he said as he uncorked the bottle.

'Wouldn't you like to know.'

'I must be soft in the head, bringing you here. I expect the two of you will gang up on me now.' Cassie made a threatening gesture with a table knife. 'Do you like her?'

'Of course. I think she likes me too.'

'Naturally. You're quiet and polite and well brought up. Well, let's hope she gets the wrong idea. It might shut her up for a bit. Babička! Come and have some wine!' There was no reply, except for the sound of frying. Viktor sat back and gestured round the room.

'It's not that I'm mean,' he said, indicating the well-worn carpet, the second-hand furniture, and the ancient sewing machine, incongruously set off by a modern stereo player and an upright piano in gleaming mahogany. Cassie noticed a framed photograph on the sideboard of a young man holding a little boy, both of whom looked like Viktor. 'She won't let me help her. It's her way of punishing me.'

'Well, you can't expect her to condone what you do. Any more than I do.'

'God, what a prig you are sometimes.' He handed her a glass. 'We arrived here with one small suitcase and no money. Czech currency's useless in the West anyway. Marta lost all her savings in the post-war devaluation, she ended up selling all her jewellery to bribe our way out of the country. Stuff that had been in the family for years.'

That explained a lot, thought Cassie. Every time he deprived some ageing *bourgeoise* of her trinkets, he was getting a bit of his own back.

'She refused to take any handouts, so she ruined her eyes on that machine over there. That damned whirring noise was the first thing I heard in the morning and the last thing I heard at night. When I was about ten years old I decided I'd had enough of being poor. By the time I was fourteen I was picking up fifty francs in an afternoon. I saved it all up until it was worth something and then I handed it to Marta in an envelope. She gave me the hiding of my life and put the lot in the poor-box when no one was looking. She told me then that she wouldn't take a sou from me, and she's never relented, except to send dollars to Prague, the biggest poor-box of them all. Which means that I can't spend it on myself, either. How can I live in a smart place and drive a sports car and all the rest of it when she lives like a pauper?'

'Why don't you give in and get a job for a while, just to please her?'

'For a while? You mean until she croaks?'

'Yes. No. I mean—'

'She'd live for ever, out of sheer bloody-mindedness. And stop lecturing me. It's bad enough having to put on an act for this kid who's coming over.' His face broke into a malevolent grin. 'Of course. What a brilliant idea . . .'

Marta waddled back into the room with all the dignity of a dowager duchess and cleared the table of her sewing things, throwing a tablecloth over it. Viktor poured himself another glass of wine.

'Cassie's simply dying to meet Eva,' he said. 'She's offered to show her round Paris. Isn't that nice of her?'

'Really?' Marta's face broke into a delighted smile. 'But my dear, that's so kind! Viktor's so unreliable, and I can't walk far because of this wretched leg of mine. Well, I must say, that's a weight off my mind. What a charming suggestion.'

Viktor sat back in his chair, evidently well pleased with himself.

'It's my pleasure,' said Cassie, determined not to bat an eyelid. And then, equally determined to retaliate, 'Can I ask you a favour in return?'

'Of course, my dear.'

'Could I use your sewing machine? I volunteered to sew some tunics for the school production of St Joan next term and doing them by hand takes so long.'

'You volunteered?' echoed Viktor, patently amazed.

'It was an impulse. I thought it would help pass the time during the vacation. They're already cut and pinned. It's just straightforward seams.'

'No problem. You can come round any time that suits you. I'm always in. It will mean we can have a nice long chat.' She gave Viktor a look which made it plain that his presence would be superfluous.

'Why don't you just do them for her?' said Viktor, smelling a conspiracy. 'She can give them to me and I'll drop them off to you.'

'I'm afraid my eyes get tired these days,' said Marta, affecting to ignore this remark. 'Otherwise I'd offer to stitch them myself. Perhaps you'd like to run yourself up a few little skirts while you're here.' She rummaged in a wicker chest and drew out a couple of yards of salmon pink crimplene. 'This piece was left over from a suit I made for one of my regulars. It would just do nicely.'

Cassie didn't dare look at Viktor, terrified that she would start giggling again and hurt the old girl's feelings. Marta whipped out a tape measure and slipped it round Cassie's waist and hips, clucking at her lack of centimetres.

'I'll cut it a bit on the large side,' she said, 'to give you room to put on a few pounds. This skirt is very short, my dear.'

'That's the length we wear them in London. I meant to take all my hems down when I arrived, but I never got round to it.'

'She pretends not to notice when men stare at her in the street,' interjected Viktor sourly. 'She lives in a little world of her own. Don't you, Cassie darling?'

'Please make it a little bit longer,' said Cassie. 'Down to about here.' She indicated the normal Parisian hemline, a good two inches lower than its English equivalent.

'You're wasting your time, Babička. She'll never wear it. She buys all her stuff from Yves St Laurent.'

'Of course I'll wear it,' insisted Cassie, flinging him a shut-up look.

'I'm going to make a few things for Eva to take back to Prague with her. There's no choice in the shops out there. She sent me her measurements. Perhaps you'd choose some fabrics for me so I can get busy before she arrives. You would know what young girls like much better than I do.'

'What about your tired old eyes?' said Viktor.

'Some things I can do with my eyes shut.' She hobbled back to the kitchen to dish up the meal.

'You don't know what you're letting yourself in for,' said Viktor curtly. 'She's a lonely old woman, she'll witter on for hours on end to anyone who'll listen to her. You'll have Munich and the war and the Communist takeover coming out of your ears. Elderly Slavs are all dotty, didn't you know? The Czechs are nearly as bad as the bloody Poles. Don't blame me if she drives you up the wall.'

Cassie turned away to hide the involuntary smile of antici- pation. Little by little, she would find out all about him, delve into his life the way he had delved into hers, dismantle all his pieces and put them together again. It was what he wanted, really. He couldn't lose face by telling her things, himself, but he didn't mind Marta doing it for him, because Marta was a sentimental old gasbag, to use his own charming epithet, and he wasn't accountable for anything she said. Bringing her here was as near to a self-revelation as he had ever come, and the fact that it had happened 'by accident' was pure camouflage.

To have invited her would have seemed like too much of a concession; he had been waiting for just such a chance opportunity as this.

Yes, little by little she would find out all about him. There was more than one way to make love.

EIGHT

May 1968

Chantal stirred in her sleep as Alain, awake since dawn, heard his mother's gentle tap on their door. Relieved that it was time to get up, he heaved himself gingerly out of bed.

'*Chéri?* What time is it?'

'Early. Go back to sleep.' She sat up in bed and groaned. 'Remember what the doctor said.'

'I'll get you some breakfast.'

'You'll do no such thing. Lie down again. I'll bring you a bowl of coffee in a moment.'

'No.' She shuddered in disgust and forced a cheerful smile. He mustn't think her feeble and self-pitying. But she felt so horribly ill . . .

'Tea then. Chocolate. Whatever you want.'

'I don't want anything. I'm sorry to be like this, Alain. Just when we need all the money we can get. We'll never get a place of our own at this rate . . . '

'Don't apologise. It's not your fault.'

'Maybe they'll give me something at the hospital today, so that I can go back to work.'

'Don't worry about work. We'll manage.'

'Oh, Alain! You're such a good husband to me.' She sat up in bed too suddenly, and her intended embrace was aborted by a wave of nausea that sent her rushing from the room. Hearing his mother clucking and fussing in the hallway, Alain pulled on his overalls and decided to skip both his ablutions and his breakfast.

'I'm off,' he said, giving his mother a brief kiss, just as Chantal emerged, whey-faced, from the bathroom. 'I won't be home till late, by the way. Don't save dinner for me.'

'Again?' demanded Jeanne. 'What is it this time?'

'Just a meeting with some comrades.'

She exchanged glances with her daughter-in-law. 'So there *is* a splinter group,' his mother accused him. 'Alain, for God's sake, remember what your father told you. With Chantal off work, you can't risk—'

'It's all right,' began Chantal stolidly, but Jeanne thundered through her interruption like a non-stop train.

'Don't you realise what this poor girl is going through? Haven't you any consideration?'

'Don't interfere, Maman,' said Alain tightly, adding, 'Chantal, if you ask me not to go to this meeting then I won't go.'

He almost hoped she would. But yet again she disappointed him.

'Of course you must go,' she said staunchly. 'I shall have your mother here with me. And I'll be fine by tonight. I'm sure they'll give me something to make me feel better. You mustn't disappoint your friends.'

He squeezed her hand, ignoring his mother's baleful look of disapproval. The family obsession that he was setting up a *groupuscule* of extremists served to divert them from more mundane suspicions. But then, even if Chantal did suspect, she would never say so. She was too sensible for that. Sometimes he wished she would shriek abuse at him, burden him with querulous demands, complain about the infrequency of their lovemaking. He bitterly resented her loyalty and forbearance, and the sight of her suffering filled him with pity and revulsion.

Reluctant to clock on early, he hung around outside the factory gates, smoking a cigarette, till the shift started to arrive, already weary with the prospect of another long monotonous day in the prison-like complex of long, low buildings, linked by ramps and covered walkways, pulsating with the inhuman din of machinery. 'Why don't you occupy the factory till my father meets all your demands?' Some hope. Especially now that he had passed up his chance to attack the system from within. He had stubbornly refused to stand as shop steward and Rivière had duly been elected, another blinkered party-liner who would do exactly what he was told. Fellow-renegades had accused Alain of political naïveté, and many of the rank and file thought he had let them down. Perhaps they were right. But it had seemed the only point of honour he had left.

His shift seemed interminable. As usual, he toyed with the possibility of defaulting on his meeting with Armelle, in the way he might have picked at a scab. He felt almost as sorry for her new boyfriend as he did for himself. But the sheer frustration of his life craved some release. Better to take it out on her than on his wife. Two of Chantal's workmates questioned him during his meal break and conveyed messages of advice and sympathy. It seemed like a female conspiracy to increase his sense of guilt. By the time he set off for his rendezvous he felt like a condemned man being granted his dying wish, because this time, every time, he convinced himself that this would be their last encounter.

As he emerged from the Odéon Métro station, an aggressive-looking youth thrust a pamphlet into his hand. Still lost in thought, he didn't bother to read it, walking head down along the Boulevard Saint-Germain towards his agreed meeting place with Armelle, a café on the corner of the Boul'Mich' and the rue des Écoles. Spotting her running towards him, he raised the sheet of blue paper in salutation, but instead of throwing her arms around him in welcome she snatched the leaflet out of his hand, spat on it, and tore it into shreds.

'How can you read that *Occident* shit?' she demanded. 'Why didn't you give the bastard a punch on the nose?'

'I didn't realise. I thought he was one of your lot.'

Sighting another leafleteer on the opposite side of the street, Armelle cupped her hands to her mouth.

'Fascist!' she shrieked. 'Collaborator! Capitalist flunky!'

Alain grasped her firmly by the arm. 'Calm down. What's the matter with you? Are you looking for a fight?'

'Yes!' She turned on him. 'Aren't you?'

'Not necessarily. What's going on?'

'You'll see. Come on.'

With some misgivings, he followed her into the Sorbonne courtyard where a throng of students were chanting slogans. He felt immediately out of place, hostile.

'We're here to protest about the lock-out at Nanterre,' explained Armelle, above the din. 'Just because we tried to protect ourselves against attack from those *Occident* vermin, the lousy Dean's gone and shut the whole place down. We were well prepared for them there, and they knew it. We had catapults, clubs, helmets, we put down oil so their cars would skid. But the cowards didn't show their faces. We might have known they'd turn up here instead.'

She waved excitedly at someone she recognised, a dark, curly-headed youth with a cut lip and the beginnings of a black eye.

'René! What happened to you?'

He grinned lopsidedly. 'I decided to relieve one of our friends outside of his sack of pamphlets.' He pointed to the remains of a small bonfire. 'Did you read what they said?'

'That right-wing pornography? No.'

'Oh, it was very amusing. It called for the suppression of Bolshevik agitators, especially dirty foreign Jews like Dany Cohn-Bendit. They're going to carry him to the German frontier by the scruff of his neck, they say. Over our dead bodies, eh?'

Armelle looked around her, eyes sparkling, her fingers closing round Alain's arms like a vice.

'There must be at least four hundred of us here already,' she said. 'More than a match for *Occident*. Why don't we take a few of them hostage?'

René roared with a good-natured laughter.

'They're pathetic, that's why,' he said cheerfully. 'They're not worth the bother. Why so glum, Armelle? As you say, they're outnumbered. We've got them on the run.' He gestured expansively and returned, smiling, to his group.

'Typical,' muttered Armelle. 'I wonder about him sometimes. Some people can't take anything seriously, not even the revolution.'

'Let them enjoy their fun,' said Alain sourly. He found

students *en masse* loathsome. 'Win or lose, this lot will still get their allowances from Papa. And wind up as the bosses of tomorrow. It's just a game for them.'

'Well, it's not a game for me!' flashed Armelle. Tightening her grip, she dragged him into the interior of the building. He felt instantly intimidated by the long corridors and high ceilings and the musty schoolroom smell. The whole place was a temple to class privilege.

'How long before they close the Sorbonne too?' she demanded. 'What would *you* do if my father tried to lock you out?' She ran ahead of him, disappeared into a doorway, and emerged carrying a wooden chair. 'You'd break your way back in, wouldn't you? Wouldn't you?'

'Perhaps,' conceded Alain. 'But Nanterre is a totally different situation from a factory. For one thing—'

His words were drowned by a splintering crash as Armelle raised the chair over her head and brought it down on the floor.

'What are you doing?'

Another crash, which dislodged one of the legs. She wrestled to pull it out of its socket and handed it to him, before wrenching out another for her own use. 'If those scum out there try to attack us, we'll be ready for them. And the police too, if they try to break it up. Give the *salauds* a taste of their own medicine.' She brandished the splintered stump of her chair leg and ran back into the courtyard with Alain in hot pursuit, fearful that she would run out into the street and take on the whole of *Occident* single-handed.

'Armelle,' he shouted self-consciously, feeling like the hapless owner of a badly trained dog. 'Stay near me. Don't get yourself hurt.' Her eyes were full of the blind, glazed glitter of fantasy, so familiar to him from their lovemaking.

'Then protect me!' she hissed melodramatically. 'Protect me with your life!'

The crowd in the courtyard had grown, more students flooding through the gates every minute. Marshals had been posted at the entrance to keep enemy infiltrators at bay. Word spread round the assembly that no one was to leave; a giant sit-in was to be organised.

The heady atmosphere of unrest was titillating, seductive. Inexorably, Alain felt himself being sucked into it, with the same passionate reluctance that drove him to make love to Armelle. If only this were the factory, if only the silent, apathetic majority could be fired into collective action – spontaneous action, not just a sheep-like response to some official union directive. It was so easy for these kids, undrained by years of drudgery and despair, to think they could change the world. He was consumed with bitter envy and a shameful longing to be one of them.

Several people had by now followed Armelle's example and found themselves extempore weapons, although the atmosphere was still festive rather than warlike.

'They can manage without us for a bit,' said Armelle at last, with the satisfaction of a general surveying his troops. 'This way.'

'Where are we going?'

'Somewhere private.' She ran back into the building, along the corridor, and up a broad stone staircase, checking the doors to the right and left as she went. Finding an empty room, she ushered him inside and closed the door.

'Forget it,' said Alain, several jumps ahead of her. 'Anyone could walk in.'

'Not if we build a barricade,' said Armelle, busily piling up chairs. 'Help me!'

The noise of chanting from outside grew louder. 'To forbid is forbidden! To forbid is forbidden!'

'It's forbidden, of course,' goaded Armelle. 'Like everything else in this shitty place, it's *interdit*. Well?'

She perched herself giddily on the stack of chairs and began writing in lipstick on the window above the double doors, slowly, concentrating on forming each letter back to front: ZONE LIBÉRÉE. Then she jumped down from the swaying edifice and into Alain's arms.

It was a *zone libérée*, and he was her prisoner. He felt like a fish struggling on a hook, his mouth full of spiked bait. She dragged him this way and that, playing with him, torturing him, reeling out and retracting the line, pushing him out of her and forcing him to re-enter her half a dozen times, half a dozen different ways. By the time she finally released him, he felt as if he were swimming in his own blood. It was like a kind of death, and yet it was the only time he felt alive.

'You're a brute,' she sighed contentedly, stretching out luxuriously on the cracked brown lino as if it were a feather bed draped in silk. The noise outside had reached fever pitch, but she seemed not to hear it, lost in her own raucous thoughts. 'I hope Rob doesn't notice my bruises,' she continued, inspecting her hip bones. 'The floor was so hard. I can hardly move.'

'You're a bitch, Armelle. Is he out there somewhere? Are we supposed to fight over you, is that it?'

'No, no, he's distributing leaflets at the Renault factory today. If he's got any left over, he might even catch the late shift at MerTech. I'm very careful to protect you, Alain. He'd kill you if he found out. Me too, probably. He's in love with me, you know. He wants me all the time. And he's so big . . . everywhere. Much bigger than you.'

'Good for him.'

'But nothing happens, unless I think of you. Do you think about me when you're in bed with your wife?'

'That's enough, Armelle. Get dressed, for God's sake. What's going on out there?' He crossed to the window and looked down at the scene below. 'Something's happening. Christ, look at that.'

Armelle rushed to his side, clapped her hand to her mouth, and hastily retrieved her nether garments.

'Let's get out there,' she said. 'It's beginning.'

'It's not just police,' muttered Alain, to himself. 'It's the CRS.'

'The same CRS they use to break up strikes. The same CRS that beat up the miners. They're your enemy too, Alain, not just ours. They're the enemy of all the workers.'

Alain felt his skin prickle. He hated all police, but the riot squads symbolised state oppression in its crudest, most blatant form. Suddenly it didn't matter that they were students out there, people he disliked and mistrusted on principle. For once they had a common foe.

He tore down their makeshift barricade and raced downstairs, with Armelle at his heels. 'Here,' she panted, handing him the chair leg. 'Defend yourself.' But before they could

211

reach the scene of the action they were accosted by a brace of student union reps, wearing UNEF armbands.

'No violence,' said one of them, holding out his hand for their weapons. 'It's been agreed that they'll check our identity cards and let us go.'

'Let us go?' repeated Armelle, incredulously. 'This is *our* territory, the police have no right coming here. You're surely not going to let them get away with this?'

'We don't want people to get hurt. Specially the women. Don't play into their hands.'

'He's right,' muttered Alain, relinquishing his club. 'They're brutes, Armelle. They'd jump at any excuse to beat people up.'

'Coward!'

For reply, Alain pulled her hand behind her back and twisted it. She screamed with pain as her grip relaxed and she dropped her weapon on the ground.

'Control yourself,' he said, through clenched teeth. 'And stop showing off, for once.' It annoyed him how easily he had been swept along, how her ravenous quest for excitement had infected him, clouded his better judgement. He reminded himself that this confrontation was irrelevant, gratuitous, that it had nothing to do with him. But he felt cheated, none the less. Petulant now, Armelle followed him towards the gates, where black-caped riot police checked their papers and let them pass. Immediately they stepped into the street, Alain felt a heavy hand on his shoulder.

'Into the van,' rasped a coarse voice.

Alain looked at his aggressor with unconcealed distaste. 'On what charge?'

'Either you get into the van, or we put you into it.'

'I'm coming too,' protested Armelle as Alain was manhandled into the back of a 'salad-shaker', so called because of the steel mesh over the windows.

'Not you. Just him. Now beat it.'

Black-gloved hands pushed her roughly to one side as the doors of the vehicle were slammed shut. Armelle began screaming abuse.

'This way,' said a voice in her ear. It was Claudine. Armelle fell into her arms, sobbing with rage.

'Traitors,' she wept. 'They lied to us. We should have stood and fought. We should have—'

'This way,' repeated Claudine urgently. 'You'll see why in a minute.'

They ran behind the vans, towards the Boulevard Saint-Michel, and Armelle saw to her delight that the police convoy had ground to a halt. Outraged fellow-students were ripping the iron gratings from around the trees on the pavement and hurling them into the path of the vans, blocking their progress and jamming traffic in both directions, while other young people, alerted to the police treachery, were advancing from all directions equipped with bottles, ashtrays, and crockery from nearby cafés, which rained loudly against the sides of the vans, as if to give hope to the unseen prisoners inside. Meanwhile, fresh contingents of police were approaching the area on foot, riot shields and truncheons at the ready.

'*Libérez nos camarades!*' went up the shout as the crowd advanced, hurling missiles. But Armelle, recklessly, hurled herself instead, in a vain attempt to break open the door of one of the vans. Her arm was almost wrenched from its socket as a black-clad robot pulled her away. Incensed, she spat and kicked, unaware, till the blood ran into her eyes, that she had been struck on the head. As others ran forward to join in the fray, she felt a brief, blissful surge of elation, cruelly thwarted by another blow which knocked her unconscious.

She came round in a room she did not recognise with her head in Claudine's lap. A folded handkerchief was pressed against her temple.

'Where am I?'

'Two comrades carried you here. The apartment belongs to one of them. They've gone back to look for more casualties. Luckily the police had their hands too full to pick you up. Are you all right?'

'Just angry,' hissed Armelle. 'This is war now, Claudine. This is finally the end of all that non-violence shit.' As if to illustrate her words, another inert body was brought in, a boy bleeding profusely from the nose.

'Lie still,' said Claudine, as Armelle tried to stand up and offer assistance. 'You might pass out again.'

Dizzily, Armelle obeyed. 'What's going on out there?' she demanded of one of the rescuers.

'All hell's broken loose. They're sealing off the Latin Quarter. You'd better hole up in here till tomorrow. They're arresting everyone they can lay their hands on. I've had a word with the concierge. She saw for herself what they did, so she's on our side. She's offered to feed us tonight, and anyone who wants to can use her phone.'

'Do you want me to ring your family?' asked Claudine.

'God, no. Ask for Pilar, don't speak to anyone else. Tell her what's happened and ask her to get word to Rob.'

'What about Alain? Won't his wife be wondering what's happened to him?'

'Oh, I shouldn't think so,' said Armelle, smiling to herself. 'She'll think he's with a woman, that's all.'

Viktor sat brooding over his drink on the terrace of Le Colisée in the Champs-Élysées. It was crammed, as always, with tourists, bags and cameras and jackets slung carelessly over the backs of chairs while their owners enjoyed the sunshine, and by now he should have enriched himself handsomely at the expense of their insurance companies. But out of sheer perversity he hadn't done so, cutting off his nose to spite his face in a fit of self-indulgent ill humour.

He looked at his watch. Cassie would be at his apartment by now, but he always kept her waiting on principle. He begrudged the time she spent with other people, as if to demonstrate her independence of him. Her life had become a disciplined structure of time-killing routines, every day mapped out like a military manoeuvre, crammed with lessons, lectures, rehearsals of *St Joan* – she had even taken to doing Marta's shopping. Exhaustion seemed to be her goal. Sometimes she would doze off prematurely after dinner, condemning herself to another sleepless night, but Viktor could never bring himself to wake her.

Seeing her fall asleep was like watching a flower open. He would have expected her to curl up into a little ball with a thumb in her mouth, but as her limbs loosened she would crook one knee and throw the other leg over the side of the settee, she would part her lips, revealing the soft pinkness within, she would fling her arms above her head in a posture of abandon... And then she would wake, quite suddenly, as if she had heard him thinking, and the bud would close up tight again. He would remind himself that in a couple of months she would be going back home, and by then she would be over the worst of her crisis and able to cope on her own, and some of it, at least, would be thanks to him, which would have been the only good deed he had ever done in his life if he hadn't done it for purely selfish motives.

Leave well alone, Viktor. She's a nice girl, and you're a lousy criminal. She's damaged, and you're destructive. As yet there's no real harm done, so let's keep it that way. Having an affair with a girl like Cassie was a bit like trying to rob a bank – big-time stuff, riddled with pitfalls. The bigger the pay-off, the greater the risk. He had survived this long by not getting greedy, by knowing his limitations. And now, thanks to her, he had begun to feel like a loser, a third-rate crook chickening out of the make-or-break job that would set him up for life.

He hailed a cab, imagining her waiting for him. Every day she looked slightly different; the shadows under her eyes were fading, and she had begun to put on weight, all her sharp angles melting and blurring into each other, playing tricks on his memory, defying his expectations. Every evening he would make her recount her day in detail. The terrifying memory lapses were now a thing of the past, her recall was almost perfect. It was like hearing a child recite its time-table correctly: it filled him with absurd parental pride. Cassie never asked what he had done, by way of tacit disapproval, and so he would invent tortuous crimes, just to annoy her, knowing that she would retaliate, wanting her to.

'Marta says you never write to your father,' she had challenged him. 'Why not?'

'Ask her.'

'I did. Now I'm asking you.'

'If I wrote to him, I'd write the truth. She's always banked on me not being able to.'

'Meaning?'

'Don't make me spell it out. She must have told you I can't spell.'

'I could help you.'

'I don't want your help.'

'I know you don't. That's the whole point. I've been waiting for a chance to get back at you. You just wait.'

The next night she had produced a lurid paperback from her bag in the middle of a crowded restaurant. *Sex Slaves of Baghdad* was real under-the-counter stuff. He couldn't begin to imagine where she had bought it.

'How's this for an incentive? Listen to what you're missing ...'

She had read out an explicit passage, in a schoolmarmy Janet-and-John voice, to the rapt attention of neighbouring diners, and wouldn't stop till he had promised to let her coach him. And she had held him to it. He had made good progress, if only because the book was too cheap and silly to be threatening. Fortunately there was nothing quite as unerotic as bad pornography; unfortunately laughter was a powerful aphrodisiac, for him if not for her ... Oh, to hell with excuses. Tonight he would get it over with. With luck, it would be a fiasco, and that would be that. He would walk into a house full of money and come out of it empty-handed, just as he had done once before, thanks to her.

The cab took for ever to get home. The Left Bank was one big traffic jam, with police vans everywhere. Viktor paid off the driver and continued his journey on foot. The area surrounding the Sorbonne was sealed off; he was obliged to forsake his normal short cut and walk the long way round. Despite his immaculate suit and tie, he was stopped by the police and required to show his papers. Viktor fished in his pockets, amused that for once he had no stolen property on him.

'What's going on?'

'You live in the 5*ème*?'

'That's what it says.'

'Proceed.'

'Is there some trouble?'

'Only local residents allowed access to this area.'

'Why?'

'Subversive activity by foreign extremists. Nothing to worry about. All under control.'

'Thank you, officer,' said Viktor, retrieving his *carte d'iden-tité*. 'It's such a comfort to know that you're there to protect us. I've never trusted foreigners myself.'

Perhaps Cassie hadn't been allowed through. Except that she usually approached from the south, via the Métro. He quickened his step. Mme Bloc was lying in wait for him as usual.

'*Bonsoir*, monsieur.' She simpered grotesquely through unnaturally white dentures.

'Madame.' Viktor treated her to a dazzling smile. 'Has Mademoiselle arrived?'

'Did you hear the news? What a to-do! Young people nowa-days . . .'

'Did she get here okay?'

'I let her in but she left again a few minutes later.'

'Did she say where she was going?'

Mme Bloc shrugged, to indicate that she minded her own business, but seeing Viktor's worried frown she relented, adding, 'I happened to see a note pinned to your door, while I was sweeping the staircase . . .'

Viktor took the stairs two at a time. She had written it in large, clear capitals.

WITH ROB. HURRY. CASSIE.

Viktor took down the note and put it inside his piano stool before changing out of his suit. If there was some student demo in progress, Rob had probably got himself beaten up again. Cassie would be doing a replay of her angel of mercy act, the two of them yakking away in English . . .

He arrived to find the door to Rob's apartment open. He was sitting next to Cassie on the bed; her arm was around his shoul-der. She jumped up and kissed Viktor on each cheek.

'Did you hear what happened?' demanded Rob gloomily. 'There's been a riot at the Sorbonne. Armelle's been hurt.'

'What about you?'

'I'm all right. I was leafleting out at Billancourt. I hitched a lift back to the Place d'Italie and walked the rest of the way. I never knew anything about it till Cassie told me.'

217

'Don't tell me Armelle dragged *you* along to a demo,' accused Viktor, inspecting Cassie for damage. 'I warned you—'

'No, of course she didn't. I was just leaving the Lemercier place when the phone rang. Some friend of Armelle's spoke to Pilar and said to tell Rob that she was hurt and was spending the night under cover and not to tell Odile or her father. That's all we know. So I thought I'd better wait here till Rob got back.'

'We've just been up to the Latin Quarter,' said Rob, 'but we couldn't get near the Sorbonne. There were police on every corner checking everybody's papers. Just as well I had the hair-cut. They were looking for any excuse to pick people up. I don't know what the hell to do next.'

'There's nothing you can do. Why do you suppose she sent you that message?'

'To stop me worrying of course.'

'To start you worrying, idiot. She's just making a drama, as usual.'

'Spend the evening with us,' said Cassie. 'There's no point in sitting and brooding on your own.' She squeezed Rob's hand. 'Armelle will be all right. If she was badly hurt, her friend would have said so.'

'They've closed the Sorbonne,' muttered Rob, 'just like she said they would.'

'So she's got what she wanted at last,' said Viktor.

'What she wanted? Are you kidding? The last time the Sorbonne was closed was in 1940, by the Nazis!'

'Please, Viktor,' said Cassie. 'Rob's upset.'

'I feel like getting drunk,' growled Rob, standing up. 'Let's go to Clément's.'

'We can't take Cassie there,' said Viktor.

'Why not?' demanded Cassie.

'Because it's a dive, that's why.'

'I don't mind,' said Cassie, looking expectant.

'She'll be okay with us,' said Rob.

'No. The place is running alive with tarts.' Viktor coloured slightly. The last thing he wanted was to have some former bedmate proposition him in front of Cassie.

'Friends of yours?' taunted Cassie, reading his face. 'I'd like to meet them. Work out the secret of their charm.'

'Easy. They've got big tits,' said Viktor, running a withering eye over Cassie's lack of curves. 'Perhaps Rob and I should go there on our own. Make a night of it. How about it, Rob? How about a nice, uncomplicated, unneurotic fuck? It would do us both the world of good.'

'Don't listen to him, Cass,' said Rob, embarrassed, seeing her lips tighten. 'He's only joking.'

'No I'm not. Can't pick myself up a woman with her breathing down my neck, can I? Talk about the skeleton at the feast.'

'What's up with you two?' demanded Rob, momentarily forgetting his own troubles.

'Nothing,' said Cassie, with sudden venom. 'Absolutely nothing's *up* between us. That's the whole trouble, isn't it, Viktor darling?'

'Shut up,' snarled Viktor.

'Have a nice evening, *chéri*. Perhaps it'll put you in a better mood. And I hope you get the bloody pox.'

'No chance.' He pulled a packet of condoms out of his jacket pocket and threw them at Rob.

'Three each. Will that be enough, or should we pick up some more?'

'Cassie—'

The door slammed.

'You bastard. Why did you have to upset her like that?'

'If it worries you, run after her. Put your arm around her. Squeeze her hand.'

'So that's what bugging you, is it? Are you crazy? I can't believe you're jealous.'

'Jealous? I'm deadly serious. Look, why don't we swap partners? That way we'd all get what we deserved. How about it? Go on, run and catch up with her.'

'What's got into you? She loves you, can't you see that?'

'You don't say? Well, you should know. All those cosy little chats in English . . . '

'We don't talk about *you*. Don't be paranoid.'

'What do you talk about then?'

'Armelle, mostly, if you must know. I was just telling Cassie, Armelle needs to get away from all this heavy political stuff. Learn to relax, to be herself. Come the summer, we're going to cut loose. Italy first. She wants me to meet her mother. Then we'll work our way round Europe, take a year out, maybe more. If these peace talks work out there's bound to be an amnesty. Then I could take her back home with me ... Go on, laugh.'

'Why should I laugh? It's not remotely funny. At least you know what you want, for what it's worth.'

'I want peace, that's all. Not just out there. In here. What do you want? A million francs?'

'Two would be better. The next best thing to a rich daddy is dirty, sordid, disgusting money, the more the better. Armelle should collect quite a pile one day – you should do well out of it. And then there's Cassie. Did she tell you? Her grandfather settled ten thousand pounds on her the day she was born. No wonder she can afford to despise me. I'm only a common criminal, after all.'

'Look, go after her and tell her you love her. Why are you so scared to admit it?'

'For God's sake. Whose side are you on? Hers or mine?'

'Both. I want you to be happy.'

'You're a romantic.'

'So what's wrong with that?'

'Let's hope you never find out,' said Viktor. 'Let's go and get drunk.'

Eva could just see herself on the front page. A tiny smudge, identifiable only by the banner she was holding aloft, emblazoned, 'Of our own free will'. Just looking at it gave her a thrill, not just of remembered excitement but of lasting pride that she had been part of it. Wenceslas Square on May Day had been like a forest of Czech flags, waving above innumerable human trees, not just saplings like herself but gnarled old specimens like Karel, walking tall for the first time in years, unable to resist the beauty and the blandishments of his old childhood sweetheart, hope.

She took home a copy of the paper to show him, only to find that he had already bought one and cut out the photograph, to send to Marta.

'Did you see me?' asked Eva, sitting beside him at the table. She pointed at the relevant blob. Karel peered myopically.

'Is that you? I must mark it with a cross. In fact, I'll mark myself with a cross while I'm about it.'

'Whereabouts were you?'

'I've no idea. But then neither has the old girl.' He closed his eyes and dropped the pen at random. 'That'll do.'

Eva smiled to herself and put on her apron.

'No need to cook for me,' he said. 'I'll fix myself some bread and sausage when I get home from the meeting. Don't wait up. The last one went on half the night.'

'Aren't you hungry?'

'I speak better on an empty stomach. Some other old fogey's gone down with laryngitis, so I said I'd take over. They might as well listen to me as to him, I suppose.'

'You mean you're nervous.'

'Self-conscious, yes. I don't enjoy raking up these old ashes. My story hardly does me credit.'

'But everyone else is in the same boat, surely?'

'Far from it. To listen to some of them, you'd think they were heroes.'

'You've always been too hard on yourself.'

'And on everyone else. Eva . . . I've been meaning to talk to you, about your trip. I want you to do something for me.'

Eva sat down again, knowing by the shifty look in his eye that the something concerned Viktor.

'Here I am, about to tell a bunch of strangers things I've never even told my own family. Not surprising, really. Why should I care what they think of me? Same with those memoirs. Who's ever heard of Karel Brožek? It might as well be a pen-name.'

'Go on.'

'All these years, I've taken the line: a father like me is just a liability, let him get on with his life and forget me. If it wasn't for my mother, we'd have lost touch. You know he never writes. There wasn't much love lost between us, when he was a child. I was never cut out to be a father.'

'There you go again. Why must you always run yourself down? You've always been a good father to *me*.'

Eva's mother had never told her her real father's identity, having traded her silence in return for a good job and financial

221

handouts. Eva had learned to accept this, but only because Karel had filled the breach. Perhaps it was easier to love someone when you didn't feel obliged to do so.

'You made it easy for me. You *wanted* a father. Viktor didn't. By the time I married Milena, he was used to having her to himself and getting his own way in everything. I didn't want him to grow up to be a spoilt brat and a mummy's boy, so I started laying down the law, the way my father had done. I grew up in awe of that man. I wanted my son to have the same kind of respect for me. God, that child had a will of iron. Beating him was worse than useless.'

'I dare say he deserved it,' put in Eva drily. Although hardly the most patient man in the world, Karel had never raised a hand to her.

'I tried to love him, you know,' he continued gruffly, 'but it wasn't easy. And not just because he was a little monster, either. I couldn't forgive him, or his mother, for preferring each other to me. All this time, I've been happy for him to reject me because it justified me rejecting him.'

'But you didn't reject him!'

'Didn't I just. Viktor knows it, even if you don't. It's been like a long-distance game of tit for tat, but now it's gone on long enough. He can think what the hell he likes of me after this. I don't expect him to change his opinion, but I'm damned if I'll carry on making things easy for him, or for myself.' He got up and fetched his manuscript. 'It's only a first draft, of course, and nowhere near finished, but I thought, if you could type a copy for me . . . would you take it to Paris with you? I want him to read it.'

Eva hadn't been prepared for this. So that was what had kept him working late into the night. He had been writing an apology to his son.

'Of course I will,' she said uncertainly. 'If you're sure that's what you want.'

'Sure isn't the right word. It'll probably make things even worse between us. Well, if it does, that's just too bad.'

So it wasn't a plea for forgiveness, after all, more a desire for confrontation. The truce was over; it was time to fight again.

'And whatever you do,' he added, 'don't let my old fool of a mother read it first. I don't want him getting the story second hand from her. She'll just twist everything. He can bloody well judge – or misjudge – for himself.'

Eva heaved her typewriter into position. It was an ancient pre-war machine which Jan had discovered mouldering in the office basement and renovated for use on *Spring Tide*.

'Hand it over, then,' she said briskly, holding out her hand. 'There's no time to lose, is there?'

'Monsieur Brožek just went out,' muttered Viktor's concierge protectively. Her favourite tenant never used to have any visitors, and now either that skinny blonde or the big American were forever in and out of the place as if they owned it.

'I know,' said Cassie. 'He said he'd be along later. So I'll wait for him if you don't mind.'

Grumbling under her breath, Mme Bloc mounted the staircase, rattling her keys like a sabre, and opened the door with all the goodwill of a gaoler. Cassie switched on the television, lit one of Viktor's cigarettes, and prepared to sit it out till he got back. He probably thought she had fled back to her room to weep off his latest insults in private. And then tomorrow he would expect her to meet him as usual and act as if nothing had happened. If she didn't, that would be tantamount to admitting he had hurt her. So she would let him get away with it. The cycle went on and on and on.

She had made a fool of herself, walking out in a huff like that. She should have laughed it off; that would have been the cool thing to do. But she didn't feel like being cool. Tonight she would have it out with him once and for all. Either he wanted her or he didn't. And whether he did or not, he wasn't entitled to make her feel ugly and unattractive in front of another man, especially Rob.

It had been a filthy day. Ragged from a bad night, she had lost her temper with all three classes, reducing one unfortunate child to tears. On the way out, a CAL activist had collared her and demanded her presence at some stupid meeting or other, and instead of inventing an excuse, she had issued a brusque negative, provoking an accusatory harangue. Odile had been particularly dense and, claiming to be short of change, had left her ten francs short. Then there had been all that hassle with the phone call, and seeing poor Rob in a state over Armelle. The last thing she had needed was any more shit from Viktor. As for the old cow Mme Bloc . . .

No use. It was definitely starting again; it had not been a recovery, merely a remission. The colours might be brighter, the noises clearer, all her perceptions sharper, but the barrage of heightened sensations had left her bruised, raw, sensitised. She needed somewhere soft and safe to retreat to, something that shielded her from a blinding, deafening world, someone she could hide behind. And instead she had Viktor, who knew all her weak spots and homed in on them ruthlessly, who gave her no respite, no relief.

'Pull yourself together, Cassie.' She would have those words etched on her tombstone. What an absurd idiom that was. It had always suggested a hunched, precarious posture, one hand clutching defective knicker elastic and the other a fly-away hat. Alternatively, 'Loosen up, Cassie.' That had been Wilfred's favourite phrase. Whatever it meant, it was the opposite of pulling yourself together. Bits of you dangling all over the place, everything on show. Impossible to do without a double dose beforehand.

The temptation to pop a pill was almost unbearable. She knew where he kept them. He had shown them to her often enough and tormented her with them and bet her a thousand francs that she would take one in the end, and sometimes, when he was being particularly vile, he would count them, just to check up on her. Yes, they were still there, in his sock drawer. One hundred and twenty-three tranquillisers and fifty-eight sleepers. Serve him right if she took the bloody lot. He'd probably be heartily relieved if she did just that. She was becoming a millstone round his neck. That was why he didn't want to go to bed with her. He was worried that he wouldn't be able to shake her off, that she would hang round him indefinitely, cramping his style and nurturing neurotic notions of lasting love. And he was absolutely, humiliatingly right.

Except that she wasn't in love with the person other people knew as Viktor. That was just the imposter who protected his privacy. The real Viktor, the one she had excavated and reassembled, the product of many patient hours of research in Marta's apartment, was somebody else altogether, so close that she carried him everywhere in her head, so far away that she despaired of ever reaching him.

She went into his bedroom and lay down experimentally on top of his bed. It was a single. He had once told her that he never brought girls home. That was some small consolation. Tonight, when he got back, drunk or not, she would force a showdown, she would make him really, really angry, she would engineer the most stupendous row, and then . . . then they would end up here, in this bed. The thought of it was like sitting finals; it sent the panic motor into overdrive . . .

She shut her eyes. It was no big deal. She knew what to do, after all. She hadn't even *liked* Wilfred, and she'd managed to fool him all right. Everyone made such a fuss about sex, but it was just a mechanical skill, after all, like driving a car or using a typewriter. You didn't have to like doing it to be proficient at it. Prostitutes didn't enjoy it, and they had to be good at it to stay in business. It was the only possible way forward. Things couldn't go on like this. If she was going to lose Viktor anyway, she might as well go down fighting.

But she had never in her life made love – or what passed for love – without a couple of preparatory pills. Just a couple couldn't do any harm, they would help her relax. This was an exception, surely. Except that he would know. He would take one look at her and know as surely as if he could smell them on her breath. She wasn't going to give him that satisfaction.

She gritted her teeth and tried one of the useless relaxation exercises the shrink had taught her. Endless bilge about sandy beaches and lapping waves and breathing and stretching and relaxing, all delivered in a voice that pinged at the end of each sentence, like a cash register. It hadn't worked, of course. She had made sure of that, littering the beach with dead jellyfish, pumping the sea full of raw sewage, filling the air with decay . . . She pulled back the covers, kicked off her shoes, and got inside. Breathe in. She could smell Viktor. Not his rather florid aftershave, which went with the awful watch and cufflinks, but a naked, night-time smell, somewhere between warm bread and damp earth. Breathe out. She drew the sheet over her head. Breathe in.

She could smell herself now, and then Viktor again, and then herself, and then both of them at once, their combined scents eddying in a miniature whirlpool, filling her lungs with warmth. And stretch. The word had reminded her of racks and rubber bands and the misery of PT lessons. S-t-r-e-t-c-h. In this secret cocoon it sounded different, slow and sensual. She curled her toes round the bottom of the mattress and threw her arms above her head. And re*lax*. It had been like an invitation to die, it had reeked of submission and surrender. But here it felt lush and languorous . . .

Her clothes felt tight and sticky. She wriggled out of them under the bedclothes and threw them overboard. That was better. She could feel every lump and bump in the mattress, the slight slipperiness of the starched linen, the myriad tiny breezes created by every move, every sigh. The springs made little mews of pleasure as she stretched and relaxed, opened and shut, rose and fell, not just inhaling him now, but swimming in him, this way and that, feeling him all around her, sucking the air out of him, drinking him dry. Not loose any more but tight, so tight that her breath came in shallow gasps as she splashed and leapt and dived and swam, faster and faster, slithering and struggling, pursuing, escaping, floating, drowning, dying, living . . .

Startled by the sound of her own voice, she rolled on to her stomach and screamed again and again, into the pillow, muffling but not muzzling, making primitive music out of what she could not see. It was the cry of a newborn animal, alive, triumphant, confused, afraid. Quietly, at the top of her voice, Cassie screamed and wept, and slept.

She awoke just after midnight, to find herself still alone. Her first reaction was to get up and dressed and away, before Viktor got back. But then she remembered. It was going to be all right . . .

Stay put, Cassie. Then you won't be able to change your mind. If he came home drunk, so much the better. Viktor was easier to handle when he was plastered. Soppy and soulful and sentimental ... Her veins tingled with a sudden surge of adrenalin. She had always assumed that retreat came naturally to her. Except that it didn't come naturally; it was a learned response, the product of years of false conditioning. Conflict was what she had always craved. Viktor was proof of that.

Loving Viktor was the nearest she had ever got to being happy. It was bound to take a bit of getting used to, like wearing new shoes. If she winced her way through it, eventually all the sore bits would create tailor-made callouses, till being happy didn't hurt any more ...

She slithered back under the bedclothes and waited.

'Are we leaving already?' asked Rob, as Viktor flung some money down on the table.

'I am. What about you?' He indicated a bored-looking hooker standing by the bar, all high heels and backcombed hair. 'I'm sure she can accommodate us both.'

'You're not serious.'

'Watch me.'

'Hell, Viktor, what about Cassie?'

'What about her? She doesn't own me. And besides, whores don't count. Sure you won't tag along?'

Rob shook his head in predictable, gratifying disgust. Viktor jerked his head at the girl and followed her out. How long had it been? Too long, that was for sure. He was getting faddy. He was like someone starving to death for want of a sugared almond ...

The girl had a decent place in the rue Monge. She was obviously doing well. Viktor paid her over the odds, to keep her on her toes. This way he was unquestionably in control. No love, no loss. No delight, no danger. No romance, no regrets ...

No nothing. God. What was wrong with him? As if he didn't know ...

'That's enough.'

'Relax.' She carried on placidly with what she was doing. For her, the problem was routine, profitable, curing it was part of the job ...

'I said, that's enough!'

He pushed her away from him roughly and stood up,

unable to bear it any longer. 'It's all right,' he muttered, shoving some extra money at her. 'It's not your fault.'

But it wasn't his fault either. It was Cassie's. She was like some dreadful, disabling disease that was eating him from the inside out, destroying his peace of mind and body, leaving nothing but a useless husk. And he had let it happen, as if to punish himself, and her.

Furious with himself, he went straight home and poured himself a large slug of Cognac, which he knocked back in one swallow. He refilled the glass and kicked open the door of the bedroom, intending to drink himself to sleep.

'Viktor?'

He switched on the light, making her blink, reminding himself of the first time they had met.

'What are you doing here?'

'I fell asleep.'

'Sorry I woke you.' He switched off the light again, not wanting her to see him, afraid that his failure was written all over his face.

'Wait a minute.' She reached for the bedside lamp and flicked it on. 'You don't have to sleep in there.'

Her blonde hair was fanned out all over his pillow and her arms and shoulders were bare; her clothes were lying higgledy-piggledy on the floor, as if she had taken them off in a hurry. He felt a rush of desire, crippled almost instantly by a vivid, vicious vision of humiliation. 'It's all right,' she would murmur, relieved, triumphant. 'It doesn't matter . . .

'I'm sorry I got upset,' she continued. 'It was silly of me. I want to make it up. I'm fed up with quarrelling all the time. Viktor . . . don't you *want* to?'

What terrific timing the girl had. Tonight of all nights . . .

'Am I ugly, or what? What's the matter with me? What's the matter with *you*?'

There was no mockery in her voice, but he heard it none the less. He felt the familiar brutal need to hurt her.

'Look, I don't like the woman to make the first move, okay? I've told you that before. It's cheap and it doesn't suit you. It's a turn-off. Now either go to sleep or get dressed and I'll take you home.'

228

He shut the door and went back into the living room, where he polished off the rest of his drink to the sound of her crashing about like an angry elephant. A few moments later she emerged, white with rage.

'Did you really pick up a girl tonight?'

'Of course not. I'm a boy scout. I live a pure and celibate life.'

'Because if you're shagged out, just tell me and I'll understand. I wouldn't mind so much if it was just that.'

'How very broad-minded of you. Well, since you insist . . . someone else beat you to it this time, I'm afraid. But never mind. Perhaps I'll fancy you tomorrow. Full marks for trying.'

'There's not going to be a tomorrow.'

Her face was pinched, livid.

'Stop dramatising. Here, have a drink.'

'Screw you, Viktor Brožek! Stay away from me in future, do you hear?'

'With pleasure. But you can't go home on your own. It's two o'clock in the morning.'

'Now why does that sound familiar? Isn't this where we came in?'

'Cassie—'

She slammed the door hard enough to disturb the piano strings, which let out a muffled murmur of protest. And by the time Viktor's grumbling conscience had sent him down to the street in pursuit, she had vanished into the night.

NINE

'Where's Alain?'

'He'll be along to visit you soon,' said Jeanne. 'He sent you these.'

She thrust an enormous bunch of flowers at her daughter-in-law. Chantal plucked at them listlessly.

'I'd rather he had come himself.'

'You know how men are,' blustered Jeanne, unused to lying. 'Afraid of hospitals. Albert's just the same. But he sends his love.'

'I feel I'm letting him down. I'm afraid he's . . .'

Chantal bit her lip, remembering her resolution to keep her fears to herself. If Alain *was* being unfaithful to her, it was hardly surprising, in the circumstances; confiding in his mother, or her own, would only store up trouble for the future.

'Don't upset yourself. It's bad for the baby. A few days in bed and you'll be fine.'

'It'll be at least a week, they said. Perhaps longer. I feel so useless, lying here.'

Jeanne's laboured smile began to twitch at the edges. But luckily Chantal didn't seem at all suspicious of Alain's absence. Already she had learned to expect no better of her reluctant husband. She heaved a sigh of relief as she spotted Chantal's parents approaching, laden with more flowers.

'Hello, Maman,' chirped Chantal. 'You've just missed Alain. Look at the lovely bouquet he brought me.'

She was a tough, determined little thing, thought Jeanne

approvingly. Her submissive manner masked a hidden strength. She would need it, with a husband like Alain.

'Poor boy,' clucked Chantal's mother in Jeanne's ear. 'I expect he's worried sick.'

'Um ... naturally,' mumbled Jeanne. 'Well, I'd better leave you together then. I'll pop in again this evening, Chantal.'

As soon as she was safely out of the ward, her matronly beam collapsed into an anxious frown. It was so unlike Alain to stay out all night. If he had missed the last Métro after his meeting, he would surely have telephoned a friend or neighbour, if only for Chantal's sake. Just as well they had kept the poor girl in hospital yesterday; she would have been frantic with worry. How could Alain be so thoughtless? She wouldn't half give him a piece of her mind when he finally showed up ...

She arrived home to find the tiny flat full of angry voices. Half a dozen young men were all talking at once, gesticulating wildly.

'What's all this?' she demanded of her husband, alarmed.

There was a sudden, awkward silence, broken by a sheepish, uneven chorus of 'Bonjour, madame.'

'We got word while you were at the hospital,' said Albert stiffly. 'Alain got himself involved in that student riot yesterday. He's been arrested.'

'Arrested?' Jeanne sat down. 'What for?'

'For nothing,' put in one of Alain's workmates. 'Just for being there.' He turned to Albert. 'The union should be supporting him, not abandoning him!'

'He had no business going to the Sorbonne!' thundered Albert. 'If he wants to get mixed up with a bunch of bourgeois brats, that's not the union's problem.'

'Albert—' remonstrated Jeanne.

'Keep out of this!' He turned to a tall swarthy fellow who seemed to be the group's elected spokesperson. 'I told you before, I heartily endorse what Jacques Rivière has told you, and if you're not satisfied, you can bring the matter up at the union meeting on Monday.'

'Too right we'll bring it up on Monday! And if the union won't stand by a member who's been unjustly arrested, then there are plenty of comrades who will be prepared to act independently!'

'Wait a minute,' interjected Jeanne. 'When did this happen? After the meeting last night, or before?'

'Meeting?' The young man looked puzzled.

'We know all about your secret meetings,' put in Albert sourly.

'Our meetings aren't secret. And there wasn't one last night. Look, those bastards only let him make one phone call. All he cared about was getting word to Chantal so that she didn't worry. Alain didn't tell me to go and see Rivière, or to waste my breath on that old fart Georges Leroux, or to ask favours of you either. He didn't ask me to bring these mates with me. They came of their own accord, to show solidarity. You say you don't want our help, you say you won't give us help. So be it. We'll act on our own.'

They filed out of the flat in an orderly procession, jaws set in grim determination. As soon as they were gone Jeanne flew at Albert.

'Well? Are you just going to sit there? We must do something!'

'I might have guessed what he was up to,' growled Albert. 'Where do you suppose he's been going two and three times a week? He's still seeing that little student bitch! Which would be bad enough if all he was doing was sleeping with her. But now he's started dabbling in student politics he can take the consequences, not look to his union to support him!'

'To hell with the union! You're his father, aren't you? And God knows, you've been unfaithful to me often enough. When I was pregnant with Françoise—'

Albert gave a bark of exasperation. 'You know who's behind all this nonsense at the Sorbonne, don't you? Fascist infiltrators, posing as anarchists. Foreigners who care nothing for France.' He waved a copy of *L'Humanité* in her face. 'The Party has officially denounced these so-called revolutionaries at Nanterre and has warned all workers against listening to their propaganda. And now I find that my own son is mixed up with this rabble! He's a traitor to his class!'

'And meanwhile that poor girl's lying there in hospital with a threatened miscarriage! I shall go down to the police station myself and demand to see him! I'll get him out of there somehow!'

'Don't you know the law of the land? They can hold him for ten days before he gets to see a lawyer, let alone his mother! Leave him to cool his heels for a bit. It will teach him a lesson. As for Chantal, you might as well tell her the truth. This won't be the first time he lands up in gaol if he carries on like this!'

He grabbed his jacket and cap and stormed out. Jeanne was about to give chase when her knees gave way, and she sat down, trembling all over. Best not to meddle. Best to leave it to Alain's mates. They were men, they would know what to do.

Debout les damnés de la terre!
Debout les forçats de la faim . . .

The basement of the Opéra police station resounded to yet another tuneless rendering of the 'Internationale'. The overcrowded cell stank of urine and stale tobacco fumes. Alain, bleary-eyed from lack of sleep, accepted a cigarette from René, the curly-headed philosophy student he had met briefly in the Sorbonne courtyard. In the last eighteen hours his cheerful face had become depressingly familiar.

'Did you get through to your folks?' said René, who appeared to be enjoying every minute of his ordeal.

'They're not on the phone. But I left a message with a friend. What about you?'

'Oh, my mother threw a fit.' René grinned unrepentantly. 'Bang goes that car they promised me for my twenty-first. But I think she was relieved that I was in one piece. She said a friend's daughter was in hospital with a broken jaw.'

Alain's thoughts flew to Armelle again, and back to Chantal, where they belonged.

'We should refuse to leave this place, except together,' put in another inmate, a gangling young man with a picture of Chairman Mao on the front of his teeshirt. 'Otherwise some of us will be kicked out while the rest are left to rot. Does anyone disagree?'

'We can do more good out there than in here,' muttered somebody else. 'In any case, I didn't do anything. I was minding my

233

own business, that's all. I was just watching. I told them I was just watching.'

'He told them he was just watching,' mimicked the Maoist, reproducing his plaintive whine exactly. 'Poor baby.'

'Shut up. I'm not one of your lot.'

'We should all stick together now,' put in somebody else. 'Communists, Trotskyists, Maoists, anarchists, and pussy-footing moderates too.'

'The revolution can't succeed unless we do,' agreed René, offering the innocent onlooker his last cigarette.

'The revolution can't succeed without the workers,' muttered Alain irritably.

'We know that. We've been leafleting factories all over the place.'

'We've been bounced out all over the place, you mean,' interjected somebody else. 'Some union heavy threatened to beat me up last week.'

'So, what's your answer?' demanded René of Alain. 'You're the only worker here. We're listening.'

All eyes were suddenly on him.

'Spontaneous action,' said Alain tersely. 'Like you had yesterday. Nobody organised it, it just happened. Nothing worthwhile ever happens if someone's trying to control it.'

'And do many workers think like you?'

'We don't get as much time for thinking as you do. Intellectuals get all the credit for revolutions. But it's the non-intellectuals who make them happen. When the workers decide they've had enough crap, that's when they'll act. They won't sit around for hours discussing it to death, they'll just go ahead and do it.'

Heads nodded reverently. Alain felt absurd, patronised, and resolved to say no more. But at that moment a contingent of policemen appeared, to a chorus of abuse. Three names were read out, one of them René's.

'Where are you taking us?' he demanded, as two pairs of burly arms hauled him out of the cell. 'We refuse to leave this place except together. We—'

A savage blow to the mouth cut him off in mid-sentence. Amid furious yelling from the other inmates the three were carted off. Opinion varied as to their likely fate, with about half predicting brutal interrogation, and the other expeditious release, the result of parental string-pulling. When Alain's own name was read out half an hour later, he had no doubt that the former must be true.

He was almost disappointed when he found himself hauled into a makeshift courtroom, where a disgruntled magistrate, summoned away from his weekend, found him guilty of causing a public affray and dispensed a thirty-day suspended sentence. Alain felt an insane desire to argue, and if it hadn't been for Chantal he might have succumbed to the lure of martyrdom and lashed out at the nearest policeman. As it was, he accepted the judgement meekly enough, telling himself again that this wasn't his struggle, wishing it was.

He emerged from the police station to find a barrage of newspapermen, onlookers and well-wishers holding placards bearing the legend, 'CRS – SS' and 'Libérez nos camarades'. He blinked as a flashbulb blinded him and opened his eyes to see a tearful Armelle.

'Alain!' She ran forward and embraced him passionately. 'Did they hurt you?'

'No, I'm fine. What about you?'

Armelle indicated the sticking plaster on her temple. 'I was unconscious for hours. I think they may have cracked my skull. We spent the night in a safe house, but I sneaked out early this morning and checked at all the police stations till I found where you were. I've been so worried about you. Thank God you're safe!'

She kissed him again just as another flashbulb exploded. Alain shielded his eyes with his hand. 'I've got to go home,' he said.

'Home? But things are just starting to happen! Can't you phone them and tell them you've got things to do? You can't go home now! Look at what they did to me!' She tore off the sticking plaster and displayed an ugly swelling. 'Don't you care?'

'You should see a doctor,' said Alain woodenly. 'I've got to get back. Chantal will be getting anxious.'

He walked away from her, in the direction of the Métro, but

she didn't seem to understand. She ran alongside him, gabbling all the while.

'Why do you suppose they let you out? Because both the students' and the teachers' unions forced their hand, that's why! All the younger profs are on our side! We've put forward three demands. That they re-open the Sorbonne, withdraw the police, and release those arrested. And already they're starting to cave in, already they're—'

'Armelle!' A girl ran to catch them up. 'We've just got word. The magistrates have sent four people to prison.'

'What?'

'It's true. Guys who attacked the vans yesterday.'

'Like we did,' muttered Armelle. 'The bastards. They're just looking for scapegoats. Did you hear that, Alain? Because you were unjustly arrested, the people who tried to defend you are being victimised! And all you can think about is running home to your wife!'

Her eyes were hard and cold as ice. This was his golden opportunity to be free of her for ever. If he turned his back on her now, she would despise him as a weakling, she would never trouble him again. All he had to do was walk away.

'I've got things to do,' he heard himself saying. 'You want the workers on your side, don't you? Well, the unions never stop attacking the students. I'm going to stand up at the union meeting on Monday and tell them what I saw, put forward a motion supporting you. I want to be sure of a big turn-out. So the more people I can talk to between now and then the better.'

Appeased, Armelle threw her arms around him. 'Of course. You're right. Why did you use your wife as an excuse? To hurt me? To make me feel jealous?' Her eyes were alight again, glittering with malice. Alain didn't answer. She lowered her voice. 'Can you get away on Tuesday afternoon?'

'I don't know . . . I'll try.'

'Come straight to Cassie's place at the usual time. I'll be waiting.'

He kissed her long and passionately. It was like trying to quench thirst with neat spirits. Then he set off, heavy-hearted but light-headed, for home.

***

236

Armelle arrived back at Rob's apartment to find a note pinned to the door: Have gone out looking for you. For God's sake stay put and wait for me.

She smiled to herself and put it between her teeth.

'Do you think the concierge believed you?' asked Claudine, while Armelle got out her key. Like the three other displaced comrades from Nanterre, she was carrying a crate full of bottles. Armelle let them in and shut the door.

'Of course she believed me. Why shouldn't we have a party on a Saturday night? She took the ten francs fast enough, didn't she?'

They began unpacking the bottles – most of them empty, some full of petrol.

'We need a funnel,' decreed Philippe, an intense, fanatical young man with a quiet, precise voice and a deceptively calm manner. As a Maoist, he was conversant with guerrilla warfare techniques, and had deserted his own tight-knit group to disseminate knowledge to the masses. A committed advocate of terrorism, he was regarded by many as a psychopath, and even Armelle had found him humourless and sinister, till today. But that savage blow on the head had altered her perception of him.

'I don't have a funnel,' she said.

'A jug then. Something to pour with.'

Rather sheepishly, Armelle unearthed a delicate milk jug in Sèvres porcelain. 'It belonged to my mother,' she began defensively, but no one was listening, all attention riveted on Philippe as he filled the jug with petrol, poured some of it into an empty bottle, and inserted a length of wick, plugging the neck with a wad of rag.

'That's all there is to it,' he said, starting on another one. 'And for God's sake be careful. No matches or cigarettes, okay? Once you've made them, put them back in the box and keep them upright till we find somewhere to store them.'

Four pairs of hands got busy.

'Perhaps it won't come to a fight,' reflected Armelle disconsolately. 'I can't believe they'll be stupid enough not to give in to our demands.'

'They won't give in,' said Philippe confidently. 'They've got to show who's boss. And they think they can do it with brute force. That's why we have to have arms.'

Arms! The word sent a shiver of delight down her spine.

'Your head is bleeding again,' said Claudine. 'Why did you take that plaster off? Here.' She handed Armelle a handkerchief, but Armelle waved it away.

'I want to see what they did to me every time I look in the mirror,' she said. 'I want to remind myself.'

She got up and went into the bathroom, to inspect the oozing wound for herself. The damage had been done not so much by the baton itself as by the tortoiseshell hairslide it had smashed into her head. Armelle squeezed a blob of blood on to her finger and smeared it over her fashionably pale lips, licking them clean slowly as if to give herself a taste for it. It was becoming real at last. This was her longed-for chance to hit back, to make people realise she was a force to be reckoned with. No one had ever taken her seriously, not even Rob, but soon all that would change . . .

'Where's Armelle?'

It was Rob's voice. Armelle ran out to greet him, her face falling as she saw that Viktor was with him.

'Well, well, well,' said Viktor, picking up one of the bottles. 'It's a Molotov cocktail party.'

'Get him out of here,' hissed Armelle.

'Jesus Christ,' said Rob, taking her head between his hands. 'What happened to you?'

'The police gave me a present. So we thought we'd give them one back, next time we meet.'

'Who's he?' demanded Philippe, eyeing Viktor suspiciously.

'A friend,' said Rob, 'and what the hell do you think you're doing, making those things in my apartment? Do you want to get me deported?'

'I invited them,' said Armelle.

'Well, you can invite them out again. You're not seriously going to throw those things at the police?'

'Why not? What do you expect us to do? Turn the other cheek?'

'You didn't see it, Rob,' put in Claudine. 'They were beating people up right and left. Armelle got off lightly.'

'They're even worse than American police,' interjected Philippe, not taking his eyes off his work, 'and that's saying something.'

'You ever been to America?' demanded Rob.

'No thanks. It's a Fascist country.'

'How the hell do you make that out?'

'Do you mind if I smoke?' put in Viktor malevolently, getting his lighter out of his pocket. Philippe snatched it from him.

'Get out of here, Viktor,' snapped Armelle. 'And if you dare breathe a word to anyone . . .'

'We'll work you over,' finished Philippe. 'Understood?'

'Why don't you do your dirty work in your own place?' snarled Rob. 'I want all those bottles cleared out of here, pronto. And you too.'

'I said they could spend the night,' protested Armelle. 'Everyone's taking in as many comrades from Nanterre as possible. They'll only get picked up if they try to go back to the campus. There's a meeting tomorrow, to plan a big demo for Monday.'

'If we're not welcome here, we'll go,' said Philippe coolly, standing up. 'I thought you were one of us, Rob. Or rather, Armelle thought you were one of us.'

Armelle clung to Rob and began weeping piteously. 'My head hurts,' she said. 'Please don't let me down. I told them we could count on you.'

Rob raised his eyes to heaven.

'Let's get out of here,' he said. 'We've got to talk. You people can stay at least until we get back.' He shepherded her out of the flat.

Intrigued, Viktor examined one of the bottles.

'So this is war, then, is it?' he asked sarcastically. 'And there's me thinking you lot believed in peace. I must have misunderstood.'

'It's self-defence,' said Claudine.

'It's retaliation,' Philippe corrected her. 'Why should we appease the aggressor? You saw what they did to Armelle. She was unarmed, and a woman. They enjoy violence. We merely employ it.'

Viktor yawned hugely. After Cassie's dramatic exit, he had

done serious damage to the bottle of Cognac and fallen asleep fully clothed on the settee, only to be woken by Rob at the crack of dawn. He had spent the morning with him – ostensibly to help him look for Armelle, but in reality to keep him out of trouble – but despite the lurid accounts of CRS brutality from groups of angry students, out in force in the bars and cafés all around the Latin Quarter, he remained disaffected. The issues at stake were too trivial to engage his sympathy, and his dislike of the police was almost perfectly balanced by his scorn for their hapless victims.

'You want jam on it, don't you?' he remarked. 'You've got it cushy, all of you. The system's designed to protect people like you, to make sure you get the best jobs and the best deal for your kids. What have you got to complain about?'

'That's exactly what we're complaining about!' protested Claudine, carefully stowing the bottles back into the crates. 'Injustice! The whole education system is corrupt. It's just a factory to keep the state supplied with spare parts! It's just—'

'I'll leave you to destroy it, then,' said Viktor, bored already. There was time to get in a few hours' kip before Cassie arrived, as she surely would. She was a sucker for punishment, thank God. The stubborn little cow wouldn't give up till she had got what she thought she wanted.

His room was exactly as she had left it, the pillow still bearing the imprint of her head. She was the first woman ever to have lain on that bed. It represented a kind of virginity; perhaps that was why he was scared of losing it. He thought of her stiff and tense and determined, doggedly turning the elaborate tricks that old pervert had taught her, desperate for approval and affection. It would be so pathetically easy to hurt and humiliate her, to ridicule her attempts to please him as a way of covering up his own inadequacies. Having sex was one thing; making love was quite another. He had never in his life made love.

Another wave of first-night nerves rippled through him. He knew all about sensations, and nothing about feelings. He had no idea how to make a woman happy. If he picked a girl up, it was without the slightest intention of ever seeing her again –

he despised those who gave it away even more than those who charged for it. And he had never been taken in by the better class of whore who charged extra for pretending to enjoy it.

Cassie had his problem in reverse. She saw sex as a duty, not a vice, something you got marked out of ten for, part of the monstrous exam of living. What kind of chance did they stand together? It would be a disaster. And if it wasn't a disaster . . . that was too terrifying to contemplate.

He sat down on the edge of the bed and began, wearily, to undress, leaning forward automatically to pick up a couple of pairs of clean silk socks lying on the floor. The top drawer of the tallboy was still open. Viktor was fanatically tidy. It annoyed him how five minutes of Cassie's presence reduced a room to total disarray. But she had no reason to open that drawer unless . . .

He knew before he looked to check that the pills were gone. It was the crudest, most obvious way of getting her own back. She would arrive doped up to the eyeballs, displaying the impenetrable vacuous calm that took her beyond the reach of hurt or happiness. It was a form of infidelity, to punish him for last night, the most despicable form of blackmail.

No. She was bluffing. It was one of her melodramatic gestures, her way of rejecting him, of telling him she didn't need him any more. If only he could be sure of that, he might find the guts to do the decent thing and let her go . . .

'I don't think I can make it to this meeting after all,' said Eva, finding Jan waiting for her after work. 'I've got a lot of typing to do for Karel before I go away.'

'But everyone's going,' said Jan.

Eva hesitated. 'Everyone's going' was always irresistible. There was nothing worse than hearing about things second hand.

'All right, then,' she said. 'But I must go straight back home afterwards.'

'Isn't Karel out tonight?' hinted Jan.

'Yes. But I can't ask you back. I'm not halfway through that manuscript yet and I have to get it finished before I leave.'

'It's a bit of an imposition, isn't it?'

'So what's new? I don't mind. It's so important to him. Anything to keep him in a good mood.'

Jan looked at her uncertainly. 'Has he said he doesn't want me coming round any more?'

'Why should he?'

'After what I wrote in *Spring Tide*, I thought that perhaps he—'

'Oh, he let off a bit of steam. You know how twitchy he gets about any criticism of the Party. He's still an old diehard at heart. He's always having arguments with other members of the club, especially that chap who gave you the interview.'

'So I've blotted my copybook, have I?'

'You were bound to, sooner or later.'

'Sorry if I made trouble for you at home.'

'What makes you think that?'

'You've just been a bit distant, lately. As if you were worried about something.'

Eva coloured. 'I've got a lot on my mind, that's all. With this trip coming up . . .'

'I'm going to miss you, you know. I'm afraid that when you come back you'll be . . . different.'

'Perhaps that wouldn't be such a bad thing.'

'It would be for me.'

'What's that supposed to mean?' asked Eva, fishing for what she didn't want to hear.

'That I love you just as you are.'

He spoke quietly, with dignity. The words didn't embarrass him the way they did her. She badly wanted to say them back at him, to see his face light up in surprise and delight, but instead she muttered crossly, 'I can't imagine why. You're much too intelligent for me. You could do a lot better, you know.'

'Tell that to your stepfather.'

'I like him disapproving of you,' said Eva, only half joking. Jan's diffident manner hid a blistering disrespect for authority, as his outspoken editorial had shown.

'That's a clever young man,' Karel had conceded grudgingly. 'But if you're wise, you won't get too involved with him.'

242

'I'm not involved,' she had insisted, as if to convince herself. 'We're just friends, that's all.'

'He doesn't realise what he's getting into with this magazine of his. Prague is a demagogue's paradise at the moment. There are far too many people sounding off in public about things they don't fully understand. And some of them are undoubtedly CIA plants. Jan could get himself into serious trouble, and you too.' It had been meant as a warning, but it had had the effect of a dare.

By the time they reached Old Town Square a huge crowd had already gathered around the mighty black statue of Jan Hus, burned at the stake as a heretic five centuries before and the inspiration for a new era of fearless self-expression. The atmosphere was heady, as always, making Eva feel part of something huge and powerful, yet personal and accessible, in a way the old dogmas had never been. She was heartily relieved that Karel wasn't with them, because the 'young hotheads' were having a field day.

'The Communist Party is and always will be a power-hungry structure which oppresses the workers it claims to represent!' declared the first speaker, his amplified voice bouncing off the ancient stone, soaring like a prayer towards the twin towers of the Church of Our Lady of Tyn. 'We have cause to be grateful to the Party for many things – our housing shortage, our antiquated transport system, our worthless currency, our low standard of living! Meanwhile the privileged few still live in luxury, buying unobtainable goods with equally unobtainable hard currency. And they call this socialism!'

Eva felt a wave of unease. It was the first time she had heard the Party openly pilloried in this way. Surely there was no need, now that it had undertaken to reform itself from within? Could Karel possibly be right when he talked of Western agitators stirring things up?

Another speaker called for the establishment of free opposition parties, a plea endorsed by a representative of the newly founded Group of Committed Non-Party Members, which was still an illegal organisation but publicised its existence with impunity. This was followed by a call for resumption of diplomatic relations with Israel and condemnation of the repressive regime in Poland, both direct challenges to established foreign policy. Every speech was met by loud and lasting applause.

'Did you agree with all that?' Eva asked Jan afterwards.

'Not all of it, no. But I don't just want to hear stuff I agree with. What matters is that people should feel free to stand up and state their views and try to influence others without fear of persecution.'

'But won't the Russians object if people are allowed to attack the Party in public? Won't they blame Dubček for letting things get out of hand?'

'Nothing's out of hand. Nobody's advocating a return to capitalism, or that we break off relations with the Soviet Union. You think socialism can't survive a bit of healthy opposition? You've been listening to Karel again.'

'You accuse me of listening to him, and he accuses me of listening to you. I do have opinions of my own, you know.'

'Then you can tell me all about them while I see you home. I promise I won't invite myself up.'

'No. There's no need.'

'But I want to.'

'And I don't want you to.'

Jan didn't look surprised, but a shadow crossed his face, robbing it of its familiar mantle of good humour. He kissed her goodnight with less than his usual ardour and turned abruptly to go.

'What's the matter?' said Eva, perversely.

'I wish you'd be frank with me, that's all. I'm not a fool.'

'I've always been frank with you. Right from the beginning.'

'Things have always been a bit one-sided, and at first I d-didn't mind. But now . . . '

'Why are you stuttering? You never stutter with me.'

He couldn't look her in the eye, and she knew in a flash what he had been building up to. Throughout all her mental meanderings as to the whethers and hows and whens of breaking things off with Jan, it had never once occurred to her that he might beat her to it. Yet again, she had underestimated him.

'Eva, I don't know how to say this, but I think perhaps we ought to—'

She silenced him with a kiss, suddenly afraid that if she lost him she would lose everything, that the whole fragile pack of cards would come tumbling down.

'Come home with me,' she said impulsively. 'Karel won't be back for hours.'

'But you said . . . '

'It's all right. I want you to. I always *wanted* you to. Come on.'

She held hold of his hand very tight in the tram going home. Life was full of doubts, nothing was certain. You had to take risks, or you'd never do anything at all. Everything that was happening all around them was founded on faith and optimism; if you stopped to analyse things too much you were done for. It was a time for confidence, not caution.

She suppressed a craven hope that Karel might not have gone out after all and felt a surge of reckless relief when she read the note he had left for her: Back around midnight. Don't wait up.

She showed it to Jan.

'I'm sorry I've been a bit preoccupied lately,' she said. 'If you must know, I've been thinking about you. Us.' She made a helpless gesture to compensate for her lack of words.

'Do you mean that? Or are you just feeling sorry for me?'

'Sorry for you? I respect you more than anyone I know.'

'Do you? Poor Jan, he's so stuck on me, I mustn't hurt his pride . . . '

'It's not like that!'

'You know what's the matter with you, Eva? You've got a low opinion of yourself. You can't understand why I love you, can you? Sometimes I think you despise me for it.'

'That's not true!'

But it was, of course. Trust him to know that. She sat down beside him and put her arms around him, ashamed of her lack of confidence in him, and in herself. Looking over his shoulder she could see Viktor staring at them with that sardonic, superior smile.

'Yes, it is true,' she corrected herself in a small voice. 'I feel so ordinary. And at first I thought you were ordinary too. But you're not, are you? So perhaps I'm not either.'

She stood up and pulled him to his feet and towards her bed, away from that mocking gaze, closing the curtains around them.

'I love you,' he said again. And still she couldn't bring herself to say it back. But from now on she wouldn't need to.

'Cassie! Come in.' Pilar ushered her into the kitchen where she was in the throes of preparing dinner. 'Have you had any news from Armelle?'

'Armelle?'

'Have you found out where she is?' demanded Pilar, looking at her curiously. 'Have you heard any more since that phone call yesterday?'

'Oh . . . no.' Yesterday seemed a hundred years ago. 'But I'm sure Rob will find her.'

'Then what brings you here on a Saturday afternoon? Is something wrong? You look as if you've been crying.' She gestured at Cassie to sit down. 'I'm up to my eyes. It's eight for dinner tonight. Would you like something to eat? Have some *foie gras aux truffes*.'

'No thanks,' shuddered Cassie. 'I'm not hungry.'

'What's up? Man trouble?'

Cassie nodded.

'You're not pregnant again, are you?'

She shook her head.

'What happened?'

'Nothing. That's the whole trouble.'

'What do you mean?'

'Can I sleep on your floor for a few nights? I'll give Madame her lessons as usual but I'm not going into school. I need to lie low for a bit.'

'Because of Viktor?'

'I don't want him following me. I don't want him to know where I am. He's gone too far this time.' She dissolved into a volley of English epithets which required no translation.

Pilar sat down next to her and put a motherly arm around her shoulders.

'Of course you can stay. Poor Cassie. What did he do to you?'

246

Cassie bowed her head in the characteristic gesture that hid her face behind a curtain of hair.

'Sometimes ... sometimes he's so good to me I can hardly bear it. He's the only person who's ever made me feel I mattered. But the rest of the time he's so hard and cold and cruel, almost as if he hates me ... ' Her voice tailed off.

'Men are all the same,' soothed Pilar knowledgeably. 'What does love mean for them? Sex, that's all. The rest of the time, they treat you like dirt. It's normal.'

She began chopping mushrooms, blissfully unaware that she had misdiagnosed the problem, while Cassie struggled to hold on to her anger. It would be so easy just to go round there this afternoon, as arranged, and feign amnesia. They had a tacit pact not to drag one day's disputes into the next. She had been vile to him often enough, after all. Except that she would abuse him in bursts of uncontrollable bad temper, whereas Viktor's jibes were delivered in cold blood, made bearable, almost welcome, by the knowledge that he would make up for them later by being nice. Viktor was at his most lethal when he was being nice, if only because you knew it couldn't last, that it was just the prelude to more pain.

But this time she wouldn't play ball. She would prove to him, and to herself, that she didn't need him any more. And if he needed her, he would bloody well have to admit it. 'Anything I want, I help myself,' he had said. Well, now he would have to. He thought she was weak and dependent, he thought she had no pride. And up till now, he had been right ...

'You'd better go up to my room,' said Pilar, 'before Madame gets back from the hairdresser. Did you bring any clothes with you?'

'Just some underwear and a toothbrush. I was in a hurry. If Viktor calls round here, for God's sake don't tell him where I am. Or Armelle. Or Rob. Or anybody.'

'You're better off without him. Armelle says he's *un type dégueulasse*.'

'She would do,' said Cassie, bristling. 'She made a pass at him once and he told her to get lost. She's never forgiven him for it.'

Pilar looked at Cassie pityingly. 'Armelle says it was the other way round, *chérie.*'

'What?'

'He tried to get her into bed and she told him she wasn't interested.'

'That's nonsense. He can't stand her.'

'Then perhaps that's why.' The gate squeaked. 'There's Madame. Quick, go upstairs.'

Cassie did so. This wasn't running away. What was that phrase the French used? *Reculer pour mieux sauter.* Retreating, the better to advance.

Damn him to hell. What a bloody hypocrite he was, neglecting the dubious charms of her miserable body while he got on with raping every last corner of her mind . . .

Armelle Lemercier, Nanterre activist, embraces her very good friend Alain Moreau, Trotskyist militant, at the Usine MerTech at Boulogne-Billancourt, owned by Mlle Lemercier's father. A practical demonstration of workers and students uniting?

'Is this true?' demanded Albert rhetorically, waving the newspaper in Alain's face.

Alain had no need to look at the photograph, which showed worker and student in a torrid Hollywood clinch. It had been the cause of much ribaldry on his shift, most of it tinged with wry admiration. Screwing the boss's daughter was clearly viewed as infiltration, not collaboration, the next best thing to screwing the boss himself.

'You look for truth in a rag like that?'

'What if Chantal sees it? Or the girl's father?'

'The photograph proves nothing.'

'You take me for a fool ? Suddenly everything starts to make sense. All these months of lies and evasion, all this anti-social behaviour of yours. Lemercier's daughter! If you take my advice, you'll keep your trap shut at this meeting. You'll have no credibility. Now that everyone knows where you've been getting this juvenile taste for revolution—'

He broke off as another man walked into the urinals and grinned knowingly at Alain. 'You've got quite an audience out there,' he observed jovially, unbuttoning his flies.

248

'Can't remember the last time I saw such a good turn-out.'

Alain's face remained impassive, but his shirt was sticking to him underneath his overalls and he could smell his own sweat. If it hadn't been for that photograph, he might well have chosen to keep a low profile and left it to others to do all the talking, ever wary of hogging the limelight. But now he had no choice. If he didn't speak up, and loudly, he would look apologetic and ashamed.

The meeting was indeed packed, much to Albert's chagrin. Georges Leroux called it to order and supervised the passage of a long list of pettifogging, jargon-ridden motions, recommended by the executive and seconded by their usual flunkeys, the sheer boredom of the proceedings designed to keep all but the usual diehards well away. By the time Alain's proposal was finally read out – 'That we officially condemn police brutality at the Sorbonne and urge the National Executive of the Confédération Générale de Travail to call for mass demonstrations in support of the students' – most of the rank and file would normally have drifted off. But not today. Even the most apathetic worker was susceptible to sensation. The photograph had not only fuelled curiosity, but humanised the rather dour political activist, tinged him with mystery and sin. Any worker who could seduce Lemercier's daughter had struck a blow for the weak against the strong. Chantal's absence from work obviated the need for tact. Most of the women shared the view that she had trapped Alain into marriage, while most of the men approved of adultery on principle.

'Those of you who can remember the Nazi occupation', began Alain, proposing the motion, 'would have seen on Friday that Fascists are still with us, here in Paris, in the shape of the CRS. Their function is to curtail civil liberties, to silence the voice of the people with brute force, to break up any assembly which presents a threat to state power. The students' demands may seem remote to us, in our world of work. But their struggle for just representation, for freedom of expression, for the right of each individual to make his voice heard above the din of the capitalist machine – this is our struggle too. Like us, the students are governed by faceless bosses and represented by bureaucratic unions. Like us, they're fed up with petty reform and tired of listening to bullshit. If they can be suppressed by violence, then so can we, and that makes us comrades-in-arms. Defeatists will tell you that we have to work within the system, that compromise is a necessary evil. But I say, nothing's impossible. Nothing's forbidden.'

'And he's proved it!' yelled a voice from the floor. There was a burst of spontaneous applause and a few raucous cheers.

Jacques Rivière promptly rose to his feet to oppose the motion. He quoted *L'Humanité* at interminable length, denounced the students as the dupes of a handful of foreign extremists, and read out a report claiming that police had been injured in an unprovoked attack and been obliged to retaliate.

'I spoke to union headquarters only this morning,' he thundered. 'The CGT is categorically opposed to any display of public solidarity with the students, who have no understanding of the problems facing workers and who merely indulge in politics as a hobby to while away the time until they accept a job in Papa's firm.'

'Perhaps we should have more working-class students, then!' yelled a heckler. 'Then perhaps our kids won't end up slaving away their days in a dump like this!'

The rest of Rivière's speech was drowned out, and the chairman decided to call for a quick vote, anxious to bring the meeting to a close. There was, predictably, overwhelming support for Alain's proposal, not that this emotional excess troubled the wily Georges. It might just become expedient to support the troublesome students – for the union's benefit, not theirs.

Viktor ordered another drink, looked at his watch, and tried to work out what day of the week it was. He had last seen Cassie on Friday night, three hangovers ago. So today must be Monday.

He had left her to stew in her own juice on Saturday, but next morning he had weakened and gone round to her room armed with an outsize box of those disgusting Swiss milk chocolates she liked. After much futile banging on the door, he had been informed by the friendly Moroccan that Mamzelle was not in, a claim which was later confirmed by the concierge who hadn't seen her since the previous day. Viktor had demanded access to her room, on the grounds she might be ill, seized by a sudden sickening fear that she had taken an overdose. A ridiculous notion, of course. He had found all her clothes and belongings in place, proving that she hadn't gone far, and had steeled himself to wait there for her till she showed up. But claustrophobia, or cowardice, had soon set in, so he sought solace in the nearest bar, resolving to lie in wait for her outside Alphonse Cluny next day.

According to the school secretary – a withered crone, not immune to flattery, who had been grotesquely helpful – Mlle Blakeney had telephoned that morning to report a *crise de foie*, and was not expected back for several days. A call at the Lemercier residence had proved equally unproductive. The maid had told him the same story as the school: Cassie was ill and would not be in for the rest of the week. After another abortive visit to her room he had spent a frantic afternoon phoning every hospital in Paris, convinced that she had finally managed to get herself run over. No such luck.

He drained his glass in one swallow and pushed it across the bar for a refill. The whole bloody lot of them were part of the conspiracy. Rob had denied all knowledge of her whereabouts and told him he had had it coming to him. Marta had accused him of maltreating the poor little thing and launched straight into one of her lectures. Both had seemed sufficiently worried about her to convince him that they weren't lying. Time and again, he had tried to drive her away, and now that he had finally succeeded he was filled with a sense of injured innocence. How could she treat him like this?

Monday afternoon. A café in Saint-Germain. A meaningless detail of time and place: he might just as well have been in Timbuctoo at midnight. Dammit. He was crying. He must be very drunk indeed. He pulled a paper napkin out of its holder and wiped his eyes, but the tears were like acid; they flowed backwards into his nasal passages and down his throat, choking him. And then suddenly everyone in the café was making fun of him, mimicking him, choking, spluttering, weeping, fighting their way out into the street, only to retreat back indoors, gagging into scarves and handkerchiefs. Before Viktor could question this strange behaviour, a young man burst inside, his clothing torn, his face bleeding. Wheezing painfully, he ran downstairs into the basement, only to return immediately, staggering, fighting for breath.

'Take him upstairs!' somebody shouted. 'Tear gas is heavy, it sinks.'

'It stinks, you mean,' muttered Viktor, washing down the noxious fumes with another glass of brandy, letting the tears course down his cheeks unchecked. What a wonderful excuse. What a wonderful, wonderful excuse. He could cry as much as he liked, and no one would think any the worse of him. 'Vive la CRS!' he hailed them jovially, as two of their number burst into the café, truncheons at the ready. 'Take off your masks and have a drink!' Swaying slightly, he got up and offered them his glass.

'Out!' They began manhandling people into the street. 'Everybody out of here! This area to be cleared immediately!'

There was a general frightened flurry to obey. Viktor shrugged and sat down again, tears plopping into his glass.

'You,' rasped one of the policeman, taking in Viktor's bedraggled, unshaven appearance. 'Papers.'

Viktor searched blindly in all his pockets before finally producing his identity card, his wet cheeks glistening with a drunkard's smile of idiotic bonhomie.

'Brožek? What kind of name is that? What are you? Another fucking German Jew?'

They hauled him to his feet, took hold of an arm each, and dragged him into the street, where reinforcements were mustering.

'Got a troublemaker here,' sneered one of them. 'Another lousy foreigner come to shit on France.'

The air was thick with a yellow haze of tear gas, sirens wailing, people running in all directions, screaming and shouting. Viktor doubled up in agony as a heavy boot kicked him in the groin, and another sent him sprawling from behind. Gestapo boots. KGB boots. Not that there was any difference. Boots that stamped on anything that stood in their path, that reduced human beings to ants. Instinctively, he curled up into a ball and covered his head with his hands. But at that moment there was the noise of a distant commotion and the boots headed off, leaving him groaning.

'Breathe in,' said a voice. Someone was holding a damp rag over his mouth. It tasted of lemon juice. 'It helps neutralise the gas.' Viktor sat up dizzily and recognised the young man who had fled into the café.

'Thanks for taking the heat off me back there. You saved my skin. I'm on the blacklist. Are you all right?'

For an answer, Viktor rolled over and vomited copiously on to the pavement.

'Here. Your papers.' His companion stuffed them into his pocket and helped him to his feet.

'Place Denfert-Rochereau!' yelled a man on the other side of the street. 'Everyone together! Everyone to the Place Denfert-Rochereau!'

'Can you walk?'

Viktor nodded. Having ejected a large quantity of alcohol, his senses were returning with a vengeance, vengeance being the operative word.

'What the hell's going on?'

'We were having a peaceful march, that's all. As soon as we got near the Latin Quarter we found the bastards waiting for us. We weren't ready for them. But next time we will be.'

'Next time?'

'Tonight, with luck. As soon as we can regroup.'

'I'll show them who's a dirty foreigner,' hissed Viktor, shaking off the supporting arm. 'I'll teach them to put their fucking boots in my face.'

He was still drunk enough not to care about the futility of it all, not to remember that the boots always won in the end, that only the uniform changed. Some ancestral memory of Nazis marching over the cobbles of Prague, of the midnight tread of Stalin's arrest teams echoing on stone steps, of a small country trampled underfoot, stirred him to belated thoughts of revenge.

He grasped his companion's hand and shook it.

'To the Place Denfert-Rochereau,' he said.

'To the Sorbonne!'

It was as if the Lion of Belfort was addressing the crowd through the loudspeakers ranged all around it. The Place

Denfert-Rochereau, a vast square with half a dozen main roads leading off it, was an impossible site to police. However many CRS turned out, there would not be enough of them to block every exit.

Rob kept a firm hold on Armelle's hand, determined not to let her out of his sight. That first whiff of tear gas had warned him what to expect, taking him back to that day last fall when ten thousand students had marched on the Army Induction Centre in Oakland. Now, as then, the police were vastly outnumbered, and it scared them. Frightened policemen lashed out brutally, indiscriminately, more concerned for their own skins than any notion of law and order. And yet the sight of a frightened policeman, however ugly, made people feel strong and brave. There must be at least fifty thousand students here, all determined to reclaim their lost territory. No matter that the Sorbonne was like a fortress: the Bastille had fallen on just such a day as this. No matter that they had been driven back once already by truncheons and gas: their numbers had doubled and trebled since then. Win or lose, he was part of it now.

'To the Sorbonne!' The words were drowned in a mighty roar as the Lion egged them on towards victory. No, not just a roar. Rob looked up to see army helicopters hovering overhead, like vultures. The crowd moved off *en masse* towards their goal, shoulder to shoulder, impenetrable.

It was a long march. The sound of chants and slogans merged into cacophony, like an orchestra tuning up before the performance. Soon the music would start, and the lyrics wouldn't matter any more. He felt the hot, tight grip of Armelle's hand and shut his mind to the newspaper photograph, the recurring image of two bodies entwined, with himself as an impotent peeping Tom. He had seen it quite by chance, lying open on the counter of his local café where he had taken a solitary breakfast. Armelle never ate in the mornings. He had challenged her immediately, but she had talked her way out of it.

'I went to the police station to find out about some comrades,' she had said. 'Next thing I knew, Alain was all over me. What was I supposed to do? Beat him off? I decided it was time to bury the hatchet. I want his people on our side.'

'And just what does burying the hatchet involve?'

'He has a big following at the factory. He could be useful to us.'

'Which gives you an excuse to carry on seeing him, is that it?'

'You don't trust me, do you? The only person on earth I've ever trusted, and he doesn't trust me.'

And then she had opened her arms out to him and lured him back into bed. 'Don't look for a reason to stop loving me. Don't desert me like all the others. You're the only one of them who's not like my father, the only one who's loyal and good and strong.' It had been better than he had ever known it, almost as if his suspicion had fired some need in her. But afterwards the worm of doubt had begun to gnaw again.

It was a relief when the action started, drowning out his thoughts. As the student army reached the Latin Quarter it was met by a volley of tear-gas canisters, exploding into ugly clouds of orange smoke and sending the students scattering in all directions.

'Stay close to me!' yelled Rob, hearing a war cry from Armelle. 'Don't let me out of your sight, do you hear?'

They were better prepared this time. Soon all the side streets leading towards the Sorbonne were manned as barricades were improvised with lightning speed. Rob joined two other men dragging parked vehicles into the centre of the road while Armelle, following his instructions, ran a hundred metres to the rear of him and got to work with the crowbar she had liberated from a building site, grunting in delight as she released the first cobblestone. Soon others had joined her, working quickly, methodically, forming a human chain, passing the ammunition to the fighters in the front line, now protected by a bulwark of cars, uprooted streetsigns and dustbins. Already a second barricade was growing, a few metres behind the first, and beyond that, the beginnings of a third. Someone carrying a bucket shoved something sour into Rob's mouth.

'Get back!' he yelled, spitting out the slice of lemon as Armelle reappeared, breathless, at his side. 'Keep digging up those *pavés*! Do what I say, damn you!'

Meekly, Armelle obeyed him. He was bigger, stronger; he could throw harder, faster, farther, and for the moment he was unquestionably the boss. As long as he kept fighting, she would keep taking orders, and as long as she kept taking orders she would be safe. The bandage on her head was like a dreadful warning. If any of those bastards touched her this time, he would kill him with his bare hands . . .

'CRS – SS!' went up the battle cry as a column of masked police advanced, wielding truncheons. A hail of cobblestones thudded against the plastic riot shields, one after another, almost as fast as bullets from a gun, as the human conveyor-belt kept up a continuous flow of ammunition. There were shrieks of delight as the assailants turned and fled, and a chorus of 'bravo's' from an upper window, where an elderly couple appeared, arm in arm.

'There's food and drink in here for those who want it!' bellowed the woman. 'I hate those Fascist scum as much as you do. Go to it, *mes enfants*!'

'You see?' shouted someone in Rob's ear. 'They're on our side!'

'So two old crackpots are on our side,' muttered Rob, returning Armelle's wave, the signal that he was okay. 'Big deal.'

'You don't understand the French. You don't know our history, our traditions. It's the spirit of the Commune all over again. And they're not crackpots. All workers have cause to hate the CRS. Whenever there's a strike or a demonstration, those thugs are given *carte blanche*.'

Two policemen ran forward to carry one of their injured number to safety. Immediately, a further volley of cobbles rained down on them.

'Stop that!' yelled Rob. 'The guy's hurt!'

'You think they have any chivalry? If a student falls, they kick him while he's down. Don't be soft!'

As if to endorse his words, the rhythm of 'CRS – SS' was taken up by an orchestra of spoons and saucepan lids, as other well-wishers opened their blinds and leaned out of the window to cheer on their young champions. Responding to frantic signals from Armelle, Rob ran back to join her. A group of girls was clustered around a transistor radio.

'They've just called in reinforcements from Rheims and

Orléans,' said Armelle, breathless with excitement. 'Doesn't that prove we're winning?'

'All it proves', said Rob, 'is that it's only just begun.'

'That's it,' said Alain, as the Radio Europe announcer announced the latest casualty figures. 'I'm going up there.'

'But you're on early shift tomorrow!' protested his mother. 'It's nearly ten o'clock!'

'Why bother to talk to him?' interjected Albert, rustling his newspaper. 'He cares nothing for his wife in hospital, but he's worried sick that his fancy woman might have got what's coming to her.'

'Be reasonable, Alain,' pleaded Jeanne. 'There are thousands of students on the streets. You'll never find her.'

'This is nothing to do with Armelle. It's a matter of principle. You heard that news bulletin. If over four hundred police have been injured, at least twice that number of students will have been hurt.'

'But they don't mention any students being hurt!'

'You think they would go to hospital to await a visit from a gendarme? Don't you realise we are living in a police state?'

'Don't exaggerate! I'm no lover of the CRS, but this time they were provoked.'

'Who told you that? Georges Leroux? And who told him? Why do you all need someone else to tell you what to think, what to believe? Come with me now, and we'll see for ourselves!'

Albert re-immersed himself in his paper. Alain slammed out of the flat. He had been itching to go into town all evening, but his duties as a husband had prevented him. He had found Chantal very poorly, for all her stubborn insistence that she was feeling much better; the doctor had taken him to one side and warned him gravely that the chances of a miscarriage were still high. The poor little cow was all but strapped down, forbidden to move from her bed even to visit the lavatory, enduring her ordeal with a bright, brave smile that was full of naked fear. His presence seemed to cheer her. He had felt obliged to stay as long as they let him, and hadn't realised, till he heard the news, just how much he had been missing. He had been wrong to write off Armelle and her comrades as dilettantes. Tonight they had proved that they weren't just talkers.

But by the time he emerged from the Odéon Métro, choking on the gas which had sunk into its tunnels, the battle was over. Burning barricades could be seen beyond the cordon of police and army trucks. There were fire brigades and ambulances on every corner, but no sign of any casualties; those who could walk would no doubt have fled rather than invite arrest. Groups of bystanders stood round muttering and shaking their heads, covering their mouths with scarves against the lingering acrid smoke.

'There were bodies all over the place,' said one woman, ghoulishly 'I reckon a few of them must be dead.'

'Police?' enquired Alain.

'Students. Once the CRS got past those barricades it was a massacre. I saw it from my window, across the street. Three of them lamming into one young girl. I've just had one of them barge into my flat, checking to see whether I'm harbouring any criminals, if you please. No search warrant nor nothing. It's a disgrace . . . '

Alain headed straight for Armelle's apartment, anxious to reassure himself that she was still in one piece. There was no light at her window. He stood outside for a long time, waiting for her to arrive, disappearing into the shadows as he sighted her at the head of her tattered regiment, a group of about a dozen students, carrying bottles of wine and beer. She had that flushed, euphoric look that came from a day's successful conflict. It had filled her with an erotic charge that illuminated her like some sexual aureole. A man had his arm round her protectively, recognisable as Rob only by his height and his hair. The hirsute California dreamer had gone, to be replaced by a hardened combat veteran, his face and hands black with dirt. The look on Armelle's face was one of abject admiration and pride. While they had been at the barricades, Alain had been sitting in a hospital ward, humouring a pregnant wife, being polite to his in-laws, dreaming of escape. He felt like a trapped fly buzzing against the window pane, exhausting itself in futile attempts to fly through glass.

A moment later the light went on, but no one closed the shutters. He could hear music playing, and laughter. Rob and Armelle perched themselves on the window sill, silhouetted against the bright interior, kissing. They looked happy. Not for the first time, Alain found himself wondering what it felt like.

Workers and students unite. If they did, it would be at most a temporary affair, an exercise in mutual exploitation, as doomed to failure as his false, forced relationship with Armelle. He lived in a world of harsh, inescapable realities; she performed on a stage, ad-libbing as she went, postponing real life till some nebulous future, enjoying a youth he had never known.

He stood a bit longer in the dark, watching the flickering images. Then he caught the last Métro home.

'What did I tell you?' said Karel, switching off the radio. The alarming news that Russian troops were heading for the border had provoked a flurry of speculation, despite official assurances about 'routine manoeuvres'. 'I put it all down to that meeting in Old Town Square the other night. I suppose you and that boyfriend of yours were cheering your heads off all the way through.'

'If you're talking about Jan, please use his name, at least.'

'Jan ought to know that to change the system you have to work at it from the inside. That's what Dubček's been trying so hard to achieve. And now the whole ship is being scuttled by impatience. Why do you suppose he was summoned to Moscow that very same night? You can bet they told him to draw in the reins or else.'

'That's not what the newspaper interview said,' put in Eva, although she knew full well that it hadn't been an interview at all. The questions and answers had been prepared in advance and circulated to all the media, just like the 'interviews' of old.

'You expect him to admit he's had a bollocking?' ranted Karel. 'He knows he's got to be careful what he says, which is more than you can say for most people. At this rate it won't be long before the censors are back in business.'

'Well, that's what you'd like, isn't it? You've always had your doubts about free speech.'

'Don't get cheeky with me, young woman. Free speech is a two-edged sword.'

'But you can't limit it! It either exists or it doesn't.'

'Moderation, Eva. Moderation!'

'How can you talk to me about moderation? God, if anyone was ever a "young hothead", you were. Or perhaps fanatic would be a better word.'

'If you're going to throw those memoirs in my face . . .'

Eva started bashing away at her typewriter again, leaving Karel to mull over her accusation. Perhaps she had a point. That meeting in Old Town Square was no different, in essence, from the Communist rallies he had attended after the war. Like the youngsters of today, he had been looking for a guiding star, fired by glorious hopes for the future. And now the wheel had turned full circle. Young people like Eva and Jan were demanding freedom with the same fervour as he had once sacrificed it.

'What's this word supposed to be?' demanded Eva, pointing at his manuscript. 'Your writing is atrocious. Here, you might as well dictate it to me. It would save me a bit of time.'

Chastened, Karel cleared his throat, embarrassed to be speaking his own words out loud.

'"At the time, it seemed to us as if individual liberty did not matter,"' he began. '"The war stopped us thinking of ourselves in isolation. It taught us the value of sticking together in the interests of survival."'

Eva's fingers flew over the keys automatically, her face registering no expression.

'"Material things seemed trivial to those who had tasted hunger, faced death, lost their nearest and dearest. We had to have a vision of something noble and inspiring to sustain us. My generation was inured to martyrdom, stunted by suffering. We acted in good faith and paid the price of our mistakes."'

Eva stopped typing.

'And now you're worried that we'll do the same? Democracy doesn't have to mean capitalism, you know. Just as socialism doesn't have to mean a one-party state.'

'You think they would agree with that in Moscow? They

won't hesitate to use force to suppress what they see as a counter-revolution.'

'Force? You think the West would stand by and watch them invade us?'

'You think they would lift a finger to stop them? Nobody's going to risk starting another war.'

'God, you're depressing me! I might have known you'd turn out to be a wet blanket.'

'I don't want to see a lot of good work undone because of a few irresponsible people putting their own selfish ambitions before the national interest.'

'Are you having another go at Jan?'

'I don't approve of that paper of his. It's inflammatory. Just as well nobody reads it.'

'Don't you believe it. We circulated five thousand copies. And next month it's going to be ten!'

'There won't be a next month at this rate.'

'And if there isn't, you can say, "I told you so"!'

Karel opened his mouth to prolong the argument and realised just in time what he was doing. 'I told you so' reminded him of his mother, whose predictions of doom had come so depressingly true. Expecting the worst was a self-fulfilling prophecy, 'I told you so' a retrospective curse.

He patted Eva's arm in a gesture of truce and took a solemn vow never to say it. Being proved right was the prerogative of pessimists, the vice of victims, the booby prize for surviving tragedy . . . Being proved right would make him feel like a traitor. From the depths of his superstitious soul, he wanted to be proved wrong.

TEN

Rob didn't wake up till two in the afternoon, to find Armelle's side of the mattress empty and cold. They had slept in the little room, ceding the large bedsitting area to their overnight guests, who still littered the floor like so many felled corpses. Only Claudine was vertical, picking her way between the sprawled bodies in a desultory attempt to clear up the remains of the previous evening's celebrations.

'*Salut,*' she greeted him. 'Did you sleep well?'

'Where's Armelle?'

'She didn't want to wake you. She's gone to address a *Comité d'Action Lycéen* out at Neuilly.'

'Don't get rid of those bottles,' growled a sleepy voice behind her, as Philippe returned to the land of the living. 'Gather them up and put them over there, in the corner, till I get some more petrol.'

'Gather them up yourself,' snapped Claudine, abruptly relinquishing her housewifely role.

'Is there any coffee in this place?' demanded another of the men, stretching luxuriously to release a pretty little blonde, who promptly got up and started filling a saucepan with water. Claudine raised her eyes to heaven.

'A meeting at Neuilly?' queried Rob, trying to sound casual. 'She didn't mention it to me.'

Claudine affected not to hear him and disappeared into the bathroom. There was a general, furtive exchange of looks. Not for the first time, Rob had a feeling that everyone else knew something he didn't. And it didn't take three guesses to know what the something was. God, why did loving someone eat up your guts like this? He had come to Europe to screw around, to have the time of his life, to do what the hell he liked, and now here he was, more shackled to Armelle than ever he had been to Ginny, wanting Armelle to be *like* Ginny . . .

Useless to pretend he wasn't jealous. He was even jealous of Claudine, which was every bit as petty as Armelle being jealous of Viktor. Not that he had ever confided in Viktor the way Armelle evidently did with Claudine. Once or twice he had come pretty near it with Cassie, but he had always backed off at the last minute, ashamed to admit to any insecurity. He had made a habit of bumping into her on her Sorbonne days and suggesting coffee, but all they ever did was exchange trivia and invent new howlers for her to teach Odile, who was now word perfect on ordering her breakfast – two very thin slices of testicle wiz strawbuggery jam. Cassie certainly hadn't tipped him off that she was planning on running out on Viktor, not that this news had come as much of a surprise. Viktor had well and truly asked for it, and Rob hoped she made him sweat; the bastard didn't know when he was well off.

He left the apartment and walked the short distance to Viktor's place, hoping to kill time until Armelle got back. Viktor answered the door immediately. He was unshaven and had evidently slept in his clothes, which were filthy and torn.

'Oh,' he grunted ungraciously. 'It's you.'

'Don't tell me *you* were in the Latin Quarter last night.'

'I suppose I must have been.' Viktor held out his blackened hands. 'Disgustingly dirty, those cobbles. Can't think what street cleaning's coming to.'

'Couldn't resist taking a shot at the police, huh? Just wait till I tell Armelle. Perhaps she'll decide you're not a Fascist after all. Whereabouts were you?'

'God knows. I was pissed before I got there. And then afterwards some little tart from the science faculty hauled me off to an all-night party.'

'Does that mean Cassie's still under cover?'

'I hope that's all it means,' said Viktor irritably. 'I'm starting to get worried.'

'She's probably staying with a friend. I could ask Armelle . . . '

'I told you specifically not to say anything to Armelle. I can do without any snide remarks from her. If she doesn't turn up soon, I'm going to report her missing.'

'Isn't that a bit over the top?'

'Perhaps. But I'd never forgive myself if . . . ' he shrugged.

'If what?'

Viktor poured himself a drink. 'Oh, you might as well know. She's got these sleeping pills. Hundreds of them.'

'So? Lots of people take sleepers.'

'You don't know her like I do. There's no telling what she might do.'

'You mean an overdose?' It was unlike Viktor to be so morbid. 'Aren't you flattering yourself just a little bit?'

'On the contrary,' snapped Viktor, knocking back the contents of the glass. 'If she's done it, it's only to spite me.'

'Have you checked the hospitals?' said Rob, still unable to take this fear seriously. It was gratifying to see the hard-bitten Viktor in such an untypically anxious state. He had it bad, all right. Good for you, Cass.

'Of course. The ones in Paris, anyway. Bitch. I'll kill her when I get my hands on her.'

'Why don't you try being nice to her for a change?'

'Nice? That's your department. I'm not nice, in case you hadn't noticed. And if she thinks she can turn me into someone *nice*, she's got another think coming. Look, do me a favour and clear off, will you? I never meant to tell you all this. You two can have a good laugh about it together when she finally shows up.'

'Let me help you look for her, at least.'

'No.'

'Why not?'

'Because I don't want *you* finding her, okay? I feel enough of a fool already.'

'You don't have to feel a fool with me. Hell, I've got problems too, you know.'

'I don't doubt it. Up to her old tricks, is she?'

'What's that supposed to mean?'

'Where is she today?'

'Back at the apartment, sleeping off yesterday. I'd better get back there. Let me know how you get on.'

He left quickly, angry with Viktor for guessing the truth, angry with himself for lying. When Armelle got back from wherever she'd gone, he wouldn't ask any questions. Not because he wasn't jealous and possessive and suspicious, but because he was too damned proud.

'What did he say?' demanded Cassie.

'The usual,' shrugged Pilar. 'He just asked if you had been here and I told him no. That's all.'

'How did he seem?'

'Very polite. He's not bad-looking, is he?'

'He didn't seem ... worried? Or upset?'

'Not particularly.'

'And he didn't leave any message?'

'No. How long is this going to go on? You've got to face him again sooner or later. Or tell him to get lost. Which is it going to be?'

'I don't know,' muttered Cassie, knowing only that she couldn't stick this for very much longer. Not so long ago, sitting in a small room for hours on end would have been routine, normal. She hadn't bargained for feeling so bored. Even giving Odile her lessons had seemed a welcome respite. 'What's happened to Madame Lemercier? It's already twenty past four.'

'Didn't I tell you? She said she might be a little late today. She was having lunch out at Billancourt with Monsieur and a buyer from England. She wanted to practise her English, she said.'

Cassie's stomach did a double somersault. 'She never said anything about it to me.'

'Monsieur just happened to mention it over breakfast and Madame invited herself. I don't think he was very pleased. He said that the man spoke perfect French and she would only make a fool of herself.'

'How true,' muttered Cassie, torn between delight and abject horror, imagining Odile trotting out her party pieces in public.

This wasn't meant to happen until she was safely on the other side of the Atlantic.

'There she is,' said Pilar, hearing the gate creak. 'I bet she keeps you at it till twenty past six now. Or docks your money by half an hour.'

She went to open the door. Cassie shut her eyes and prepared herself for the onslaught. It would be quite a lark to get the sack, she had always known there was that risk. She didn't regret it. It had been fun. Rob and Armelle would fall about laughing; she would be the heroine of the hour.

'Good afternoon, madame,' said Cassie, faltering as she saw that she had a man with her, recognisable from the framed photographs she has seen as Armelle's father. His coarse, florid complexion and stocky build gave the expensive suit an air of fancy dress; he looked like a farm labourer all got up for a wedding.

Odile was very flushed. There were angry red blotches on her neck and she had chewed all her lipstick off.

'Mademoiselle Blakeney?' His voice was cool and courteous. It gave nothing away.

'Monsieur?'

'You little bitch—' began Odile, but her husband silenced her with a look and gestured at her handbag. Odile produced her leather-bound vocabulary notebook, jam-packed with the essential phrases she had learned, and handed it to her husband, visibly quivering with the effort of keeping her mouth shut.

'You recognise this?'

'Yes.'

'You admit that it was compiled under your instruction and supervision?'

'Yes.'

Mme le Censeur's harangues had been good practice for this moment. Cassie swallowed a lump of unease and steeled herself to enjoy it.

'Then you will not dispute that this record gives legal evidence of intent to defraud,' he went on. 'My wife tells me she has signed receipts from you totalling one thousand four hundred and forty francs. Either you pay back this amount in full

266

within the next seven days, or I shall inform the police and press charges against you. In any event, I shall be writing a formal letter of complaint to the Lyceé Alphonse Cluny, to the Ministries of Education both in France and in England, to your college, and to your parents, if only to protect other unsuspecting pupils from your predilection for obscenity and foul language. Good-day, mademoiselle.'

'Fuck off, you filthy little cunt!' screeched Odile, unable to contain herself any longer.

Bertrand Lemercier had the grace to look embarrassed. 'Please go,' he said, raising his voice above another volley of abuse which included several interesting idioms Cassie didn't know.

'Perhaps Madame should give French lessons,' she managed to say, before the door slammed shut behind her.

I'M SORRY. PLEASE FORGIVE ME. VIKTOR.

The words didn't look quite right, but then nothing he wrote ever looked quite right. This was no time to worry about spelling. If she was in, he would have to steel himself to say the words instead, except that they were bound to sound sarcastic. Either way she probably wouldn't believe him. The truth was always less convincing than a lie.

He tapped on the door and put his ear against it. Not a sound. He tried the handle, with some vague notion of forcing the lock, but it opened instantly. The room was empty but the bedcover and pillows were lying on the floor, and there was a faint but unmistakable smell in the air.

'What the . . . oh. It's you.'

Armelle stood for one absurd moment in the doorway, clutching a roll of pale-blue lavatory paper. Her hair was all over the place, her lips swollen, and her cheeks pink and puffy. She looked as if she had just been screwed out of her spoilt little skull.

'What are you doing here?' demanded Viktor. 'Or is that a stupid question?'

'Cassie invited me.'

'You and who else?'

'I don't know what you mean.'

267

'This place stinks like a cheap brothel.'

'Well, you would know.'

'So this is where you do your whoring. Well, well, well. What it is to have friends.'

She turned her back on him and began putting the bed to rights, trying to play it cool. But there was something rigid about the set of her shoulders. She was scared.

'Viktor . . . please,' she began in a small, sad voice. 'Please don't say anything.'

'Where's lover-boy?'

'He's gone. I should have been gone too, but I fell asleep.' She made a helpless gesture. 'Can't you just forget it? What's the point in hurting Rob?'

'Perhaps you should be asking yourself that question.'

'You've wanted to break us up right from the beginning,' she hissed, going on the attack. 'You can't bear to see anyone else happy, can you?'

'I can't bear to see a little slut like you—'

'I'm not a slut!'

'A little slut like you making a fool of a decent guy who's mad enough to trust you.'

'It's your word against mine. He won't believe you.'

'Then perhaps he'll believe Cassie.'

She turned round, eyes blazing. 'Don't try to drag her into this. She's not mean and spiteful like you. And don't be such a bloody hypocrite. I bet you're not faithful to *her*.'

This accusation struck a raw nerve, not because it was true, but because it wasn't.

'Get out before I throw you out,' snarled Viktor. 'And don't ever bring your boyfriends here again, do you hear me?'

'You've no right to order me about. This is Cassie's room, not yours.'

'Here,' he rooted in his pockets and threw some money at her. 'Go to a hotel next time. Somewhere on the other side of Paris. Somewhere safe, where Rob won't find out.'

'A moment ago you were going to tell him!'

'Perhaps I haven't got the stomach for it. Perhaps I wouldn't enjoy making him suffer. I leave that to you.'

She looked at him oddly for a moment. Then she bent to pick

up the notes and made great play of counting them before snapping her takings into her bag.

'Why did you really give me that money?'

Viktor didn't answer, hating the sudden knowing smile playing on her lips. Calmly, she set about primping herself in the mirror, brushing her hair and renewing her make-up. To think of that little slag contaminating Cassie's lonely little room, leaving her stench in the air, making a fool of the only man he had ever called a friend. It was as if she had defiled two out of the three people in the world he gave a damn about.

Seeing his stare reflected in the mirror, Armelle turned round. 'Why did you really give me that money?' she repeated.

Viktor didn't need to answer. It had been a gesture of explicit, specific, calculated contempt. And she had understood it immediately, like the whore she was.

'Poor Viktor. Does he want something Cassie won't do? Does he have a hidden weakness for little sluts like me?'

For an answer, Viktor delivered a stinging blow to her cheek. Her eyes flickered in excitement.

'If you lay another finger on me, I'll scream.'

'Go on,' said Viktor, advancing, appalled at the effect she was having on him. 'It'll give me a good excuse to throttle you.' He slapped her again, harder this time.

'Take your hands off me. I'll tell Rob.'

'Tell him. Tell him what you were doing here in the first place. Tell him why I gave you a bloody good hiding.'

'You wouldn't dare.'

He flung her to the floor, knelt astride her, and pinned down both her arms.

'Time somebody did. God, you're disgusting.'

'And you're pathetic,' she snarled. 'You dirty thief! I'm not afraid of you!' She jerked her head up and spat in his face. Viktor promptly spat back at her and yanked her to her feet by her hair.

'You brute! Go on, rape me. Tear all my clothes off and fuck me to death. That's what you want to do, isn't it? *Isn't it?*' Viktor let go of her abruptly. 'What's the matter with you? Can't you get it up?' She reached for his crotch, making him recoil as if from the bite of a poisonous snake. 'You're scared.

Scared you can't do it.' She unzipped her dress and stepped out of it. 'And I'm going to *prove* you can't do it.' Slowly, striptease-style, she discarded a chaste white bra and panties, keeping her eyes fixed mockingly on his flies.

It was crude, transparent blackmail, to guarantee his silence. She didn't want him, any more than he wanted her. He didn't want *her*. He just wanted *it*, thank God. He would have preferred a woman with her head in a bag, a nameless, faceless fuck, but failing that, she would have to do.

He turned her round roughly, bent her over and took her from behind, like the bitch in heat she was, but mainly so he wouldn't have to look at her, despising her, despising himself. 'If I charged you a hundred francs, would you reconsider?' Cassie had taunted. Oh, he'd wanted her all right, more than he had wanted anything in his life. That was the whole trouble . . .

He had expected it to be over quickly, but it seemed to take for ever, almost as if there was some blockage, some denial that this was happening. He had a giddy sense of watching his own performance, voyeuristically, through a hole in a wall. What an ugly, degrading business it was, like two constipated bodies trying to shit into each other. Armelle was stiff and wooden, flinching with each thrust as if in pain, breathing noisily through her teeth, making out that she was hating every minute, and he hoped to God she was.

A final overwhelming wave of revulsion robbed him of control, catching him unawares, momentarily halting his reflexes – not that there was anything he could have done in the time available. It was one of those split seconds of horror that lasts the rest of your life. And then one door opened and another door closed, for ever.

'I don't like that cough of yours, my friend,' said Miloš. 'When did you last have an X-ray?'

'More recently than you last practised medicine. Stop fussing. It's all this public speaking that's done it. A touch of laryngitis, that's all.'

'Hmm. Eva tells me you promised to give up smoking while she was away.'

'You mean she's set you to spy on me, I suppose.'

'As soon as I get my reinstatement, you're my first patient, agreed?'

'Not if I can help it.'

Miloš watched despairingly as Karel expended three matches on his evil-smelling pipe and sat puffing away like a dirty old train.

'And what about you?' demanded Miloš. 'You should be brushing up on your subject too. Think of it! In a few months' time you could be back in a proper job, using your brain, doing the work you were trained for.'

'I'm happy as I am.'

'Happy? You've done nothing but moan for the last eleven years.'

'Perhaps I enjoy moaning.' He began scribbling calculations on the back of his tobacco wrapper. 'Let's see. Twenty thousand crowns for every year spent in gaol equals one hundred and sixty thousand ...'

'That should keep you in cigarettes for six months at least.'

' ... Assuming they declare my conviction null and void, of course. We're still guilty until proven innocent, you realise. Twenty-five per cent to be paid immediately, the rest over ten years ... That makes forty thousand down and twelve thousand per annum. Enough to leave Eva well provided for.'

'Why so morbid tonight? Are you planning to die, at long last?'

'It was a recent decision. Once you started harping on about X-rays, I knew my days were numbered.'

'And that's your excuse for letting your brain rot, is it? You want to waste what's left of your life making cardboard boxes. Shame on you.'

Karel took a long defiant drag of smoke. 'Once you have a good job, they've got something over you.'

'They? Who's "they"? *They* will be accountable to *us* in future.'

'And to whom will *we* be accountable? It's easier to keep your integrity when you've got nothing to lose. Time I went home.'

'So early? You *are* feeling poorly.'

271

'I'm just a bit tired, that's all.'

He shook his friend's hand and made his way out of the *hospada*, leaving Miloš to finish his beer for him. His meal hadn't agreed with him, and had left a tight, burning sensation beneath his ribs which made him feel breathless. Ironically, his renewed zest for living had increased his tendency to hypochondria, and a morbid fear that his days were numbered made it tempting to overdo things. He ought to ease up a bit. The last thing he wanted to do was to lumber Eva with another invalid to care for.

As he climbed the stairs he cocked an ear for the tapping of the typewriter, but could hear only the drone of neighbouring radios. The initial panic about troop movements had been buried under a wave of fresh optimism, but no one risked missing a news bulletin these days.

He opened the door. The living room was deserted, but the light was on. Two sets of used crockery lay on the table, bearing witness to a recent meal.

'Eva?' he called through the curtain. 'Are you in there?'

'I was asleep,' said a small voice.

'It's not eight yet. Are you ill?'

'No. I . . . I went to bed early.'

'Who was your guest?' As if he didn't know. His cough broke again, making him feel wretched.

'Jan came for supper. Are you all right?'

'I could do with a hot drink, that's all. Don't worry, I'll make it for myself.'

'I'll be there in a minute.'

A nice strong cup of tea laced with rum would settle his chest better than anything. And it always tasted better when Eva made it. He unlaced his shoes and sat down heavily, wheezing painfully, suddenly too exhausted to move, but the sight and smell of the greasy plates made him feel nauseous, so he got up and cleared them away. She was always sneaking that boy back here and feeding him, as the eagle-eyed *domovnice* had not hesitated to tell him. Her innuendos had been less than subtle, and Karel had braced himself more than once to deliver a fatherly lecture. But when it came to it he had been too embarrassed to broach the subject. How could he discuss such things with a girl of eighteen who wasn't even his real daughter? And besides, there was no way to stop it happening; to forbid would only be to encourage. And so he had held his peace, knowing all the while that yet again he had failed her as a father, but then he had never been much good at being a father, even with his own son.

The curtain moved briefly, and Eva appeared in her dressing gown.

'You look dreadful,' she said, rather irritably. 'Are you sickening for something?'

'Nothing a drop of the hard stuff won't cure.'

Her brow was furrowed; she seemed preoccupied.

'Did you and Jan have a row?'

'What makes you think that?'

'He left pretty early, didn't he?'

'That doesn't mean we had a row.'

'Mmm. Pity.'

'What's that supposed to mean?'

'That you've been seeing rather too much of him lately, that's all.'

'I work with him. I see him every day.'

'Which will only make it even more difficult to shake him off when the time comes.' Eva marched off into the kitchen and began clattering dishes loudly in the sink. Too weary to follow her, Karel raised his voice so that she could hear him. Might as well say something now, while he had the chance. 'You only have to look at the lad to know that he's besotted with you. And you don't feel the same way about him, that's equally obvious. You ought to make a clean break, before you break the poor boy's heart.'

Eva came back into the room.

'Don't be ridiculous.'

'I mean to say, he's a nice enough chap, but he's hardly love's young dream. And that stammer of his—'

'You make him nervous, that's all,' she said quickly, interrupting him. 'He never stammers with me.'

'You know your biggest failing, Eva? You're incorrigibly soft-hearted, like your mother. She married me because she felt sorry for me. Don't you go doing the same.'

'There's no need to shout!' hissed Eva.

'I'm speaking quite normally, apart from this damned cough.' He cleared his throat noisily. 'Why are you so jumpy this evening? All I meant to say was that you could do better, that's all. Until your mother died you'd never had a boyfriend. You've no one to compare him with. That's no reason to settle for the first man who comes along.'

'Drink your tea.' She shoved the cup at him, eyes flashing.

'Let me say my piece. I should have had a talk with you long ago. Several times that old bag downstairs has called me to one side and said that you – that you and Jan – well, you can guess what she said. I meant to bring it up before, but I knew you'd accuse me of having a nasty suspicious mind. Nevertheless . . . ' he faltered briefly under her furious gaze ' . . . nevertheless, it's my duty as your guardian to warn you that even the most innocuous kind of boy has no scruples when it comes to . . . to getting what he wants, and if I know you, you won't have the heart to say no to him. If you were in love with him, that might be a different matter, but as it is . . . '

'Stop it!' Eva dropped her dishcloth on the floor and threw her head back in exasperation. 'Don't say another word. *Please.*'

Something panicky in her expression filled him with alarm.

'What is it? Are you trying to tell me something?' Eva shut her eyes and bit her lip. 'Good God. He hasn't got you into trouble, has he? If he has, I'll, I'll—'

'Of course not! Oh, this is hopeless. He can hear every word you're saying!'

Eva strode across the room without another word and pulled the curtain aside. Karel closed his eyes in acute embarrassment.

'Good evening, sir,' said Jan stiffly. He had put his jumper back on inside out, and his hair was sticking up on end. 'I'm afraid we weren't expecting you back till later.'

'Evidently,' growled Karel, taking a scalding sip of tea. 'Seems my little sermon came too late.'

Jan looked at Eva and Eva looked away.

'Everything you said was true,' said Jan quietly. 'I'm g-glad I heard it. Not that you said anything I d-didn't know already.'

Eva took his arm and held on to it, like a lioness guarding her cub.

'And how exactly were you planning to make your getaway, young man?' demanded Karel, recovering himself. 'I happen to be a very light sleeper.'

'He would have stayed until morning,' put in Eva, glaring. Poor Jan blushed scarlet.

'Just how long has this been going on?'

'It was my fault,' put in Jan stolidly. 'I talked her into it.'

'It was my own decision! I would have told you, except that I knew you wouldn't understand!'

'I understand perfectly!' roared Karel. He turned to Jan and wagged a finger at him. 'If I find out you've set foot in this place again behind my back—'

'That's right!' shouted Eva. 'Set the concierge to spy on us, just like the good old days!'

'If I have any more cheek from you, young woman—'

'Can I have a word with Eva?' cut in Jan, putting a restraining hand on her shoulder. 'It won't take a minute.'

Karel grunted assent, glad of a breather. It was his duty to rant and rave, but somehow he had no heart for it. If it was anybody's fault, it was his own, for burying his head in the sand. And now he had probably done more harm than good. Thanks to his ill-timed remarks, she would stick to the boy like glue.

They began speaking in agonised whispers behind the curtain. Karel got up, intending to go outside for a few moments. But then he heard Eva's voice, saying 'No! That's not true!' And then, 'How can you believe that? How can you believe anything that silly old fool says?'

Karel crossed the room on tiptoe, and stood as close as he dared, ears flapping.

' . . . just for a little while,' Jan was saying. 'Next week you've got your holiday. Then we'll wait another month or two, till you decide how you feel.'

'I know how I feel!'

'It's easy to get carried away at the moment. With all this excitement going on, it's difficult to analyse your feelings properly.'

'Speak for yourself.'

'All right then. I've got a lot to prove. All these years I've gone along with the system, minding my own business, keeping my nose clean, trying to stay out of trouble. And now suddenly I'm saying what I think, taking risks, finding out who I really am. I want you to do the same. We're both changing, Eva. We have to let each other change, not hold each other back.'

'Everything was all right till he walked in.'

'Everything wasn't all right and you know it. He just said the words for both of us, that's all. Look, part of me wants to tell him to go to hell, to ask you to marry me. I know you'd say yes, just to defy him. Do you think I'd pass up a chance like that without a good reason?'

Karel padded back to his chair, chastened, not wanting to hear any more. A few minutes later Jan emerged alone.

'I'm sorry about what happened tonight,' he said. 'If you're still angry, please take it out on me, not on Eva. She's upset.'

'Oh, I'm not going to beat her, if that's what's worrying you. Though perhaps I should. I daresay there was blame on both sides.'

'We've agreed to be just friends for a bit. To give Eva a chance to decide what she really wants.'

'And what do *you* really want?'

'I don't want her to settle for second best. Because there's no need, not any more. At least, I hope there isn't. That's what we both have to be sure of. Otherwise it won't work.'

'Hmph. So that's why she's crying her eyes out in there, is it?'

'She said to tell you she'd like to be left alone for a bit. Well . . . I'd better say goodnight, then.'

Karel cleared his throat and held out his hand. The boy had a strong, confident grip which belied his modest, unassuming manner.

'Don't get me wrong,' he growled, by way of apology. 'I want her to settle down. I don't want her to waste the best years of her life tied to an old wreck like me. I want her to be happy, that's all.'

'So do I,' said Jan.

Cassie stood tongue-tied for a moment while Viktor squeezed a protesting Jack back into the box and Armelle draped herself, Greek-goddess-style, in the bedspread.

'He raped me,' she announced sullenly, fumbling one-handed for her cigarettes.

'Is that true?' enquired Cassie frigidly, turning to Viktor. He held her gaze for a moment before discarding it abruptly, like a used match.

'Have you ever known Armelle tell a lie?'

He crossed to the window and stared out at the grey roofs with his hands in his pockets. Cassie tried to feel angry, or shocked, or upset, but all she could manage was a frozen calm, a bleak, bitter satisfaction. She ought to laugh really; the whole scenario was straight out of Feydeau. Of course, the reason you laughed at farce was that in real life it wouldn't be remotely funny.

'He threatened to tell Rob,' went on Armelle. 'I was so frightened I didn't dare resist.'

'Tell Rob what?'

'What do you suppose she wanted your room for?' muttered Viktor. 'To admire the view?'

'Oh my God. You're not still . . . You've got a bloody nerve.' She fixed Armelle with a look of icy contempt, consciously focusing her attention on her, pointedly ignoring Viktor. 'How dare you use my room behind my back?'

'Don't *you* start! Why does everyone feel they have the right to judge me?' Armelle began weeping piteously. 'I was so careful!' she wailed. 'I thought you were teaching Odile till six! I never meant to do any harm! I would have told you about Alain, I wanted to. But I was frightened you might tell Rob! And now you will, just to get your own back.'

'Oh, stop whining,' snapped Cassie. 'What do you take me for? Put some clothes on, for God's sake.'

Armelle stubbed out her newly lit cigarette and abandoned her pretence at modesty, casting the bedspread aside while she dressed. Cassie watched her, coldly appraising her physical perfection. Even in a situation like this, Armelle couldn't help flaunting herself. Every movement and posture was studied, practised, full of arrogant grace. Cassie would have liked to scratch her eyes out, in a theoretical kind of way. But she wouldn't give Viktor that satisfaction. The only way to pay him back was to show she didn't care.

Armelle addressed Viktor's back, sniffing, her dignity somewhat restored.

'If you tell him now, I'm warning you, he'll kill you. He'll beat you to a pulp.' Viktor didn't deign to acknowledge this threat. 'I'm sorry Cassie,' went on Armelle. 'There was nothing I could do. It wasn't my fault.'

'Please go.'

Cassie stood stiff as a board while Armelle gave her a sisterly embrace and beat a hasty retreat.

'You too,' said Cassie. 'I don't want to hear any excuses. Just get out and don't come near me ever again.'

She sounded as if she meant it, if that wasn't too much to hope for. He couldn't have planned things better, really. He could never have brought himself to do this to her in cold blood. 'I'm sorry. Please forgive me. Viktor.' He put his hand in his pocket and screwed up the piece of paper in a tight, angry ball. The words had been as hollow as one of those meaningless deals people did with God at times of crisis: Please let her be all right and I'll never do anything wrong, ever again. And now she was all right; she was more than all right, damn her.

'You're admirably calm, I must say,' he said, turning round. 'I'm impressed. How many of those damned things did it take?'

'None. I flushed the whole bloody lot down the loo. Which is what I should have done in the first place. Now clear off, will you?'

Whether she really meant it or not, this was his heaven-sent opportunity to be rid of her for good, to shed the crushing burden of her dependence. No, not her dependence. His. Somewhere along the line she had turned the tables on him, manipulated him as surely as Armelle had done, forced him to act against his better judgement. But not any more.

'You mustn't blame Armelle,' he said, shrugging. 'It's not her fault that she's so damned sexy. I just couldn't help myself.'

'Spare me the post-mortem. I'm not interested.'

'It won't stop us being friends, will it?' he goaded, twisting the knife. 'I do hope we can be adult and mature about this. It was just a physical thing. There's really no need to be jealous.'

'Goodbye, Viktor.'

She opened the door wide, freezing him with a chilling, glittering calm, a million degrees colder than the kind that came on prescription. It suited her.

'I adore it when you get angry with me. It makes me feel loved. And you do love me, Cassie, don't you? Don't you?'

She didn't answer, but her eyes betrayed her, telling him all he needed to know, giving him the strength to walk away. He had never heard her weep, and he didn't want to.

'Talk, talk, talk,' grumbled Armelle. Rob yawned. The Boul'Mich' had become an open-air political bazaar, with groups of students clustered all along its length, engaged in round-the-clock discussion about tactics and objectives. There had been no more clashes with the police since Monday night's bloodbath; just endless marches and demonstrations, each one bigger than the last. After three interminable days of non-violence, Armelle was getting bored.

'This is a waste of time!' she yelled, as an earnest Communist student urged an end to confrontation.

'A committee of elected representatives should seek a negotiated settlement!' he bellowed. 'We have assurances of support from the trade unions if we proceed in a calm and orderly fashion.'

Armelle jumped up and down in fury. 'He's asking us to sell out!' she yelled, through cupped hands. 'We sit here talking on the pavement while the police still occupy the Sorbonne and innocent people rot in gaol! While five hundred people nurse their injuries unavenged! We must fight back, as the Vietnamese people are fighting back! What kind of revolution do you want, comrade? I'll tell you. One the Party can control, as always!'

'Cool it,' muttered Rob. 'We don't have to listen to him. Why don't we go back home for a couple of hours?'

'Go home? You realise what's going on, don't you? The revolution is being betrayed!'

'What's the matter with you? The police are leaving us alone. For the last three days we've marched all over Paris and they haven't made a move. Because they know that public opinion is on our side. That's progress.'

'Progress? Don't be so gullible. There's some dirty deal going on behind our backs, can't you see? Why do you suppose the CGT is suddenly backing us? The PCF is trying to take control!'

She returned a signal from a nearby group, where Philippe and his cohorts were mercilessly heckling a well-known Communist writer, who had arrived with a couple of minders in a gleaming official car, expecting adulation. Rob took refuge in his instrument.

'Hailstones in May, what a surprise,
 They melt into blood and bring tears to your eyes,
 We're black and blue, the cobbles are red . . . '

He struck a jarring discord.

'We make love in the streets, but we make war in bed . . . '

She was at it again, shouting herself hoarse, working herself up into a frenzy. Polemics gave Rob a headache even in English; in polysyllabic French they had the mind-numbing effect of a CRS truncheon. He was tempted to leave her to it for a while. It didn't look as if there would be any trouble tonight. Clearly the police had been told to back off. Now that workers and schoolchildren had swelled the ranks of the demonstrators, they would be wary of inviting more bad publicity.

He ambled over to her for one more try. 'I've had enough for one day. I'm going back to the apartment.'

'Mmm? You go ahead. I'll be along later.'

'You and how many others?'

'Okay. See you.'

'For Christ's sake. Listen when I speak to you!'

'I'm sorry.' She pulled down his head and kissed him. 'I'm just very tense at the moment.'

'I know a good cure for that.'

'Please, Rob. I'm not in the mood.'

She hadn't been in the mood since that glorious Monday

night. And now it was Thursday. Rob felt another wave of gut-rotting suspicion and made a determined effort not to show it.

'Look, I'll meet you back here at six, okay? Don't go running off anywhere without me.'

She nodded and squeezed his hand, and ran off to join Philippe's group. Resigned, he strode off, shouldering his way through the crowds of onlookers who had come to witness the free street entertainment. Police vans were still in evidence, but discreetly so, their inhabitants skulking out of sight. Poor bastards. In tranquillity, it seemed a waste of energy to hate them. They were only obeying orders, after all. The real villains, the politicians who pulled the strings, never put themselves in the front line, here or in Vietnam or anywhere else. And yet, when you saw the CRS advancing, dehumanised by goggles and masks and shields, hating them was easy. Too easy.

Rather than go home he wandered down towards the Seine, heading for his favourite spot, opposite Notre-Dame, strumming away at his home-made song.

'Hating's so easy, killing is too,
Living and loving's much harder to do,
Peace feels like death, life feels like war,
Revenge is illegal, injustice is law,
Hailstones in May, what a sur—'

'Cassie!'

She was standing on the edge of the embankment, staring into the water, as if contemplating whether to jump in. She looked round, startled.

'Oh. Hello.'

'Where have you been hiding yourself all week?'

'I went away for a few days. Actually, I ought to be getting back. See you.'

'How about a drink?'

'I'm in a bit of hurry, actually.'

'You didn't look in a hurry a minute ago. Are you all right? What's the matter?'

'Nothing. I'm absolutely fine.'

'What about Viktor? Is he absolutely fine as well?'

She looked away. 'Have you spoken to him recently?'

'Not recently, no. I've called round there a few times, but he's never in. What's going on between you two?'

She blew her nose. 'Oh, you might as well know. It's finished. Thank God. Look, I really must go.'

She tried to walk past him, but he caught hold of both her hands and pulled them behind his back, bringing her face level with his chest. She was rippling with suppressed tears.

'Go on,' he said. 'Cry. Let it go.'

'Please, Rob. I have to . . . I have to . . . oh shit.'

'That's right. Don't fight it. It's okay.'

It took a real bastard to make a girl cry like that. It reminded him of the way Armelle had wept over Alain. He held her close for several minutes till the tears subsided.

'D-don't tell him I c-cried. P-promise.'

'I won't say a word. Look, let me take you home. Then you can tell me all about it.'

'No. I don't want to.'

'All right. Don't tell me all about it. But I'm still going to take you home.'

'There's no need. Honestly.'

'Shut up, Cass. Do as you're told.'

Sullenly, she obeyed him. Careless of his tight budget, he hailed a cab, as she had once done for him, and bundled her into it. He remembered what Viktor had said about the sleeping pills, remembered her teetering posture on the edge of the Seine, and knew that he couldn't risk leaving her alone in such a vulnerable state. Perhaps he could act as a go-between, help them patch things up.

'There's no need to come all the way up,' she said, as he paid off the taxi, overruling her attempts to beat him to it. 'There are seven flights.'

'Look, when I was hurting, you looked after me. Now it's my turn.'

Grudgingly, she led the way up the stairs.

'Christ, this must keep you fit,' he said, panting.

'I don't notice them any more. But I won't miss them either.'

She opened the door. A suitcase lay on the bed and a cabin trunk stuffed with books and clothes stood in the middle of the room.

'You're moving?'

'Yes.'

'Where to?'

'I'm going home.'

'When?'

'Tomorrow.'

'Because of Viktor?'

'Of course not! It's nothing to do with him!'

'Then why?' She didn't answer. 'What about your job?'

'I don't have a job. I've been suspended. They've called in all the girls' exercise books to check out what I've been teaching them.'

'What?'

'Odile wrote to the school. She found out about me conning her. Armelle's father says if I don't pay back the cost of the lessons he's going to have me up for fraud. It's nearly fifteen hundred francs and I don't have it.'

'Christ. What a bitch.'

'It's my own fault. I had it coming.'

'Look – Viktor would give you the money.'

'Are you kidding? I'd rather go to gaol.'

'Does he know the trouble you're in?'

'No. And don't you dare tell him. I honestly don't want to talk about it. If I hadn't bumped into you back there—'

'Come back to our place tonight. Armelle—'

'I don't want to see Armelle!'

'Listen to me. She'll be furious when she hears about this. She'll put you in touch with a lawyer who'll give you free advice. Sounds to me like her father's just trying to scare you. Why give him the satisfaction of running away?'

'I don't want any help from Armelle, okay? Or you. Or anybody. I can manage on my own.'

Ignoring her, Rob sat down on the bed and patted the space next to him. But she shut the lid of the trunk and perched herself on that instead, not looking at him, fidgeting with the hem of her skirt.

'What did Viktor do to you this time?'

'What do you think?'

So that was all it was. Stupid bastard. How could he risk

losing a girl like that for the sake of some flea-bitten whore?

'Cassie, he thinks like a Frenchman. For them, it's no big deal. Don't over-react.'

Her eyes flashed coldly. 'It's easy to talk. How would you feel if you walked in and found Armelle with somebody else?'

'You mean you actually caught him in the act?'

'Go on, tell me. What would you do, if it had been Armelle?'

Rob hesitated. There were times when you had to preach what you couldn't practise, and this was one of them. 'That's not the point. Viktor screwing some little tramp isn't the same thing as Armelle cheating on me.'

'Why isn't it?'

'Well . . . for one thing, he's a man.'

'For God's sake!'

'Okay, so there's a double standard. I'm not defending it, I'm just saying it exists. Sex is different for men, that's all.'

'I might have known you'd make excuses for him!'

'I'm not making excuses. But if you love him, you have to—'

'Let him make a fool of me? Put up with any amount of shit rather than risk losing him? Is that how much *you* love *her*?'

'Yes! I mean, no! That is . . . I'll bet he's every bit as miserable as you. I'm not condoning what he did, far from it, but—'

'For Christ's sake stop sticking up for him! You can't believe a bad word about anyone, can you? You trust everybody. Even Viktor! Even Armelle! God, what a pair we are!'

She turned her back on him, as if wishing the words unsaid. Rob pulled her round to face him but she wouldn't meet his eyes.

'Meaning what exactly?' he demanded, his voice suddenly harsh. She shook her head. He took it between his hands and forced her to look at him. 'Meaning *what*?'

'It's your own fault for coming back here. I wasn't going to say anything. If you hadn't gone on and on and on at me I wouldn't have—'

'Cut the crap, Cassie. Just tell me.'

But by then, she didn't have to. It was as if he'd known all along.

* * *

'That's your girl, isn't it?' hissed one of Alain's workmates, nudging him. 'Aren't you going to say hello?'

Armelle was haranguing a man twice her size, supported by cheers from her cronies. Alain scanned the group, looking for Rob, but he wasn't there.

'Not with you lot watching. I'll see you later, okay?'

They grinned and headed off towards the Mutualité, where they had arranged to meet up with other workers. Alain hung back, waiting for Armelle to finish speaking, then raised his hand discreetly and caught her eye. After a moment, she joined him.

'*Salut!* How many people have you brought with you?'

Her brisk, comradely manner gave nothing away.

'About thirty. Not counting the union delegation. They'll be giving you their official support, you'll be glad to hear. Special instructions from the CGT. Congratulations.'

Armelle nodded cynically. 'We've been waiting for them to jump on the bandwagon. Now we've proved we're a force to be reckoned with, they'll try to take all the credit. They make me sick.'

She accepted a cigarette and drew on it hungrily. She seemed on edge.

'They're pragmatists, not idealists,' shrugged Alain. 'And once they've got what they want out of this, they'll sell the students down the river. Do your people realise what they're up against?'

'We know that all kinds of dirty deals are going on behind our backs. We were ready for the police last night, thousands of us, till the UNEF marshals broke the whole thing up. Traitors. I could have cried. Tomorrow night we're planning an all-out attack to liberate the Sorbonne. Spread the word, will you?'

'You can count on us. My mates are getting pretty pissed off with marching up and down and singing the "Internationale". They're looking for some action.'

Her eyes lit up in anticipation. Then, abruptly, she dropped her voice to a murmur. 'We have to be a bit careful. I think Rob suspects something.'

'Because of that picture in the paper?'

'Partly. What about your wife?'

'What about her?'

'I don't want to break up your marriage, Alain. You know me better than that.' The old sugary spite was back in her voice.

'You don't understand how working-class people live,' said Alain coldly. 'For you, everything's a drama. Chantal knows that I would never leave her for you. As long as you know that too.'

It was the answer she wanted. She set no value on what was accessible; she was like a poor girl dreaming of princes.

'We can't use Cassie's room any longer,' she continued, in the same furtive undertone. 'Wait for me tomorrow at the café, but don't be surprised if I don't turn up. *D'accord?*'

She ran back to join her friends. Seeing Rob's tall figure striding towards Armelle's group, Alain suppressed a desire to expose her there and then and walked quickly away. He did not witness the sudden intense dialogue between them, did not see Rob pull Armelle roughly by the arm and lead her away. And did not hear the subsequent chorus of knowing, heartless laughter.

'What's going on?' demanded Marta, handing Viktor a sheet of notepaper. 'This arrived in the post this morning.'

Viktor looked at the signature and handed it back to her. 'Read it to me.'

'Why didn't you tell me?'

'Just read it!'

'"Dear Marta, I'm having to go home earlier than planned due to a sudden emergency. Please don't worry, it's nothing serious. I hope Eva's visit goes well, and I'm sorry I won't get the chance to meet her. Thank you for all your kindness to me. Love and best wishes, Cassie."'

Viktor poured himself a glass of wine.

'What's this emergency?' demanded Marta. 'Is somebody ill?'

'I haven't the faintest idea.'

'It's you, isn't it? You're the emergency! You've finally driven the poor girl away.'

286

Viktor didn't answer. The news of her departure was a shock. No, a relief. Now he wouldn't have to think about her any more. Wouldn't have to fight the temptation to go after her, or wrestle with the hope that she would come back to him. Now he could finally go back to the way he was before . . .

'The first decent girl you've ever met and—'

'That's enough, Babička. I don't want a lecture, okay? It's over.'

'This is postmarked yesterday. Perhaps she hasn't left yet. Why don't you go round to her place and see if you can make it up? Once she's gone, you won't get another chance.'

'Another chance to do what? Ruin her life? Or let her ruin mine?'

Marta threw the letter down in exasperation. Viktor picked it up and put it in his pocket.

'She was so looking forward to meeting Eva,' lamented Marta. 'She was going to take her to the lycée for a day, and show her round the Sorbonne and take her shopping and . . . oh, get out of my sight.'

'Don't start, Babička, please.'

'That girl believed in you!'

'Touching, isn't it? She even started teaching me to read, so I could get myself a lousy job. I'm not going to change, not for her, not for anybody. I like my life. I chose it.'

'You mean it chose you.'

'I know, I know. I'm lazy and stupid. I've heard it all before.'

'You're neither and you know it. When are you finally going to stop trying to get your own back for things that happened years ago? We lose all our money and possessions, so you have to help yourself to other people's. Your father gets arrested on a trumped-up charge and twenty years on you're still breaking the law just to prove that you can get away with it. Your mother—'

'What's with all these sudden theories?'

'They're not sudden,' said Marta stiffly. 'They're obvious.'

'Since when? You've been talking about me behind my back and she's been trying to *explain* me!'

'What if we have? We both love you!'

'Then more fool you!' He got up and made for the door.

'Don't you dare walk out while I'm talking to you! If you do, you needn't bother to come back!'

'Don't make me laugh. I may be a shower of shit, but I'm all you've got!'

'And I may be a foolish old woman, but I'm all *you've* got! And I'm all you'll ever have, if you carry on like this!'

She flopped down into an armchair in a crumpled heap, looking suddenly very old and sad and frail. Viktor wished she would take that leather belt to him and make it quits. But those halcyon days were past.

'I'm sorry, Babička,' he said wearily. 'I treated her badly. I couldn't help it. You know what I'm like. It would never have worked.' Marta grunted, unimpressed, and blew her nose. 'I could have got her to forgive me. She always does, just like you. But I didn't. Because she's better off without me.'

Marta glared at him over the top of her handkerchief, as if silently acknowledging this truth. The look was full of disappointment – which he was used to – and contempt, which was something new.

'Couldn't you have waited another few weeks?' she said coldly. 'It was such a relief, knowing that Cassie would take care of Eva. I knew I couldn't rely on *you*. She was going to take her to the ballet, and Versailles, and—'

'I'll do it.'

'You and your promises. If you show me up, I'll never forgive you.'

'I won't show you up.'

'You make me sick, Viktor. I'm tired, I think I'll go to bed early. There's food in the kitchen if you want it.'

'I'm not hungry.'

'Please yourself.'

She hobbled off into her bedroom, leaning heavily on her stick, leaving the air thick with reproach. Viktor let himself out, glad to have got that little ordeal over with. Time to go home and change into working clothes. A visit to the opera would soon get him back into his stride. A nice crowded foyer full of fat wallets and three soothing hours of Mozart. And then tomorrow he would go to the races and help himself to a few winnings. There was nothing like betting on a sure thing.

'Your American friend is waiting upstairs for you,' announced Mme Bloc, intercepting him in the hallway. 'He said you were expecting him and so I had to let him in . . . ' She cocked her head expectantly.

'Er . . . thanks.' Viktor shoved five francs at her, disconcerted. Rob was the last person he wanted to see. He had been avoiding him all week, knowing he wouldn't be able to meet his eye. Bloody friends. Who needed them?

'Rob?' he called as he let himself in.

'About time, you bastard!'

'Now wait a minute . . . '

The first blow was so sudden that Viktor lost his balance and fell over.

'I don't care about Armelle,' snarled Rob. 'You can fuck her all you want from now on. Get up, damn you! I haven't finished with you yet.'

Viktor struggled to his feet and held up his hands in a gesture of surrender, seized by an almost comic sense of *déjà vu*. It had started with a fight, and it would end with a fight. A nice touch, that.

'Hit me all you want. I deserve it. Look, I don't know what she told you, but—'

'Oh, she gave me all the crap about you raping her. Trust you to know how she likes it. Rape really turns her on.'

'For God's sake, listen to me—'

'Shut up. Like I said, this has nothing to do with Armelle. Otherwise I'd go round and beat up Alain as well. This is for *Cassie.*'

Another vicious punch to the jaw sent him reeling.

'I'm not going to hit you back,' said Viktor, staggering to regain his balance. 'I've got no quarrel with you.'

'You gutless little shit. How could you do that to her?'

'It was easy, really. First I took her clothes off, and then I bent her over, and then—'

Instinctively, he put out an arm to save himself as the next blow sent him crashing to the floor. He felt a sudden, sickening snap and a wave of nausea, but no pain. The pain would come later. He shut his eyes and began laughing, hoping that Rob would finish the job and beat him senseless. But no such luck.

He heard the door slam, and footsteps running down the stairs, and then the black, empty silence of perfect freedom.

ELEVEN

'Here we are,' said Cassie, as the taxi drew up outside a big, grey, double-fronted house. It looked solid, impregnable, reassuring. She would never have believed that she would feel so glad to be home.

'Are you sure your folks won't mind me turning up like this?'

'Of course not. The house is always full of people. One more won't make any difference.'

Rob had crashed out on Cassie's floor the previous night, but not before a heart-to-heart that had lasted well into the small hours. The assumption that they would never see each other again had loosened both their tongues; by morning the bond of shared secrets made it hard to say goodbye. Rob had already announced his intention to 'hit the road', anxious to get well away from Armelle. Knowing he had never been to London, Cassie had offered, shyly, to put him up and show him round – which was as good an excuse as any to give each other moral support.

'It would be one in the eye for Viktor and Armelle,' she had said, with a glimmer of malice. 'They're bound to jump to the wrong conclusions.'

Or the right ones, thought Rob, still unsure if she had been warning him off or leading him on. 'Why don't we swap partners?' Viktor had taunted. Perhaps it wasn't such a bad idea.

Rob helped the driver haul the cabin trunk out of the taxi, while Cassie rang the bell, to no response. She fished around for her keys and opened the front door, revealing a wide, gloomy hallway lined with dark panelled wood.

'Looks like they're out,' she said. 'Leave the trunk down here while I find us two spare beds. Mummy lets my room out to students during term-time. And they're always having people to stay. I suppose I should have warned her we were coming, but I couldn't face explaining over the phone.'

'Will your parents be mad at you?'

'They never get mad. They'll write the whole thing off as a lot of silly fuss about nothing.'

'Lucky you.'

'Yes. I know I am.'

Rob followed her up the stairs. A very dusty antique bureau stood on the first-floor landing, flanked by two huge hideous urns, chipped and scarred with deep cracks and full of dead flowers. The carpet was threadbare, the wallpaper scuffed and grubby, and the air smelt of old books, like a college library.

Cassie opened a couple of doors, put her head round them, and, seeing evidence of house guests, led him up to the top of the house.

'We'll have to sleep in the nursery, I'm afraid. Mummy never puts anyone in there. The roof leaks.'

She showed him into a large, mansarded room smelling strongly of damp, home to a geriatric rocking-horse, a dismantled clockwork train set, and a dilapidated doll's house. Battered books, broken toys and jigsaw puzzles were stacked randomly on sagging shelves; two single beds were arranged asymmetrically, to avoid the leaks from the roof. Buckets and bowls were dotted all around the floor; the ceiling was peppered with drainage holes and mottled with dirty brown stains. Cassie flopped down on one of the beds.

'Sorry about this. You don't mind sharing a room, do you?'

From any other girl, it would have sounded like a come-on. But the question was anxious, apologetic, devoid of innuendo. She trusts me, thought Rob, despondently.

'Won't your parents object?'

'Even if they did, they would never say so. You must be starving. I'll see what I can find and bring up a tray. Make yourself at home.'

A yellowing calendar hung on the wall, depicting an old master for every month; it still showed Constable's 'Hay Wain', illustrating September 1959. A cluster of dolls lolled together on the floor beneath, looking old and tired. Rob bent to pick one of them up, imagining Cassie playing with it as a child, making its eyes click open and shut. They were china blue, to match what remained of its baby-blonde hair, most of which had been cut off, leaving the scalp peeping pinkly through the ravaged tufts, testimony to some tiny tantrum. The room struck him as claustrophobic, redolent of a confined, bookish childhood and a lack of fresh air. Even on this mild evening it felt chill in here, as if it had never been touched by the sun.

Cassie returned a few minutes later with a tray of odds and ends and a decanter of whisky. She splashed the Scotch into two cloudy tumblers and got stuck into a packet of chocolate digestives, while Rob ate a ragged remnant of overcooked chicken and adorned a pile of stale cream crackers with hard butter and crumbly cheese.

'What did they say to you at immigration?' she said through a mouthful of biscuit.

'That I only had a tourist visa and how long was I staying and did I have a return ticket back to the US. So I showed them my *permis de séjour* and told them I was going back to France. They gave me a month. Reluctantly. Those guys really hate draft resisters.'

'Except that you're not, are you?' She leaned forward, took off his spectacles and put them on herself, removing them almost immediately as her eyes began watering.

'I am in principle,' said Rob, retrieving them. 'That's what matters.'

'Why did you really leave?' She topped up his glass, inviting indiscretion. Oh, what the hell, thought Rob. He'd told her so much already, she might as well know the whole story.

'It's the easy way out, failing a medical. If your parents know the right people they can rig it. Or get you into the National Guard. All perfectly legal and hypocritical. I don't hold with that. If you don't want to fight, you should get out or go to gaol.'

'But your medical wouldn't have to be rigged.'

'You're missing the point. I needed to make a protest. And besides, I wasn't just protesting about the war.'

'What then?'

Rob shrugged, embarrassed. 'After my brother got killed, my family expected me to do all the things he would have done. Go to college, get a good job, settle down with a nice girl. I'd always looked up to Mike, wanted to be like him. So I went along with it. And then one day I woke up and thought, I didn't choose any of this, this isn't me. I had to get away to find out who I really was.'

'It doesn't work, you know,' muttered Cassie. 'You feel different when you're away from home. It's like having two identities. But underneath you're still the same person, whether you like it or not. The minute I walked through that door I felt like a child again.'

And for the moment, that was what she wanted to be, thought Rob. A child again. A wish which all his instincts warned him to respect.

'It's nearly midnight,' she said, inspecting her watch. 'They've probably gone to the country for the weekend. Have a bath if you like. It's the second door on the left, downstairs. I hope you don't mind lukewarm water. The geyser's been on the blink for years.'

She gathered up the debris of their meal, leaving Rob to make his tepid ablutions in a massive, draughty bathroom, equipped with decaying loofahs, moth-eaten towels and a coffin-sized oak chest containing hundreds of back numbers of the *Times Literary Supplement*. By the time he returned Cassie was sitting up in bed, reading.

'I brought up a radio from downstairs,' she said, indicating a Mark One bakelite model. 'Will it disturb you if we have it on for a bit? You know what a raving insomniac I am.'

'What do you want to listen to?'

'I couldn't care less as long as it's not music. It might set me off again.'

After some knob-twiddling, he tuned into a soporific documentary about the life cycle of the fruit bat; in twenty minutes

294

or so, Cassie dropped her book and dozed off, while Rob lay wakeful, endlessly reliving his last encounter with Armelle. He was a lousy lover, she had said, striking at the heart of his deepest insecurities. He was boring and unimaginative and conventional. Being with him was like being married.

This orgy of introspection was mercifully interrupted by Cassie gasping and moaning, twisting and turning, fighting for her life against some demon of the night. Rob got up and caught hold of one of the flailing arms.

'It's okay,' he murmured. 'It's just a dream.'

'What time is it?'

'Ten after two.'

She switched on the bedside light and sat up.

'Once I wake up I can never get off again,' she said irritably. 'Would it bother you if I read for a bit?'

'Don't worry. I can't sleep either.' The radio was still on, but the station had stopped transmitting. Rob began fiddling with the knobs again, filling the room with a Babel-like discord, stopping short as he heard a voice speaking in French.

'Listen.'

' . . . Every street around the Sorbonne is filled with CRS in full combat gear. Negotiations between student leaders and government spokesmen have ended in deadlock and, as I speak, the barricades are manned for action. Throughout the evening thousands of young workers have made their way to the Latin Quarter to swell the ranks of the students. After many hours of uncertainty, it seems that the order has finally been given to clear the area . . . '

'Plus ça change,' muttered Cassie, flicking over the page of her book.

Rob felt a pang of something like homesickness. Only a few days ago he had been in the thick of it; now it was going on without him. The reporter's voice rose excitedly, like a sports commentator, yelling into the microphone to make himself heard above the background noise.

' . . . And now I can see the CRS advancing towards us. Missiles are being hurled at the police from upper windows as local residents join in the fray. It's hard to see . . . there's water

295

everywhere ... the demonstrators have turned on the fire hydrants to disperse the suffocating fumes of tear gas ... ' The voice collapsed into a splutter and another one took over.

' ... And here in the rue Saint Jacques, the police are backing off under a hail of bottles, bricks and Molotov cocktails ... no, they're just regrouping, ready to storm the barricades again ... ' There was a loud bang. 'They're now shooting gas grenades through the open windows, in retaliation against the onslaught from above. And now back to my colleague in the rue Gay Lussac ... '

' ... I have in my hand an empty canister which provides proof positive that CS gas is now being used against the demonstrators ... '

'Christ,' said Rob. 'That's the stuff they use in Vietnam.'

'This is a highly toxic gas, which produces violent and incapacitating symptoms. It is normally used only in combat situations and ... '

Some music started playing.

'They've pulled the plug on him,' said Rob, searching quickly for another channel. 'The bastards are going to start killing people.'

'Don't worry about Armelle. She'll be all right.'

'I'm not worried about her.'

'I know. It's political, not personal.' It was one of Armelle's stock phrases. But for Rob, it had always been personal. In his mind's eye, he could see the barricades burning, flames shooting twenty feet into the sky as the petrol tanks of the overturned cars exploded like bombs, showering debris. He could see a policeman clubbing a fleeing student about the head till the body slumped at his feet, only to receive more vicious blows; see the blood gushing out of Armelle's head, staining the cobbles; hear the wail of ambulances and cries of pain.

' ... the CRS are now engaged in a house-to-house search for those who have fled the burning barricades. Anyone with dirty hands or injuries is liable to arrest. A convoy of police vans is moving away from the scene, full of dejected prisoners, many of them bleeding ... '

They sat listening till the broadcast ceased at dawn. There had been four hundred and fifty arrests and three hundred and sixty casualties; some two hundred cars had been destroyed. Eye witnesses reported that police had stormed a Red Cross post and beaten up the medical personnel, dragging the wounded back out into the street and manhandling them into the vans. Local residents complained that they had had their doors kicked in and that innocent people had been assaulted and taken off for questioning. Many schoolchildren and young workers, as well as students, had apparently been hurt. Finally, Dany Cohn-Bendit had come on the air and challenged the unions to prove what side they were really on by calling a general strike.

'It makes Monday night seem pretty tame,' said Rob, almost regretfully.

'Good job you weren't around,' said Cassie. 'You're one of those foreign agitators they're always on about. At least this way you've still got your permit.'

Rob grunted, preoccupied. Cassie waved her hands in front of his face to attract his attention.

'You wish you were still there, don't you?'

'Yes. In a way.'

'So do I,' she said.

Rob had paid the rent up to the end of the month; Armelle saw no reason to move out before then, not that she spent much time in the apartment. Another vicious night of street fighting had achieved a major victory – the withdrawal of police from the Sorbonne, which was now being occupied night and day. This belated placatory move by the Government had done nothing to defuse the situation. Fortified by its moral victory, the revolution was getting into its stride. The 'Sorbonne Commune' was in permanent session and offered shelter to all who sought it. Food was cooked and served round the clock, to sustain the soap-box orators and their disciples, an operation financed by voluntary contributions from the public. Inevitably this free-for-all had attracted an assortment of hangers-on – vagrants, hippies and drug pushers – but there was no non-Fascist way of excluding them. *Occident*, enraged by the occupation, had made an abortive attempt to storm the citadel; since then a group of self-styled mercenaries had been recruited to discourage would-be invaders. The leather-clad *Katangais* gang, armed with knives and chains, were a law unto themselves, but their menacing appearance had achieved the desired effect.

While Armelle was with Alain, or fighting the police, or touting for revolutionary funds, or taking her turn on the podium, or applauding and heckling by turns at the Odéon Theatre – now requisitioned by the students to house a vast public teach-in – she was able to pass herself off as happy. Only Claudine had been privy to her tears. Philippe and Co. had dispersed, leaving Armelle in sole occupation of both rooms; Claudine had stayed on, at her friend's invitation, to provide sisterly support.

It had been a good day. The two girls had joined a march on the big Renault factory at Boulogne-Billancourt – one of MerTech's major clients – where students had managed to converse with workers through locked gates and bring work to a standstill, much to the chagrin of the CGT, whose recent one-day strike, rigidly controlled and organised, had been designed as a negotiating lever for wage demands, not as a commitment to the revolution.

'Shall I make us a nightcap?' asked Claudine, yawning.

'If you like,' said Armelle grumpily. 'I'm not tired.'

She lay down on the bed, looking up at the pencil sketch Rob had done of her, which was still pinned up on the wall. It was a romantic head-and-shoulders pose, not the nude she had asked for. That was typical of Rob. Prudish and possessive. He didn't like the thought of anyone else seeing her naked, even in a picture.

'God, you're beautiful,' he had told her, over and over again. Beauty. It was like a perfect apple with a core full of maggots, eating their way slowly outwards. Well, now he knew that she was just a little slut. It was almost a relief. Now she could hate him, just like all the others. She jumped up, tore down the picture, and ripped it into shreds.

Claudine handed her a mug of hot chocolate, and began picking up the pieces.

'Bitch,' hissed Armelle.

'Are you talking to me?' said Claudine mildly.

'She just did it for spite, that's all. She didn't care how much she hurt Rob, as long as she got back at me for bloody Viktor.'

'Can you blame her? You can't expect her to do you any favours.'

'Well, she has done.'

'Poor Rob. He was never one of us, you know. I don't think he ever cared about the revolution. Only about you.'

'Well, it made a change from Alain. With him, it's the other way round.'

'It's sexual politics again,' said Claudine, resuming her favourite theme. 'Women always end up on the sidelines, one way or another. Look how it was at the Odéon last night. It's supposed to be an open platform for anyone and everyone to present his views. His views. Hardly any women stood up. But every man who spoke had some adoring female applauding him. It's the same at the Sorbonne. They're like a lot of sheikhs strutting around a harem. We're the ones who ought to go on strike. What use is the revolution if women are still going to be inferior?'

'Then why don't you stand up and say so?'

'I told you before. I'm a coward. I'm afraid of ridicule. But it would be different if there were several of us. If we would only stick together, instead of looking for male approval, then men couldn't divide and rule any more. It would be harder for them to control us and bully us and turn us against each other. Easier for us to develop our confidence and formulate our own ideas and demands.'

'You mean, form a women's group? They'll write us off as a bunch of lesbians . . . sorry.' Armelle never missed an opportunity to make an 'accidental' slip of the tongue.

'Does that worry you?' said Claudine calmly. 'Because if it does, perhaps I'd better move out. I'd hate to damage your reputation.'

'What do you take me for? I don't give a shit what people say about me.'

'There's safety in numbers. I've been talking to Sylvie and Yvette, and they feel the same way.'

'Sylvie Poujol? That little scrubber?'

Claudine made a gesture of exasperation. 'Whose side are

you on? Marcel threw you over for Sylvie. Like Étienne threw me over for you. That doesn't make any of us scrubbers. We've been conditioned from birth to be rivals when we ought to be allies. Can't you see that?'

'Okay, okay. I just wish it wasn't her, that's all. I never liked her, even before Marcel. And I dare say the feeling's mutual.'

'This isn't about friendship, it's about solidarity. Anyway, how about if I invite them over one evening? Just so that we can knock some ideas around?'

Armelle made a *moue* of half-hearted assent. Men had always been the enemy, after all. As for Claudine and Sylvie and Yvette . . . they were only women.

Eva's pact with Jan precluded their seeing each other alone, but he had broken it to say a brief goodbye.

'I meant what I said about you writing a piece about Paris,' he said. 'But that doesn't mean I want you getting involved in these riots. Their police sound even worse than ours used to be. So steer clear of the "young hotheads", do you hear me?'

The cover for the next issue of *Spring Tide* bore a cartoon showing a disconsolate Czech policeman, cap in hand, applying to join the French CRS. The caption read, 'At home they won't let me beat people up any more!' And now she wouldn't be there to help print and distribute it. It had gone against the grain to hand over her typewriter to another volunteer, but perhaps it was just as well she was going away. The last ten days had been awkward for both of them.

'I can't get out much these days,' Marta had written, 'thanks to this wretched ulcer on my leg, but Viktor's English girl-friend, Cassie, will be meeting you at the Gare de l'Est and bringing you back here. She is tall with long fair hair, but don't worry about recognising her – she has seen the photograph you sent and will be looking out for you . . . '

It had been too much to expect, of course, that Viktor would deign to collect her himself. No doubt he regarded her visit as an imposition. And yet all the hard currency in her purse had been sent, at one time or another, courtesy of Viktor, and more than likely she wouldn't be allowed to pay for anything, on the same basis. Like it or not, it put her firmly in his debt. She would have to be nice to him, however arrogant and insufferable she found him. On balance, she hoped he would be. It would reduce her sense of obligation.

Eva was stiff and itchy from twenty hours' travelling; the third-class couchette had left her feeling as if she had been kicked all over. As the train drew in, she lifted her suitcase off the rack, taking care not to jar it. Marta had told her not to bring many clothes, she would run her up a new wardrobe, but the case was weighed down not only with Karel's manuscript, but with a heavy glass bowl in Bohemian crystal, which, being export quality, had cost Eva precious dollars.

She stepped out on to the platform and began walking slowly towards the ticket barrier, looking this way and that for any sign of Viktor's girlfriend. The station was deserted, it being early on a Sunday morning, and after standing with her luggage for a few minutes, she parked herself on a bench. France had a curious smell – a pungent cocktail of tobacco, garlic and public lavatory, overlaid with a tantalising aroma of new bread and real coffee. A group of young men were flyposting on a wall, right under the eye of a uniformed station official. Eva was puzzled to see that the posters were just blank white sheets of paper. After a few moments, an elderly man carrying a suitcase stopped, contemplated the empty space, put down his luggage, and responded to the unspoken invitation by scrawling a grotesque cartoon of General de Gaulle wearing a Hitleresque moustache, while Eva watched, fascinated. Having finished his sketch, the artist stood back to admire his handiwork and noticed her looking at him. He grinned broadly and made a mock bow, assuming her approval; the simple gesture made her feel instantly at home, because in Prague, these days, strangers smiled at each other in the street, bound by a sense of common purpose.

For some obscure reason, the station clock had no hands – Eva was not to know that local anarchists had removed them, a symbolic anti-authoritarian gesture copied from the days of the Paris Commune. Not having a watch, she had no idea how long she had been waiting, but it seemed like at least half an hour. Another ten minutes or so trickled by. How much longer should she give it before starting to make her own way? She

301

had Marta's address written down, but venturing into the labyrinthine Métro system seemed foolhardy and a taxi would surely cost a fortune. Nervously, she got her hand mirror out of her bag and gave her face a quick dab of powder. God, what a sight. She spat into a well-worn block of mascara and began thickening up her eyelashes, blinking painfully as the brush caught the underside of her eyelid, releasing a spurt of tears.

'Sorry I'm late.'

She jumped to attention, startled, not immediately recognising the speaker. Through a blur, she saw a man wearing dark glasses.

'Welcome to Paris.' He extended his left hand. The other was invisible, except for its fingertips peeping out from a plaster cast resting in a sling. 'Is that all the luggage you've brought?'

He picked up the suitcase.

'Careful,' said Eva. 'It's fragile. I brought some crystal for Marta. You . . . you're Viktor, aren't you? I was expecting your girlfriend.'

'She had to go back to England,' he said shortly. 'What with all these riots and so forth, her parents wanted her at home.'

'Karel was a bit worried about me coming,' nodded Eva. 'But it would have taken more than that to put me off. What have you done to your arm?'

'What does it look like? I broke it. Don't tell the old girl I was late, will you? We'll say the cab got stuck in traffic.'

'Er . . . of course. I hope I haven't put you to any trouble.'

'No, no, I love getting up early on Sunday mornings. Come on.'

A taxi was waiting for them outside the station, with its meter still ticking away. Automatically, Eva began converting the number of francs into crowns – at the unofficial rate – and felt duly horrified.

Viktor offered her a cigarette, which she declined, and lit one himself, filling the cab full of smoke. Eva's eye, still trying to eject the gobbet of mascara, began watering anew at this onslaught.

The dark glasses made him look rather sinister, like a gangster, and seemed pretentious in view of the overcast weather. Eva craned her neck out of the window, hoping to catch sight of some famous landmark, but she couldn't see much except traffic, which seemed to be nearly all private vehicles, not public transport as at home. As they stopped for a red light, a silver-blue open-topped sports car drew up alongside; a girl about her own age, still wearing evening dress from the night before, was driving it with superb nonchalance.

'Do you have a car?' she asked Viktor.

'No. I prefer cabs. Why?'

'I just thought everybody did, in the West.'

'If there's somewhere you want to go, I can always hire one. I'm honour-bound to satisfy your every whim.'

'There's no need,' said Eva politely, picking up the mockery in his voice. 'I'm sure I can find my own way around.'

'That's a relief. I'll hold you to it. But don't let on to Marta.'

'I'm sorry if she's been putting pressure on you,' said Eva placidly. 'I won't say a word.'

'Good girl. If you need any money, let me know. Those city tours are a rip-off. And watch out for pickpockets, won't you? The crime rate in Paris is something shocking. All part of the decadent Western way of life. Then there are the white-slave traffickers. You feel a little pinprick on your arm and next thing you know you're in some Arab brothel. Now, there's an original way of defecting. And make sure you steer clear of the police. They're on the lookout for foreign agitators. Specially Reds like you. One look at your papers and you'll be hauled off for questioning on suspicion . . . Are you sure you'll be all right on your own?'

If he was trying to be funny, it was at her expense. There was a bored, derisive edge to his voice, and his manner hovered uncertainly between the off-hand and the provocative. Eva struggled to find some witty rejoinder and failed.

'Forgive me,' he continued, with a self-castigatory gesture. 'I promised Marta I'd be nice to you. Not making a very good job of it, am I?'

'Well, it must be a nuisance, having to disrupt your schedule for me.'

'I don't have a schedule at the moment.' He tapped the plaster cast with a knuckle. 'Thanks to this thing.'

'You're off work?'

'Yes.'

'Can't you write with the other hand?'

'No,' he said curtly, as if it were a silly question.

For the rest of the journey he was silent, sitting back in his seat, dragging away on his cigarette like a junior edition of his father. So far he was exactly as she had imagined him – cold and supercilious. But knowing she had no gift for backchat, she decided that her best line of counter-attack would be stubborn, infuriating good humour. It had always worked with Karel, whose black moods were water off a duck's back. Perhaps his arm was giving him pain. Or perhaps he was missing his girlfriend. Or perhaps ... Why was she making excuses for him?

Eventually the cab drew up outside a decaying apartment block rendered with peeling stucco, not unlike the one Eva lived in. She had been expecting something a great deal smarter, having always assumed, as indeed Karel had, that Marta lived quite comfortably. The old lady was standing with her front door open, having sighted them from her window. She pinioned Eva in a tearful embrace.

'You look so like your mother,' bleated Marta. 'Doesn't she, Viktor? Isn't she the image of poor Věra?'

'Yes,' said Viktor shortly. 'Look, I'll leave you two to talk. See you later.'

Marta ushered her into a cramped, cosy room. To Eva's disappointment a large crystal bowl filled with fresh fruit held pride of place on top of the television set, but Marta expressed herself ecstatic at Eva's gift. She was soon overwhelming her with hospitality, twittering like a bird in her eagerness to make her feel welcome. Eva began to relax. Here was someone who was genuinely pleased to see her, poor old thing. There were endless queries about Karel, and the situation at home, Marta's eyes alive with hungry curiosity. Eva kept her answers cheerful and optimistic, not mentioning Karel's bad chest or the anxieties about Russian troops. This was a time for good news.

'Was Viktor late meeting you? I was getting worried.'

'No, he was already waiting for me. But the train was a little late. And then the traffic was bad.'

'He told you about Cassie?'

'He said that she had to go back to England.'

'Such a pity. You would have liked her. I'd even taught her a few words . . . Still. Viktor will take good care of you.'

'Yes,' said Eva, smiling brightly. 'Yes, I'm sure he will.'

Bertrand Lemercier had dismissed the one-day strike as a minor inconvenience which would save him a day's wages. Negotiations with the union had been proceeding well; with luck all outstanding matters would be settled before his visit to America at the end of the month. Well, perhaps not all outstanding matters . . .

Armelle Lemercier, Nanterre activist, embraces her very good friend Alain Moreau, Trotskyist militant, at the Usine MerTech . . . It might have been himself and Madeleine all those years ago, an over-indulged, headstrong beauty in the arms of a rough young worker. Their faces were merged in a kiss, but he could almost see her mocking smile, his anxious frown. Undoubtedly she had seduced him, and not the other way round: he had experienced a stab of fellow feeling for her luckless victim. In consequence, he had chosen to ignore his daughter's liaison with MerTech's leading troublemaker, if only to thwart her hope that he would make himself a laughing stock by sacking the fellow, or forbidding her to see him again.

He got out of bed carefully, taking care not to wake Odile, not so much out of consideration for her beauty sleep as from a desire to avoid having to talk to her. With every day that passed he disliked her more, for her avarice, her discontent, her lack of warmth. And yet, those were the very qualities that had attracted him to her. She had seemed a safe bet – a woman as coarse and materialistic as himself, who understood his baser needs, who in no way resembled his adored first wife, who would never have the power to hurt or humiliate him. Above all, a woman who would protect him from Armelle, and Armelle from him.

'Bertrand?'

'Go back to sleep. I'm going into the factory in time for the early shift. There are rumours of wildcat action.'

'But you were supposed to come with me to the clinic!'

305

'Well, I can't. Not today.'

'Why not? Because you're afraid of what they might say? I can tell you that already. There's nothing wrong with me. There's never been anything wrong with me.'

She got out of bed, harridan-like in her rollers and hairnet, and stood, arms folded, between Bertrand and his reflection in the full-length mirror.

'Congratulations,' he said, calmly adjusting his tie. 'I rejoice for you.'

'Doctor Braque specifically asked to see you. How are we ever going to have a child if you refuse to cooperate? If there's something wrong with you—'

'There's nothing wrong with me. I have a daughter.'

'Do you? What makes you so sure?'

With cold precision, he slapped her across the mouth. 'Shut up.'

'That's right. Hit me and prove what a big man you are. You're a brute, Bertrand. In bed and out of it. No wonder your first wife left you.'

'If you find me so distasteful, by all means do the same. The marriage contract provides for all your needs. I married you for a son. If you cannot provide me with one—'

'You married me for sex! And by God, I've kept my side of the bargain.'

'And charged me through the nose for it. I must go.'

'You refuse to see the doctor?'

'I have no need of one.'

'So if I were to get pregnant . . . you'd have no doubt that the baby was yours?'

'Do not force me to divorce you for adultery, Odile. It would substantially reduce your portion. And invite the possibility of *crime passionel*. Don't think you can make a fool out of me.'

'No, of course not. I leave that to your daughter. If that's what she is . . . '

'That's enough!'

'Not only that, she tries to make a fool of me as well! I've never been so embarrassed in all my life! I'd lay money she put that little English cow up to it!'

'If so, their little plan could only have worked with a singularly ignorant and unintelligent pupil.'

'Ignorant and unintelligent, am I? Well, you should know!'

She proceeded to revile him in gutter French while Bertrand completed his *toilette*, affecting not to hear her. Eventually she threw an ivory-backed hairbrush at him, catching him on the back of the head and squealing in triumphant terror as Bertrand advanced towards her, his eyes hard and cold. There was a brief tussle on the floor while he tore off her nightgown, shut his eyes, and fought to obliterate the memory of bliss, the dizzying sense of melting into his own flesh, lust transmuted into a kind of sacrament, blessed relief from months of bitter loneliness mingled with poignant, agonising guilt. Fourteen-year-old Armelle waking from a troubled dream, hungrily returning his embrace, screaming with terror at the sudden inexplicable pain, firing his unstoppable desire. And yet she had clung to him afterwards and wept, as if some stranger had been the culprit, misinterpreting his self-disgust as rejection. 'Don't be angry with me, Papa. Don't go away, like Maman. Don't stop loving me . . .'

And he never had. He had married Odile out of love for Armelle, but she would never understand that. He had half hoped that she would expose him, punish him with the public disgrace he so richly deserved. But predictably, she had kept their secret, driven by a guilt and shame even deeper than his own. If he had suspected then, for one single moment, that she might not be his daughter, he might have felt marginally less culpable. But the experience would have been sullied, diluted, less profound. Even now, he could not bear to think that any other man could have created such perfection.

'You've ruined my nightdress,' muttered Odile crossly, inspecting the torn silk. She straightened up and Bertrand noted with disgust that she was running to premature seed. Her thighs were already wider than her hips, her breasts had begun to sag, and her buttocks were pitted with cellulite. Three years ago, she had seemed young enough to save him.

Odile flounced off into the bathroom. Such confrontations left her unmoved. Like Bertrand, she had grown up in a violent home where abuse was routine and a thick skin a prerequisite for survival. She was more of a comfort to him than he liked to admit, in that she knew the very worst of him and thought it normal.

His driver was waiting for him outside the house, the morning papers crisply folded on the back seat. The news was not good. In the wake of Monday's strike, a rash of spontaneous unofficial stoppages was spreading like wildfire across the country. With this threat in mind, he had called an extraordinary meeting with union representatives for that afternoon, determined to avert any attempts to cash in on the prevailing industrial unrest. His intended assault on the American market made the long-delayed overtime deal and the installation of new plant more vital than ever.

As the gleaming Citroën swept through the factory gates he observed, with some satisfaction, that a group of young agitators attempting to distribute subversive literature were having little success. The early shift streamed past them, unwilling, no doubt, to be duped into losing any more of their meagre income. Most of them dropped the leaflets without reading them, leaving them to sink ignominiously into the puddles left by the overnight rain. It seemed like a good omen.

That afternoon's meeting got off to a slow start. As always, Bertrand said little, leaving his yes-men to do most of the talking. A good hour was wasted in preliminary waffle, with both sides agreeing that the recent clashes between the students and the CRS had no relevance to the problems facing the workforce at MerTech.

'Evidently not,' interjected Bertrand impatiently, making everybody jump. 'Would I ever call the police into these premises? Would I ever stand by and watch them attack my employees with truncheons and tear gas? I would remind you that I was once a working man myself. The one-day strike was a waste of everybody's time, except as a gesture of contempt for the incompetent way the Government has handled the whole affair. Let's get one thing straight. All a worker is interested in is wages, working hours, and job security, not the mindless polemics of overgrown schoolchildren. If there are any revolutionaries at work in this factory, I have no doubt that the union can keep them in check.' He looked meaningfully at Georges Leroux. 'So let's get down to facts and figures.'

He sat back again, listening to the dogs he paid to bark on his behalf. The role of employer still felt like an ill-fitting coat, several sizes too big for him. He was a doer, not a talker.

'Ultimately, these enhanced demands are against the men's best interests,' droned Bertrand's chief accountant. 'They would make it economically impossible to install the new plant which we need to enable us to keep up with our competitors. A fall in productivity would result, orders would be lost, and workers laid off.'

'New plant designed to cut how many jobs?'

'New plant designed to save jobs. An extra ten per cent per overtime hour backdated to January and multiplied over the next financial year would reduce our investment budget by approximately—'

'You can prove anything with statistics,' interjected Georges Leroux, rapping the desk. 'We both know you'll recoup your losses one way or the other. If you want the deal, you have to pay what it's worth. And give guarantees for the future.'

Guarantees that would be so skilfully worded as to be meaningless. Georges loved to blind his members with words. Words could make any compromise look like a triumph.

The haggling went on for the rest of the afternoon, with Georges and his cohorts attempting to capitalise on the threat of further action, and management, following Bertrand's cues, making frequent allusions to the crumbling authority of the union and the prevalence of Trotskyist agitators.

'The best way to disarm such people', countered Georges, 'is to settle the grievances they feed on. I can guarantee that this improved deal will be voted in by a huge majority. If you want to pull one over wreckers like Alain Moreau, you have to show the workers which side has more to offer.'

'Moreau?' enquired Bertrand blandly. 'Who's he?'

'How many are with us?' demanded Alain, never taking his eyes off his work, well aware that his flunkey of a foreman had been told to watch him like a hawk.

'At least two hundred.'

'Anyone against?'

'I think they're mostly waiting to see what happens. Should we call a meeting?'

'No. I don't want to talk people into anything. Just pass the word round and tell them that they're free to join in or not. It's not an instruction, it's an invitation. If enough people oppose us, so be it – it's up to them to take their own action.'

Word flitted from ear to ear like a bee growing huge with pollen. The one-day strike had been 'official'; yet another thing you had to do whether you wanted to or not. But this was different. This was unauthorised, voluntary, a chance to disobey, or at least stand back and watch while others did.

Albert stood stolidly at his lathe, his face betraying no emotion. He couldn't bring himself to condone wildcat action. But he wasn't going to stick his neck out to condemn it either. He wasn't a steward any more, thank God. He had no duty to tell tales. Strange how you could almost hear the buzz of excitement above the din of the machinery. It took him back to the heady days of mass strikes and occupations. He remembered the intoxicating recklessness, the sense of integrity that came from sticking together, the collective pride born of a common struggle. Alain had never known that exhilaration. He had been prematurely disillusioned by the double-dealing and hard-headed pragmatism of professional negotiators like Georges, the new breed of collaborators masquerading as partisans.

The hooter sounded, signifying the end of the shift. All he had to do was go home quickly, knowing that many others would follow his example. There would be no betrayal in it, no shame; it would not be like crossing a picket line. Uncertainly, he clocked out and made his way to the bicycle sheds. But people were moving sluggishly, indecisively; those ahead of him kept looking behind, those behind him were splitting off into groups, talking and gesticulating, waiting . . .

Then the hooter blared out again, long and loud. For a moment, nobody moved. The hated sound that governed their lives had acquired a new note of defiance. It sang on, taunting them, daring them to ignore it now when they had obeyed it reluctantly for so long.

Slowly, inexorably, the tide turned. People walked back the way they had come. Albert stood indecisively for a moment. If they'd voted for this, he'd have gone along with the majority, wouldn't he? Well, this was a vote of sorts. If he turned his back on this, he would be no better than a scab.

By the time Lemercier emerged from his lair, safe behind the smoked glass of his chauffeur-driven car, the banners were out. Every long, low building bore the same legend draped from window to window: USINE OCCUPÉE. They parted the gates for him with the utmost courtesy, and waved him on his way. Then they padlocked them safely behind him.

'Three hundred francs,' said the pawnbroker, evidently unimpressed.

'But it's a solid-gold Rolex!'

'I'm allowing for that.'

The guy ought to be a fence, thought Viktor sourly. But what the hell. It was only short term, after all. He would redeem the watch as a matter of principle, not because he gave a toss for the thing itself. He thrust his good hand into his trouser pocket and brought out three pairs of jewelled cufflinks. Might as well get it all over with at once. The honest merchant inspected these closely.

'Are they hot?'

'If they were I'd know better than to bring them to you.'

'I'm bound to tell you, you'd get more from a jeweller.'

'I'm aware of that. But I don't want to sell them.'

'I can't give you much.'

'Then it will cost me that much less to buy them back.' Viktor tapped his plaster cast. 'I'm self-employed. Can't earn a sou till this thing comes off. Then I'll be taking the whole damn lot off your hands, pronto.'

All those weeks of not being 'in the mood' had taken their toll. Viktor had counted the money in his piano stool that morning and found barely enough to pay his next month's rent. He had never bothered to save for a rainy day, for fear of losing his edge; now less than a thousand francs stood between him and a major cloudburst.

At least it was a genuine reason not to work, rather than a

311

feeble excuse. Trying to operate with his left hand would have been asking for trouble; in addition, having an arm in a sling made you dangerously conspicuous. The niggling suspicion that he had lost his nerve could be shelved for a few weeks longer, displaced by the much greater fear that his hand would somehow rot and atrophy inside its plaster casing, emerging stiff, weak and clumsy, never to regain its former agility, despite all the talk of physiotherapy and it being a nice clean break. The awkward angle of his fall had snapped both radius and ulna, necessitating a cast which immobilised the arm from fingers to elbow, imprisoning him for a minimum of six weeks. Viktor had instinctively mistrusted the doctor, a smug, author-itarian figure who had refused point blank to set the arm until the patient sobered up. By the time the excruciating pain had driven Viktor to seek help, several hours after Rob had left him laughing, he had been very drunk indeed.

A thousand lousy francs. Still, there was plenty of other stuff he could hock, and Eva wouldn't cost much to entertain, except in terms of time. And, deprived of his other entertain-ments – either from lack of funds, or lack of an arm – he had time on his hands.

Poor kid. He had promised himself he would be nice to her, but the sight of her sitting on that bench, looking so uncannily like Věra, had put him on the defensive straight away. She had the same round, rosy face and short, buxom build, the same air of being between smiles. A vivid image of her mother had pro-voked an equally vivid image of his own, hurtling him back to good times and bad times, all of them equally painful. He remembered Eva as a gurgling infant, sitting on his mother's lap in that foul little room, grinning from ear to ear, while Věra beamed and said, 'Which hand?' and gave him the biggest, reddest apple he had ever seen . . . the taste of it had flooded his mouth, seventeen long years on.

Watching her, unobserved, had been like watching a fire dancing in the hearth, throwing up fleeting, flickering images, drawing the eye deep into the heart of the flames, luring him towards a hot pit of memories, burning down the barricade that protected him from his past. He had walked away from her before she spotted him and taken refuge in the nearest café,

emerging half an hour later with an irresistible need to antagonise her. But evidently she wasn't the touchy type. If in doubt,
she took refuge behind that jolly, dimpled, maddening, disarming smile.

Yesterday he had endured a day of excruciating boredom,
trailing round the sights. Her ingenuous delight in everything
touched and irritated him by turns; her cheerfulness was both
a comfort and a reproach.

'Paris isn't as beautiful as Prague, of course,' she had said.
'Or perhaps I'm just prejudiced. What do you think?'

'I don't know. I can't remember Prague.'

'I suppose you must feel as if you've always lived here.
Specially as you're a French citizen.'

'Not by choice. Marta arranged it all while I was still too
young to object. That doesn't make me French.'

'You mean you still feel Czech?'

'I didn't say that.'

'What do you feel then?'

'God, don't you ever stop asking questions?'

'I'm interested, that's all. I would have thought that having
two nationalities ought to give you the best of both worlds.'

Or the worst, thought Viktor, not deigning to comment on
this fatuous assumption. His avowed loathing of France and
all things French had started off as a sour-grapes reaction to
the unspeakable misery of being an alien. Those early weeks at
the *école maternelle* had been worse, much worse, than the
year he had spent being bullied and victimised in Prague.
Unable to understand a word of what was going on, he had sat
there seething with frustration and humiliation while a well-
meaning teacher shouted and made sign language and the
other children sniggered in derision. By the time he had ceased
to be a circus freak, he had cultivated a perverse delight in
being different. If he couldn't join them, he would have to beat
them.

He would always be a foreigner, and therefore inferior; more
inferior than most, a native of a subjugated, impoverished
country, a country people ran away from because it didn't bear
living in. Except that people did live, or rather exist in it. Drab,
grey regiments of puppets, pulled by strings from Moscow. A

passive nation, drained of spirit, purged of honest men, governed by fear, and betrayed by every friend it ever had.

He might be ashamed of being Czech, but he was still much too proud to be French. Like a badly tamed animal, he had bitten the hand that fed him, spat out the charitable crumbs, and foraged for himself. 'France has been good to you,' Marta would remind him, fuelling his disgust. Gratitude was the ultimate emetic. He had piled on France all the fury he felt towards his homeland, affecting allegiance towards a place he had no desire to see ever again. Not that Marta had ever witnessed these spurious avowals of patriotism, which were strictly for the benefit of the chauvinistic natives. He was like a disgruntled husband, showering praise on a discarded mistress just to spite his wife.

'Karel's very proud of you, you know,' Eva had continued. 'I get fed up with hearing about how clever you are.'

'I'm not clever.' He was beginning to hate this charade, not so much because he wasn't a lousy accountant but because he wasn't even a lousy thief, because he was nothing at all. 'I'm just good at my job, that's all.'

'Do you enjoy it?'

'Yes. I mean, no. That is . . . it was Marta's choice of career. Not mine.'

'What would you rather do?'

'Oh . . . play the piano, I suppose.'

'Wouldn't Marta have let you study music?'

'We couldn't have afforded it. And besides, I wanted a job that would pay well.'

'Pity about your arm. I would have liked to hear you play.'

'You're not missing anything. I've never learned properly.' He flexed the tips of his imprisoned fingers as if itching for the freedom of the keyboard.

'Does it hurt?'

'Now and then.'

'How did it happen?'

'Same way the black eye happened. I got into a fight and fell over.'

'What was the fight about?'

'Nothing important.'

314

'I thought at first you might have been injured during the riots.'

'Sorry to disappoint you.'

'I wish you'd tell me more about your night on the barricades. Jan wants me to write a piece for *Spring Tide*. That's our new magazine, for students and young workers.'

'Jan?'

'My boyfriend.'

'You mean your lover?' He had meant it as a tease, to make her blush. Eva had 'virgin' stamped all over her.

'That's none of your business. But as it happens, yes he is.'

'Tut, tut, tut,' said Viktor, not quite believing her. 'So the permissive society's reached Prague now, has it?'

'Not at all. He wants to marry me. I'm thinking about it. Satisfied?'

'You're much too young to get married.'

'I'm eighteen.'

'Never! I thought you were only sixteen.'

'You know perfectly well I'm not.'

'Oh well, if you're eighteen you'd better get married as soon as possible, before you end up on the shelf.'

'I didn't say I was going to get married. I said I was thinking about it.'

'Careful. Your smile's slipping.'

'I'm trying to be friendly. I know it's a bore for you, me being here. You've made that perfectly clear.'

'Now what on earth gave you that idea?'

'I'm not as stupid as I look, you know.'

'How could you be?'

'God, you're so like your father it isn't true!' It was the first time she had exploded out of her persistent good humour. It made him like her better.

'Is that a compliment?'

'Tactless and sarcastic and insensitive and—'

'Rude. I'm sorry, Eva. I shouldn't have said that. Of course you don't look stupid.'

' . . . and manipulative. Once you've drawn blood, you rush to find the sticking plaster. Don't go all cute and innocent on me, I'm wise to all that. I feel as if I've known you for years!'

That was the most unnerving thing about her. She already knew all kinds of things about him, including things he didn't know himself. She sat there like a parcel wrapped in stout brown paper, packed with things he had mislaid or lost or wantonly thrown away. It was as if she was saying, 'Do you want this stuff or not? It might not be worth much, but it belongs to you.'

'Where's Eva?' asked Viktor, finding his grandmother alone.

'I sent her down to the shops, to stock up. Already there's no sugar left.' She indicated six full bags with some satisfaction. 'She's a good girl. She's made three trips already. Here, you can help put these away.'

Sighing, Viktor stowed several kilos of flour, beans, dried milk, rice and pasta on to a high shelf.

'For God's sake, Babička. What a fuss. You'd think war had broken out.'

'It could happen. Civil war. If you ask me, the Communists are planning a coup, just like they did at home back in forty-eight. Next thing you know they'll have people's militias on the streets. They won't be happy till they've forced de Gaulle to stand down. To think such things could happen in France!'

'De Gaulle? He's not still alive, is he? I thought he was just a waxwork.'

'Be serious, Viktor! If you read the newspapers – There she is.'

Eva arrived, panting, with two bags full of tins.

'There was such a queue!' she said. 'Worse than at home. The shelves were practically empty. I just grabbed what I could.'

'This is ridiculous,' said Viktor.

'I've lived through enough shortages in my life not to take any chances. Thank you, Evička. Oh good, you got some soap. It's a terrible thing, not to have any soap. And some toilet paper! Where did you find it?'

'A little shop on the other side of the Place d'Italie. I tried six other places first and they were all sold out.'

'You're a treasure. Viktor, switch on the news while I put on the potatoes. Sit down, Eva, you've done quite enough.'

'Don't worry,' teased Eva, exchanging glances with Viktor. 'I won't let you starve. When I get back to Prague, I can always send you food parcels.'

Marta didn't see the joke.

'The way things are going, you can expect two refugees seeking political asylum,' she said, with the utmost seriousness. 'To think that you're re-creating democracy while we're hell bent on destroying it. People in the West don't know when they're well off.'

She hobbled off into the kitchen, muttering. Eva grinned, evidently enjoying the fun, and switched on the television. Her robust good nature seemed to fill the room like the smell of home cooking. Viktor found himself smiling back at her.

Despite his lack of interest, he was obliged to pay attention, in order to translate for Eva. The students had lost the headlines, swamped by the tidal wave of industrial action. There were shots of idle shipyards and occupied factories, and interviews with union worthies pledging pious support for 'the will of the people'.

No more petrol deliveries are expected after today. Public transport, both by rail and road, is likely to cease by the weekend, and airlines are under pressure from anxious tourists, who risk being stranded in the wake of action by air traffic controllers.

'Poor Eva,' murmured Viktor. 'How dreadful if you get stuck in the wicked West.'

It seems likely that the strike will also affect ferry services. Queues of vehicles are already building up at channel ports, where many holidaymakers, both in France and England, have been waiting since yesterday in the hope of returning home early.

Cassie had timed her departure well, thought Viktor. Even now, he half expected her to turn up one day at her usual time and behave as if nothing had happened. And now she wouldn't be able to . . . thank God.

Refuse collection has already ceased in most areas. Action by teachers may result in pupils being sent home from school,

*with serious consequences for lycéens due to sit their baccalau-
réat next month. Panic buying has set in, as anxious shoppers
gut the shelves of stores and supermarkets.*

'Look, there's Eva!' said Viktor, as a group of rabid-looking
women were shown laying siege to their local Viniprix.

'Where?' asked Marta.

'See that short fat one over there . . .? No, she's gone. But it
was definitely her.'

'No it wasn't,' protested Eva. 'She was much slimmer than
me.'

*To avoid a run on the banks, withdrawals will be limited to five
hundred francs as from tomorrow morning.*

'Viktor, you'd better go along to the Crédit Mutuel this afternoon and clear out my account. Though God knows, the franc
won't be worth having for much longer. We might as well
spend the lot before they devalue all our savings . . .'

' . . . just like they did in forty-eight,' chorused Viktor and
Eva, before collapsing into mutual mirth.

Marta cracked a smile. They seemed to be getting on
together better than she had hoped. Viktor had been in such a
filthy mood ever since Cassie's departure that she had begun
to despair of his ever being civil again; so much so that she had
sat down and written a letter to the poor girl, care of the Lycée
Alphonse Cluny, in the hope that they would forward it.
Viktor would be furious if he knew. He would have called her
an interfering old busybody, which was exactly what she was.

*Postal services have been severely disrupted by lightning walk-
outs.*

There was a shot of piles of neglected sacks of mail, piled up
like sandbags in an unmanned sorting office.

'Oh no!' said Marta.

'What is it?'

'Nothing.'

*Television broadcasts may be the next casualty if ORTF work-
ers vote to strike in support of their claim for a forty-hour week
and an enhanced minimum wage. Meanwhile . . .*

318

The screen went blank.

'That was a quick vote,' said Viktor.

'It's a power cut,' said Eva, testing the lights.

'And the potatoes aren't cooked!' wailed Marta.

'We'll make do with bread,' said Eva.

'But I haven't put the meat on yet. Oh dear! We'll have to open one of those tins!'

Eva took over, preparing a scratch meal under Marta's instructions. As usual, Viktor just picked at it.

'What's the matter with your appetite?' demanded Marta, as if she didn't know.

'It's just this bloody arm playing up again. Stop nagging.'

Marta had taken a grim satisfaction in his injury, the result of some drunken brawl or other, no doubt provoked by him. It reassured her to know that he would be going straight, willy-nilly, until Eva's visit was safely over.

'Where are you two off to this afternoon?' she prompted, as she cleared the table.

'How about the Gare de L'Est, while there's still time?'

Eva slapped his plaster case with her napkin.

'When you come to Prague, I shall be just as horrible to you.'

'Eva's invited us both for next summer,' ventured Marta. 'She's certain they'd grant us a visa—' Catching the look in Viktor's eye, she changed tack abruptly. 'I'll have dinner ready at seven. Get out in the sunshine and enjoy yourselves.'

'Are you coming out to play, Eva?' lisped Viktor, provoking a warning glare from Marta. God, being nice was such a drag. He would have to find some way to shake her off.

'You can play hookey this afternoon,' said Eva pleasantly, as soon as they were out of the house. 'I'm beginning to find my way around. So you don't have to nursemaid me. We can meet back here, at half past six. Marta need never know.'

'Okay.' Perversely, he felt annoyed that she had pre-empted him. 'So . . . where are you going? In case you get lost and I have to come looking for you.'

'The Sorbonne. To see the occupation. I told you, I'm going to write about it.'

'You can't go there on your own. It's full of all kinds of dead-beats. Tramps, drug addicts, criminals . . .'

'I'll be very careful.'

'You can imagine what Marta would do to me if anything happened to you,' said Viktor, adding ungraciously, 'I suppose I'd better take you. Come on.'

There were no cabs in sight. What little fuel was available was being put to profitable use, ferrying stranded tourists to the Belgian border. Viktor was glad of the excuse to use the Métro – he hated to look mean – but on finding the local station picketed by transport workers, they had no option but to walk. It was bright and very warm, with more people about than was usual at this time of day, and a lot less traffic. Sacks of rotting refuse baked in the hot sun, and posters were plastered on every spare bit of wall. A mighty fist gripping a spanner was captioned 'Power to the People'; de Gaulle was portrayed in CRS combat gear with his boot in a student's face. For all his cynicism, Viktor had no doubt as to whose side he was on. It pleased him to think of idle workers taking their leisure in parks and cafés purged of tourists, claiming the city as their own. Paris, that most arrogant, elegant and snobbish of capitals was being repossessed by its people. The bosses were on the run.

'Poor Marta,' giggled Eva. 'She seems really worried.'

'She's in her element. What are you going to do if you can't get back?'

'Walk, if I have to.'

'How touching. It must be serious with this Jan.'

'It's nothing to do with him. Why does everyone suppose that I'd like to stay? Those old cronies of Marta's drive me up the wall with their talk of arranged marriages.'

'Arranged marriages?'

'For five thousand francs you can buy a husband of convenience, apparently. They even offered to have a whip-round.'

Viktor roared with laughter. 'And I was only going to charge you two thousand. Does that mean you're going to turn me down?'

'Things are changing at home, you know. Not so long ago, I would have done anything to emigrate to the West. But I don't feel that way any more.'

'Then perhaps you're the one that's changed.'

'No. People don't change. They just discover things about themselves that were always there. Not just me, everybody. It's hard to explain what it feels like. You'd have to go there to understand.'

'You'll never pull it off you know. Any more than they will here.'

'You're sounding just like your father again.'

'For God's sake. If you say that once more . . . '

'I'm sorry. I keep forgetting.'

But she hadn't forgotten at all. She was like a dog, nipping at his ankles, jumping clear before he could kick her. She smiled again, in mock contrition, and he ruffled her hair.

'How many days till you go home? I'm going to make myself a chart.'

'You make me feel so welcome, Viktor. How can I ever repay your hospitality?'

They had to queue to get through the gates to the Sorbonne's central courtyard, which was thronged with pilgrims paying their visit to Mecca. The tricolours had all been removed, to be replaced by black and red flags; the venerable statue of Victor Hugo was draped in revolutionary scarlet. Slogans had been daubed on every wall and demagogues of every persuasion bellowed their conflicting messages to an ever-shifting audience, with portraits of Che Guevara and Mao and Stalin and Trotsky in uneasy juxtaposition. Puzzled, Eva made notes in her head. What did these young people admire about Stalin? She was about to ask Viktor to translate the words of one of that demigod's disciples when a young man appeared from nowhere, grabbed her hand, and bore her off. She looked back at Viktor, waving to indicate her abduction, but he was engrossed in conversation with a girl and didn't seem to notice. The boy began speaking to her in French and, not understanding him, Eva just smiled, which seemed to satisfy him. He scooped up another girl with his spare hand and, following her example, Eva grabbed hold of the nearest male, who collared the next available woman, and so on until they were part of a human chain that snaked its way through the marble halls in an unbroken cordon of solidarity, taking up the chant, 'Paris, London, Rome, Berlin, We shall fight and we shall win . . . '. Prague wasn't mentioned, of course. According to Jan, the French students dismissed their Czech counterparts as reactionaries, dupes of the 'bogus bourgeois freedoms' they themselves despised. But rightly or wrongly, they had fought at the barricades for what they believed in, and this place was surely the ultimate testament to free speech. If she had been able to speak their language, she too could have had her say . . .

Gradually, she fell into the spirit of it, not because she had been converted to their cause, not because she believed or even understood the rant and cant all around her, but because she wanted to collect the moment, like a seashell, as a lasting memento of a brief holiday.

Viktor, meanwhile, had failed to dodge an eagle-eyed Armelle. He might have known that bitch would be here.

'What happened to you?' she demanded, indicating Viktor's arm.

'What do you think?'

'Rob did that?' Her eyes lit up.

'He did it for Cassie,' he added witheringly. 'Not for you.'

She tossed her head. 'That figures. You know he's gone to England with her?'

Viktor kept his face absolutely deadpan. 'Yes,' he lied.

'I reckon she was after him right from the start. Looks like she made a fool of both of us. They'll make a lovely couple, don't you think?'

'Yes. They're very well suited.'

'So . . . how's business?'

'Bad, evidently.'

'Never mind. There's free soup and bread all day long for anyone who wants it. The public have been so generous, the money's simply flooding in. Here. Buy yourself a whore.'

She shoved a fifty-franc note at him. Only then did Viktor meet her eyes and see that they were huge with unshed tears. A bubble of involuntary pity broke through the surface of his scorn.

'Don't blame me,' he said quietly, handing the money back to her.

'I wish I could,' she said.

* * *

'How's it going at the factory?' demanded Armelle, a few days later. Claudine had just got back from MerTech, whose strike committee had offered indefinite shelter to a group of student activists wanted by the police. Armelle had been specifically excluded from the escort party, on Alain's instructions.

'I wish you could have been there,' said Claudine tactlessly. 'They made us very welcome. They even allowed Étienne and two of the others to address the workers. While they were speaking a CGT delegation arrived at the factory gates, wanting to do the same, but they voted not to let them in! It was glorious.'

'And my father?'

'He's upped his offer again. The union executive have recommended acceptance. But the workers threw it out. Collective power or nothing.'

Armelle hugged her in delight.

'And Alain?'

'He said he was sorry he couldn't make it last night, and he'll do his best for tomorrow. But if he's not here by eight, don't wait in for him.'

Armelle's face crumpled.

'Try to understand,' soothed Claudine. 'It's difficult for him to get away at the moment. There's so much going on. People expect him to be there.'

'Papa will never forgive him, you know,' said Armelle, attacking what was left of her thumbnail. 'He'll get his own back somehow.' There was a strange, bitter note of hope in her voice.

'It's all very well organised,' continued Claudine. 'The wives take in food every day, there are film shows and discussions, and a crèche so women workers can join in the occupation. And to think this is only part of it. Nine million on strike! De Gaulle is finished now. And everything he stands for. We've finally proved that capitalism doesn't work.'

'Don't count on it. The CGT are desperate to do a deal. A revolution would cook their goose nicely. They've just

323

published their demands. Look.' Armelle threw the evening paper at her. 'A minimum wage of a thousand a month. And a forty-hour week. And retirement at sixty. The usual crap.'

'Cheap bribes. They make me sick. People aren't going to be bought off that easily. Not now they've proved that they have all the power. Not now they're united. It's happening, at last. What's the matter?'

'Nothing.'

'Armelle, the man's married. You're wasting your time.'

'You think I want to be anyone's wife? Don't insult my intelligence. Now he's got his precious revolution he doesn't need me any more.'

'So? There are plenty more fish in the sea.'

'Perhaps I've gone off fish. I'm buggered if I'll hang around here tomorrow waiting for him to stand me up. All he wants me for is sex. All anyone wants me for is sex.'

'I don't, you know. In case you were wondering.'

'Why not?'

'What?'

'I said, why not? What's wrong with me?'

'Nothing's wrong with you! I just don't want you to think that I . . . that I . . .'

'Why are you blushing?'

'Because you're embarrassing me. Stop it, Armelle. We're good friends. I want it to stay that way.'

Armelle shrugged, went into the bathroom to take a shower, and emerged naked. Claudine looked away.

'Do you think I've put on weight?' demanded Armelle.

'I hadn't noticed.'

'The bloody Pill makes me retain water. I think I'll stop taking it.'

'Don't be silly. You'll get pregnant.'

'Not if I'm careful who I sleep with.'

'Armelle . . .'

'I've been wondering what it would be like. Why don't you show me?'

'Don't do this to me, Armelle. You're just playing games, you know you are. Don't use me to punish them.'

'Come and lie down next to me. We won't do anything you

don't want to do. Or anything I don't want to do. That's a promise.'

For the first time there was nothing to be afraid of. No monstrous invasion of her body, no shadow of remembered shame. It was new, and untainted, and effortlessly easy. She wondered why she hadn't thought of it before.

TWELVE

The Blakeneys made Rob very welcome, in their own over-powering way. A pair of vague, affable intellectuals, they prided themselves on being modern, progressive parents. Cassie's laconic account of the Lemercier débâcle had met with amused tolerance, not horror, and Rob got the distinct impression that she would have much preferred them to get mad.

'When they hear you're resisting the draft, they'll be all over you,' Cassie had warned him darkly. 'Not to mention your stint on the barricades. They're suckers for anything like that.' It was almost as if she were setting him up. Certainly she seemed to take a sly delight in watching them put him through his paces.

'Do come and say hello to so-and-so,' Mummy would gush, forcing Rob to relate his recent exploits and making him feel like a prize phoney. Cassie's own lack of participation in the riots was tactfully glossed over, with everyone persisting in the bland assumption that she had been cheering her comrades on from the sidelines and generally having a perfectly thrilling time.

Inexorably, Cassie withdrew back into the safety of her shell. At least home was the devil she knew. Here there was no danger, no excitement, no challenge, no risk. Just empty security and the old creeping defeatism. Poor polite, patient Rob. He must be bored to tears. She had known he would be. Mummy meant well, of course. She obviously thought that she and Rob were sleeping together, and was bending over backwards to appear approving and make him feel at home, especially as Cassie herself had made little effort to entertain him. It was easier, as always, to let her mother take charge, and besides, it wouldn't be for long. She should never have invited him here in the first place. He had come because he was worried about her, not because he enjoyed her company, and one day soon he would sling his guitar over his shoulder and move on, leaving her lonely.

He broached the subject of his departure one Friday afternoon, just as they were preparing to leave for a weekend in the country. The parents had gone ahead with a carful of guests, leaving Cassie and Rob to follow on by train. Blakeney dinner parties were interminable at the best of times, but this one would last two whole days, a prospect which filled Rob with gloom. He couldn't believe that Cassie enjoyed these sterile gatherings any more than he did, but she had accepted Mummy's well-meant invitation with her usual infuriating diffidence. It was hard to believe that this subdued, compliant creature was the same Cassie who had rescued him from the *Occident* thugs and held her own with a bully like Viktor. At home she seemed passive, flaccid, colourless, although Rob soon came to realise that it was all an act, and a bloody-minded one at that. She would sit there tonight looking vague and vapid; later on, in the privacy of their room, she would reduce him to helpless mirth by mimicking all the guests in turn with savage accuracy, proving that she hadn't missed a thing. Except, perhaps, her own motives for playing it dumb. If so, it was high time she turned her merciless powers of observation on herself.

'I really appreciate all the hospitality,' Rob began, choosing his words carefully, 'but I don't want to outstay my welcome, and—'

'You mean you've had enough,' said Cassie, with a certain perverse satisfaction.

'Haven't you?'

'I'm used to it,' she shrugged, rather petulantly. 'And anyway, I haven't got much choice.'

'Yes you have. Why don't we hitch south for the summer, via Ostend?'

327

'We? Look, I'm sorry I put you on the spot by asking you to come to London with me. But I'm perfectly all right now. You don't have to feel responsible for me any more.'

'It's not that. I don't want to go without you.'

'And I don't want to cramp your style.'

'Stop making excuses. I'm not trying to lay you, if that's what's worrying you.'

'I know you're not.' She made it sound like a reproach, wrong-footing him with her usual deftness.

'But only because you made it clear I didn't stand a chance. Your "keep off" sign's about ten feet high.'

'What "keep off" sign?'

'Come off it, Cassie. You're the most unapproachable girl I ever met. No wonder Viktor was terrified of you.'

'That'll teach me to confide in you in future,' she snapped, with a flash of her old asperity. 'As for being unapproachable, I practically threw myself at him, remember? So I'm hardly likely to make the same mistake with you.'

Rob sighed, exasperated. The more he watched Cassie on home ground, the more certain he was that Viktor wasn't wholly to blame for what had happened. She gave out false signals all the time, usually deliberately; she had a gift for putting others in the wrong, for playing the innocent victim, for cutting off her nose to spite her face.

'I know what you're playing at, Cass. You want me to give up on you. And you want to make sure that when I do, you can blame it on your parents, like you always blame everything on your parents.'

'I *don't* . . .'

'Nothing's ever your fault, is it? That's the reason you and Viktor had so much in common. Talk about soulmates. No wonder you both ended up as losers.'

'Stop it!'

'You came here to hide, didn't you? Nobody can get at you here, because Mummy and Daddy will fight all your battles for you, like they always have done. They'd rather not, you know, but you'll make damn sure they do. You like having them make all your decisions for you, preferably the wrong ones. That way it's down to them when you mess up.'

328

He'd been thinking it for days, but had balked at saying it, inhibited by his status as a guest, his role as Mr Nice, his innate dislike of confrontation. She had been counting on that. But he cared about her too much to let her get away with it.

'That's not true!' exploded Cassie, but the denial rang hollow. She was much too intelligent not to have worked it out for herself, long ago. Yielding to a sudden impulse, Rob picked up his haversack. This would only work if he did it quickly, brutally, before she managed to out-talk him. 'Have a nice weekend,' he said. 'And say goodbye and thanks to your folks for me.'

'Where are you going?'

'I told you. Ostend. Are you coming?'

'But . . . but the parents are expecting us! They've invited all their weekend cronies to meet you!'

'Don't kid yourself. They'll have a much better time without us. And we'll have a much better time without them. Yes or no, Cassie? I can't force you. Nobody ever forces you to do any-thing – you're just ace at making it look that way.'

Cassie glared at him speechlessly, furious that he had blown her cover. She had made a stooge out of everyone all her life – her parents, the doctors, Wilfred, even Viktor – only to have Viktor give her a taste of her own medicine. Not that it had cured her. She had thought she was through with soft options, and yet the minute things went wrong she had come running home to her trusty scapegoats, just to give herself the same tired old excuse for failure. As for Rob . . .

'What is it you're really afraid of?' he persisted, reading the mutinous look on her face. 'That I *won't* try to lay you?'

She drew breath to deny it and let it collapse into an okay-you-win sigh.

'Perhaps.'

'I give up,' said Rob, making as if to go.

'Don't do that,' she whispered, catching hold of both his hands and holding up her face for a kiss.

He let her make the running, still unsure exactly what she wanted. It was a slow, sad, sincere kiss, a kiss that said you're right, and I'm sorry, and thanks, and above all, yes, a yes that tasted of defiance, not compliance, a yes that surprised her as well as him.

'I'm still in love with Viktor, you know,' she muttered awkwardly. 'If I've been unapproachable, that's why. Partly, anyway. I don't want either of us to get hurt.'

'Neither do I. This is strictly for laughs, okay?'

He kissed her again, enjoying it this time. There was an element of revenge in this, no doubt, for both of them, but it was sweet in the most positive sense. This was about affection, not passion, comfort, not conquest.

'I've never done it for laughs,' said Cassie, apologetically. 'I don't know how.'

'Come to think of it, neither do I. But we can always try.'

'No. Don't try. And I won't try either. I'm fed up with trying, aren't you?'

But she found it almost impossible not to. She was painfully anxious to please. He had to teach her to be selfish and lazy, muttering 'No need' and 'Not yet' as much for his own benefit as hers. It didn't seem urgent, just essential; something that had to be done now, right away, but not quickly. It was like dismantling a wall, brick by brick, before stepping across the vanished divide, it was like walking the long way home. Gradually she wound down, forgot what she was doing, lost herself, let it happen by accident, just in time.

'That was . . . fun,' she murmured. 'It was . . . *easy*.'

That's all you know, thought Rob, relieved. Perhaps he wasn't such a lousy lover after all.

WITH THE SOVIET UNION FOREVER — BUT NOT A DAY LONGER!
LONG LIVE THE USSR — AT ITS OWN EXPENSE!

Karel watched the vast throng of students march, banners held high, down the length of Wenceslas Square, shaking his head in despair. That they had chosen to hold this demonstration on the first day of Premier Kosygin's goodwill visit was proof, to his mind, that they were hell-bent on self-destruction. The reform programme depended heavily on Russian support – not just in terms of ideological tolerance, but in the more practical matter of a badly needed hard-currency loan. What did these young people hope to gain by such a crass display of anti-Soviet feeling?

His deep-rooted paranoia began sending up new shoots. The CIA were definitely behind all this. Not because they wanted to foster the cause of democracy, but because they were trying to provoke a crisis. A massive repression, enforced from Moscow, would have infinitely more propaganda value than 'socialism with a human face', which might just prove too successful for comfort and spread to the class-ridden, capitalist West. That was this country's tragedy. There was no one it could trust. Riding a wave of hopeless, helpless rage, he took a deep, deliberate breath and reminded himself that he was jumping to conclusions again, that years of persecution had warped his mind. But knowing that didn't seem to help.

The police stood by, watching, making no move. Western journalists were taking photographs, to bring untold joy to their anti-Communist readers. Karel was willing to bet that there wasn't one demonstrator in a thousand who wanted a return to capitalism, but that was how it would be interpreted abroad.

'Good evening, sir.' It was Jan.

'I might have known you wouldn't be far away,' grunted Karel.

'I was wondering if you'd heard from Eva.'

'Not a word. There's a general strike in France, in case you didn't know.'

'I've been following the news every day. I hope she's all right.'

'My mother will keep her on a short rein, don't worry. She's less likely to get up to mischief there than she is at home.' He doubled up with a sudden, vicious fit of coughing which tightened the band of pain around his chest.

'Are you all right?' Jan put a supporting arm under his elbow.

'Thank you. I'm quite all—'

His words were lost in a gurgle of viscous phlegm.

'Please let me help. Can I take you to the doctor?'

'No, no. It will pass.'

'Let's find somewhere to sit down.'

Karel wanted to protest, but he couldn't find the energy. Taking nearly all his weight, Jan led him into the nearest *restaurace*, which was deserted, with all the staff standing in the window watching the marchers go by. A sympathetic manager agreed to provide some fortified tea, for which Jan insisted on paying.

'I'm a slave to this blasted bronchitis,' muttered Karel, fumbling for a cigarette.

'Don't you think that might set you off again?'

'Rubbish. The smoke soothes my lungs. Whenever I try to cut down, I have trouble. Besides, I just went for an X-ray and got the all clear.' But he shoved the packet back in his pocket none the less, sending a folded piece of paper fluttering to the floor. 'I'm grateful for your help, young man. But I'm not dead yet.'

'You dropped this,' said Jan, bending to retrieve it.

'Have a read,' growled Karel. 'They were dishing them out at work this morning.'

'"Workers beware – Anti-socialist agents are at work in your factory." Anonymous, of course.'

'As if we didn't know where they're coming from.'

With an eye to the future, perhaps, certain prominent conservatives had got their second wind and mounted a virulent anti-Dubček campaign.

'"These unscrupulous people want to restore capitalism by revisionist means. They seek to deceive you for their own mercenary interests. Under the slogan of 'liberalisation' the following bourgeois intellectuals plan to fight their way into the leadership and seize power . . . " All these names are Jewish, of course. This is blatantly anti-Semitic. Surely nobody's going to fall for this kind of thing. It reeks of Stalinism.'

'When in doubt, blame the Jews. It's a tried and tested formula. I shouted myself hoarse at work this morning. I think that's what did for me.' He glared. 'I know you and Eva have got me down for an old reactionary, but at work I'm considered a rampant liberal. It makes me feel quite schizophrenic. Not that I expect the working classes to listen to me. I'm only a "formerly" after all.' The term encompassed the wide cross-section of people who had fallen from grace in the last twenty years, all of whom had 'formerly' held responsible jobs.

Jan thought for a moment.

'How about if I gave you a hundred copies of *Spring Tide*?

The new issue is carrying a feature on the anti-reform campaign and dealing with each of its claims in turn. Perhaps . . . perhaps it would save your voice.'

'Hmph. I didn't agree with that editorial of yours.'

'You mean you've read it?'

'Some girl shoved a copy at me yesterday. It gave me something to look at on the tram.'

Jan smiled. 'Have some more tea,' he said.

The crowd around the Gare de Lyon was stupendous but, despite the throng of bodies, there was almost perfect silence as people waited for the presidential broadcast to begin. Armelle and Claudine were on tenterhooks. If de Gaulle resigned, as he was expected to do, the way would be open for a new Government of the Left – some patched-together coalition stinking of compromise and double dealing that would put the revolution on ice for ever. If he held on, then the way was open to bring him down by force, and with him all the loathsome structures of law and order.

Claudine felt Armelle's nails digging into her palm, drawing blood. At moments like this she was afraid for her; in the last week Armelle's earlier ebullience had hardened into cold-eyed fanaticism. However much they achieved, she would feel short-changed; in politics, as in love, she was never satisfied.

At last de Gaulle's ponderous tones came on the air, emanating from the innumerable transistor radios dotted throughout the crowd, all turned up to full volume. Over-amplification distorted the old man's words, and he spoke very slowly, as if to compensate for this.

'Je ne me retirai pas.'

He would not stand down. In the middle of a tempest, he proposed to walk on water. In the face of a general strike, he affected to believe that the majority of French citizens would support him in a national referendum. A hush fell over the assembly as the broadcast ended, like the momentary lull at the end of a concert, while the audience considers its verdict.

'Adieu de Gaulle!' One voice at first, and then several, and then a deafening, rhythmic roar, an unequivocal message to the representatives of the Government, the unions and the

employers, who were at this very moment engaged in top-level talks, united in their desire to find a peace formula. There would be no peace, no surrender while de Gaulle clung to power.

On the other side of the square, Albert Moreau, standing next to his son, knew in his bones that this was the beginning of the end. Unlike most of these young demonstrators, he could remember the Popular Front occupations of thirty years before, when workers' control had been within their grasp. But they had abandoned their revolution, traded power for better pay, established the unalterable premise for all future disputes – that a worker's soul was for sale. It would happen again: while there were families to be fed, every man would have his price.

But not yet. A huge collective impulse propelled the crowd northwards to the Place de la Bastille, to broadcast its own message long and loud. A contingent of young warriors was already armed with pickaxes, shovels and iron bars. Many were wearing crash helmets and face masks. For them, no doubt, the news had been welcome.

Alain felt a thrill of exhilaration. The period since the factory occupation had been the happiest of his life. Even Chantal had noticed the difference in him; he seemed more attentive, less resentful, more like a real husband. That crushing sense of isolation had gone. All the people in this crowd were his comrades. Like him, they were all powerless individuals discovering the euphoria of collective strength. Nothing could destroy this. Not government, nor unions, nor bosses had any armoury against the combined will of the people. This was unstoppable.

'What's happening?' demanded Eva impatiently. Viktor hadn't wanted to come, of course; but the threat that she would go on her own, if necessary, had done the trick as usual.

'He's refusing to quit. Stupid old fart.'

Eva was more confused than ever. Some people evidently regarded de Gaulle as a Western-style Novotny, representing discredited values and presiding over injustice and decay, while others appeared to revere him as a Masaryk-like figure,

334

symbolising patriotism, integrity and wisdom. The truth was presumably somewhere in between.

'I'd better take you home,' added Viktor. 'There's going to be trouble. This lot are out for blood.'

'Can't we follow the crowd and see what happens?'

'I can tell you what will happen. Sooner or later, the police will break things up. People won't disperse until they do. It's all stage-managed, you realise. The police beating up workers and students is good publicity for the so-called revolution.'

'I never know what side you're on.'

'Oh, I'd like to see this lousy Government on the run. But the next one will be just as bad. Still, you know what they say. A country gets the government it deserves. Come on.'

The temptation, in this crush, to slide his left hand into the nearest pocket had been almost overwhelming. But these were ordinary people, most of them on strike; workers now outnumbered students at any public protest. He hadn't sunk that low yet, even if his funds had.

'I don't want to go back yet. Marta's invited a couple of old girls round to play cards.'

'That sounds like a lot of fun,' observed Viktor heartlessly, and then, 'Look, I'd take you somewhere, but with the banks being on strike, I'm a bit short of cash.'

'I'll pay,' volunteered Eva. 'I've hardly spent anything since I got here.'

'Hang on to it. It's worth three or four times as much at home.'

'At home,' he had said, a slip of the tongue that seemed to bode well. Tonight, she had hoped to broach the subject of the memoirs. So far, any mention of Karel had provoked a glazing over of the eyes, and a pointed change of subject. But she couldn't leave Paris with her mission uncompleted. Time was running out, in more ways than one.

'Oh, don't look so hangdog. You can kill a couple of hours at my place if you like, till they've gone. Have a glass of wine, listen to some music. Would you like that?'

That was exactly what she would like. She had been hoping that he would invite her, give her the chance to observe him on

335

his own territory and to talk to him in private. But knowing Viktor she merely shrugged, as if indicating that if that was all that was on offer, it was better than nothing, softening her pretended indifference with her usual bright, cryptic smile, ignoring the increased tempo of her heart, shutting her mind to the images that tormented her.

He didn't speak much during the walk home, but by now Eva was well used to his silent moods. His bursts of chatty good humour were counterpointed by dark periods of silent gloom, which Marta put down to his bust-up with the girlfriend. In fact, Marta's eulogies about Cassie ('Such a well-brought-up girl. So polite. So considerate. I had such hopes . . . ') had grown more than a little tedious. Strange how hearing good of people put you right off them. No doubt similar things would be said about her in time. ('Such a busy little bee. She did all my housework and shopping for me, I hardly lifted a finger all the time she was here. And so patient with Viktor!')

She hadn't wanted to like him. She had expected someone arrogant, sarcastic and superior, and he could be all those things, not to mention touchy, impatient and just plain rude. But he could also be kind, attentive and generous, qualities which were all the more potent because he rationed them so ruthlessly. Like Karel, he repaid effort. Perhaps the sinister force of habit made her appreciate difficult people more than easy ones, like Jan.

'Madame Bloc, this is my sister, Eva, from Prague. Madame Bloc, my concierge.'

Eva smiled prettily and shook hands, evidently struggling to keep her face straight.

'What's so funny?' asked Viktor, as they mounted the stairs.

'The beady eye. She reminds me of old Nováková, our caretaker. Is that why you told her I was your sister?'

'Is what why?'

'To stop her gossiping.'

'I tip her not to gossip.'

'At home it's the other way round. The concierges are paid to inform. Or rather were. Nováková spies on me all the time. She hangs around on the landing, listening to me typing "subversive literature". She tells all the neighbours I have loose morals. She—'

'Loose morals?'

'Because of Jan. I smuggled him in a few times, while Karel was out at his meetings.'

'How romantic.'

Romantic. That was one thing it hadn't been. It had been uncomfortable, awkward, and disappointing, perhaps because neither of them had much of a clue what to do. It had left her dissatisfied, and impatient, and wanting more.

Viktor pulled the cork out of a bottle of red wine and filled two tumblers.

'No thanks,' said Eva. 'Do you have any coffee?'

'No. Force yourself. I hate to drink alone.' He thrust the glass at her. *'Na zdraví.'*

'Na zdraví.' She sat down at the piano. 'This is beautiful,' she said, running her fingers up and down the keys. 'How much does something like this cost?'

'A lot,' shrugged Viktor irritably.

'And all these records. And the stereo.' She lifted the lid of the machine. 'Can we play something?'

'Help yourself.'

'No, you choose.'

'What sort of thing do you like?'

'Whatever will put you in a good temper.'

Ignoring this stricture, Viktor pulled down an Otis Redding album, filling the room with the melancholy strains of disappointed dreams. Eva sat sipping the dark, bitter wine, looking around her curiously. The room looked unlived-in. There was no table to eat at, and no chairs to sit on, just a sofa – not that the piano left room for much other furniture. But there were no books either, no newspapers, no photographs, no pictures.

'How long have you lived here?'

'About five years. Before that I had a smaller place, downstairs. Before that I was in the bloody army. And before that I lived with Marta.'

'How many rooms?'

'Three.'

'You could make it really nice.'

'I don't want to make it really nice.'

'Why not?'

'I can live anywhere. I don't believe in getting attached to things. It's just a roof, that's all.'

'You can't live anywhere with that piano. It needs a room all to itself.'

'Then I'd have to live without it, wouldn't I? God, the fuss Marta made about losing her precious piano when they kicked her out of Prague!'

'Is that why you bought her another one?'

'Oh, she practically starved herself to buy a worm-eaten second-hand thing so that I would have something to practise on. It was so clapped out it wouldn't hold its pitch for more than five minutes. So once I started earning, I got rid of it and bought her a decent one. Not that she ever plays it.'

'Yes, she does! She plays it all the time.'

Viktor looked surprised. 'Never when I'm there.'

'Why not?'

'Oh . . . she wasn't very pleased the day it turned up. She disapproves of me spending money, she still counts every penny. It's nothing new, her hoarding food, you know. She's neurotic about it. I never keep anything to eat in the house. As for the rest of this stuff, if I lost the lot tomorrow, it wouldn't worry me in the least.'

His tone was over-emphatic, as if he were expecting her to argue.

'Well, you'd be all right, wouldn't you? You've got a good job. You could always replace things.'

'My job? Oh, yes, I keep forgetting. My job.'

He didn't like his job, of course. Perhaps he felt trapped, just as she had felt trapped in hers, until recently.

'Perhaps you ought to change it. Try doing something else.'

'I can't do anything else. Besides, I enjoy spending the money. Spending it, not having it. Having it's something else altogether.'

'What's wrong with having it?'

'It ties you down.' He replenished his glass. 'You're not drinking.'

'I don't want to get drunk.'

'Oh, don't be such a goody-goody. Did he knock all the stuffing out of you as well?'

'What do you mean?'

'Did you have to creep around the place very quietly so as not to upset him? Did he beat the shit out of you when you answered back?'

'No! Of course not.' It was the first time Viktor had ever referred to the past.

'Don't you dread the sound of his key in the lock when he comes home at night? Wasn't your mother afraid of him?'

'Of Karel? That's absurd. He's such a softie!'

'How touching. Isn't it wonderful, what prison does for the soul?'

'That's not fair.'

'Forget it. I'm glad he's turned into such a cuddly, lovable old thing. I remember your mother. She deserved a lot better. I was sorry when I heard she'd died. I wondered if he'd done the same to her.'

'The same as what?'

'The same as he did to mine. She had no family, you know. Nobody to turn to. She could have left him if it hadn't been for me. But she had nowhere to go.'

'You're wrong.'

'How do you know? I suppose you've heard *his* version.'

'She loved him till the day she died. My mother could have told you that. And he loved her too. He still does. That doesn't mean they made each other happy. *My* mother made him happy,' she continued doggedly. 'But there was never any passion . . . not on his side, anyway. Karel—'

'Forget it. I don't want to talk about it, okay? I wish I'd never brought it up.'

'Why do you bear him such a grudge? Was he really such a terrible father?'

'Good gracious no. I was a terrible son. Lazy, stupid, lacking in respect, fonder of my mother than I was of him . . . He's the one who bore a grudge. I don't blame him, I'd probably be exactly the same. Not that I'd ever be stupid enough to marry, let alone have a child.'

'Is that why you broke it off with Cassie?'

'Look, I don't know what fairy story Marta told you but—'

'She sounds too good to be true. Not your type at all.'

His eyes flashed, warning her, daring her.

'So what is my type?'

'You need a woman who can live without passion, like my mother. Or one who can stand a lot of pain, like yours.'

'She didn't stand it, evidently. She threw herself under a tram.'

'A car ran her over. That's not the same thing.'

'Stop telling me things you can't possibly know.'

'You can't possibly know them either.'

'I've been waiting for this. The big reconciliation project. Save your breath. I'm not interested.'

'Why not? Because you want to hang on to your prejudices?'

'I'm entitled to my prejudices. God knows, I can't be more prejudiced than he was.'

'He learned the truth the hard way, too late. Is that what you want to do?'

'So he's mellowed. So I was only a kid and I got him all wrong. So it all happened years ago. Fine. I accept all that. Go back to Prague and tell him whatever you like so he can die happy. Just get off my back, will you?'

Eva fell silent. She could well imagine what Milena had had to put up with from Karel all those years ago. He was as stubborn and unyielding as only those who mistrusted their own judgement could be. In an uncertain world, unalterable truths gave people something to cling to. Hence the power of narrow doctrines of every sort, religious and political and personal, which clearly defined good and bad, right and wrong, which exploited both love and hate, which suppressed doubt, stifled tolerance, fostered lies and destroyed freedom.

'All right,' she said. 'I won't say any more about it. The only reason I brought it up is that Karel wrote everything down for you to read, because he felt you had a right to know. But if you're not interested, I won't show it to you. In any case, you wouldn't understand.'

So he'd written everything down for him to read, had he? That was a nice touch. That just about summed it up. The message, whatever it was, was wrapped up tight, tied with innumerable knots. She was right. He wouldn't understand.

She returned his scowl with that characteristic look of placid defiance, as if to say, 'Go ahead. Take it out on me. I don't care.'

'Poor Evička. You might have known I'd shoot the ambassador.'

'I'll survive.'

'Nothing gets to you, does it? Or is it just put on? I'd just love to see you tiddly.'

'I don't like the stuff. Living with Karel's enough to put you off booze for life.'

'Go on, be a devil. We can get paralytic together. It's the only way to seal a friendship.'

'I don't think Marta would be very pleased if I rolled home drunk.'

'You could always spend the night here. I'll phone her and say you're not well.'

'Oh, very funny. You can imagine what she'd think.'

'What would she think?'

Eva began blushing furiously, much to Viktor's amusement.

'You're quite safe, I promise. She put me on my honour not to molest you. Not that I ever would.'

'That's very reassuring.' Her mouth compressed into a thin line.

'What's the matter?'

'Nothing.'

Whoops, thought Viktor, reading her face. That hadn't been very tactful. She was obviously as vain as the next woman, despite being such a lump. A wholesome, cosy, unneurotic lump, motherly, wifely, but not, alas, sexy.

'You're a very pretty girl, Eva,' he said, in a belated attempt to repair the damage.

'Don't be ridiculous.'

'You've got lovely skin and hair and eyes . . .'

'Oh, stop it, Viktor. I'm not stupid.'

'And I like that dress Marta made you.' It was a short cotton shift with cut-away shoulders in a pink candystripe. Cassie had chosen the material in Printemps.

'Thank you.'

'Jan's a lucky guy.'

'That's enough.'

'I'm not trying to chat you up.'

'I never thought you were.'

'What I mean is, I'm being sincere.'

'That makes a change.'

He caught another tantalising glimpse of the daunting glare that kept Karel firmly under her thumb.

'You're a nice kid. I like you. Even though I didn't think I would.' He gave her one of those crooked, rakish smiles of his. It reminded her of that mocking photograph on the wall at home.

'I know the feeling,' she countered, 'I didn't expect to like you either.' He shrugged modestly, as if to acknowledge his own irresistibility, fuelling her mounting irritation. The compliments had been a sop, insults by any other name. He took her for a fool.

'All my life I've been jealous of you,' she continued, wanting to jolt him out of his complacency. 'I so badly wanted a father. I worked really hard at being Karel's daughter. But he always preferred you, even though he wouldn't admit it, even though you couldn't care less.' She tried to stop there, but the words kept coming. 'It was the same for my mother. Milena led him a dog's life, but he still loved her more. He'd have traded my mother and me in any day of the week if he could have had you two back . . . ' She subsided into simmering composure, as if a thousand bubbles were straining against the cork. 'Sorry, I forgot. You don't want to know all that.'

Once, behind their mothers' backs, he had stolen a soggy biscuit from her chubby little fist, not because he was hungry – even though he probably was – but because, in his misery, he wanted to wipe that eternal gummy grin off her fat little face. She had watched, open-mouthed, with saliva dribbling down her chin, while he put it between his teeth, tormenting her. For one satisfying moment he had thought she was about to howl in protest, but at the last minute he had relented and given it back to her, producing an uncertain half frown like the one she was frowning now. He felt a wave of helpless, soppy affection for her.

'Don't sulk. I can't help teasing you, you ought to know that by now. And I'm sure my poor old dad is very fond of you. In his way.' He gave her a placatory peck on the cheek, which flushed several shades darker.

'I expect so. I might as well go now.' She stood up, evidently regretting her outburst.

'I thought Marta was playing cards tonight?'

'I'm in the way here. I'm fed up with you doing me a big favour all the time. I'm sure you've got better things to do with your time. Like getting drunk, for example.'

'What's all this about? You're not usually so touchy.'

'Everyone underestimates me. Everyone except Jan.'

'Cheer up. You'll be seeing him again soon.'

This seemed to be the wrong answer. She looked away, biting her lip, as if wrestling with some dilemma.

'Or is that the problem?'

'What?'

'You never talk about him, except when you mention the magazine. Is something wrong between you two?' She shrugged, looking at her feet. 'Is he messing you about?'

'Why should *he* be messing *me* about?'

'Why don't you tell your big brother all about it?'

'You're not my brother. And I'm not a baby. Stop making fun of me.'

'I'm not making fun of you.'

'Poor, plump, puddingy little Eva. That's what you're thinking, isn't it? Why do people always judge by appearances? Why should looks matter?'

'They don't.'

'They do. If I was tall and slim and blonde, you'd treat me differently.'

'Then thank your stars you're not tall and slim and blonde.'

'I don't want you feeling sorry for me.'

'I'm feeling sorry for myself, if you must know. If I've put you down, that's the only reason. I'm always rude to people I like. Have a heart, Eva. Smile. You're so good at it.'

He put an arm round her and gave her a conciliatory squeeze; after some initial stiffness she pressed her head into his shoulder, and he kissed the top of her head. She was soft and warm and cuddly and comfortable and it seemed quite natural to sit like that for a few minutes, sealing their truce. He would quite miss her, when she was gone. She'd been surprisingly good company. She'd never once split on him to Marta, sitting patiently in dingy bars, nursing a soft drink, when he should have been taking her to god-awful boring places like the Louvre and bloody Napoleon's tomb. The least he could do was be nice to her for the rest of her holiday.

'Viktor?'

'Yes, Evička?'

'I...I...nothing.' Another furious blush.

'What is it?'

She didn't answer, shutting her eyes and tilting her face up to his in a silent, agonised plea.

It took him fractionally longer than it should have done to realise what she was after. Poor, plump, puddingy little Eva. Why hadn't he realised before? She had gone and got a crush on him. She wanted him to kiss her goodnight.

He fought not to show his amusement, anxious not to cause her further offence, touched by her desperate lack of subtlety. It couldn't do any harm. Gently, he put his mouth against hers, intending something chaste and respectful and brief, but she hung on like a limpet; short of beating her off, there was nothing he could do except reciprocate. He tried to disengage himself tactfully but she wouldn't let go, clinging to him stubbornly, making it impossible for him to retreat without hurting her pride. What she lacked in experience, she made up for in enthusiasm. She was clumsy and guileless and in the most tearing hurry, and ... oh God. She meant business.

'Eva ... I really don't think—'

She stopped his mouth with another passionate kiss. Really, she was an amazingly randy little thing. They said the plain ones usually were, not that Viktor had ever put the theory to the test. If he'd suspected for one minute that she felt this way, he would never have risked bringing her here.

Eva knew it was now or never. It was the first time they had ever been alone together, and it might be her last chance. No point in waiting for him to make the first move, she had no illusions about that. She would probably regret doing this, but not half as much as she would regret not doing it. She had to know what it was supposed to be like. From the minute she first saw him at the station – no, long, long before that – she had been imagining this moment.

This wasn't my idea, Viktor reminded himself. This was for her benefit, not his. That exonerated him. He had better make a decent job of it, for her sake, so that she would feel good about herself afterwards even if he didn't. At least everything seemed to be back in full working order. Presumably because he didn't love her. For the first time, but not the last, he wished to God that he did.

'You're late,' clucked Marta. 'I was getting worried. They've set fire to the Bourse, did you hear?'

'No,' said Viktor, not daring to look at Eva, certain that Marta would smell a rat. God help him if she did. She would probably expect him to marry her.

'They tried to occupy the Ministry of Justice,' continued Marta. 'And the Élysée Palace. Luckily the police have headed them off. What a dreadful world we live in . . . Well, now you're safely home, I can go to bed. There's some coffee in the pot if you want it. Goodnight.'

She retired to her bedroom, yawning.

'Would you like some coffee?'

'No thanks. Look, Eva, I . . .'

'Please don't say anything. Don't spoil it.'

'I feel responsible. I honestly never intended—'

'I know you didn't. Don't worry. I'm not going to get any crazy ideas.'

'You're a terrific girl, Eva, really. But the thing is, you're going home next week, and—'

'No need to remind me. I'm not after a French passport, if that's what you're thinking.'

'I wasn't thinking any such thing.'

'Yes, you were. It's written all over your face.' Her voice was without rancour. She put a finger to his lips to silence his denial and opened the door.

'Goodnight, Viktor.'

'Yes. Well. Goodnight, then. See you tomorrow.'

'See you.'

He walked homewards, in a daze, thinking not about Eva but about Cassie, imagining a loss a million times worse than the one he had already endured. Yes, that was what he had been afraid of. 'Some people are meant to make each other miserable.' You could say that again. He stopped briefly outside his block and, after a second's hesitation, walked on, intending to find himself an anonymous bar. He didn't want to be alone. Once he was alone, he would start brooding about the things that Eva had told him. Not that she had told him anything he hadn't known already. His mother had been an impossible woman, he would no doubt have sided with his father against her, given half a chance. She had been like a leech, draining him of strength, and yet he would have given her his last drop of blood rather than abandon her, as she had abandoned him. The only way he could forgive her was by fixing the blame on his absent father, his alter ego and fellow-victim, locked into a love that threatened to destroy itself and him.

Saint-Germain was seething with activity. The thwarted demonstrators had evidently returned to base, and barricades were being thrown up at random – no longer with a view to reclaiming lost territory, but as a gratuitous challenge to the police, still confined to their strategically parked wire-netted vans, ready to disgorge their growling occupants like so many savage dogs. People were busy with axes, chopping down plane trees to reinforce the barricades, now sorely short of overturned cars – no one with any sense parked in the Latin Quarter these days – but rich in uncollected garbage, exuding noxious fumes almost as deadly as CS gas.

'*Salut.*' A young man greeted him with a wave of a crowbar. 'You look like a veteran.'

'You might say that.'

'Does the other arm still work?'

'I expect so.'

'Come and join us, then. We could do with an extra hand. Can you manage to drag a few of those dustbins over here?'

The instant camaraderie was like a dam against the tide of unwelcome thoughts.

'If it'll help.'

'It should be starting pretty soon. The bastards are getting twitchy. They're going to come at us from over there.' He pointed to the far end of the street. 'Once they get within three metres of this barricade, we're going to hit them from above. We've got girls posted on the fourth floor with Molotovs.' He handed him a gauze mask soaked in bicarbonate of soda. 'Best of luck.'

The cheerful guerrilla slapped him on the back, thinking he was one of them. Well, why not? It was better than going home.

'Nothing's happening yet,' complained Armelle, looking down into the street. Rows of petrol bombs stood ready in the two front rooms, both of which gave a good view of the battle-ground below. An art student friend of Philippe's had made free with his parents' apartment; they were currently sunning themselves on the Côte d'Azur, unaware that their premises had been converted into an ammunition dump. But other residents had lent out their premises knowingly and willingly; the most unlikely people had shown support for the cause, just as the most unlikely people had betrayed it.

'Give them time,' called Claudine from the next room. 'They're probably waiting for reinforcements before they attack.'

Armelle filled the last few bottles, carelessly spilling some of the precious fuel, now in short supply. Preoccupied, she wiped her wet hands on her blouse.

'We should be occupying government buildings, not fighting on our own territory,' she yelled back. 'We should have captured the TV and radio stations.'

With these major goals within its grasp, the revolution had lost its impetus as warring splinter groups argued over tactics and objectives and withdrew their members from the targeted buildings, shattering the unity that would have guaranteed victory.

'Relax,' said Claudine, rejoining her. 'You're nervous as a cat.'

'Why don't we attack first for a change, instead of hanging around waiting for the police to call the tune? What's the point in waiting till they're ready?' Armelle struck a match, set light

347

to one of the bottles, and chucked it haphazardly out of the window. There was a satisfying bang as a flurry of fire shimmied across the darkened street.

'Don't waste ammunition,' said Claudine calmly. Armelle was in one of her mordant, reckless moods. She wasn't just fighting the CRS but the whole treacherous world. 'You could have hit one of our own people.'

'Our own? Who exactly are they? There's no one you can trust these days. I sometimes think the real enemies are within our own ranks—'

Another impassioned harangue against real and imagined traitors was interrupted by a loud knock on the door. Claudine went to answer it.

'Who is it?'

'Was it you that threw that thing into the street?' bellowed an angry male voice.

'What's it to you?'

'It hit me on the arm. You nearly set me alight. Watch what you're fucking doing!'

'Wait a minute,' said Armelle, approaching. 'Viktor? Is that you?' She opened the door.

'Christ almighty. Mademoiselle Molotov herself. I might have known.' The sling on his arm was charred; he was soaking wet from head to foot. 'Someone turned a fire hydrant on me, to stop me frying.'

Armelle dissolved into peals of laughter. Claudine joined in. Viktor, who had raced up the stairs in a rage, found himself doing likewise.

'What are you doing round these parts?' demanded Armelle, dabbing at him with a teatowel.

'I was just taking a walk and one of your lot shanghaied me.'

'Poor Viktor. Why don't you stay up here with us? This is a billet for the weak and feeble. Women and one-armed men welcome.'

'Perhaps you'd better have a bath,' put in Claudine, practically. 'I'll try to find you some dry clothes.'

'Is this place yours?'

'We borrowed it,' said Armelle. 'So don't go pinching anything, okay?'

Viktor retired to the bathroom, wriggled monodextrously out of his wet things, and lowered himself gingerly into the hot water, dangling his damaged arm over the edge. He felt suddenly immensely tired. Eva was the sort of girl you ought to cuddle up with till morning. She was a funny kid. Red hot one minute, and then back to her old, placid self the next. You would never believe it to look at her. Perhaps she wanted a final fling before she settled down with the boyfriend back home. He hoped that was all it was. She was born to get married and have a whole tribe of sturdy kids that she could knit woolly vests for and feed full of *knedlíky*.

Eventually he must have dozed off, waking abruptly to the clammy embrace of condensed steam and the sound of a commotion in the street below, signifying the start of the attack. He dried himself, wound the towel round his waist and padded barefoot into the living room, where Claudine was throwing missiles out of the window.

'I've put out some things for you in the back bedroom,' she said, turning round briefly. 'Hurry up. We could do with some help.'

He peered next door to find Armelle perched on the window ledge, a taper in one hand and a bottle in the other. She looked round briefly but she didn't seem to see him; her face was twisted and her eyes glazed, as if she were possessed by some evil spirit. Viktor left her to it and located the bedroom, where Claudine had laid out some clean, if ill fitting, clothes. It took ages to dress, as usual, manoeuvring the dead weight of his arm into the sleeve and fastening the buttons one-handed. Out of habit, he opened a few drawers. There was some quite decent jewellery in an onyx box – a couple of gold chains with crosses, a string of pearls, and a pair of diamond stud earrings. Enough to fetch in a few hundred francs. He fingered them briefly. Their owner would undoubtedly get more from her insurance company than he would from a fence. Even if she didn't, it was no great loss. It was all so easy to justify. And he shouldn't need to justify it, because that was halfway to admitting that he didn't want to do it, even though he did.

He dropped the trinkets abruptly as a bloodcurdling shriek sent him rushing towards its source, nearly colliding with

Claudine in the hallway. Armelle was screaming blue murder, dancing like a dervish, vainly trying to extinguish her burning blouse with her bare hands. Her hair had ignited and her face was lost behind shooting yellow tongues of fire.

'Go and get help!' barked Viktor, pulling Armelle on to the floor and trying to smother the flames with a cushion. 'Quick!'

Galvanised by horror, Claudine raced to do his bidding while Armelle, obeying some primitive reflex, struggled blindly to fight him off before finally falling back, semi-conscious. Relieved that he had extinguished her clothing, Viktor didn't immediately notice the puddle of spilt petrol beneath the window or the lighted taper lying on the ledge, till some sixth sense drew his eye to the flame, reflected in the deadly pool below and in the glass of the neighbouring bottles. Unable to lift Armelle's dead weight one-handed, he grabbed hold of a foot and began dragging her out of the room towards safety, bracing himself for the explosion. But the bang, when it came, was so loud that he didn't hear it.

Viktor opened his eyes to see two men standing either side of his bed.

'Where am I?'

'In hospital. For the moment.'

It hurt to breathe and he had a filthy headache.

'When can I go home?'

'Your name is Viktor Brožek?'

'If you say so.'

'We want to ask you a few questions.'

A nurse came in at that moment and took his pulse, halting the conversation for a moment.

'He's still in shock. Can you wait outside for a few moments? I have to consult with the doctor.'

Reluctantly, they left.

'What happened to the girl?' asked Viktor.

'She's in intensive care. Badly burned, I'm afraid. You were lucky. Do you remember anything?'

'Not much.'

'The blast knocked you unconscious and you inhaled some smoke, but the firemen got you both out in time. Just as well they were already in the area. You'll be up and about in a day or two.'

'Who were those men?'

'Detectives. I'm sorry. All the casualties are being questioned.'

His first reaction was that he hadn't done anything. He distinctly remembered putting that jewellery back in the box. Even if they searched him, he had nothing on him.

'How did they know my name?' He had left his ID in the pocket of his sodden jacket.

'They seem to know a lot of people's names.' She shrugged expressively and left the room, returning a few moments later with a young, harassed-looking doctor.

'Do you feel up to answering a few questions? I can put them off for a day, but not much longer.'

'What am I supposed to have done?'

'Do you really need to ask me that?'

'But I . . . ' The rest came out as a cracked laugh. Of course. He was guilty of subversive activity. Armelle's little accident had brought fire brigade, ambulance, and of course, police, rushing to the scene. Only fools got caught all right. And it took a very special kind of fool to get caught for a crime he hadn't even committed.

'Might as well get it over with.'

'I'll tell them they can have five minutes.'

The two men came back and drew up a chair each on either side of his bed.

'Your name is Viktor Brožek?'

'So you said.'

'You are not French born.'

'I'm a French citizen.'

'Cohn-Bendit calls himself a French citizen,' observed his interlocutor sourly. 'Monsieur Brožek, not to put too fine a point upon it, you are in deep shit. My advice to you is to co-operate with us. That way we can go easy on you.'

'I didn't do anything.'

'You were in the apartment when the explosion took place, evidently. What were you doing there?'

'I was taking a bath.'

'How fastidious. It's dirty work, building barricades, isn't it?'

'Someone turned a fire hydrant on me. I got soaked. The girls lent me some clothes.'

'Girls? How many of them were there?'

'Girl. In the singular. The one who got burned. There was nobody else there.'

'I thought you said girls.'

'You misheard me. I don't have to answer these questions. I demand to see a solicitor.'

'If you're innocent of any crime, you have nothing to fear by talking to us. If you're not, you'd do well not to be obstructive. When did you first arrive in this country?'

'1951.'

'And do you have many foreign friends?'

'Foreign friends?'

'Mademoiselle Lemercier is well known to state security. Do you share the same German anarchist friends?'

'Look, I hardly know the girl. I don't mix with students. You can check me out, I work as a waiter at the Chez Clément.'

'Mademoiselle Lemercier has a known predilection for the company of working men. You have been seen together on more than one occasion. Most recently at the Sorbonne, where money was seen to change hands between you. The lady has been under surveillance for some time.'

'What is this – a police state?'

'This other girl you mentioned. What was her name?'

'I never mentioned another girl. There were just the two of us.'

'So you admit to being on intimate terms with Mademoiselle Lemercier?'

'Look, I didn't even know she was there. I told you, I went up to have a bath and the next thing I knew—'

The nurse reappeared to say their time was up, winking at Viktor behind their backs. They exchanged nods and then one of them droned the formal words of caution, adding that a police guard would remain outside his door until his removal to custody the next day. Meanwhile, he would do well to jog his powers of memory, before questioning began in earnest.

'Are there any relatives you would like us to contact?' asked the nurse, when they had gone.

The thing Marta had always dreaded, and now it had happened. Worse, it had happened while Eva was here.

'My grandmother. But I don't want her to get a fright. What time is it?'

'Just after two a.m.'

'Can you leave it till the morning? And just tell her about me being in hospital? Not about the police?'

'Give me the number.' She squeezed his hand. 'Bastards,' she said.

'About time! Chantal's been worried sick!' Jeanne took her son's filthy jacket from him. 'We were beginning to think you'd been injured. Or arrested again.'

'Chantal?'

'They've discharged her. She's in the front room. She's to have plenty of rest and no stress. I'll leave you alone for a little while. Be nice to her.'

Chantal was lying on the settee. Resisting the urge to spring to her feet, she held out her arms in welcome. Alain kissed her woodenly.

'Thank God you're all right,' she said, hugging him. 'I was so afraid you'd been hurt.'

'How are you?'

'Much better. They say the danger's past. It's so nice, being home again. I missed you terribly. Tell me about last night. Was it as bad as they say?'

Alain swallowed the hard knot at the back of his throat.

'It was pretty bad, yes. One of the girls got burned.'

'One of the girls from the factory?'

'No. Armelle.'

'Oh, Alain!' Her distress seemed genuine. 'I'm so sorry!'

It had been daybreak when he heard the news, passed by word of mouth from barricade to barricade. He had rushed to the block in question to find a window on the fourth floor blown out, and several policemen guarding the premises and questioning all comers.

'I went to the hospital,' he said. 'I couldn't go in – the place was swarming with police. So I hung around across the road till I saw her father come out. I asked him how she was, and . . . ' His voice tailed off.

He would never forget the look of devastation in Lemercier's eyes, the cold fury in his voice. 'You will have no further use for her, I fear,' he had hissed, almost triumphantly. 'Her face is like a lump of raw meat.' For a moment, he had thought the old man was going to strike him, and he would have understood, even welcomed it, because he was entitled to hate him, after all, even though it wasn't his fault. Or was it?

'She's going to be badly scarred,' Alain resumed. 'She'll need plastic surgery. How's that for revenge?'

'Revenge? You think so little of me?'

It would never have occurred to Chantal that the revenge might be his, that his horror would be underpinned by a monstrous, inadmissible sense of release and retribution.

'It was myself I hated, not her,' said Chantal, 'for forcing you into marrying me, for making you so unhappy.' She bowed her head. 'I got pregnant deliberately, Alain. Because I knew it was my only chance. There. Now you know.'

It was an admission, not an apology. She had fought with the only weapons at her disposal, just as he had done. He had never thought of her as a fighter before. He had spared her the truth because he thought she wasn't strong enough to take it, but he was the one who had been weak.

'There's something you have to know as well,' he said, seizing the moment. 'All these months, I've wanted to be free of you. Not because I loved Armelle. I wanted to be free of her as well. I feel as if I'd wished this on her. If anything had happened to you, I would have felt the same. When Maman said you were home, I thought for a minute that you must have lost the baby. And it would have been my fault.'

'I'm fine. The baby's fine.'

'I'm not going to see her again, Chantal. I can't bear the thought of seeing her like that.'

'She wouldn't want you to.'

'That's not the point. It's finally over. I'm glad it's over, I can't help it. She was like a curse. It was all part of the anger. I can't explain . . . '

354

'You don't need to explain to me. It's all right.'

He laid his head against her heart, drawing strength from her. It was good, for once, to be home. Chantal stroked his hair, placed his cold hand on her warm belly, and reminded herself what a lucky girl she was.

'Viktor! I came straightaway! To think you've been here all night and nobody told me.'

'It's all right, Babička. I'm okay.' His voice was hoarse and cracked from the effects of the smoke; he still felt dizzy and nauseous.

'Eva's outside. They would only let one of us in at a time. Why have they given you a room to yourself? It must be serious!'

'Sit down and keep calm. They just kept me in for observation. There's nothing wrong with me.'

'When are they letting you out? You must come back to my place so that I can look after you.'

'Listen. This is my own stupid fault. I was in the Latin Quarter last night and—'

Marta patted his hand.

'The little nurse told us about you saving that poor girl's life. That was very brave of you, Viktor. I'm proud of you. Even though you should never have taken such a foolish risk.'

'You can say that again. The place was chock-a-block with Molotov cocktails. I'm under arrest.'

'What?'

'For assaulting the security forces, conspiracy, and God knows what else.'

'Viktor!'

'Keep your hair on. I'm innocent. For once in my life, I didn't do anything. But the evidence is all stacked up against me, and the only people who could testify in my favour won't be crazy enough to come forward. The girl I rescued is on some police blacklist or other. But she's got a rich daddy, so they've decided to make do with me instead.'

Marta seized his hands, her eyes staring straight ahead, eighteen years into the past.

'I've got some money saved. We'll get you a good lawyer.'

'There's no need for all that. I'm going to plead guilty.'

'You're what?'

'If I don't co-operate, they're going to throw the book at me. This way they'll let me off with a lighter sentence. The alternative is kicking my heels on remand for God knows how long while they drum up a case against me. And once they start poking around and asking questions about me, who knows what they might find out? It's not worth the risk.'

'You mean . . . you're going to go to prison?'

'I'd have gone to prison anyway, till they brought me to trial. And they'd have taken their time about it, believe me.'

'But what about bail?'

'Not a chance. They're trying to make an example of people. Specially foreign agitators like me. Don't panic. They're not going to torture me or send me to a labour camp. It's no big deal.'

'I don't believe this! It's not possible!'

'Don't cry, Babička. I'm innocent, remember. I thought that would cheer you up.'

'I'd rather you weren't! I'd rather they'd caught you picking someone's pocket! Then at least you would have deserved it!'

Viktor patted her hand, trying to keep up the pretence of nonchalance. She was right, of course. If he'd been nicked fair and square, he could have been more philosophical about it. Innocence weighed much more heavily than guilt. But he was too well versed in street wisdom to fight the system. He had too much to hide. And there was no point in taking it personally. This was standard police procedure, after all. Help us, and we'll go easy on you. Cop a plea, and we'll reduce the sentence. Stitch up a few of your mates and we might even let you go . . . No. He might be a thief but he wasn't a nark.

'Are you going to be okay for cash?' he went on. 'Because if you're not, get rid of the piano.'

'Never! It was a birthday present!'

'Not yours. Mine.'

'What do you take me for? All these years I've been putting money aside, in case you ever got into trouble . . . '

'Then pay off Madame Bloc, will you, so she doesn't re-let my apartment. I'll pay you back when I get out, even if I have to rob a bank to do it.'

'You'll be the death of me!'

'Rubbish. You've been through worse than this. And if the police come round and ask you any questions, just act senile. It shouldn't be hard.'

'How can you joke at a time like this?'

'Don't be such an old misery. I could do with a rest. At least they can't make me break stones, or stitch mailbags. Not for a couple of months, anyway. I shall milk this bloody arm for all it's worth.'

'To think we came here for justice and freedom!'

'The two things don't always go together. Luckily for me. Now go home and stop worrying. I'll get word to you where they take me.'

Marta creaked to her feet.

'You're right,' she said, reverting to her habitual stoicism. 'Don't antagonise them. Just concentrate on getting out as quickly as you can.' She bent to kiss him. 'At least you're not hurt. The nurse said you could have been killed. That you risked your life to pull that girl clear.'

'Rubbish. She fancies me, that's all.'

'You're incorrigible.'

'Let's hope so.'

'Be careful what you say to Eva, won't you?'

'Of course I will. Now go.'

Eva didn't appear for several minutes. Marta had obviously been filling her in. She gave him a rather forced dimple-to-dimple grin, delved in her shopping bag, and handed him a bag of apples. Big, bright red ones . . .

'Thanks. Sorry this had to happen while you were here.'

'Sorry it had to happen at all. Marta says the police framed you. How can that happen in a democracy?'

'It's too complicated to explain. It was my own stupid fault for getting involved. Just as well you weren't with me.'

'What will they do to you?'

'Send me down for a few months, I expect. Don't look so

horrified. Prison can't be any worse than *service militaire*. I'll survive.'

'Will you write to me?'

'I'm not much of a one for letters.'

'Can I write to you?'

'If you like.'

'When are they taking you away from here?'

'Some time later today.'

'Will I be able to visit you?'

'I doubt it. Look, Marta's got some concert tickets for tonight. Cassie booked them weeks ago. Mind you don't waste them. And help yourself to my records before you go. Take as many as you like.'

'Thank you. I'll miss you, Viktor. Perhaps you'll come to Prague one day.'

'Don't count on it. But I'll miss you too.'

'About yesterday. I hope you don't think that I'm a . . . a . . .'

'Never for a minute. You made my day.'

'You're a dreadful liar.'

'No, it's true. Too bad we won't get a chance to do it again. You're a smashing girl, Eva. I'm sorry I was such a sod to you at times.'

'Don't apologise. I'm used to it, remember?'

He reached for her hand, pulled her on to the bed and kissed her very thoroughly, to give her something nice to remember him by, leaving her pink and almost pretty.

'Fancy a quickie before the nurse comes back?'

'Viktor!'

'Oh well. I thought it was worth a try. Look after yourself, won't you? Have a safe journey back. And good luck with the magazine.'

'I'll send you a copy.'

'I hope things work out between you and Jan.'

'Yes. Well. Perhaps.' She reached into her bag again. 'I should have given you this right at the start. Your father made me promise. But there was never a good moment. I know you don't want it, but perhaps reading will help pass the time.' She handed him a buff folder. 'That man outside searched my bag,

358

so he might take it off you. Be sure to ask for a receipt. It's a hundred and forty-six pages.'

'I'll do that.' Christ. A hundred and forty-six pages all in Czech. They would take him for a spy.

'Don't let them get to you,' said Eva, thickly. 'Remember, truth will prevail.'

Fat chance, thought Viktor.

'Of course it will,' he said.

'Papa?'

'Don't try to speak. I'm here.'

Her hands were heavily bandaged, but the burns on her face and chest had been left open to the air, the red, raw, ravaged flesh glistening under a layer of ointment. The worst of the damage had been done by the vaporised petrol, rising like a deadly gas from the warmth of her body, waiting for its chance to ignite. Bertrand looked away in disgust. The sight of her made his stomach heave, and the worst was still to come. They proposed to keep her heavily sedated for the first week or so. After a month, skin grafting could begin. And then it would be a matter of time and patience and skill. They had tried to tell him she was lucky: lucky that her rescuer had beaten out the flames before they turned her into a human torch, lucky that he had pulled her clear of the subsequent inferno, lucky, lucky, lucky, that she was *alive*. But Armelle would not think herself lucky, any more than he did. He would have grieved less over her grave.

His lawyers were already hard at work. In view of Armelle's appalling injuries, they foresaw no problems with the authorities. Any charges against her would almost certainly be dropped; if not, the worst that would happen would be a suspended sentence. They had assumed, naïvely, that Bertrand would want to assist and reward the fellow-activist who had saved his daughter's life. They had actually expected him to thank him for condemning her to a hideous future, not realising that every tragedy needed its scapegoat. His instructions had been instant and unequivocal. Let her so-called saviour take the rap.

'Maman...'

'She's on her way. I'm having you moved to a private clinic in Neuilly. You'll have the best man.' He wanted to add, 'And he'll soon have you looking good as new,' but the lie stuck in his throat. She would be healed, repaired, remodelled, but her beauty had gone for ever. She shut her eyes, still dopey from the drugs, still ignorant of her loss. No man would ever want her again. That was the only solace.

As Rob had predicted, the Blakeneys took their sudden disappearance in their stride. Cassie had phoned them, sheepishly, from Ostend, to say that she wouldn't be back for several weeks and asking them to forward any mail or messages *poste restante*. Rob knew that she was still hoping that Viktor would make contact, and hoped for her sake that he would ... but not just yet.

All the while the postal services were on strike, she could put his continuing silence down to that. But within a few days of their departure from London they discovered, via an English newspaper, that the crisis had ended as suddenly as it had begun. One moment there had been the threat of civil war, with troops on full alert, ready to impose martial law on an unruly populace. The next, the Champs-Élysées had been thronged from the Concorde to the Étoile with pro-Gaullist demonstrators, in scenes unparalleled since the Liberation.

A million voices had chanted 'France back to work!' and 'Forward with de Gaulle!' as the silent majority erupted, abruptly, into a deafening roar. The unions had reached a settlement with the Government, workers had voted to accept it, students had retreated in squabbling disarray, and everyone had resumed their normal business with typically French sang-froid. While police set about removing the few remaining strike pickets, the whole of Paris queued at the newly replenished petrol pumps to take off for the Whitsun holiday, leaving disconsolate militants to continue their campaigning to no avail. It was all over. Armelle would be devastated, thought Rob. But at least he could stop worrying about her getting hurt.

The following week they arrived in Rome to find a redirected letter, bearing a French stamp. Cassie tore it open and read it avidly, her expression hovering between regret and relief.

'It's from Viktor's grandmother,' she said, showing it to Rob. 'You can read it if you like.'

The letter was three weeks old, dated the day Cassie had left Paris.

> ... Needless to say, Viktor hasn't told me what happened, but whatever he said or did to hurt you, I know he bitterly regrets it. I have never seen him so wretched, not since his mother died. He denies it, of course, as he did then. He has to convince himself that he doesn't care. No doubt he managed to convince you too. For Viktor, love is a frightening thing – he lives from day to day because he has no faith in the future, or other people, or himself. I'm a sentimental old woman, and I hate unhappy endings. If you're half as miserable as he is, please don't be too proud to let him know it ...

Rob sighed.

'So when are you off?'

'You don't have a very high opinion of me, do you? Every time he whistles, I jump. Trust him to get Marta to do his whistling for him. And trust Marta to try to make me feel guilty ... Don't let me weaken, will you?'

'Is weaken the right word?'

'For the moment, yes. That is, I'm not strong enough to weaken just yet. Does that make sense?'

'More or less.'

'If I went back now, things would just be exactly the same as they were before. I've got to prove to myself that I can live without him.'

'And if you can't?'

'If I can't,' she said grimly, 'he'll never find out.'

If she ever went back to him, it would be a sign of success, not surrender. And if she didn't, the same formula would apply. With an effort, she tore Marta's letter up and put it in the nearest litter bin, so that she couldn't re-read it. Not that she needed to. She knew she would remember every word.

Paris, 6th June 1968

Dear children, [Marta had written]

God knows when this will reach you. No doubt the postal workers will want to spin out their overtime as long as possible. Everything is more or less back to normal here, but there are still shortages, so I am glad I stocked up.

The place seems so empty without you, Eva. I'm sorry you had to come at such a bad time. It can't have been much of a holiday for you. God only knows what you must think of the West – to think that I thought you would be impressed! I expect you are glad to be home. France is clearly going to the dogs . . .

There was no mention of Viktor, other than that he was 'very well, and sends his love'. Marta had agreed to write to Eva separately, care of her workplace, to let her know what had happened in court. There seemed to be no point in worrying Karel. But so far nothing had arrived. This letter, the first since the strikes, had taken ten days to reach its destination, delayed by the huge backlog of mail.

Perhaps Viktor hadn't got her letter yet. She had meant to make it brisk and matter of fact, but it had come out several shades softer than she had intended. 'I think about you often,' and 'I wish we could have had more time together,' were surely innocuous-enough sentiments, even if her behaviour hadn't been. It seemed mean-spirited to pretend that she didn't care for him, just to spare her pride.

She didn't regret what had happened. It had been the first step on a bold voyage full of infinite possibilities, a step she would never have dared to take but for the last few months of self-discovery. And Jan had been part of that. She hadn't been disloyal to him. She had simply been true to herself.

Strange, how quickly one got greedy. Too far, too fast. It was Karel's favourite phrase. But when you knew there wasn't much time, you went as far as possible, as quickly as you could; the alternative was to settle for nothing. She felt trapped in a spiral of limitless longing, of sublime dissatisfaction. And yet part of her remained resolutely earthbound, potting her dreams like pickles in a jar, to tickle a winter palate with remembered sun.

Wrenching her mind back to the present, she returned to her typewriter and read through her piece for the umpteenth time.

THE PARIS SPRING – a personal view

It read like an obituary, and perhaps it was. Eva had felt little empathy with the confused, conflicting aims of the French Left, but she was disappointed that so much should have boiled down, so quickly, to so little.

> Even as this issue of *Spring Tide* goes to press, the last bastion of anti-Government resistance has fallen as French police evacuate the Sorbonne, where student activists had vowed to hold out to the last claiming that the French Communist Party, and the Communist-controlled CGT, had 'betrayed the revolution'. But despite the routine use of tear gas and truncheons, resistance was less than had been anticipated and reports suggest that the vast majority of students are weary of conflict and anxious to resume lectures and tutorials. A recent poll indicates that the elections at the end of this month will result in a landslide victory for the Gaullists. This goes to show how suddenly and dramatically the tide of national events can turn against all predictions and expectations . . .

Eva crossed out her last sentence. It drew a false analogy. And it sounded unintentionally ominous. There was no comparison between events in Paris and the quiet revolution taking place at home. The whole tenor of the French situation had been destructive. There had been no unity of purpose, no clear programme for the future. The malcontents and the manipulators had joined forces briefly, with opposing aims in view; the manipulators, inevitably, had won.

Here, everyone wanted the same thing. Well, almost everybody. Despite there being a wide spectrum of opinion, people were generally united in their support for the Action Programme. The only disputes were about how much, how soon. And the ever-growing threat of a clampdown, enforced from Moscow, had had the effect of drawing people together. The much-resented presence of Warsaw Pact troops on Czechoslovak soil – just for 'routine manoeuvres', of course – had engendered not fear, but a collective determination not to give in to bullying, despite, or perhaps because of the cautious stance of the leadership, caught between the devil of Soviet intervention and the deep blue sea of public opinion.

'There's a letter from Marta,' said Eva, jumping up to greet Karel. 'It was addressed to both of us, so I opened it.'

Karel read it with a vague, abstracted air. Typically, he was not expecting any sudden overtures from Viktor, which perhaps accounted for his low spirits. Eva would have given anything to cheer him up. Since her return, he seemed permanently preoccupied and looked deathly tired all the time; he was smoking more than ever and that dreadful hacking cough of his had been driving her mad.

'You ought to see the doctor again,' she had said. 'Get yourself some time off work.'

'If I take time off work, I can hardly turn up for meetings, can I? It's just a touch of catarrh, that's all.'

'Are you sure that's all it is?' As always, she found it difficult to voice her deep-rooted fear out loud. Having watched her mother die of cancer, Eva nurtured a morbid dread of Karel going the same way.

'While you were away, I had a thorough check-up. For your sake, not for mine. Miloš fixed it up, through this doctor friend of his, who sees private patients on the side. For hard currency, of course. It's a good racket. I don't approve, mind, but I didn't want to risk some official quack pensioning me off before my time.'

'And?'

'He gave me an X-ray and there's nothing there. So you're stuck with me for a few years yet.'

'You're not lying to me, are you?'

'Why would I bother to tell you, if I was lying? When I finally croak, it will be to get a bit of peace from your nagging.'

Karel looked over her shoulder and read through her piece.

'What do you think?' demanded Eva.

'That perhaps you should have stayed put.'

'The troops aren't going to do anything. It's just intimidation, that's all.'

'Is that what Jan says?'

'I haven't asked him. When will you realise that I can think for myself?'

'Is it really over between you two?'

'I told you. We agreed not to see each other till the end of the month.'

'And then?'

Eva didn't answer. What had happened with Viktor should have shunted Jan into the sidelines for ever; perversely, it seemed to have had the opposite effect. His rigorously just-good-friends behaviour had been driving her to distraction.

'I don't know yet.'

'We had a few beers together, while you were in Paris,' continued Karel. 'He has integrity, I'll say that for him. And courage. Too much courage.'

'Meaning what, exactly?'

'Eva, he's getting in very deep. He was sounding me out about what I'd be prepared to do if there was an invasion.'

'An invasion? But he's always said it could never happen!'

'I know a recruiting officer when I see one. I was in the Resistance, remember. Oh, he skirted round and round the houses, but I know what he's up to. Already they're trying to find sites for underground printing presses and radio transmitters and safe houses for potential political prisoners. To identify people who are willing to stick their necks out. To form contingency plans for co-ordination and sabotage.'

'He admitted all that?'

'Of course not. He was very careful not to. But I've been there before. I can read between the lines. If anything happens, Jan is going to be right in the thick of things, you mark my words. This little magazine of his is just the tip of the iceberg.'

'Why are you suddenly telling me this?'

'To warn you. Once you two are back together, you'll both

be tarred with the same brush, even if he tries to keep you out of it.'

'So much for him being . . . what was it? A lame duck.'

'He has more to prove than most people.'

'Just because of the way he looks? Just because he's got a stutter?'

'Don't jump to his defence again. I told you, I respect the lad. He's got guts. But don't make the mistake my first wife made. He's got "labour camp" written all over him.'

'You're one to talk! You're a founder member of Club 231. Are you going to end up back in gaol as well? Because in that case I might as well be hanged for a sheep as a lamb.'

She picked up the typewritten sheets and reached for her bag.

'Where are you going?'

'I promised Jan I'd drop this in to him tonight. We start running it off tomorrow.'

'Don't be back late, will you?'

'He might want to suggest a few changes. I don't know how long it'll take. Don't wait up.'

'I might have known. You can't resist forbidden fruit, can you?'

'For goodness' sake. Ever since I got home you've been back to your miserable old self.'

'And ever since you got home you've been different. Touchy. Restless. Is there something you're not telling me?'

'Here we go again. I'm not pregnant, if that's what you're driving at.'

'I wasn't thinking of that. Is it something to do with Viktor?'

'Viktor? I don't know what you mean.'

'Then why are you blushing?'

'Oh, for heaven's sake. I've got to go.'

And she ran off down the stairs, leaving him wondering.

'Roll up, roll up,' said Armelle. 'Don't be shy. Come and see the freak show.'

'How are you?' asked Claudine, doing her best not to look away. Armelle's face was a piebald mess of old and new skin which had healed unevenly, pulling her mouth out of shape.

She had no eyebrows or lashes, and the singed remains of her long chestnut hair had been cut very short. 'I've been every day, but they wouldn't let me in. They told me you didn't want any visitors.'

'I've had a bellyful of visitors. The police, mostly. Don't worry. I didn't shop you.'

'Nor did Viktor,' said Claudine, drawing up a chair. 'He got three months. It was in the paper. I wanted to come forward, but my parents wouldn't let me. I feel really bad about it. They just picked on him, that was all. It wasn't fair.'

'Serve him bloody right. He was overdue for a spell in gaol. Stop looking at me like that. I know I'm ugly.'

'I was expecting it to be worse. I didn't run away, you know, if that's what you've been thinking. Viktor sent me to fetch help. When I heard the explosion, I panicked. I thought you were both dead.'

'Pity we weren't. I'll never forgive that bastard for pulling me clear.'

'How can you say that? If it hadn't been for him—'

'Look, why don't you just bugger off? You've seen me now. You've satisfied your curiosity.'

'I don't blame you for being angry. So would I be, if it happened to me. I wish it had been me, instead of you.'

'It would have been wasted on you. You never had any looks to lose.' She plucked irritably at the bedspread with a bandaged hand. 'Alain hasn't been near me, of course. I expect he's too busy earning his new improved wages. The factory's humming like a happy little hive. God, people are such sheep.'

'How much longer will you be here?'

'Another couple of months. They want to take the skin off my thighs and try to stick it on to my face. I'd tell them not to bother, except that all this fancy treatment is costing my father a fortune. That's the only thing that makes it worth while.'

'You'll get your looks back. And even if you don't . . . I still love you, Armelle.'

'How kind. I can't afford to be fussy now, obviously. Maman wants me to go to Italy to convalesce. I suppose she thinks I'm not a threat any more. That's all she knows. I've still got two tits and a hole between my legs.'

'I wish there was something I could do. I feel so helpless.'

'I don't want you to do anything. It was my own stupid fault. I don't need your pity.'

'I need yours. I went to pieces after it happened. I just wanted to die. I kept vomiting, I came out in a rash, I couldn't sleep. Don't punish me by sending me away. The last few weeks have been such hell.'

She burst into tears. Sighing, Armelle relented, mollified by the sight of someone more pathetic than herself.

'Stop blubbering for God's sake. You can visit me if you've nothing better to do. Come back tomorrow, will you? I'm tired.'

Tired wasn't the word. She was exhausted to the marrow of her bones. She had lost everything, personally and politically. The revolution would never happen now. It had all been a gross illusion, fired by its own death-wish. 'Power to the imagination.' It was the slogan of a masochist bent on his own subjugation. The imagination robbed you of all content, enslaved the brain with chaotic longings, tormented you with impossibilities.

A few stalwarts would carry on regardless of course, banging their heads against a brick wall, content – no, preferring – to be a minority. But they would never win. Perhaps that was what had attracted her in the first place. The inevitability of defeat.

As soon as Claudine had gone she reached for the mirror she kept illicitly under the pillow and looked defeat straight in the eye. They had warned her it would get worse before it got better. Part of her face still felt numb, as if she had been to the dentist; the rest of it itched and tingled unbearably. She couldn't remember the accident, thank God. Her amnesia had proved useful: her inability to give any meaningful evidence had spared her the ordeal of interrogation and an expensive lawyer had done the rest – an expensive lawyer who hadn't lifted a finger to help Viktor.

Well, that was his lookout. Her survival programme left no room for gratitude. Those early days of why-me? paranoia had been saturated with hatred for everyone who had conspired towards her survival. Every time she felt her anger slipping, it seemed like the first step towards capitulation. She had no desire to be one of those brave, smiling, cheerful victims who gibbered thanks and counted blessings and sucked up to the bloody doctors and nurses, none of whom gave a damn in any case. To them, this was all in the day's work. For all they knew she had been ugly to begin with. They had expected hysteria, no doubt, and had the chemical equivalent of a strait-jacket ready in some handy hypodermic. Unimpressed by her sullen fortitude, they were waiting, eagerly, for a delayed reaction. Well, she would prove them all wrong.

Defeat was a state of mind. The struggle wasn't over yet. Not by a long chalk.

A hundred and forty-six pages, all in Czech. The police had duly confiscated the manuscript, in the hope of finding something incriminating. He had had to make a fuss to get it back; that in itself had made it precious.

It was slow going, but he had time on his hands. A proficient reader might have polished it off in a day and dismissed it as the maudlin, rambling outpourings of a broken-down old man. But when you had to sweat over every line it was hard to dismiss the results of your labours as worthless. On the surface it was a disappointingly factual account, describing events which were by no means unique, which had happened to thousands of other innocent people. But squeezed between those closely typed lines was a subtext that required no reading skills, that revealed a man who had admired and resented his father, who feared and mistrusted the woman he loved, and who heartily disliked himself. A cynic encumbered with ideals, a misanthropist burdened with a heart. It was like scraping paint off a window, painstakingly letting in the light, wanting to look through it to what lay beyond, not realising till it was too late that you were staring at your own reflection in the glass.

Looking back, I ask myself how I could have been so blind. Perhaps it was because my work was an escape, a way of compensating for the humiliations of the past, a means of proving myself. I would have convinced myself black was white, rather than admit I was wrong. I became that most honest of liars, one who deceives himself.

Viktor knew exactly what he meant.

THIRTEEN

July/August 1968

'Sorry I'm late,' said Jan. Eva had been at her post since first thing that morning, on a baking hot day, and now it was nearly six. 'How many signatures have you got so far?'

'I've lost count. The queue started as soon as I got here.'

'It's the same everywhere. The response has been fantastic.'

Eva smiled at an old woman in a headscarf, appending her name to the petition in slow, arthritic script. A line of people stood patiently waiting behind her, ordinary working people who normally left politics to the activists, the students and the young. The whole of the last weekend in July had been devoted to a countrywide signature campaign, made urgent by the imminent top-level talks between the Czechoslovak leadership and the Soviet Politburo. The recent spate of virulent propaganda in the Russian press left no room for doubt as to the purpose of the meeting.

Even people who hadn't read the impassioned article in *Literarni Listy* were eager to endorse it. You didn't have to be educated, or an intellectual, to understand what it was all about. It was a message to Moscow, telling them to back off. It was a plea to Dubček, assuring him that the people were united behind the reform programme and urging him not to give in to intimidation. It was a declaration of intent, for and on behalf of every Czech and Slovak, summarised in the four rousing words, Socialism! Alliance! Sovereignty!, and above all, Freedom!

'I'll take over now,' said Jan. 'I've left some stuff at home for you to type, if you're not too tired.'

'Of course I'm not.'

He was sure of her now although, ironically, Eva wasn't so sure of him. She was no longer the most important thing in his life but, on balance, she preferred things that way.

'Thanks. I'll be along in a couple of hours, as soon as Hela relieves me. See you later.'

Eva had been quick to take advantage of Karel's temporary absence. Under doctor's orders he had been exiled to a mountain spa, much against his will. No sooner had she waved him off at the station than she had moved Jan into the apartment, much to old Nováková's disgust. And they had been making up for lost time ever since, as if aware that time was running out.

'Don't be too late, will you?'

He smiled and squeezed her hand, and she felt it again, that sudden lurch of fear. Not just of invasion, but of what could happen to Jan. He had signed the notorious *Two Thousand Words* in June, an impassioned manifesto appealing to the leadership to honour its commitment to reform, and assuring it of popular support against the threat of foreign intervention. It had been immediately denounced by the Soviet press as an anti-Communist document. For all that the vast majority of the population wholeheartedly agreed with the sentiments expressed, the seventy people who had signed it – many of them well known, others, like Jan, obscure – were now marked down by Moscow as self-confessed counter-revolutionaries.

Karel was right. She might not be in love with Jan, in the romantic sense, but she was certainly in love with what he represented. For the moment, that was all that mattered. Certainly it mattered more than Viktor not answering her letters. In a way, she was glad he hadn't. She was less glad that he hadn't written to his father, although Karel refused to admit his disappointment.

The tram queue was a-buzz with talk.

'A woman in our block's been hoarding food,' one woman was saying disdainfully to her neighbour. 'I said to her, you ought to be ashamed. It's the kind of thing that leads to panic.'

Eva smiled to herself, remembering the gutted shelves of Marta's local *alimentation*.

'Perhaps she really believes that West Germany is planning to invade us,' suggested someone else, provoking a roar of laughter. It was like that all the time, these days. People trying to keep up each other's morale. Strangers speaking in the street like old friends. As Jan had said, this was the best time yet. It was better than those early, heady days of spring; much better than the impatient, carping ones that followed. But could a wall of signatures hold back tanks? Weeks after the 'routine manoeuvres' had ended, Soviet troops were still in residence. 'We shall fight', sneered the cynics, 'to the last drop of ink.' But Eva still clung to the stubborn hope that the pen would prove mightier than the sword.

'There was a visitor for you,' said Nováková, accosting her at the foot of the stairs, rattling her keys like a sabre. 'A young man,' she added disapprovingly.

'Oh? Did he give his name?'

'I didn't ask. It's none of my business, I'm sure. He said to tell you that he'd call back later this evening.'

'Thank you.' It could be any one of a dozen people, delivering copy for the magazine, or wanting a word with Jan. Yawning, she went upstairs, hauled out her typewriter, and got down to work.

'Your father is here to see you, mademoiselle. Shall I show him in?'

The private clinic in Neuilly was run on the lines of a luxury hotel. Visiting hours were unrestricted, but Armelle refused to see her father except by appointment, and invariably kept him waiting like some importunate courtier seeking an audience with his queen.

'Yes, please,' said Armelle. Claudine, Sylvie and Yvette prepared to leave the room.

'No,' said Armelle. 'I want you to stay here.'

The girls looked at each other dubiously.

'Are you sure?'

'I can't do it on my own. He's always relied on me being too ashamed to tell anyone. If you're here, it will prove that you already know.'

She was trembling all over. Claudine sat down again and took her hand.

'Are you certain you want to go through with this? Are you sure it won't make things worse?'

Armelle shook her head vehemently.

'They couldn't be worse. You haven't seen the way he looks at me lately. Or rather, doesn't look at me. You can all bear to look at me – why can't he?'

She was making good progress, so everyone claimed. Good enough for her to leave hospital tomorrow. The grafts had taken well and, although further plastic surgery would be necessary, short admissions would be sufficient in future. They would be glad to see the back of her, no doubt. She had hardly been a model patient. But ironically, she was terrified to leave the safety of this hated place, to go out into a world where she had once been admired and see people stare, or point, or turn away.

The embryonic women's group had held its first meeting in this room, a month ago, signifying Armelle's first contact with the outside world, apart from the long-suffering Claudine. She had forced herself to face her former rivals, particularly the much-despised Sylvie, just to prove she wasn't afraid of them, although, of course, she was. Continuing painful surgery meant that it often hurt to speak, forcing her into the role of listener. They had worked their way through Claudine's list of topics, made plans for extending the group next term, and begun drawing up a manifesto of their objectives. But invariably the agenda broke down into anecdotal discussions, illustrating the all-pervasive despotism of men. Armelle was glad she had an excuse not to participate in these self-revelatory sessions. Watching the three of them parade their hang-ups – all of which seemed supremely trivial – enabled her to look down on them, a negative but effective way of boosting her own precarious self-esteem. They were weak, silly, female . . .

And then one day a quarrel had erupted between Sylvie and

everyone else on the subject of abortion, a subject on which Sylvie held inexplicably right-wing views which the others put down to her Catholic upbringing. Outnumbered, Sylvie had overstated her case, become ridiculously emotional, and finally burst into tears, stunning them all with the statement that she would give anything, anything, to be able to have a child, but she was sterile. Not as the result of a bungled abortion, which they had all immediately assumed, but because of long-standing, untreated gonorrhoea contracted in early childhood.

She had never told anyone before, she had sobbed. It made her feel dirty and ashamed. She was convinced that nobody would ever want to marry her, and so she deliberately sought out men she didn't even like, who would be no loss.

Appalled, Armelle had exchanged glances with Claudine, reminding her of her vow of secrecy, recalling the words she had stubbornly refused to believe: 'It's not just you. You're not alone.' And suddenly, incredibly, irresistibly, she had heard herself saying the same to Sylvie. 'It's not just you. You're not alone.' It had been like lancing a huge, festering boil.

Afterwards, she had badly wanted to complete the process by forgiving him. She had wanted to throw her arms round him and say, 'I still love you, Papa. I can't help it. Please love me too.' But she couldn't forgive him. Not for what he had done to her in the past, but for what he was doing to her now. If he had really loved her, he could have looked at her, still found some beauty in her damaged face, or at least had the grace to dissimulate. But his visits were brief and painful, his eyes permanently downcast as if he were paying his respects at her tomb. Without her mother's beauty, she was nothing. He would rather she had died.

Bertrand Lemercier looked disconcerted to see three other women in the room and turned immediately to go, saying he would return later, but Armelle called him back. He bent to kiss her, very briefly, closing his eyes as he did so.

'Everything's ready for you to come home,' he began stiffly. 'I've arranged for a nurse to come in every day. Or if you prefer, she can go to Italy with you for the summer.'

'I don't want to go to Italy. I prefer to go to the house in Provence. I've invited my friends here to join me.'

'That's not possible, *chérie*. Odile is there for the month of August, with her mother and sisters. But in September—'

'I want the house in Provence for the summer. Then I want my own apartment, in Paris. I want my independence. I'm not greedy. I'll settle for thirty thousand francs a year.'

'This is no time to talk about money, Armelle. It goes without saying that all your needs will be provided for.'

'I don't want my needs provided for. I want to run my own life. I've earned every penny. Whores get paid – why shouldn't I?'

Claudine watched him closely, but his expression gave nothing away.

'We'll discuss your allowance another time. You know I can refuse you nothing at the moment. But your mother is looking forward to seeing you and—'

'If I see Maman, I'm warning you, I'll tell her. I'll tell her everything. Everything. Just like I've told my friends here.'

For the first time since the accident he looked her full in the face, subjecting her to the old, incapacitating contempt. His eyes were suddenly hard and cold, excluding everyone else in the room. Armelle felt her voice dry in her throat.

'And if she doesn't tell her, we will,' put in Claudine, sensing her hesitation. There was a murmur of sisterly support.

She waited for him to say, 'I admit nothing. You have no proof,' to brazen it out to the end, to pit his superior strength against hers. Inadmissibly, part of her still craved humiliation. But then his expression changed from the comfortingly familiar implacability to something she had not bargained for. Relief. Relief that was like a slap in the face. This was his chance to pay her off.

'As you wish,' he said shortly.

'I want Odile and her menagerie out of there by tomorrow,' said Armelle, rallying. 'And you can pay the first instalment into my bank account tomorrow. Otherwise . . . '

He left before she could finish, before either of them could weaken. She knew then with crushing certainty that she would never see him again.

Viktor wandered round Prague in a daze, watching Marta's photographs come to life as monochrome melted into muted colour, set against a wash of ochre and russet, and static, silent images were animated by shifting light and sound. While other visitors consulted their Baedekers or listened attentively to the drone of the guides, Viktor searched out scenes from the family album, like a bloodhound sniffing a trail.

He had tried to manipulate Marta into suggesting this trip, but she had seen through him immediately.

'You just want me as a front, don't you? So that you can pretend that I dragged you along as my escort. You'll do this thing properly, Viktor, or not at all.'

She had been only too ready to believe that the purpose of this visit was to seek out his long-lost father. It was a simple reason that she could understand; to have denied it would have provoked questions he couldn't even answer himself.

He had had no choice but to come, which wasn't the same thing as wanting to. Did a salmon know what drove it to swim upstream in search of its spawning ground? He had had to go right back to the beginning, so that he could take a big long run at the future . . . if there was any.

'We'll be watching you, Brožek,' they had said. He could still feel eyes boring into his back everywhere he went. His visit to the Embassy, for his visa, had no doubt been duly noted; as a known Red he would never be sure when they were watching him and when they weren't. The next time he chatted up a jewel-encrusted widow or helped himself to a superfluous wallet, he could be walking straight into a trap of his own making. And three months of gaol (nearer two with remission, but it had felt like three, all the same) was not an experience which he cared to repeat too soon. It might not have been the Ruzyne prison, or the Vojna labour camp, but it had been quite bad enough. So a sabbatical had seemed to be the obvious short-term solution. But that still left a meantime. And meantime he had been left with a huge pile of jigsaw pieces that he couldn't hope to fit together unless he found the missing picture on the box.

Marta had offered to finance the trip, but he wouldn't let her.

He had got a good price for his piano, and he could always buy another one once he started work again. 'We'll be watching you, Brožek.' Give it a few months, and they'd get fed up with it. But meanwhile . . . he needed that meanwhile.

He came to the Charles Bridge quite by accident, wandering aimlessly without map or guidebook, relying on half-forgotten memories to guide him. Tourists gaped at the twin rows of mighty sculptures all along its length, admired the magnificent view of the Vltava valley, looked up in wonderment at the towering splendour of Hradcany Castle, took photographs . . . It was here somewhere. He looked to the right and left, impatient now, and was almost ready to retrace his steps, thinking he must have missed it, when he recognised the statue of St Vitus, not knowing it was St Vitus, its historical significance limited to one wintry afternoon in 1946. He sat down just to the left of that heaving mass of stone, as his mother had done before him with her small son standing between her knees, staring at his unseen father lurking behind the lens.

It was like a paper chase, with photographs scattered all over Prague, leading him onwards. Panting, he climbed to the viewing platform at the top of the Letna Hill and looked down dizzily on the panorama of domes and spires and gables, parapets and pillars, towers and turrets, transfixed not by the architectural feast below him, spanning six centuries, but by the knowledge that he had seen this view before, as a five-year-old, solemnly grasping a gigantic father's hand. He tracked down the statue of Jan Hus in Old Town Square, the backdrop to a yellowing snapshot taken by a friendly passer-by showing himself flanked by his mother and Věra, her new baby in her arms, all of them looking unaccountably cheerful. It was a Sunday afternoon outing that had stuck in his memory, if only because it was the last one he could remember, the lull before the storm that had split his life in two. The memorial bore the familiar legend, 'Truth will Prevail'. He remembered Věra spelling out the words to him. *Pravda vítězí.* Had it been a promise or a threat?

He had to ask directions to the Smichov district where he had lived with his parents and, once there, was unable to locate his former home. But he found a street that looked familiar and walked the length of it several times, peeping through the high double windows, imagining the dark panelled walls beyond, the slippery polished floor, the glittering frozen raindrops of the chandelier suspended from the lofty ceiling. Other images crowded in: the stuffed bear he had taken to bed with him, snatches of long-forgotten lullabies, the comforting glow of the wood stove, the smell of a roasting goose, his mother's lemony scent, his father's laugh. Had his father ever laughed? He must have done, once, because he could hear it quite distinctly, a warm dry chuckle echoing through the corridors of the past.

Slowly, the fragments began to acquire a recognisable shape, like a shattered ornament reconstructed from innumerable smithereens. Insidiously, the stranger began to feel at home, as his ear attuned itself to the babble of voices speaking his mother tongue. Wenceslas Square was alive with talk. People stood in clusters, conversing with almost Latin animation, openly, without fear, and congregated in crowded bars and taverns where the walls no longer had ears.

Viktor eavesdropped his way down the long, wide boulevard, self-consciously at first, aware that his clothes marked him out as a foreigner, feeling like a spy, until one speaker noticed him loitering within earshot and drew him into the discussion, soliciting his opinion as a visitor. The chorus of surprise that greeted his perfect Czech was followed by a barrage of questions. Did people in the West understand what was happening here? What did they think of it? It was a desire to inform, not a need for approval, that motivated their eager explanations; Viktor got the impression that they felt almost sorry for him, exiled to a country less privileged than theirs. The sullen submissiveness of the last thirty years had been shucked off like a chrysalis; the air whistled with the whirr of wings. Would he care to sign a petition? The Russians had to realise that they couldn't kick Dubček around, that the whole nation was right behind him ... Not even a hardened cynic like Viktor could resist such infectious confidence and optimism. It made him feel humble. It made him feel proud.

He was a stranger in this place, and yet he belonged to it, in the way an adopted child will always belong to its natural parents. More than that, he felt welcome, like a prodigal son.

'Have you come back for good?' someone asked him, as if it were an obvious question. He shook his head, almost regretfully, and moved on. To prey on his own people was as unthinkable as to labour alongside them in honest socialist toil. The familiar mood of depression settled on him again. What the hell was he doing here? Could it be he was running away?

It was a summer of blazing heat and blinding light. Rob and Cassie had hitched their way across Europe, picking fruit, washing dishes, waiting tables, getting sunburned, and never thinking more than one day ahead. They only worked when the money ran out; the rest of the time they ate and slept and made love – when it wasn't too hot. While Cassie scribbled endlessly in a succession of spiral-bound notebooks, leaking boiling ballpoint all over her hands, Rob did much the same thing with a paint-brush, although it remained a minor bone of contention that he let her see his stuff and she remained secretive about hers.

'You can't paint fire with water,' Cassie had said one day, back in Athens. The easel, the canvases, the oils and the brushes had been a surprise present, bought with money she had smuggled out of England inside her bra, money she had never mentioned. It was her 'just in case' fund, she had said, casually, and she didn't need it any more. She didn't have to elaborate. The mere spending of it had been a gift in itself.

Every landscape had Cassie in it somewhere: Cassie surrounded by white sand, by silver olive trees, by glowing hibiscus, Cassie up to her neck in blue water, Cassie growing brown and plump and lazy. There was a new indolence about her, as if the sun had seeped through to her soul, as if the heat had ripened her. Rob had worried that she wouldn't take to camping, but she slept better under canvas than ever she had done indoors; she was like a creature rescued from a cage, revelling in space and light and air. In the evenings he would practise tirelessly on his guitar and she would hum along, and only then would he wonder if she was thinking about Viktor. The answer lay somewhere in those notebooks.

'What are you writing? A novel?'

'Maybe, one day. But not yet. In twenty years, perhaps,

when I'm old. I'm only making notes, so I don't forget things.'

'I can't imagine you being forty-one.'

'Oh, I can imagine you. A devoted *père de famille*, with a station-wagon and at least four kids with braces on their teeth, and a fishing rod and a neat little wife who bakes cookies and irons socks.' Rob grinned, not denying it. 'Whereas I . . . I can't even imagine me in six months' time. Or six weeks, come to that.'

They had never spoken about the nights drawing in or the long cold days ahead. But they both knew that the beauty of their arrangement was that it was temporary. It wouldn't have worked any other way.

Cassie no longer hurried to collect her mail from each new post office. She kept up a creditable pretence of having put Viktor out of her mind, and Rob knew better than to force her to admit otherwise. There was a part of Cassie that remained inaccessible, that would always be inaccessible to anyone else but Viktor; Viktor who had been crazy enough to throw away the key.

But he wasn't sore at Viktor any more. Viktor had done him a favour in more ways than one. He had set him free from Armelle and lent him Cassie for a short, sweet season, the best season of the year. Rob had been careful not to let himself fall in love with her, knowing that she couldn't reciprocate and unwilling to risk ruining their friendship. They had had a lot of fun together, and they would always remember each other with affection, but once the process of healing and renewal was complete they would have to go their separate ways – a painful prospect that was drawing inexorably nearer.

'Have you got any plans?' she said one day, broaching the taboo subject of the future.

'I've been thinking about going home and failing my medical.'

She didn't seem surprised. 'Does that mean you've found whatever it was you were looking for?'

'Not exactly. I think I probably left it behind. What about you?'

'I don't know. I mean, the rest of the world hasn't changed, has it? If everyone was like you, life would be so easy.'

'Too easy?'

'Perhaps. That's not a put-down.'

'You like things to be difficult, don't you?'

'Not deliberately. But I've copped out so often. That doesn't mean I think of being with *you* as a cop-out. But – you're so comfortable to be with. You're like lying in a nice warm bed all day.'

She lay down on her back with her head resting on his thighs, squinting against the sun.

'I wish this could go on for ever. But if it did, it wouldn't be what it is, would it? I keep telling myself, one day at a time. But it's as if there's an exam round the corner and I haven't done enough work for it, and every day that passes is another day gone, another day nearer failing. It's like having a huge calendar on the wall. Sorry. I'm being neurotic.'

'Being scared isn't being neurotic.'

'I've started thinking about him again, you know.'

'Started? Liar. You never stopped.'

'Yes, I did. Thanks to you. I began to think I'd forgotten him, and now it all keeps coming back.'

'You're never going to forget him, Cass. You don't want to. You don't want to lie in a nice warm bed all day, you don't want to be comfortable. You're a sucker for punishment. Otherwise you'd stick with a terrific guy like me.'

'Then you'd be the sucker for punishment,' she said. 'And you're not, are you?'

'Not any more. Once bitten, twice shy.'

'Are you over her yet?'

'Pretty much. I'm a lot lazier than you, remember. With Armelle I had to work at her all the time and however hard I tried it was never going to be good enough. That's not my idea of being happy. I guess Ginny and I were well suited. I just couldn't accept that at the time. Armelle would have been great for a wild affair. But do I settle for that? Not me. I want to own her, I want to make a wife out of her. Can you see Armelle baking cookies and ironing socks?'

'So will you go back to your girlfriend?'

'I don't know yet. But one day I'll settle down with someone like her, a girl I can be absolutely sure of, one who wants an

382

ordinary, reliable kind of guy. I'll wind up going back to college, making the parents proud, getting a steady job, doing right by my wife and kids. I used to think that was knuckling under to the system, but maybe that's the way I really am. Perhaps I was forced into something I'd have chosen anyway, if I'd had the choice.'

'What about your protest?'

'This isn't protesting any more. I first realised that when Martin Luther King was shot, and then Bobby Kennedy. I began to feel as if I'd jumped ship. If I'm going to protest, I've got to do it at home, where I belong.'

'I don't know where I belong.'

'I do. With Viktor.'

'Stop trying to play Cupid,' she snapped, right on cue. 'You might at least pretend to be a little bit jealous.'

'If you thought for a minute I was jealous, I wouldn't see you for dust. You really are the most contrary female I ever met. I feel sorry for Viktor sometimes. And for myself. Have a heart, Cassie. How am I ever going to get rid of you unless he takes you off my hands?'

Cassie attacked him with two puny fists, hurling cheerful abuse at him. For the moment, mock conflict was enough. The summer wasn't over yet.

Jan was late. Eva turned off the heat under the saucepans and went back to her typing, nibbling at a piece of rye bread. She had got used to her supporting role, to sharing him with other people and waiting her turn for his attention. It had made her respect him more. And respect was something you could build on.

After dinner they would make love and she would feel the same old misgivings. But then they would talk till late, and her doubts would be submerged by a fresh wave of admiration and affection. She knew not to ask too many questions, but Karel's instincts had been right. Secretly, stealthily, so as not to cause panic, tight-knit groups were preparing for the worst. In the event of an invasion, it would be vital to keep up the flow of words, to continue broadcasting and printing the truth against the inevitable barrage of lies and propaganda.

And yet, the prevailing mood was still one of stubborn optimism. Even Karel put on a brave face in public, for fear of spreading defeatism. She hoped that this holiday would do him good; he had been overdoing it lately, as if racing against some invisible clock.

Half-past seven. Hearing footsteps on the stone stairwell, she ran to let Jan in.

'Hello, Eva.'

'Viktor.' The welcoming smile faded from her face. 'I thought you were still . . .'

'I got time off for good behaviour. Can I come in?'

'Your father's not here. He's at Novy Smokovec.'

'I know. He told Marta in his last letter.'

'Well, don't just stand there. Where's your luggage?'

'At the Zlata Husa.'

'That must run expensive. I'd ask you to stay here, but with Karel away . . .'

'I budgeted for it. Here. This is for you.'

He handed over a big bottle of Chanel No. 5, bought not in Paris but at Tuzex, evidently as an afterthought.

'Thank you. But you shouldn't have wasted your money. Would you like something to eat?'

'If there's anything going. I had a *klobasy*, off a stall,' – he indicated the grease spot on his shirt – 'but that seems like hours ago.'

'Sit down. It's all ready.'

'I'm sorry I didn't let you know I was coming. It was an impulse thing.'

'You didn't have any trouble getting a visa?'

'No. You don't look very pleased to see me.'

'Why didn't you answer my letters?'

'Because I'm a terrible speller. Especially in Czech. But your letters cheered me up a lot.'

Too late, Eva regretted some of the things she'd written, careless of the possible consequences, never dreaming that he would turn up on her doorstep. He belonged in Paris, where she could consign him to the realms of fantasy, not here in Prague, invading her real life.

384

'That's why I wrote them. To cheer you up. No other reason. So . . . how long are you staying?'

'I'm not sure yet.'

'When do you have to be back at work?'

'I lost my job while I was inside. And after being cooped up for so long, I fancied a bit of freedom.'

'Well, you've come to the right place. Though that could change at any moment, you realise.'

'So I gather. I signed that petition.'

'I should hope so. Have you come to make things up with Karel?'

'Not necessarily.'

'You read his memoirs?'

'I glanced through them. I didn't have much else to do. They couldn't very well put me to work. The plaster only came off a couple of weeks ago.'

'And?'

He shrugged. 'I feel sorry for him. That's what he wanted, isn't it?'

'That's just what he didn't want! For heaven's sake don't patronise him!'

'So what do you want me to do? Kneel down at his feet and tell him how wonderful he is?'

'Hardly. I give it ten minutes before you're at each other's throats. I'll write down the address so you can go and see him.'

He lit a cigarette, looking curiously around the room, noticing the photograph of himself on the wall, sneering back at it. Eva scribbled something on a piece of paper and handed it to him.

'Marta gave it to me already,' said Viktor. 'She thinks I'm hot-footing it straight to the spa.'

'And aren't you?'

He reached for her hand. 'What do you think? It's you I came to see, not him.'

'Viktor . . .'

'I thought about you a lot, while I was in gaol. And your letters . . .'

'Stop going on about those letters.'

385

'I'm a very slow reader, you know. But that means I remember things. "I'll never forget you. I hope you won't forget me either." Well, I didn't. Here I am.'

'Eat your dinner.'

'Aren't you having any?'

'No. I'll wait for Jan.'

'Oh. I didn't realise you were expecting him. I hope I'm not interrupting anything.'

'Stop being polite. It just sounds sarcastic.'

'You're much more formidable on your own territory, aren't you? I bet the old man is terrified of you. It won't work on me, you know.'

'Viktor . . . don't.' Resolutely, she refused to respond to his kiss, keeping her lips firmly shut. But other parts of her responded none the less, invisibly. Why couldn't Jan make her feel like that? Feelings like that were for putting away in a safe place, to be examined and cherished from time to time, to be handled with care. They were too precious, too fragile for everyday use. And now Viktor would play with them, casually, thoughtlessly, till they fell apart and lost their value.

'That's enough. I'm with Jan now.'

'You were with Jan then.'

'But I'm *here* now.'

'So am I.'

'So is he,' she said, jumping up as she heard the knock on the door, thanking God he was spending the night, wishing to hell that he wasn't.

Viktor shook hands with a tall, gangling youth with prematurely receding hair, a long thin face, and pale-blue bulging eyes, wondering what on earth Eva saw in him. As if aware of this, Jan's speech impediment returned with a vengeance, making its usual disastrous first impression. It irritated Viktor to see Eva acting the devoted wife, giving Jan her undivided attention, pointedly ignoring her uninvited guest. He had expected her to welcome him with open arms, to flood him with that sunny smile of hers, to revive that seductive sense of warmth, and peace, and being wanted. He had been relying on her to make this easy for him, to give him a reason for being here, to make it difficult for him to retreat. Could she really be in love with a weedy specimen like that? If so, why had she practically raped him back in Paris? Why had she written those letters?

'I'd better go,' he said, taking the hint.

'No, don't,' said Jan, earnestly. 'I'm sorry if we seemed to be excluding you. It's just that there's a lot happening today, as you must have gathered. I hope we'll get to know each other better while you're here. Eva's told me a lot about you.' Eva's face flooded with tell-tale colour. 'How's your arm, by the way?'

'Still a bit stiff.'

'And the girl you rescued?'

Viktor flung Eva an accusatory look.

'I told Jan everything,' she said cryptically.

'She survived,' said Viktor.

'Did they send her to prison too?'

'No. She served her time in hospital.'

'You were very brave.'

'I'm not in the least brave. I couldn't very well leave her to fry.'

'Have you read Eva's piece? We had a lot of letters about it. People here find it difficult to understand exactly what the French students wanted.'

'So did the French students. But the workers knew what they wanted all right. And they got it. Let's not discuss France, for God's sake. I came here to get away from the bloody place.'

'Thank you for those records, by the way.'

'I didn't realise you'd taken any,' said Viktor, turning to Eva.

'I wasn't going to, but Marta insisted.'

'Eva doesn't have a record player, so I've got them all back at my place. She brought back all my favourites. Dave Brubeck, Dizzy Gillespie, Miles Davis . . . It was very kind of you.'

'Not at all. I've got thousands of records. If I'd known I would have brought some more with me. I came at rather short notice.'

'Why don't you join us this evening? I've arranged to meet up with some friends later on at a jazz club.'

How absolutely typical of Jan, thought Eva. She hadn't been able to lie to him; she had told him what had happened and now here he was treating Viktor like a long-lost friend, as if to say, 'I can cope with this. I'm not going to go into a huff or make him feel unwelcome. I don't own you.' It was his way of testing her. If Jan had been the possessive type this would have been so much simpler. Then she would have had no choice.

It was odd, seeing the two of them together: Viktor with his usual brash self-assurance, Jan with his peculiarly gauche charm. Viktor looked so out of place in this room, his expensive leather jacket and well-cut jeans contrasting sharply with Jan's ill-fitting synthetic suit. The smell of French tobacco and aftershave filled the room; tonight his presence would hang in the air like spent incense. And Jan would find nice things to say about him, making her feel guiltier than ever.

Not wanting to look like a jealous lover, Viktor made an effort to be nice to Eva's boyfriend, although after a while it came naturally enough. Jan wasn't the sort of guy you could dislike and it seemed churlish to turn his invitation down. The jazz club was just the kind of place Viktor felt at home in: a dark, crowded, noisy basement with first-class beer and plenty of pretty girls to make eyes at, if only to annoy Eva. Viktor ordered a round of drinks for the whole table and got stuck into his first foaming tankard. There was a dispute in progress about whether small private businesses had any place in a socialist system, with a vociferous minority denouncing this as the first step on the slippery slope towards capitalism. Viktor listened with a mixture of fascination and amusement, the only carnivore amongst lifelong vegetarians earnestly debating the nutritional value of meat.

Eventually the band started up and worked their way through a predictable-sounding medley, technically quite competent but, to Viktor's mind, too hidebound. The nucleus of the group consisted of trumpet, clarinet, drums and piano, supplemented by guest performers on an *ad hoc* basis – tonight there was a double bass. Viktor listened impatiently, improvising in his head, fingers itching.

'What did you think?' asked Jan, as the applause died down.

'It was okay. A bit unadventurous, perhaps.'

'They're only amateurs, you know. Students. I know the pianist. Why don't you have a go?'

'God, no. I haven't practised for weeks.'

'All the more reason to now,' put in Eva slyly. 'We don't have a piano at home, you realise.'

'You can play?' asked somebody else.

'A bit. But I'm rusty.'

'Go on,' said Jan. 'We promise not to boo.'

There was a chorus of convivial encouragement, making his protests sound coy. He felt a surge of the familiar goading fear he got before he pulled off a job.

'My right hand's still a bit stiff.'

'Then perhaps it could do with the exercise.'

'Well . . . if you'll buy me a drink afterwards . . .'

'You're on.' Jan went to have a word with his friend, who bore Viktor off without further ado, to a send-off of raucous cheers, and introduced him to the rest of the band.

'I usually play alone,' croaked Viktor, his voice suddenly hoarse. 'And my arm's just come out of plaster. So you'll have to cover up for me.'

'You lead, they'll follow,' the young man told him casually. 'Wait a minute while I announce you.'

He had spent most of his life being anonymous, wearing camouflage, melting into the background. It seemed strange to hear his own name spoken out loud as if he had nothing to hide. He had never played in public before, ever careful not to draw attention to himself, to maintain his invisibility. And besides, his music was something private, personal, something he chose not to share with a hostile world. But this little world didn't seem so hostile.

He started off with 'Samantha', cautiously at first and then more boldly, improvising around the melody, folding it up tight, shaking it out, turning it inside out, stretching and twisting the keyboard around it, making it his own, while his fellow musicians wove their way in and out of the labyrinth of sound. But it was the audience, not his hands, that made it happen. Ignoring the demand for an encore, he deferred politely to the trumpeter, who launched into 'Lonesome Blues' while Viktor submerged his virtuosity, taking his pleasure lazily. And then, ceding to pressure from the group, he took over again, choosing 'Dock of the Bay' this time, simply because it had been a favourite of Cassie's, although Cassie liked it straight and sad and haunting and he didn't feel like playing it that way. He took it to pieces and put it back together again, quickened the tempo, broke up the rhythms, transposed the yearning regret into seething ambition, filled it full of rage and determination. 'Wastin' time.' She had translated the words for him. 'Wastin' time' meant sitting on the sidelines, making excuses, hiding, wishing your life away.

The burst of applause brought him abruptly down to earth. He had got away with it. Even though that right hand had let him down more than once, he hadn't been caught out. Like thieving it took nerve, left him weak and elated, released some of his devils. Like thieving it was a big con. The difference was, he had given something back.

'That wasn't bad,' hissed Eva, cutting through the chorus of congratulations. 'Don't get big-headed, will you?'

'Not a chance,' said Viktor. 'I only did it for the beer.'

After two weeks of gulping pure mountain air, Karel felt a good deal better, even though he knew that two weeks at a spa couldn't halt his downward slide. Miloš's enterprising doctor friend had been in no doubt about his diagnosis. The breathlessness and searing chest pains had less to do with phlegm-choked lungs than with a diseased, labouring heart.

The knowledge had been almost welcome; he had convinced himself long ago that he had a tumour. This way, with luck, it would be quick. In the meantime, his ever-worsening smokers' cough was a useful blind. He had been labelled bronchitic for so many years that no one had taken the trouble to check his other organs. He had been able to look Eva straight in the eye and tell the truth about that X-ray. For the moment, that was all she needed to know.

'You've got to stop smoking,' the quack had said. 'It's too late to unclog those arteries of yours, but respiratory congestion could easily bring on an attack. Go to your doctor and be honest with him for once. Early retirement will increase your life expectancy. Take it easy, my friend. That's all you can do.'

Well, he had taken it easy for two excruciating weeks, vegetating in the company of a bunch of decrepit old wheezers like himself, playing endless games of cards and chess and inventing new and ingenious ways of circumventing his landlady's smoking ban. If that was a taste of taking things easy, then his life expectancy wasn't worth increasing. No, he would steer clear of the medical profession in future, make the most of the time he had left.

Doctors were all fools. He might live for years yet: long enough to get his rehabilitation at least, long enough to see Eva settled. Once the crisis had passed, she and Jan would surely go their separate ways. Theirs was like a war-time romance, thriving on uncertainty and struggle; it would not survive the humdrum atmosphere of peace.

The outlook was bright. The talks at Čierna had not, as many had feared, been a prelude to disaster, and a further meeting at Bratislava had ended in much comradely kissing, handshaking, and assurances of fraternal goodwill; in token of this, the Russian troops had finally ended their 'manoeuvres' and pulled out, amid general jubilation. The danger was past.

Nothing came for free, of course. There looked likely to be a slowing down of the reform programme and certain limitations on the freedom of the press, but in Karel's view that was no bad thing. If they proceeded carefully, all might yet be well. He might yet die happy. Well, almost happy . . .

He had come to terms with the lack of response from Viktor. More honestly, he was secretly relieved. The pressure he had put upon himself was off. In any case, his memoirs had painted a misleading picture of himself as a man of strong convictions and unapologetic candour. Not of a rather seedy old man desperately salvaging the tattered remnants of his self-respect. This way, at least, he would not be caught out in a lie, would not have to contend with a youthful, undamaged version of himself, would not risk exposing that most despicable of middle-aged vices – envy of one's own child. Yes, it was best that they remain strangers, free to indulge their illusions and delusions, to believe what they wanted to believe.

Significantly, perhaps, Eva had told him next to nothing about his son. She had certainly never admitted that she corresponded with him. Once, when Karel had found her writing a letter 'to Marta' and looked over her shoulder, as he normally would, she had bitten his head off, told him not to be so nosy and removed herself to the windowless gloom of her cubicle to finish her letter in private. It was then that he had first begun to put two and two together. Her vague, preoccupied manner ever since her return from Paris, her tendency to change the subject whenever Viktor was mentioned, and her sudden bouts of irritability – seen in the context of this secretive scribbling – had lured him into a fanciful daydream, whereby Eva and Viktor fell in love and walked hand in hand into the sunset, healing ancient rifts, cementing a new alliance, recreating the happiness he had lost.

The truth, evidently, was more mundane. Eva's renewed pursuit of Jan indicated that her feelings for Viktor, whatever they were, had either cooled or been unrequited, which was hardly surprising. Holiday romances were doomed to failure. Rather too strenuously, perhaps, she had professed herself disenchanted with the West, if only because the milk and honey had stopped flowing almost as soon as the poor girl had got there. The shiny, efficient, plentiful world she had heard so much about had shown that its prosperity was built on the sandy soil of exploitation and discontent. The same was doubtless true of the other European democracies, all of whom were beset by domestic strife. Even in America, that standard-bearer of the free world, young people, the poor and the blacks were in revolt, attacking the rotten underside of capitalism and the deeply unpopular Vietnam war. The West was too busy with its own problems to risk a confrontation with the mighty Soviet Union. If the worst happened, Czechoslovakia would find herself without allies, not for the first time in her chequered history. But if the best happened, she could put the rest of the world to shame.

After the cool of the mountains, Prague seemed oppressively hot; a lassitude had settled over the city, its mellow ochre stone glowing with reflected sun. Scaffolding marred every vista as workmen laboured to repair years of neglect, renewing decaying plasterwork and leaking roofs as part of the long-delayed refurbishment programme. Everywhere people were investing in the future, taking a new proprietorial pride in their homes and their homeland. In the countryside, peasants attacked their stone cottages with fresh paint and tumbledown weekend *chatas* were being restored and redecorated in readiness for the holiday season. After weeks of unremitting tension, spirits were high again.

Karel was glad to be back; he had managed to sneak off a day early, anxious not to miss that evening's committee meeting. Eva would no doubt be less than delighted at his premature return; more than likely she and Jan had been making the most of his absence.

Not wishing to hear this suspicion confirmed from the twitching lips of old Nováková, Karel swept past her with a cursory greeting and mounted the stairs with imprudent haste, leaving himself breathless. He stopped on the landing outside his door, coughed extra loudly to give them fair warning, and fiddled interminably with his keys before finally letting himself in.

The shock sent his heart into spasm. Unable to speak, he stood clutching the door-jamb, trying to get his breath, fighting the sudden, savage pain.

'Are you all right?' Viktor sprang forward and took him by the arm.

'I'm fine,' he gasped. 'It's the heat, that's all.' He sank weakly into his old armchair, waiting for the vice round his chest to slacken. Viktor fetched a glass of water.

'Here. Drink this.'

Karel waved it away.

'I can see you've made yourself at home,' he observed testily, indicating the open bottle of vodka. 'I might as well have a drop of that instead.'

'I'm sorry if I gave you a fright,' said Viktor, hastily complying with this request. 'Eva's gone out to the shops, she'll be back any minute. We weren't expecting you till tomorrow.'

'*Na zdraví.*' Karel tossed back the drink in one swallow, trying to get a grip on himself. 'So what brings you here all of a sudden?' he demanded ungraciously. 'Is your grandmother well?'

'She's fine. She sends her love.'

'You might have brought her with you.'

'I wanted to. But she wasn't feeling up to it. She doesn't get out much these days. Because of her bad leg. I expect Eva told you.'

'Eva never tells me anything these days. Cigarette?'

'Have one of mine.'

'And you can top up my glass while you're at it.' He inhaled greedily. 'So when are you leaving?'

'Leaving? Have I outstayed my welcome already?'

'What welcome? I didn't even know you were coming.'

'Neither did I, till the last minute. Eva said I could come any time, so I took her at her word. I assumed she had your permission.'

'Eva does exactly as she pleases. Sit down, for God's sake. You're making me nervous.'

Viktor did so, aware that he was losing control of the conversation. Just looking at his father made him feel like a powerless, angry little boy. The same overbearing manner, the same ill-concealed dislike, the same ability to crush him with a look. He hadn't changed a bit.

He hasn't changed a bit, thought Karel, still trying to collect his wits. The same hostile eyes, the same mutinous chin, the same chilling self-possession. He was acutely aware of his shabby, run-down appearance, the threadbare corduroy jacket, the scuffed shoes, the tufts of stubble his razor had missed in his haste to catch the early train. Why hadn't Eva sent a telegram to warn him? If he had known he would have dressed with care, prepared suitable words of welcome, dusted off his social graces, treated his son as an honoured guest, not as an intruder. But already the mood of the meeting seemed set. He wished he could go back into the street, mount the stairs again, and start afresh.

'So,' he said heavily. 'You came to see Eva, then.'

'Yes. She kept inviting me, and I thought I might not get another chance.'

'You've swallowed this invasion scare, have you?'

'Not exactly. But I arrived just before Čierna, when things were looking pretty bad.'

'You've been here a week already? That's half your holiday gone, I suppose.'

'Not necessarily. I'm between jobs at the moment. But I

won't be imposing myself on you. I'm staying in a hotel, in Wenceslas Square.'

'In a hotel? Isn't this place good enough for you?'

'I didn't want to put Eva to any trouble. And besides, there isn't room.'

'I've come down in the world, as you can see.'

'You never saw the place I lived in with my mother. This is luxury.'

'Luxury, eh? Well, it's no worse than your grandmother's place, by all accounts. Eva was shocked.'

'Marta refuses to move. You think I like her living in that dump?'

'I gather you've got a nice place.'

'Not by Paris standards.'

'Complete with grand piano.'

'It was a baby grand. And anyway, I've sold it.'

'Well, if you've lost your job I dare say you needed the money.'

'I didn't lose it. I fancied a change, that was all.'

'So you're unemployed?'

'We're allowed to be, in the West.'

'No wonder France is in trouble.'

'Oh, for God's sake!' exploded Viktor, in French.

Eighteen years collapsed into as many minutes. Nothing had changed. Long-lost relatives were supposed to fall on each other's necks, sobbing with sentimental joy. 'Karel thinks the world of you,' Eva had said. 'Viktor this, Viktor that, I get fed up with it sometimes.' Oh yes, he thought the world of him all right, as long as he wasn't there, as long as he could invent some version of him to suit his notion of what he ought to be. But in reality, now as always, he couldn't stand the sight of him.

'If you're going to swear under my roof, then kindly swear in your own language. Do you think in French too?'

'I don't know what I think in.'

'You speak Czech with a French accent.'

'Well, it's better than speaking French with a Czech accent.'

'So you're ashamed of your nationality, are you?'

'I didn't say that. I—'

Karel erupted into a violent fit of coughing, as a slug of vodka went down the wrong way. Viktor slapped him on the back ungently while the tears streamed down his face.

'Damn you,' Karel spluttered. 'What kind of welcome is this? Why must you always put me in the wrong?'

'I didn't expect a welcome,' said Viktor, handing him an immaculate linen handkerchief with V.B. embroidered in the corner. 'I don't expect you to be glad to see me. I didn't come here for that.'

'No.' Karel blew his nose stertorously. 'I keep forgetting. You came to see Eva.'

'She's a nice kid. We got on well.'

'You've met this boyfriend of hers?'

'Jan? Yes, I've met him.'

'Well?'

'Well what? He seems very fond of her.'

'He's the only boyfriend she's ever had, you realise. She's rushing into this thing as if he was her last chance. The poor girl's never had any fun. And now she spends all her free time hawking pamphlets and pounding that typewriter over there.'

'You didn't complain when she typed your memoirs.'

'You wouldn't have been able to read my handwriting. It was Eva's idea, you realise. I didn't want you to read them. I told her, he's got a low-enough opinion of me already. But she talked me into it.'

'I can't imagine why. I never believed you were a traitor, you know. You didn't have to convince me.'

'That wasn't the point.'

'What was the point, then?'

'I wasn't after sympathy, if that's what you thought. I just wanted to set the record straight.'

'What about? I knew you were set up. I knew they forced you to sign that confession. My mother dinned it into me every day. And then Marta took over. They made you sound like a bloody hero.'

'Well, now you know I wasn't.'

'Yes. Thank God for that.'

'I'm not making any excuses. I admitted I was a lousy

husband to your mother and an even worse father to you. Isn't that enough? What more do you want me to do?'

'What do you want *me* to do? Throw my arms round your neck and tell you that I love you? Because I can't. I can't do it.'

'No. You never could. Even when you were this high, I couldn't even get you to smile at me.'

'You might have tried smiling at me first.'

'I don't go in much for smiling. It's not in my nature.'

'You can say that again.'

'I don't know why you bothered to come.'

'I told you before, I came to see Eva.'

'Oh yes. So you did.'

I came to see Eva, Viktor reminded himself. No other reason. And she's glad to see me, even if you're not. I can see it in her eyes, in her face, I can smell it on her. If it wasn't for Eva I'd walk out of this room right now and tell you to go to hell, you miserable old sod.

Eva would be furious, thought Karel uneasily. 'Can't you even be nice to your own son? What's the matter with you?' Good questions. But the boy hadn't given him a chance. He had obviously come here spoiling for a fight, he had neither forgiven nor forgotten.

'In that case,' he growled, holding out his glass for a top-up, 'we'd better call a truce. For Eva's sake. I don't want her to walk in and find us quarrelling. "Be nice to Viktor,"' he squeaked, in a parody of feminine cajolery. '"Be nice to your father." I can't face it.'

'All right,' shrugged Viktor. And then, casually, 'Perhaps we'd better get in some practice, before she gets back. I'll smile if you do.'

'Count of three,' conceded Karel gruffly, determined not to do it first.

'One, two ... Hello, Eva.'

'Karel!' She ran over to kiss him. 'We weren't expecting you till tomorrow ... What are you two laughing about?'

'Just a private joke,' said Viktor.

'What are you doing home at this hour?' said Chantal. She was alone in the apartment, running up new curtains for their bedroom. Despite the continued prohibition on strenuous activities, she was bursting with renewed health and energy and found it impossible to be idle. There was so much to do before the baby arrived.

'I walked out,' said Alain.

'In the middle of a shift?' she said, alarmed, making mental deductions from his wage packet.

'I'm sorry. I just couldn't stand it another minute. I told them I felt ill. It was true. I feel like throwing up.'

Chantal knelt down and pulled off his boots, concerned. 'You've been looking poorly for weeks. Perhaps you should go to the doctor. Can I get you anything?'

Alain shook his head, and Chantal repressed the urge to fuss. Alain liked being pampered as much as any other man, but she had learned not to be too obvious about it. She looked after him unobtrusively, content to be taken for granted, never bothering him with domestic trivia or preparations for the baby, aware that he had more important things on his mind.

Ever since the collapse of the strike he had been understandably depressed, even though most workers seemed to believe that they had had a resounding victory. They had more money in their pockets for less work. There had been no point in holding out when everyone else all over the country was voting for a settlement; the improved offer was too good to turn down. Chantal had shared this common-sense view, although she knew better than to say so.

Placidly, she put on a pan of water for some coffee, hiding her anxiety, preparing herself for another diatribe against the bosses, the union, and the Government. She knew exactly the right responses to make, and when; she might not understand politics, but she was word perfect on her husband's opinions, as any good wife ought to be.

'Listen,' he said gruffly, as she returned from the kitchen. 'I have to talk to you. This has gone on long enough.'

He looked angry and embarrassed, addressing his words to the floor, not to her. Chantal controlled a spasm of panic with a deep breath, ever fearful of dislodging her baby. This was it, then. The moment she had been dreading. All these weeks she had kidded herself that she was home and dry, driven by stubborn optimism, fielding Alain's moods and his irritability, testing her own strength. But deep down she had always known that she would never get away with it. 'It's no good,' he would say. 'I should never have married you. I feel trapped . . . ' But for a long time he said nothing at all, as if struggling to find the words.

'I know this will come as a shock,' he said at last, 'but I've been thinking about it for a long time. I can't carry on like this.' Chantal bowed her head and shut her eyes. 'I feel such a hypocrite. Can you understand that?'

'Yes.' She kept her voice calm, dignified. 'I understand.'

'What kind of father can I be without self-respect? With every day that passes I despise myself more and more.'

Chantal got up and stood with her back to him, staring out of the window so that he couldn't see her face.

'You don't need to justify yourself to me,' she said quietly. 'I've been expecting this to happen.'

'What?'

'For a while, during the strike, I thought there was some hope for us. You seemed different. Almost happy. But now . . . Don't worry. I can always go back home. No one will be surprised, after all. I'm not going to make a scene.'

'God. Is that what you've been thinking? That I'm going to walk out on you? Though I'll have to, if you refuse to come with me.'

Chantal turned round, very slowly, as if afraid of losing her balance. 'Come with you? Where?'

'I don't know yet. Away from MerTech. Away from this apartment. Away from Paris.'

'But not away from me?'

'That's entirely up to you. I can't stay, Chantal, whatever you decide. I need to breathe.'

'But . . . What about money?'

'All I've done for the last few weeks is think about money. Every time I handed you my wage packet I thought, that's another week of my life gone. Lemercier's got me where he wants me now. That's why he'll never sack me, because he prefers to *own* me. I've tried to find work at a dozen other factories but nobody will touch me. He's made sure of that. I'm a known trouble-maker, you realise. So if I leave I'll end up on the dole. But I've got a wife, and soon I'll have a child. They can't let us starve, can they?'

'You mean . . .'

'It'll be tough. If you want security, then go back to your family. Divorce me. Everyone will understand. I won't hold it against you.'

Chantal should have been horrified but all she could feel was the heady sense of a burden lifting. She was still in with a chance.

'I've got a bit saved,' she said, sitting down beside him. 'If we went to the country we could find somewhere cheap to live. Somewhere where there aren't any jobs. Then they couldn't blame you for not working, could they?'

'On the contrary,' said Alain, 'I could complain bitterly about being unemployed.'

'And plenty of *chômeurs* do odd jobs on the side,' added Chantal, ever practical. 'Cash in hand.' Gradually the fluttering feeling in her chest subsided. This wasn't so bad. She could cope with this. She was used to being poor.

'It would give me the chance to read, and study,' continued Alain eagerly, grasping both her hands. 'Our child is going to grow up educated, Chantal. I don't mean the crap they teach in schools. I mean real knowledge. So that when his turn comes, he can fight and win.'

Chantal nodded, reassured, while he talked and planned, only half listening, not needing to. It was going to be all right. She had something he wanted after all. This child and the children that would follow it. He had nothing left, thank God, except the future.

FOURTEEN

Prague, 17 August 1968

Dear Babička,

First of all, Viktor sends his love. I have been nagging him to write to you ever since he got here, but you know what he is like. He said to tell you he'll send you a telegram to let you know when he'll be back and not to worry. I think he must like Prague better than he expected.

There was only one reason why Viktor was still here, so he claimed. But Eva knew that it was just a pretext, despite the relentless teasing and tempting and the repeated invitations to come back to his hotel.

'I'd have left weeks ago if it wasn't for you,' he would say. 'Why are you playing hard to get like this? I can see through you, even if Jan can't.'

Oh, but Jan could. Jan didn't miss a thing. He had asked her outright and she had denied it, desperate to convince him and herself, because when Viktor finally went home she would need Jan more than ever. And to make matters worse, Karel had got the wrong idea as well.

'Why do you suppose he's stayed this long? Why do you think he came here in the first place? To see you! He told me so himself.'

'He came to see you, you silly old fool. He's just too proud to admit it.'

'Rubbish! When you're not there we fight like cat and dog.'

Eva returned her attention to her letter.

Karel and Viktor fight like cat and dog. I have given up trying to keep the peace, as I have come to the conclusion that they enjoy it. Viktor threatens to leave on the next flight roughly twice a day. Three times, to my knowledge, Karel has yelled at him to get out of his sight and never darken his door again. They never actually make it up – they just carry on next day as if nothing had happened. I know you hoped for a reconciliation, but I think this is the nearest they are likely to get to it. The fact that Viktor is still here speaks for itself.

Jan and I have introduced him to all our friends and even roped him in to help out on the magazine – he spent most of yesterday distributing copies. He's all for standing up to Moscow and not giving an inch, so, as you can imagine, Karel has now got him labelled as yet another 'young hothead'. I think that's the only reason why he does it.

No it wasn't. His what-the-hell flamboyance masked a serious wish to belong, to be part of what was going on. He listened, learned, asked intelligent questions, and deferred constantly to Jan. Their friendship made her feel excluded, resentful, guilty. Every day, she lied to both of them.

Seeing Jan approach her desk, she pulled the sheet of paper out of her typewriter and began gathering up her things.

'Sorry I kept you waiting,' he said.

'No problem. I was just writing a letter to Marta.'

'I came to tell you not to hang around any longer. It looks like I'm going to be stuck here till late.'

'What do you want me to tell Viktor? Shall we meet you at the restaurant?'

They were supposed to be dining out – at Viktor's expense, of course. His continuing open-handedness – drinks all round at the jazz club, scarce foodstuffs from the Tuzex shop, a hefty donation to *Spring Tide* – was, to Eva's mind, symptomatic of his need to buy his way in, his deep-rooted capitalistic notion that everything had a price tag, even friendship.

'No, it could drag on for hours. You know how things are at the moment. Just say I'm sorry I can't make it. He'll understand. Enjoy yourself. Have a nice meal. See you tomorrow.'

He kissed her briefly and hurried off, preoccupied. The atmosphere at work was increasingly tense as harassed editors tried to conform to the new 'self-censorship' guidelines. While Soviet newspapers continued their daily onslaught against the 'enemies of the working class in Czechoslovakia', the Presidium had issued a directive to the press forbidding any counter-polemics. Journalists, spoiled by their new freedoms, were champing at the bit; much time was spent in finding oblique ways to get round the restrictions. Jan had come up with the idea of simply quoting the *Pravda* diatribes verbatim, without comment, and leaving the readers to draw their own conclusions; judging by the flood of correspondence this had generated, the readers were no fools.

Eva signed her letter and posted it on her way to Viktor's hotel. She had no intention of spending an evening alone with him, something he had been trying to engineer ever since his arrival. She would plead a headache and go home immediately they had eaten. No, that might not be such a good idea. He would insist on taking her home, and Karel was out this evening. It would be safer to drag out the meal as long as possible, so that Karel got back before her. Even if she had trusted Viktor, she didn't trust herself.

They had arranged to meet in the hotel bar. Eva sat down on a banquette and immersed herself in the evening paper, feeling rather out of place. A very pretty girl sat nursing a drink at a corner table, her eyes scanning the room expectantly. Eva knew at a glance that she was a prostitute – the high-class kind that only worked for hard currency. She was wearing a red silk blouse, with one too many buttons undone, and a very short black leather skirt; she was slim and blonde with very long legs.

The girl's face lit up suddenly in a smile of saucy recognition. Over the top of her newspaper Eva saw Viktor saunter into the bar, sit down next to her and whisper something in her ear, provoking a husky laugh. Eva affected not to notice them; after a couple of minutes Viktor finally deigned to acknowledge her presence.

'I didn't see you sitting there,' he lied. 'Have you been waiting long? Where's Jan?'

'He can't come. He had to work late. I only came to tell you. In fact, I ought to get back to the office myself. I promised to help him out.'

'Not until you've had dinner, surely?'

'I'm sure you can find someone else to keep you company.'

'What's up with you? Surely you need to eat? Or would you like a drink first?'

'No thanks. I'm not hungry. And besides, I'm fed up with you flashing your money around all the time.'

'Don't be silly. I've been getting five times the official rate through one of the porters here. Everything's so cheap compared to Paris. If you're uncomfortable sitting here, we can have an aperitif up in my room.'

'No.'

'What's the matter? What are you afraid of?'

'Nothing.'

'Then stop acting as if I'd just picked you up. Come on.'

Eva opened her mouth to protest, but she caught the girl's eye again, full of curious mockery, as if to say, 'What does he see in *her*?'

'Oh, all right. But I can't stay long.'

He took her up to the third floor and showed her into a room overlooking Wenceslas Square.

'Have a seat. What would you like to drink? Rum? Cognac? Slivovitz?'

'I told you, I don't drink.'

'Oh yes, I forgot. You lose your head on half a glass of wine.'

'Lost my head. Once. And you've never let me forget it.'

'Don't look at me like that. Anyone would think I'd seduced you, instead of the other way round.'

'I don't want to discuss it.'

'I wouldn't have laid a finger on you, you know. Nothing was further from my mind. Do you know, you're the first girl I ever slept with that I actually liked?'

It sounded like an accusation.

'What about Cassie?' demanded Eva boldly. 'Didn't you like her?'

He ran a finger round the rim of his glass, as if giving the question some thought.

'I never slept with Cassie. No, honestly,' he added, seeing the sceptical look on her face. 'It's true.'

'Why not?'

He gave that inescapably French shrug of his, one of the innumerable tiny idiosyncrasies that marked him out as a foreigner.

'Because I was scared to.'

'Scared of what?'

'God knows. Of falling in love with her, I expect. Is that what you're scared of too?'

Eva refused to meet his eye.

'Don't you understand how impossible this is for me? I never expected you to turn up like this. It was one of those crazy holiday things. And now I'm back home. You surely don't think I'd deceive Jan?'

'You're already deceiving him. You could try being honest with him for once, instead of stringing him along. He's not a fool.'

'I have been honest with him. I told him what happened in Paris before you even got here. And being loyal to someone isn't the same thing as stringing them along.'

'Karel says you're not in love with him.'

'Karel doesn't want me to get involved with an activist, that's all. Even though he's one himself. I admire Jan. I respect him. And he respects me. You don't care about me. You used me as an excuse to come here and now you're using me as an excuse to stay. If you think you can amuse yourself with me till you go back home—'

'Amuse myself? If I want to amuse myself, the lady you were scowling at in the bar is one hell of a lot more amusing than you.'

'I'm sorry I was so disappointing. But I'm only an amateur after all.'

'You can say that again.'

'Well, you weren't so hot yourself.'

'I didn't hear you complaining. Talk about begging for it.'

'I'm going back to the office. Take the lady in the bar out to dinner. Clearly she can't afford to be fussy.'

'Eva . . . ' He caught hold of her arm.

'Let go of me!'

'Why are you shouting? I'm not going to force you. That's your department, not mine.'

The jibe stung, but she let it pass. 'Please, Viktor, leave me alone. I'm sorry about what happened in Paris. It was all my fault. And I'm sorry about those letters. I never meant—'

'I know. It was just a crazy holiday thing. It meant nothing to you. I mean nothing to you.'

She stood rigid for a moment while he stroked her hair, trying to soften her into the warm, yielding, pliable Eva he remembered. For God knows what reason, she *had* loved him, if only for a moment, pouring balm into that open wound of loneliness without asking anything in return. He wanted her to do it again. To love and comfort and cherish him, just for a moment, unreservedly, undeservedly, for no reason at all.

'Please, Eva. I'm so bloody miserable, you've no idea. Please . . . '

Please. What an unthinkable thing to say to a woman. What a terrible admission of need. Please. How pathetic. How luxurious. What bliss it would be to love Eva instead of Cassie, Eva who was everything Cassie wasn't: good-natured, soft-hearted, uncomplicated, undemanding, she would take all the pain away and then . . .

'No, Viktor.' She pulled away. And then, impulsively, 'I love you.'

'What?'

'I said I love you. I said no.' She took hold of both his hands. 'Now tell me why you're so miserable. Because I love you. Tell me.'

He didn't realise he was crying till she got out a handkerchief and wiped his wet cheeks like a nanny. It would have been the most humiliating moment of his life, if she hadn't loved him.

* * *

406

'Did you hear what I said?'

Rob was miles away, as usual. He was supposed to be painting her, but Cassie knew she was merely an impressionistic smudge in the field of poppy-strewn corn, there not so much for reference as for inspiration.

'Rob?'

He looked up suddenly, losing his sun hat.

'I said, I'm going into the village, to the shops. Can I get you anything?'

'No. I'll come with you. I could do with a beer.'

She picked up his hat and put it back on his head at a rakish angle. Even at this hour of the morning the sun was savage. His nose was peeling again, his face red rather than brown. They were both a mass of joined-up freckles.

There were still another few weeks to go but Cassie's imaginary calendar on the wall was making her ever more twitchy. Even as a child she had mourned the summer holidays long before their demise, whereas Rob seemed determined to enjoy his vacation right up to the very last minute. It would sound mean to say, 'I'm starting to get bored,' or 'I'm not enjoying this any more,' or 'I've had enough of bumming around,' because none of that was his fault. But just lately she had been touchy, irritable, and Rob knew the reason why . . . or thought he did.

Viktor wasn't the solution; he was part of the problem. She had proved, as she had promised herself, that she could live without him; the temptation was to leave well alone. The fact that she didn't *want* to live without him was a symptom of her new-found greed, her reckless desire to push her luck, to court rejection and disappointment rather than curse herself for cowardice. Viktor was part of the real world, the world that was waiting to claim her. And rather than wait till the last minute, she knew she ought to run ahead and take it by surprise, if only to show that she wasn't afraid, although of course she was. But the more she thought about it, the harder it was to do anything; risks were the stuff of impulse, not deliberation.

Another bubble of frustrated energy welled up inside her. She felt sated, as if she had had three months' solid sleep. She had thought that she wanted to sleep for ever, but now she was wide awake. A painful state, as always, but this time it was the healing ache of a wasted muscle forced to stretch again, not the warning symptom of some dread disease. And she owed much of that to Rob, the sandman who had presided over her hibernation.

She would always think of him as her first lover, not her second. Thanks to Rob she had unlearned every cold-blooded manoeuvre Wilfred had taught her, gone back to the beginning and started all over again. In trusting Rob, she had come to trust herself – a self that was honest and spontaneous and generous, a self she would never have believed existed, a self she was beginning to like. Thanks to Rob, for the first time in her life, Cassie felt . . . *young*.

She put her arms around his chest and kissed him on the back of his sunburned neck.

'What do you think?' he fished, admiring his handiwork.

'Terrific.' The response was automatic. She had no idea whether his pictures were any good, but then to Rob it didn't much matter whether they were or not. The pleasure of painting them was enough.

'Are you still mad at me?' he said, grinning.

'I wasn't mad at you. I'm sorry I bit your head off like that.'

'Forget it.'

He wished he could give her a run for her money, satisfy her need for confrontation. But he found it impossible to retaliate, knowing that her bursts of irritability were focused on herself not on him. 'I'm going to miss you terribly,' she would accuse him, miserably, almost as if she wanted him to talk her into staying with him, betraying the same old craving for security. A security that would soon degenerate into boredom. Cassie would never be happy with a man she could be sure of. Perhaps Cassie would never be happy, period.

Arm in arm, they ambled along the winding dusty lane from the campsite into the village. They were in the heart of van Gogh country, shimmering with incandescent yellow heat, blazing a relentless, unstoppable trail towards a ripe, rustling autumn. It was market day, and the stalls were piled high with a kaleidoscope of vivid colour. Women who lived real lives piled raw materials into their string bags while Cassie bought peaches and figs.

'Hurry up, Cass. I'm dying of thirst.'

'You go ahead. I'll see you in the café.'

She spent some time in the *papeterie*, browsing through its limited stock of books and having a free read of the magazines before she rejoined him. There was only one café in the village, not counting an insalubrious *bar-tabac*, a tiny dark den which catered exclusively for men. The Tournesol was a chic summer place with a large sun terrace and umbrellas, catering for the seasonal visitors who kept holiday homes in the surrounding hills. Rob had got talking to a couple of girls who were sitting with their backs to the street. He was always getting picked up by strangers, as naturally sociable as Cassie was reserved. One of them was wearing a broad-brimmed sun hat, her hand curled round a tall glass of *diabolo menthe*, a bright-green peppermint fizz.

Just as Cassie caught Rob's eye, the girl turned round and smiled, her face half hidden behind large black lenses. The other half was plastered in thick matt make-up which failed to disguise her bad complexion.

'Don't you recognise me?' she said. 'Rob did, straightaway.'

Her mouth was different. The delicate rose-bud lips had lost their original shape and another pair, coarser and thicker, had replaced them. She took off the sunglasses, almost provocatively, as if to prove her identity, revealing the unmistakable green eyes.

'Armelle,' said Cassie helplessly. Her once perfect skin was creased and mottled beneath the panstick; it seemed to have shrunk in some places and stretched in others, altering the contours of her face.

'Are you enjoying your vacation? Hasn't the weather been glorious?'

'Yes. Um . . . are you on holiday here?'

'I'm convalescent, as you can see,' she purred, mocking Cassie's confusion. 'I set fire to myself. Terribly careless of me.' She stood up abruptly, leaving her drink unfinished. 'Forgive me. I'm embarrassing you. Don't worry, I'm getting used to it. I always was an exhibitionist, remember?'

'I'm sorry,' said Cassie hurriedly. 'I'm not embarrassed. Just surprised. Please don't go.'

'Poor Cassie. You've don't have to be nice to me, you know. I said the same to Rob, but he can't help it.'

'Armelle,' murmured Claudine quietly. Just 'Armelle'. But the one word must have conveyed some secret, silent message. There was a brief, meaningful exchange of looks between them. Then Armelle said briskly, 'Look, we really do have to go now, but why don't you two come to the house for dinner? You can spend the night in a proper bed for a change. You'd be doing me a favour. After all, if I can face you two, I can face just about anyone, can't I?'

The challenge was aimed at them, and not just at herself. Despite the studied flippancy, there was a note of desperate appeal in her voice.

'Of course we'll come,' said Rob.

'Good. I'll draw you a map.' Claudine produced a pen and Armelle scribbled a sketch on a napkin. The backs of her hands were pink, puckered, shiny. 'It's my turn to cook today, we've just been getting the food. Just wait till you taste my *soupe de poissons*. It's out of this world. Well . . . see you later then.'

Not content with the routine kiss on each cheek, Rob held Armelle close for a moment and said something to her in a voice too low for Cassie to hear. Then the girls walked off, carrying two heavy bags each, Armelle striding ahead, Claudine an imperceptible pace behind

'She didn't want to speak to me,' said Rob, as soon as they were out of earshot. 'The minute she saw me she got up to go. But I couldn't just let her walk away.'

'Did she tell you how it happened?'

'She was throwing Molotovs at the police. She spilt some petrol on her blouse and it caught alight. That's all I know. You turned up before I could ask any questions. You don't mind going there tonight, do you?'

'We've got to. It was brave of her to ask us.'

'She won't want sympathy. We've got to act normal. Behave just like we would if she hadn't got hurt.'

'And as if *we* hadn't got hurt?'

'I stopped hurting weeks ago. What about you?'

Cassie shrugged, rather sheepishly. She had quite lost the habit of lying. 'I don't know. Perhaps I don't want it to stop.'

'Then don't pretend. She'll only see through you.'

The invitation hung over the rest of Cassie's day like a storm cloud. Armelle was quite capable, even in her present state, of manipulating Rob's better nature, of making him feel responsible for her, of destroying his hard-won peace of mind. Cassie felt threatened, and fiercely protective. He's mine now, she wanted to say; hands off. Except that he wasn't hers. If he had been, she might even have welcomed this sudden challenge. It seemed an awfully long time since she had had a good fight. Perhaps that was what she had been missing.

Armelle was waiting to greet them, together with Claudine and two other girls. The lavishly modernised Provençal farmhouse, embellished with a swimming pool and tennis court, had been requisitioned as a summer school for Armelle's new women's group, which was all set to take Nanterre by storm.

'I'm glad you came,' she said, as if she hadn't been sure of them. She seemed more like her old self on home ground, looking exotic and dignified in a long, flowing kaftan. The bouillabaisse was, as she had promised, very good indeed, as was the rôti de veau which followed. After three months of roughing it, the whole set-up seemed terribly domesticated and bourgeois.

'I'm going to have my own apartment next term,' Armelle said, over the cheese and fruit. 'Claudine and I are going up to Paris next month to look at a few places. Unfurnished, of course. I want somewhere I can do up from scratch. I've decided to have the walls in plain white, to set off all my pictures. And a very pale green fitted carpet throughout. We found just the thing at this terrific wholesale place in Aix the other day. The antique shops round here are so much cheaper than Paris – the garage is chock-a-block already. And I must have a dining room, of course, so that I can entertain. And a decent-sized kitchen . . . '

Cassie remembered Armelle's precious collection of china and linen and knick-knacks, ballast in search of a ship. Evidently she had used her horrific accident to twist her skinflint father's arm. She was a survivor all right. Cassie couldn't help liking her for it.

'How's Pilar?' she asked.

'Same as ever. She offered to come to work for me in the new apartment. But only if I agree to pay her more than Odile! She seems to think I'm made of money. So I'll probably make do with a char and send the washing out to the laundry. It'll work out cheaper in the end. Pilar eats like a horse.'

Rob began laughing mercilessly.

'I know,' sighed Armelle, taking his point. 'There's no such thing as a good employer. But Pilar will do well out of it. Odile's bound to bribe her to stay, just to spite me. Long live the workers. Talking of which, whose turn is it to wash up?'

'Rob's!' shouted one of the girls. And as if responding to some prearranged signal they bore him off, protesting feebly, to the kitchen.

'Don't go,' said Armelle, as Cassie got up to follow them. 'I want to talk to you.' She beckoned her into the living room and shut the door behind her. Cassie wondered uneasily what this was leading up to.

'I'm sorry about what happened with Odile,' began Armelle, patting the space on the settee beside her. 'I didn't know anything about it till Pilar told me. And by that time you'd gone back to England. I would have talked to my father, told him it was all my idea.'

'It was my idea. I asked for it. I asked for what happened with Viktor as well. I didn't tell Rob for spite, you know.'

'I wouldn't think any less of you if you did. Are you happy together?'

'We're happy, yes, but we're not together, exactly. We just teamed up for the summer.'

'And then?'

'We'll always be friends, I hope.'

'That's a pity. You make such a nice couple.'

'It's not a pity to be friends.'

'Do you think he'd be friends with me? No, I mean it,' she added, seeing the wary look in Cassie's eyes. 'I'm with Claudine now. Trust me.'

'With Claudine?'

'It's not just because of my face. We were together before it happened. Otherwise I wouldn't have believed in it. I'm not ashamed of it. Do you think he'd understand?'

412

'Do you need him to?'

'I'd like him to, yes. He was the nearest I ever got to loving a man. I want him to know I'm all right. I'm more all right than I've ever been. You don't believe me, do you? You think I'm being brave.'

'What's wrong with being brave? I wish I was.'

'In some ways things are easier for me now. Before, I used to think that looks were all I had. That used to scare me. I was so angry with Viktor. I swore I'd never forgive him for—'

'Don't. There's no point in raking all that up again.'

'For saving my life. Not that the poor bastard got any thanks for it. My father didn't lift a finger to help him, you know. And by the time I started thinking straight he was already in gaol. What's the matter?'

Cassie stared at her, open-mouthed.

'What do you think's the matter? I never knew Viktor was in gaol! You might have told me before.'

'I didn't think you'd be interested,' said Armelle innocently. 'Anyhow, he must be out by now. I sent him a cheque a couple of weeks ago, to thank him. I couldn't do anything before – I didn't have the money. A thousand francs. It's not much, I know, but it's the thought that counts, isn't it? I've got so many expenses coming up, what with the new apartment and—'

'For God's sake!' exploded Cassie. 'Will you please get to the point? What happened? Where is he? Is he all right?'

Armelle's new mouth widened in the same old malicious smile.

'If only you could see your face,' she said.

Viktor couldn't sleep. Ever since his talk with Eva he had felt better, and worse. Better because he had finally told her the truth, and worse because she had returned the compliment.

'Staying here isn't the answer,' she had told him flatly. 'You'd never fit in. Even if you stop being a thief, what kind of job could you get here? With your poor reading and writing you'd end up working in a factory. You'd have to squeeze in with us, or live in digs like Jan. There's a ten-year waiting list for flats. And there won't be anything worth buying with your wages unless you pay through the nose for hard currency.

Even the Action Programme won't work miracles – it's going to take years to put things right. Be realistic. You'd never stick it. You're a capitalist through and through. In the West there are a million ways to make money. That's where you belong.'

She had been equally brutal about Cassie.

'You say she wanted to change you. But it was you who wanted to change, can't you see that? You've got to stop making excuses and blaming everything on other people. You're like a little boy trying to hide behind my apron strings.'

She had told him nothing he didn't know already. Perhaps he had just needed to hear her say it, with love. She was right, of course. When his visa ran out at the end of the week, he would cut his losses and go.

The telephone rang by his bed, making him jump. 'Hello?'

'Viktor? It's your father.'

'What time is it?'

'Two o'clock. It's happened. They've invaded.'

'What?' The shock catapulted him out of bed and on to his feet.

'I just heard it on the radio. They crossed the border just before midnight. They'll be here within a couple of hours. Not just the Russians. They've roped in the Poles, the Hungarians, the East Germans, the Bulgarians. You know why this is such a dangerous place to live? Because we're surrounded by friends.'

'I'm on my way.'

He flung on his clothes, seizing upon the news as a kind of reprieve. This was no time to be thinking of leaving. He hadn't expected this; nobody had. The troops had pulled out only three weeks ago. Everyone had assumed that the crisis was over. Bastards. They would never get away with this. People would fight back.

Jan had hinted darkly at contingency plans and Viktor had assumed he meant secret caches of guns and ammunition, as there had been in his grandmother's flat during the war. The Russians couldn't massacre the entire population. If enough people stood up to them, they could drive them back. They had to drive them back. If they didn't, there would be another massive purge. His father would be rounded up as a founder member of Club 231, Eva was up to her neck in *Spring Tide* . . .

A five-dollar tip to the hall porter produced a cab instantly out of nowhere. The streets were still deserted as people slept on, oblivious. The cab driver, who had heard the news on the car radio, didn't share Viktor's eagerness for the fray.

'The Presidium's instructed the army and the security forces not to resist. So they're hardly likely to arm the people. In any case, what can civilians do against tanks? We've seen it all before, remember. It's like the Nazis marching in all over again.'

By the time he dropped Viktor off, the lights were on all over his father's block. He raced up the stairs and hammered on the door. Eva opened it instantly and fell into his arms, fighting back the tears.

'There you are,' said Karel coolly. 'I suppose it's no use my telling you to get the hell out while the going's good?'

'None at all. What do we do now? Build barricades?'

Karel snorted. 'We're not talking about the French CRS. This is the Red Army. Barricades! You do know what a tank is, I take it?'

'I phoned Jan,' said Eva. 'They've already started printing leaflets about passive resistance.'

'Passive resistance? What good is that?'

'A lot more good than thousands dead in the streets!' thundered Karel. 'You're not in the West now! They're not going to come at us with tear gas and truncheons. They'll have machine-guns!'

'We're to start removing all the street signs so they can't find their way around,' continued Eva, rummaging in a drawer for a screwdriver. 'Jan's going straight to the Central Committee building to see what he can find out.'

'I'd better knock up Miloš,' growled Karel. 'We need to call an emergency committee meeting, to see what we old fogeys can organise. Don't expect me here when you get back. And be careful! Viktor, I'm relying on you to watch out for Eva.'

Nováková, bristling curlers like a porcupine, was prevailed upon to lend out the communal stepladder. Amazingly, she was full of encouragement.

'What a way for them to treat us! Haven't we always been

their staunchest allies? It's outrageous! Would a pot of paint be any use to you?'

By the time they sighted the first convoy, just before daybreak, Viktor had disposed of some fifty street names while Eva rechristened them Dubček Road and Dubček Gardens and Dubček Avenue and painted large helpful arrows labelled, 'Moscow – 1500 kilometres'. Other people soon joined in, everyone working together with frantic camaraderie. But the sight of the troops as they crossed the river gave a new focus for activity. In the thin light of morning people left their homes to line the streets, hurling stones and abuse at the tanks and vehicles, some weeping, some chanting slogans. Most of the soldiers were very young and looked more frightened than the populace they had come to suppress.

Viktor and Eva arrived in the city centre to find that barricades, useless or not, had been thrown up by students in an attempt to block the path of the tanks which already infested every thoroughfare like a column of monstrous ants. All around the Radio Prague building buses and trams had been overturned; inside, journalists continued to broadcast the news under siege conditions. As the tanks prepared to plough their way through the obstacles and capture the building, people hurled cobblestones, bottles and rubbish bins, anything that came to hand.

Eva and Viktor joined in the onslaught, but it was no use. Moments later the tanks flattened the obstructions, and a volley of gunfire shattered the windows. The furious crowd responded by setting fire to two munitions lorries whose occupants panicked and baled out, while others began firing randomly into the crowd. One young man keeled over, half his head shot away.

'Come away from here,' yelled Viktor, appalled. Eva was staring, horror-struck, at the victim, rooted to the spot with sudden paralysing fear. 'Karel will have my guts if anything happens to you.'

There was a loud bang as one of the blazing lorries exploded, showering flaming fragments in all directions, sending everyone running for cover. Viktor grabbed Eva's hand and retreated to the southern end of Wenceslas Square, where fresh-faced rookies, trigger-fingers itching, were still under siege from a furious populace chanting 'Fascists!' and 'Russians go home!' Many of the soldiers evidently weren't Russian but natives of other Warsaw Pact countries, although all identifying marks had been strategically removed from their vehicles; angry citizens daubed huge swastikas in their place. Meanwhile foreign journalists mingled with the crowds, interviewing people, photographing the scene, assuring everyone that all the Western democracies were right behind them.

'Much good that will do us,' muttered Eva, taking up the rhythmic chant of 'Dubček! Svoboda!' Svoboda, the Czech word for freedom, was also the surname of the revered elderly President, still inviolate in Hradcany Castle, steadfastly refusing to grant his authority to the invasion despite the summary abduction of Dubček and the rest of the leadership, who had been driven away by armoured car to an unknown destination; many feared they had been taken to Moscow, there to be tortured into surrender, or even killed, to be replaced by puppets. Transistor radios blared out non-stop news, as the clandestine stations swung into action.

'There has been no capitulation. Do not panic. Please try to reason with the soldiers. They have been told that they are here to suppress a counter-revolution at our Government's invitation. Tell them the truth.'

But by the end of the day this strategy had been abandoned as useless. Further gratuitous killings and injuries had hardened people's attitude to the troops who, well drilled by their commissars, had been inoculated against truth as part of their training. By nightfall not a street sign remained, rendering their maps useless. Every shop window was festooned with pictures of Dubček; walls bore the unequivocal message 'This is not Vietnam!' and 'Ivan, go home!' Everyone wore the national colours on their lapels, with a black ribbon attached; flags were flown at half-mast and leaflets denouncing the invasion were in open circulation. The word went out that no food or water or other assistance was to be given to the invaders under any circumstances; the soldiers were reduced to eating their emergency combat rations.

In response to this public show of defiance a strict curfew

was announced. Anyone breaking it would be shot on sight, a threat which nobody doubted; in Prague alone seven people were already dead and over two hundred injured. Rail links between Prague and the rest of the country had been cut, as had telephone and telegraph contact with the rest of the world. Visitors streamed out of the country; hotels, restaurants and places of entertainment were closed; churches were padlocked. Viktor duly vacated his room at the Zlata Husa, arriving back at the apartment with Eva minutes before curfew to find Jan already installed for the night at Karel's invitation, his digs being miles out in the suburbs. He had brought a large sack of pamphlets with him, ready for distribution first thing next morning.

'Did you go to the office?' he asked Eva, hugging her.

'Not once I saw soldiers guarding the place. I'm not typing Russian lies and propaganda.'

'You must go in tomorrow,' said Jan. 'I'm going to. The more of us show up, the harder it will be for them to take over. We can sabotage them more effectively at work than we can by staying away.'

'What about those leaflets?'

Jan turned to Viktor. 'I've arranged for a car to pick you up at five a.m. By the time you've got rid of this lot, a new batch will have been printed. The driver will have details of the pick-up point.'

'What if they're stopped?' put in Eva.

'I'm a French citizen,' Viktor reminded her, rather sourly. 'Not much they can do to me.'

'I doubt if you'll have any trouble,' said Jan. 'They've got too much else on their plate to worry about a few handbills. There are plenty more where those came from, and they know it.'

They tuned in to the radio for another bulletin, made more poignant by the knowledge that those transmitting it were risking their lives by so doing. Listeners were assured that the whole country was united in its will to resist; the scenes in Prague had been duplicated nationwide. Trade unions and government departments had declared their support for Dubček and Svoboda, and as yet no collaborators had come forward. If any did, their names would be broadcast so that everyone would know who they were. The transmission ended with the now familiar slogan, 'We are with you. Be with us.'

Viktor didn't need telling twice.

'Hello, Marta.'

'Cassie!' Marta clasped Cassie to her bosom and promptly burst into tears; Cassie, who had been unsure of her welcome, did likewise. She hadn't dared go straight round to Viktor's place, for fear that he might not be alone.

'I came as soon as I heard,' began Cassie. 'I'm sorry I didn't answer your letter. I didn't know—'

'Such terrible news. It's a tragedy.'

'Is Viktor all right?' asked Cassie, alarmed at Marta's funebral tones, noticing that her eyes were red and swollen from weeping.

'God knows. I've been trying to telephone Prague, but it's hopeless.'

'Prague? Viktor's in Prague?'

'I've never trusted the Russians. Never. I told Karel a million times . . . ' Cassie looked at her blankly. 'Haven't you heard? They've sent the tanks in.'

'Tanks? God. I came by the overnight train from Marseilles. I haven't seen a newspaper yet . . . Oh Marta, I'm so sorry!'

'I was so pleased when he decided to visit after all this time. And now he's going to end up getting himself shot! It will be a massacre, like it was in Hungary . . . '

According to Marta, they were bound to close the borders and refuse to let Viktor out. He still had Czech nationality, his French passport would be scant protection against those murderous Russians. She had already rung the French foreign office, but they hadn't been the least bit helpful.

Her garbled account was constantly interrupted by the telephone as fellow-exiles engaged her in lengthy, incomprehensible commiserations. Cassie didn't like to leave her alone in such an agitated state. She tried to submerge her own anxiety in brewing coffee, coaxing Marta to eat something, and assuring her repeatedly that Viktor would be all right.

'I knew you'd come back one of these days,' whimpered Marta, dabbing her eyes with a sodden handkerchief. 'I knew

you'd give him another chance. Please God it's not too late!'
More tears.

'If I'd known he was in trouble, I'd have come before,' said
Cassie. And then, awkwardly, 'But that doesn't necessarily
mean we'll be getting back together. Please don't try to write a
happy ending for us, Marta. Real life isn't like that.'

'No,' sighed Marta, shaking her head. 'Real life is you settling down with a nice, professional, respectable man, someone of your own class.'

'No!' Cassie startled herself with her own vehemence.

'Then what is it?'

'Real life is . . . doing what's difficult. Choosing. Fighting
back. Taking risks.'

And for the first time that day, Marta smiled.

The second day of the occupation ends with good news.
Today a thousand delegates, dressed in working clothes,
assembled in the CKD factory here in Prague for the
Fourteenth Party Congress in order to elect a new
Central Committee. This meeting was arranged at short
notice by the underground free Czechoslovak
Communist Party to prevent the Russians installing collaborators. Alexander Dubček has been duly and legally
re-elected as First Secretary and heads a new liberal leadership. Former conservative members of the committee
have lost their posts. Full details are as follows . . .

'What's the point in re-electing Dubček when he's rotting in
some gaol in Moscow?' said Viktor.

'It's the principle that matters,' said Karel.

'It shows you how useless the Russians are,' put in Eva. 'A
thousand extra people turn up for work and their so-called
intelligence doesn't even notice.'

Eva was in high spirits. The mood at the office had been defiant and determined. The sheer solidarity of the workforce had
proved unstoppable, and a rousing editorial had gone out
unchecked. Meanwhile badly translated editions of *Pravda*,
welcoming the troops as an army of liberation, had been
distributed by glum-looking soldiers, only to be consigned to
ceremonial bonfires.

420

'Your grandmother must be frantic with worry,' said Karel. 'She's probably been trying to get through ever since she heard the news.'

'Thank God she can't,' said Viktor. 'She'd only start nagging at me to go back.'

'That's good advice. We can manage without you, believe it or not.'

'Are you trying to get rid of me?'

'You're my son. I don't want anything to happen to you. I'm beginning to think you've got a death-wish.'

'Don't be ridiculous.'

'That was a dangerous thing you did today.'

'So I set fire to one lousy tank. Big deal.'

'You were lucky not to get shot.'

'No chance. I picked my victims. Two thick-as-shit conscripts straight off the farm. They didn't know one end of a gun from the other.'

'They might have missed you and killed some innocent bystander,' continued Karel. 'No more stupid heroics, do you hear me?'

'So fighting back is stupid, is it?'

Eva marched off to the kitchen, not wanting to hear any more. If Viktor did have a death-wish, it could only be because he didn't want to go home. Perhaps she should have lied to him, encouraged him to stay on permanently, taken advantage of his desperate need to escape from himself. She had had her chance on a plate and missed it. Because she loved him. And because she understood exactly how he felt. For years she had dreamed of fleeing to the West and leaving all her problems behind. And now Viktor was doing the same thing in reverse.

She heard the door slam and returned to the living room to find Karel looking sheepish.

'Where's he gone?'

'How should I know?'

'You don't look well.'

'I'm perfectly all right. And now he's out of the way, I want to ask you a question.'

He shifted around in his seat for a moment, groping for the

421

words. Eva knew in a flash what he was going to say. He had been working up to it for weeks.

'Tell me the truth. Is something going on between you and Viktor?'

'Whatever gave you that idea?'

'Don't lie to me. I can see it, and so can Jan. You're in love with him, aren't you?'

Eva hesitated a moment before answering.

'Yes. I'm in love with him. Like my mother was with you. You told me not to make the same mistakes as she did, remember? Well, I've taken your advice.'

'What are you talking about?'

'Oh, you were fond of her, I know. Just like Viktor's fond of me. But you never loved her the way you loved Milena. At the moment he wants looking after and mothering and comforting, like a big baby. But the man in him wants what you had with his mother. And I can't give him that.'

'But Milena and I . . . it wasn't a good marriage! Your mother and I were happy together!'

'I never said you weren't. Now please don't mention it again. And for God's sake stop biting his head off every two minutes.'

Evidently disappointed, Karel bowed his head. 'I've been trying to get on with him, you know. He rubs me up the wrong way deliberately.'

'He says exactly the same about you.'

'I wish we could make it up properly, before I – before he goes.'

'You've made it up properly. People fight because they love each other. You of all people should know that.'

The door flew open again and Viktor barged in.

'Where have you been?' demanded Karel.

'To buy some cigarettes,' said Viktor innocently, tossing the packet at him. 'Help yourself.'

'Well it makes a change from you smoking mine,' said Karel.

'Cassie's on the line for you,' said Armelle. Rob was installed with his easel by the swimming pool, painting the frolics of three water nymphs. Armelle contrived to look cooler than any of them, swathed from head to foot in a shimmering Indian sari, an exquisite kingfisher creation embroidered in gold. Rob jumped up and went to take the call, leaving Armelle draped elegantly over a deck chair, twirling her parasol.

'Cass? Any news yet?'

'No. Marta's in a dreadful state. I feel I ought to stay and give her moral support.'

Her voice sounded terribly far away. Rob had known when she left that she wasn't coming back, whatever happened with Viktor. She hadn't said so, but he had seen it in her eyes when he saw her off at the station, felt it in the way she made love that last night.

'How are you?' she continued, taking refuge in small talk. That was another sure sign. 'Is the weather still good down there?'

Rob glanced out the window. Claudine was throwing a beach ball at Sylvie, a frail, sad-eyed waif of a girl with a tiny waist and full, high breasts and skin the colour of dark, transparent honey.

'I'm fine. I had a long talk with Armelle last night. She told me about Claudine.'

'And?'

'She offered to lend me the money to fly home. And invited me to stay on here for the rest of the vacation.'

'Are you going to?'

'I told her it depended on you.'

'What do *you* want to do?'

'I'm easy. If you need me, I'll come straightaway.'

'I need you. But I've got to do this on my own.'

'Are you okay for money?'

'For the moment. It's not costing me anything to stay here.'

'Me neither. Well, I guess I might as well live a life of luxury while I still can. At least you can phone me here.'

'Yes. Relax and enjoy yourself.'

'Keep me posted, won't you?'

'Of course. Bye now.' She blew him a kiss and rang off.

Rob stepped back into the oven of the noonday heat. Armelle had already laid out an open-air lunch – salad, langoustines, bread, olives, wine – looking like a still life against the crisp checked tablecloth, set with chunky Provençal pottery. This was the life. While the Russians raped Viktor's homeland, anti-imperialists basked in the sunshine, saving their strength for the next Vietnam rally.

'What did Cassie have to say?'

'She wanted to know if we'd been on any good demos lately.'

'Oh Rob. Not again. Please.'

There had been a few token protests against the invasion, but most activists had been conspicuous by their absence, with the honourable exception of the Maoists. Chou En-lai had roundly condemned the invasion, but Castro had endorsed it, and the French Communist Party had remained equivocal, balking at any direct criticism of the Soviet Union.

'Speak out against Soviet intervention in Czechoslovakia!' mocked Rob. 'But only if Fidel says you can.'

Armelle shrugged peevishly. 'It's difficult to mobilise people in the holiday season. Everyone's tired of protesting, Rob. It's a bad time . . . '

A wet beach ball landed in Armelle's lap, making her squeal. Rob threw it back at Sylvie, who smiled and jumped up in the water to catch it, with a movement as sleek as a dolphin's.

'She's lovely, isn't she?' teased Armelle, as Sylvie climbed out of the pool, glistening with an emulsion of water and sun oil.

'She's not bad,' said Rob, picking up his brush again.

'We're all going into Aix after lunch. Except Sylvie. It's her turn to be skivvy. If you're staying, we really ought to ask you to do your share.'

'Sure. I don't mind.'

'Why don't you go for a swim?' said Armelle slyly.

'This afternoon, perhaps,' said Rob.

Every night the posters were removed; every morning new ones went up. Viktor had been on his rounds since curfew ended at five a.m., flyposting the latest bulletin from one of the numerous underground printing presses.

WATCH OUT FOR THESE REGISTRATION NUMBERS. THEY DENOTE OFFICIAL CARS BEING USED TO MAKE ARRESTS. IF YOU SEE ONE,

'Quick,' hissed Pavel, a baby-faced student of biology who drove like a maniac. Petrol was now virtually unobtainable· and the van, 'borrowed' from a friendly factory, ran on fuel illicitly siphoned from military vehicles. 'There's an army lorry heading this way.'

More and more people were being arrested each day for 'counter-revolutionary activities' and Jan had dinned it into them to be careful. Viktor jumped back in, wound down the passenger window, and hurled one of his handy stock of half-bricks at the truck as it passed. It glanced off ineffectually, but the gesture made him feel better. Seeing an early-morning queue for bread, now an increasingly scarce commodity, he jumped out again and distributed leaflets bearing the same information. The baker willingly stuck a poster on the inside of his window and within a minute they were on their way again.

Hopes were still high. The continuing absence of the leadership was seen as a sign that they were holding firm; the pro-Soviet collaborators installed in their place had found themselves ostracised and unable to form a new administration. Meanwhile the threat of bombardment – Prague was now ringed by three battle divisions armed with heavy artillery and rocket launchers – had produced not panic, but an increased will to resist. Although many people in possession of exit visas had used them to leave the country, they were heavily outnumbered by the thousands of Czechs and Slovaks who had cut short foreign holidays to come home and join in the struggle. All other would-be visitors were being denied entry as border controls tightened up.

These last few days had been, unquestionably, the happiest of Viktor's life. Talking with his father and Jan late into the night, while Eva slept, he had at last begun to feel accepted. For the first time ever, he had known that Karel was pleased with him, however much he ranted at him and urged him to go home. Jan was the one who asked the questions, who pumped Karel to recount his stories of the war years, to describe the euphoria of the Liberation and the hopes and disillusionment that followed. And Viktor listened, while those dry, stilted, self-effacing memoirs came to life, spiced with the mordant gallows humour that had seen his country through worse times than this. Then the narrative would cease abruptly with 'I've bored you long enough,' and Viktor would yawn and say, 'Thank God for that,' and then, in the silent, secret time between the small hours and dawn, when they couldn't possibly argue without waking up Eva in her cubicle, or Jan, curled up in his sleeping bag on the floor, they would continue their conversation furtively, whispering like lovers, using the darkness and quiet to hide behind, remembering and regretting, making their private peace.

The underground printing press had recently been relocated to an address in the suburbs where there was less troop activity than in the centre of Prague and less likelihood of a routine raid.

'Wait here while I go in,' said Pavel, parking the van outside the drab high-rise estate. 'If you see anything suspicious, sound the horn.'

There was no sign of any patrols. Viktor yawned and lit a cigarette. Yesterday's slogans were still daubed on every wall, awaiting the attentions of the daily clean-up squad; within minutes, they would be replaced. Through the open windows, a buzz of radios could be heard. Radio Vltava, the official station of the occupation forces, was universally shunned in favour of the continuing illegal broadcasts; the jamming equipment sent from Russia had been unavoidably delayed, thanks to the action of railway workers who had blocked the passage of the train. Somewhere, in one of those dingy flats perhaps, someone was risking his or her neck so that truth might prevail.

In the wing mirror, Viktor saw a car turn off the main highway and begin driving across the no man's land of waste ground leading to the housing estate. As soon as it was near enough, he automatically checked its registration number against that day's list. He found it impossible to remember sequences of numbers – like letters, they invariably transposed themselves in his mind – and at first he thought that he must have made a mistake. It wasn't a sinister black Volga, just an

426

ordinary, dusty old Skoda. But the number was definitely the same. As it drew up, opposite the van, he saw that there was a man in a raincoat sitting in the passenger seat, and two armed soldiers in the back.

He switched on the ignition, pushed his foot right down to the floor, and rammed the car as it slowed to a halt, pressing hard on his horn to the unmistakable staccato rhythm of 'Dubček, Svoboda, Dubček, Svoboda!' The effect was instantaneous. Obeying the summons, men, women and children flooded out of the surrounding blocks, gathering round the vehicle and creating an impassable cordon of bodies, stubbornly ignoring the order to make way. The soldiers fired shots in the air, but more people kept coming, some still in their pyjamas. As Viktor was hauled roughly out of the van and man-handled into the back of the Skoda, the crowd took up the slogan, giving him a rousing send-off, while whoever the men had come to arrest was quickly spirited away.

'Papers,' said the man in the raincoat, without turning around. Viktor affected not to understand his thick Russian accent. He barked an order at the soldiers, who frisked him and handed over his passport.

'You are French,' he observed, inspecting this document closely. 'But I see you were born in Prague.'

Remembering the tales of *The Good Soldier Švejk* from his childhood, Viktor adopted an expression of cheerful, co-operative idiocy. 'So I'm told. I was too young at the time to remember.'

'Address?'

'Hotel Zlata Husa.'

'I think not. Your visa expired four days ago.'

'Really? How careless of me. Time passes so fast when you're enjoying yourself.'

Lacking enough colloquial Czech to keep up this exchange, his interlocutor confined himself to issuing further orders to the soldiers, who manacled Viktor's hands behind his back. Viktor launched into a robust rendering of the national anthem but, having no appreciation of music, they responded by gagging him, and the car drove on in silence to a grey concrete block, evidently the local police station.

Not again, thought Viktor, as they shut him into a cell. This was getting to be a habit. Still, Pavel would soon find out where they had taken him, and get word to his father and Eva. He felt absurdly pleased with himself. He wasn't in the least bit afraid.

The man who came to question him was Czech, accompanied by the friendly Russian. Viktor greeted them both with a sunny, subversive smile.

'These were found in the van,' he said, showing Viktor a bundle of leaflets and posters.

'Oh, you're more than welcome to them,' said Viktor pleasantly. 'We've got plenty more.'

'Do you know the penalty for distributing counter-revolutionary literature?'

'Literature, is it? I wouldn't know. I'm not an educated man.'

'Your visa expired four days ago. You have no authority to remain in the country.'

'I don't need any authority. I was born here.'

'Where have you been staying since you left the hotel? With relatives?'

'I don't know the address. I got involved with this woman, see.'

'Her name?'

'Lolita. That's all she told me.'

'And whereabouts does this Lolita live?'

'As you say, I'm a foreigner. I don't know my way around. Somewhere near a church, with a spire.'

'Prague has hundreds of churches with spires.'

'Really? How interesting. I thought there was only the one.'

'If you wish to insist on claiming Czech nationality, we may choose to permit you to remain. But be aware, we may not choose to let you out again. Is that what you want?'

'Well, since you're asking me so nicely . . .'

The man began speaking very fast, as if to thwart the listening Russian. 'Do not force me to arrest you. You emigrated illegally to a capitalist country and you are now assisting in a counter-revolution. You will bring nothing but trouble to whoever is harbouring you.'

There followed a short exchange in Russian and the two men left the room.

Viktor kicked the door of the cell and swore viciously. He

was an undesirable alien again, in his own country this time. Get the hell out or go to gaol. 'You will bring nothing but trouble to whoever is harbouring you.' Shit. Just as he was beginning to enjoy himself.

An hour or so later the plain-clothes policeman returned, alone.

'Come with me.'

'Where are we going?'

'You are to be taken to a government facility to await deportation. Special vehicles are being provided to convey foreigners to the border.'

'But I have to get word to my . . . girlfriend. I can't just leave!'

'I thought you didn't know where she lived?'

He bundled Viktor into the front of a police car, and took the driving seat himself.

'Look, give me a break,' began Viktor. 'Just an extra day or two. Anyone would think you were on their side.'

'You think I like doing those bastards' dirty work?' spat the policeman, abruptly dropping his bureaucratic façade. 'I've got three kids. What choice do I have?' The car turned into an alleyway and screeched to a halt. 'Get out.'

'What?'

'Go home, say goodbye, collect your stuff and be out of the country by tomorrow. Otherwise, next time they pick you up I'll be the one in gaol. Do you understand me?'

'But—'

'I like what you did back there. God knows, it's the only help we've had from the West so far. Now do me a favour and go back there, will you? Remember what I said. This is my neck now, not yours.'

He held out his hand. Viktor shook it, got out of the car, and watched him drive away.

'I'm all right,' Karel told himself, pouring a slug of rum into his tea. 'It's just a touch of indigestion, that's all.' But whatever it was, it had been quite beyond him to struggle into work. He had told Eva that he had the runs, so as not to alarm her, and had promised faithfully to see the doctor. Not that he had the slightest intention of doing any such thing. Once his cover was blown they would put him out to grass, make a pathetic invalid out of him. And then Viktor would pussy-foot around him being polite and taking care not to upset him. And Eva would wear herself out, waiting on him hand and foot. And people would start suggesting, very tactfully, that perhaps he ought to resign from the committee. It didn't bear thinking about.

It couldn't be his heart. The pain was much higher than that, in his throat, as if it were being eaten away by acid. And since Viktor had been here he had been feeling so much better. Their conflicts had energised and restored him more than Věra's loving care, more than Eva's cheerful affection. He loved him for all the faults that mirrored his own, for being so irredeemably his son. And he feared for him because he had that same deep self-doubting discontent that threatened to destroy himself and others.

'He wants what you had with his mother.' God help him. But even if it ended in heartbreak, he hoped for his sake that he would find it, while he was still young and strong. Compromise and caution were for middle age. The whole Prague Spring had been like some glorious doomed love affair. He had known from the start that it would come to grief but he didn't regret a single minute of it.

He took a scalding hot swallow. The vaporised alcohol rasped his throat, robbing him of air, choking him, making him cough, driving nails of pain into his chest. And once he started coughing, he couldn't stop, he couldn't breathe . . .

Hearing the key in the lock, he struggled to control himself, fighting the instinct to expel the irritant scratching at his lungs.

'What are you doing at home?' demanded Viktor. 'Are you ill?'

'I'm fine. Why are you back so early? I wasn't—' His voice erupted into a hideous gurgle. He tried to eject the obstruction but it sank further back into his windpipe, blocking further speech. Viktor lifted him to his feet and helped him over to the bed.

'Lie down. You look dreadful. I'm going to call the doctor. What's the number?'

Karel shook his head, unable to speak. Viktor ran to the telephone. Karel sank back into the pillows, fuelling his lungs with short, shallow breaths. He had promised himself he would stay well while Viktor was here. He must think him quite enough of an old wreck as it was.

'Eva? How do I get hold of a doctor? It's my father. Yes. Right. Hurry.'

Karel opened his mouth to protest that he was perfectly all right, but another vicious spasm told him not to waste what words he had left.

'Eva's ringing the doctor from her office. Then she's coming home. Don't try to speak.'

Karel's face was was as grey as his hair, his arms were wrapped around his chest, he seemed to have shrunk into a tight ball of pain. Viktor felt helpless, panic-stricken. If only Eva were here. She would make everything all right . . .

'It's okay. You're going to be fine. Relax now.'

Karel reached out for his hand. 'Whatever happens,' he croaked, 'it was worth it.'

'Of course it was. We're not beaten yet.'

'I'm glad . . . you were here . . . when it happened.'

'So am I.'

'You know that I—'

His body convulsed in an arch of pain.

'I know. I know.'

'Viktor—' The eyes continued to stare at him sightlessly, longingly, frozen in an expression of hunger.

'Tati?' He hadn't called him that in years. 'Tati!' He shook the limp hand almost savagely. 'Come back, you old bastard! Answer me! You can't die on me now! Come back damn you!'

He couldn't weep. By the time Eva arrived he was numb, calm. His father was safe now. They couldn't frighten him, or humiliate him, or persecute him ever again. Unlike his much-loved country, he was free.

Following the return of the Czechoslovak leadership to Prague, in the early hours of this morning, Alexander Dubček has broadcast an emotional appeal to the nation.

Marta turned up the sound on the television. The famous smile had gone for ever; he looked and sounded like a broken man.

His speech was delivered in a cracked voice and punctuated by long pauses, his words inaudible above the superimposed French commentary.

> Monsieur Dubček pleaded with the people to avert a national catastrophe by supporting necessary measures to ensure the withdrawal of Russian troops. These necessary measures can only be guessed at, but it seems inevitable that censorship will be reimposed and the Action Programme abandoned as part of a 'normalisation' process aimed at restoring hardline Communist orthodoxy. The reaction of Czechs and Slovaks to the news is one of blank horror and disbelief. Many people believed that—

Marta switched off the set, too depressed to listen any more. It was like Munich all over again. The only solace was that Viktor would surely come home now. Another cold shiver of fear ran through her as she thought of armed soldiers on every street corner, bristling with weapons, waiting for a pretext to shoot. Viktor's hatred of authority had hardened, if anything, after his spell in gaol. She prayed that his natural belligerence had not got the better of him. 'Karel has got him labelled as a "young hothead". He's all for standing up to Moscow and not giving an inch . . .'

Shuddering, she sat down at her sewing machine, to give her hands something to do. Cassie would be back with the shopping in a moment; then together they would cook a meal that neither of them wanted to eat, in case Viktor suddenly arrived, tired and hungry, offering up the wasted food like some primitive ritual sacrifice to appease the gods, united by the common fear neither of them dared express.

The sudden, blessed rap on the door was unlike anyone else's. Marta jumped out of her seat, knocking over the chair; then she took a deep breath and rearranged her features, hiding her relief and delight behind a mask of so-it's-you crankiness. Viktor hated emotional displays.

'Well, don't just stand there. Come in!' she greeted him. 'You might have let me know when to expect you, I've got no food in the house . . . Viktor? What is it?'

He had meant to break the news gently, kindly, but it came out as a brutal, unadorned statement of fact. Marta went very white. Viktor sat her down and fetched her a glass of brandy.

'I couldn't stay for the funeral,' he said bleakly. 'My visa expired and they kicked me out.'

'My poor Karel. Poor Eva. Now she's all alone.'

'No. She's got Jan. For the time being anyway. Till the bastards round him up. And probably her as well. At least they can't touch my father. I'm glad he's dead, Babička. I'm glad.'

He held her close, letting her weep for both of them, envying her the relief of tears. He still couldn't feel anything. Or perhaps he was afraid to, afraid that the dam would finally burst and drown him. 'It was the real you he loved,' Eva had said. 'Not the smart-alec accountant. And not the petty thief either. You . . .'

'Well, this won't do him any good,' said Marta, blowing her nose and creaking to her feet. She retired to the bedroom and returned dressed in her heavy black winter coat and hat.

'Where are you going?'

'To church, to light a candle. Who else is going to pray for him? Did he ask for a priest before he died?'

'A priest? He was an atheist.'

'Then there's no time to lose, is there? No, you stay here. God's hardly likely to listen to you. I suppose there's dirty washing in that suitcase. Cas – I'll take it to the launderette tomorrow.'

He had seen her like this before, when his mother died. The day his mother had died, she had lit a candle and prayed. Then she had made dumplings and done a big pile of ironing.

'When I get back, you must tell me everything,' she said, blinking rapidly, subjecting him to a fierce, brief embrace. 'Everything, from the very first day. I'm glad you were there when it happened.'

'That's what he said. Just before he died.'

'And now I'm glad you're home. I don't know how I would have got through the last week without . . . You're a terrible worry to me, Viktor, just like your poor father was. God preserve any woman who takes you on. Perhaps I should say a prayer for her as well.'

She waddled off, leaning heavily on her stick. Viktor let her go, knowing that she wanted to be alone with her memories. It was true he was glad for his father, glad that he had escaped the savage purge that would surely have claimed him, glad he didn't have to witness the final collapse of the dream. But that didn't make the grief any easier to bear. Grief not just for him, but for Eva and Jan, for his country, for Marta and himself. He had never felt more alone.

And he simply couldn't make it alone. If Eva could have come back with him he would have had some incentive, but without her he would never stay the course. Oh, he could make a half-hearted stab at respectability, earn a pittance playing in some piano-bar, or a pile selling second-hand cars on commission, become as honest, and as dishonest, as the next man. But what was the point? To send Marta to a happy grave? He could do that more effectively with lies.

Eva would have shamed him into voluntary virtue. She was the kind of girl you married and had babies with. But that would have been the easy way out. And she had known it.

'Mummy? It's me.'

'Darling! How lovely to hear from you!'

'Did you get my postcards?'

'Sweet of you to send so many. What a trip! Daddy and I were green with envy. When will you be home?'

'I'm not sure yet. I've decided not to go back to college. I'm going to look for a job in France.'

There was a short silence. Cassie could tell what her mother was thinking. That it was exam nerves again. If only it were that simple.

'Didn't you get my last letter, darling? I wrote to Marseilles to let you know that everything's been sorted out. Daddy had a word with the Dean at Southwold and they're going to credit you with the full year of France. They agreed the whole thing was just a silly storm in a teacup. And remember, finals aren't the be-all and end-all these days. Southwold take all your course work into account, it's virtually impossible to fail.'

Yes, thought Cassie. That was the whole trouble. 'It's not

that. I'm sorry to let you and Daddy down, but I've made up my mind. I should have made it up before, instead of getting you do it for me.'

'But ... if you really don't want to go back to college ... what about VSO? Monica Weston's daughter is going out to teach in Pakistan ... '

Poor Mummy, thought Cassie absently. Already she's dreaming up a way of covering up for me. But this was one battle her parents couldn't fight for her, and if she lost it, it would be, indisputably, all her own fault.

'I don't want to make any definite plans just yet. I need time to sort myself out. At least a year, maybe longer.'

'You mean ... you're dropping out?'

Dropping out. A nice, fashionable label that would cover a multitude of sins. 'Cassie's decided to drop out for a year,' they would tell their friends, conjuring up an image of some saffron-robed, mantra-chanting flower child. 'She wants to get some life experience before she finishes her degree ... '

'Yes,' said Cassie. 'Yes, I'm dropping out.'

'You do realise you came into your money last month? We can't send it out to you, obviously.'

It was unlike Mummy to refer to her trust fund in such specific terms. It was like some drooling relative they kept locked in an attic, tactfully out of sight.

'I'll manage.'

'Well, darling, what can I say? It's your life. You know we've always respected your decisions. Just remember we're here if you're ever in trouble. This is your home ... '

'I know,' said Cassie, feeling, momentarily, like a child again. This was proving much harder than she had expected, but perhaps that was a good sign. 'I'll ring you again next week. I should have a proper address by then. Goodbye, Mummy. And don't worry. I'll be all right.'

Cassie walked out of the post office, glad to have burned her boats. She hadn't wanted to make the call at Marta's expense, especially as she hadn't yet told Marta she wasn't going home. Marta would have fondly assumed she was giving up all for Viktor, but Viktor was only part of it. Whatever happened with

Viktor, there was no going back to the way she was before. Or perhaps there was, which was why it made sense to block any possible retreat, to leave herself nowhere to hide.

She had fifty-three francs, no job, and six weeks left on her work permit. But her parents weren't the only ones with contacts. 'You can always stay with Claudine and me,' Armelle had said, with an omnipotent wave of the hand. 'And a permit's no problem – I know this terrific lawyer. You don't want to end up dependent on bloody Viktor.'

On the way home she bought an evening paper. The headlines had been taken over by the riots at the Chicago Democratic convention; Czechoslovakia was already old news. There was a résumé of Dubček's speech and a photograph of him looking haggard and desolate.

It was finally, tragically, over. But her first reaction, like Marta's, had been a guilty, furtive relief that there was no reason for Viktor to stay any longer, that now he would surely come home. As long as he came home safe, she would be happy never to see him again. It was one of those meaningless deals one did with God in times of crisis.

'Marta?' Cassie let herself in and went to put the groceries away, stopping short as she noticed the suitcase standing in the middle of the floor.

'I saw your things in the bedroom,' said a mocking voice behind her. 'Marta never said a word. Lying old bag.'

'W-where is she?' said Cassie stupidly, her arms still full of shopping.

'She's gone to church, to pray for my father's soul. He died yesterday, of a heart attack.'

'Oh God. Oh Viktor. I'm so sorry.'

'It's no big deal. I hardly knew him. But Marta's pretty upset. You look terrific, by the way.'

'It's the tan.'

'Freckles you mean. And you've put on weight.'

'I went back-packing. With Rob.'

'Rob's here?'

'No. Just me.'

She went into the kitchen and began putting the shopping away, kneeling in front of the open fridge, taking big gulps of

436

cold air. Don't blow it, she muttered, mentally. Don't slobber all over him. This is real life, remember. With Viktor there's no such thing as a happy ending.

'So you've had a nice summer, have you?' he said, watching her from the doorway.

'Nicer than yours, I should think.'

'I knew you'd turn up sooner or later. You took your time about it.'

'I didn't know you were in gaol. Otherwise—'

'You shouldn't have come, Cassie.'

'I know I shouldn't. But I'm here.'

She looked him squarely in the face, daring him to reject her.

'What am I supposed to say now?' he taunted, flinching under the candour of her gaze. 'That I'm sorry? That I've missed you like hell? That I love you?'

'Only if it's true.'

'If it's true I shouldn't have to say it. Did you sleep with him?'

'Of course. Do you mind?'

'Why should I mind? I'm glad he got lucky. I must ask him how the hell he managed it.'

'That's not fair. You were the one who was frigid, not me.'

His eyes flashed the way they always did when she hit a raw nerve, provoking the familiar surge of adrenalin. Cassie checked herself. His father had just died. His country had just been trampled underfoot. He was traumatised, in shock, in mourning. It wouldn't be a fair fight.

'But if you were, it was my fault,' she added. 'I can see that now. Please don't let's quarrel. Not yet, anyway. I know how awful you must be feeling.'

'I feel fine. You don't have to be nice to me just because my father's dead. Or because of the bloody invasion.'

Like all his prohibitions, it was a plea in disguise. Viktor hated her to make the first move, but only because he wanted her to. She took hold of both of his hands, willing him to meet her halfway. Their rock-steadiness had gone, every finger vibrating with pain and regret and need.

'That's what it feels like when you care,' she said softly. 'Even if it doesn't show.'

437

But it did. It showed in his eyes, in the curve of his mouth, it showed all over his face. Just as well he couldn't see himself. Just as well she couldn't see *herself*.

She had changed, thought Viktor. And yet she was still the same. What was it Eva had said? 'People don't change. They just discover things about themselves that were always there.' And about other people. There was a new warmth and confidence about her that put him to shame. All his life he had been afraid of his own feelings, and now they were all he had left.

He was different, thought Cassie. And yet he would never change. He would never be safe and comfortable like Rob, but some of his prickles had gone, or perhaps she just wasn't afraid of them any more. He was like a nettle: if you held him tight enough he didn't sting. She put her arms around him, as if to test her theory. It didn't hurt a bit.

Viktor couldn't find the words he needed but perhaps it was just as well. It was easier to kiss her than to speak. Her mouth was a warm, dark, secret place where no one else could hear what he was saying, or rather shouting, shouting from the rooftops, while she yelled back at him, deafening him, making his ears ring. And this time she wasn't doing him a favour, or settling a debt, or trying to win approval. This time it wasn't a gift or a payment either. She was too busy helping herself to what she wanted to notice how much he was stealing from her. This was big-time stuff. This was the bank raid that would set him up for life and this time he wouldn't chicken out. Like thieving, it took nerve, left him weak and elated, released some of his devils. The difference was, he had given something back . . .

Make the most of it, thought Cassie greedily. This was a new and delicious variant on Viktor being nice, all the more precious because you knew it couldn't last . . . until the next time. But then, she wouldn't have wanted it any other way. She hoped this wasn't a happy ending. She hoped this was just the beginning.

Lucy Floyd's latest novel is

BAPTISM OF FIRE

A powerful family drama, set in Cuba against a dramatic background of romance, revolution and betrayal.

Cuba in 1956 is a bubbling cauldron – an island of exotic beauty and vicious corruption. To this turbulent place comes Raúl Soler, exiled elder son of a rich landowner, to reclaim his lost inheritance by fair means or foul.

Two people stand in his way – his stepbrother Eduardo, who discovers a secret about him no one else must ever know, and Celia, would-be bride of his younger brother León, the woman in whom Raúl will finally meet his match.

Here follows a short extract from *Baptism Of Fire*, available in hardback from Macmillan.

Seeing the shiny red convertible parked in the driveway, Celia had to force herself not to run.

'When did he arrive?' she asked casually, as Emilia let her in.

'They,' Emilia corrected her grimly. 'They've been here a couple of hours already.'

'They?' echoed Celia, swamped by the fear that León had brought some woman home to meet the family. 'Who's they?'

'You'll find out soon enough,' said Emilia, adding darkly, 'My blood ran cold the minute he walked through that door. He'll bring bad luck on this house, you mark my words.'

He. Celia was too relieved to be curious. Emilia mistrusted all strangers, especially those who hailed from foreign parts like Havana; as long as León's companion was male, Celia didn't much care who he was.

'Take this,' said Emilia, thrusting a muslin bag at her.

'What is it?' said Celia vaguely, tidying a stray wisp of hair and checking if her seams were straight.

'Jezebel root. To protect your virginity.' Emilia, like Lázaro, was a devotee of the *santeria* cult, a blend of Christianity and African magic. Her quarters, adjoining the kitchen, were full of religious artefacts and charms to ward off real or imagined evils, among which this visitor evidently now numbered.

Celia stifled a giggle. 'Is he good-looking, then?'

'Don't mock,' said Emilia crossly, 'I shall put something in your bath tonight, to ward off danger . . .'

There was a burst of laughter from the salon; stuffing the muslin bag up her sleeve – Emilia could be very touchy – Celia headed towards the sound, curbing the childish desire to rush at León like a puppy greeting its master. That was the kind of thing little sisters did, and she wasn't his little sister any more. The buzz of conversation stopped abruptly as she opened the door of the huge reception room reserved for entertaining guests. She was unnaturally aware of the click of her high heels on the polished marble floor, and of a man's face looking at her intently, one side of it haughtily handsome, the other brutally disfigured.

'Celia, we have an unexpected visitor,' said León breezily, jumping up to greet her. Not long ago he would have picked her up bodily and swung her round and round; today he restricted himself to a brotherly kiss on each cheek. He indicated the newcomer, who bowed stiffly and met her gaze full on, daring her to look away. 'Prepare yourself for a big surprise. This is . . .'

' . . . León's brother, Raúl,' put in Lidia gushingly, leaning back in her rocking chair, flooding her new stepson with the favour of her smile, a false smile which Celia saw through instantly, her mind racing ahead. León's brother Raúl.

God. Papá would throw a fit. No wonder her mother was purring at the prospect. News of the rebel attack on the docks had produced a similar frisson of delight, betraying her unspoken hope that the shock might finish him off. And the unannounced arrival of his long-lost son would be a much greater shock than that. The son who had defied rescue, who had never once contacted him in seventeen years, who had committed the unforgivable sin of siding with his treacherous mother . . .

'I'm very pleased to meet you,' said Celia, rather woodenly, dreading the coming conflagration, fearful for her stepfather's health, a fear which nobody else seemed to share. León, with typical head-in-the-sand optimism, refused to take his father's heart condition seriously, while

Lidia actively desired her husband's demise and Eduardo displayed his usual sublime indifference.

'And I you,' said Raúl. He was tall and powerfully built, with an erect, military bearing; he had his father's piercing black eyes and hair and olive complexion, undiluted by the Anglo-Saxon genes so evident in his brother.

He'll bring bad luck on this house, you mark my words. Celia took an involuntary step backwards, realising too late that the stranger might misinterpret this gesture as physical revulsion, a primitive reaction, like Emilia's, to his hideous scar. She blushed, ashamed.

'Celia's terrified our father will throw you out,' put in León, making her excuses for her. 'Don't worry, *chica*. We've spent the last hour putting Raúl through his paces and reminding him how to grovel in the required manner.'

Raúl endorsed this irreverent remark with a lop-sided grimace which could have passed for amusement or derision. Lidia tut-tutted gleefully, while Eduardo smiled his usual inscrutable smile.

'Well,' said Lidia, rising. 'I must go and change for dinner. You too, Celia,' she added meaningfully, indicating that she wanted to talk to her in private. Celia caught León's eye briefly and caught a flash of discomfiture behind the determined bonhomie. This might be a mountain but León would insist on treating it like a molehill; he was incapable of taking anything seriously. *Including me*, she thought. *He's going to behave as if nothing ever happened, and expect me to do the same.* A spark of well-I-won't defiance flared up and subsided, leaving behind a dull glow of frustration.

As soon as they were safely upstairs Lidia discarded her fulsome manner like a mask.

'You realise why he's turned up after all these years, don't you?' she hissed, beckoning Celia into her bedroom and shutting the door. 'To reclaim his inheritance!'

'That's rather optimistic of him, isn't it?' said Celia, taken aback, if not exactly surprised, by this abrupt change of mood. 'I expect Papá will show him the door as soon as look at him.'

'Don't you believe it. He's never stopped hoping he'd come back. Damn! Why couldn't he have waited till the old man was dead? I've always been afraid that this would happen.'

'Well, I must say, you did a good job of hiding your feelings just now,' said Celia drily. 'I thought you seemed quite taken with him.'

'There's more than one way to kill a cat,' snapped Lidia. 'I want you to be perfectly charming to him, do you hear me? I don't want him to suspect we're on to him, we have to keep one jump ahead. Don't give me that patient, pitying look of yours, young woman. May I remind you that as things stand, I will receive all the income from the estate for my lifetime. Which means that you and Eduardo will always be provided for, firstly by me, and eventually by León. If the old man changes his will in Raúl's favour, we could all be out on our ear.'

'That's a big if,' shrugged Celia. 'He's never forgiven Raúl for not coming home once he was old enough to choose. And he's bound to assume he's just after his money. He's—'

'He's getting more senile by the minute!' interrupted Lidia. 'Who knows what the old fool might do? I'm damned if I'll lose everything I've suffered for all these years. There's one sure way to make absolutely certain your father kicks him out.'

'What's that?' said Celia, chilled by the malevolent look on her mother's face. Lidia smiled at herself coquettishly in the mirror.

'Leave that to me. Just remember what I told you. Be perfectly charming to him. Don't give him any reason to act hard done by or put us in the wrong. Don't give Enrique the chance to play him off against us. Do you understand?'

Celia felt a sudden, perverse allegiance towards the intruder. Honest hostility was one thing, duplicity quite another. She might be expert at keeping her feelings to herself, but she was quite unable to pretend to feelings she didn't have.

'I shall make him welcome,' she said carefully, 'until I have reason to do otherwise.'

YESTERDAY

Lucy Floyd was born in London of Polish-Italian parentage. She read French at King's College, London, and studied at the Sorbonne from 1967 to 1968. She began writing part time in 1983, winning the Romantic Novelists Association's Netta Muskett Award for a first novel. She has written full time since 1986 and now lives in Fulham with her husband.

Also by Lucy Floyd, writing as Teresa de Luca

By Truth Divided